WREN MARTIN RUINS IT ALL

FOR MICHAEL
—A. D.

Published by Peachtree Teen
An imprint of PEACHTREE PUBLISHING COMPANY INC.
1700 Chattahoochee Avenue
Atlanta, Georgia 30318-2112
PeachtreeBooks.com

Text © 2023 by Amanda DeWitt
Jacket illustration © 2023 by Cherriielle

Edited by Ashley Hearn
Designed by Lily Steele
Composition by Amnet Contentsource Private Limited

Printed and bound in September 2023 at Lake Book Manufacturing,
Melrose Park, IL, USA
10 9 8 7 6 5 4 3 2 1
First Edition
ISBN: 978-1-68263-598-8

Cataloging-in-Publication Data is available from the Library of Congress.

WREN MARTIN RUINS IT ALL

AMANDA DEWITT

PEACHTREE *Teen*

1
THE DANCE

There's something about decision-making and running full tilt down an empty hallway that doesn't pair well. I have approximately five seconds to get to the student council room. I can make it in four if I don't slow down. If I'm lucky, the new faculty advisor won't be there to see my dramatic entrance. If I'm not—well, I'll worry about that later.

It's this overconfident mindset that leads me to believe I can yank open the door and enter the classroom at the same time. Which might have worked. If the door hadn't been locked.

Rest in peace, Wren Martin. You will be missed.

I collide with the door, my forehead smacking neatly against a solid inch and a half of lacquered wood with a *clunk!* that reverberates through my entire skull. I stumble backward, clutching my forehead like my hands are the only thing keeping my head from splitting open.

Well, that's one way to knock.

The door opens. "Oh," Leo says, peeking through the doorway like he's expecting a package to be delivered. I can actually feel his eyes skating downward, taking in the entire scene. "Are you okay?"

Of course it's Leo, six feet and two inches worth of perfect teenage boy. Somehow it's always Leo when it comes to my humiliations, like fate arranges to put us in the same place at the same time of disaster. I'm not sure if I was cursed at birth to screw up or if Leo was cursed to witness it. Considering I'm the one who physically hit the door, I suspect it might be me.

I close my eyes and exhale through my nose. "Why was the door locked?" I say in an exemplary display of patience and restraint.

A pause. "The door was locked?" I hear its futile clicking as Leo tests it. "Oh, I guess it was. Sorry, Wren. Are you sure you're okay?"

My eyes snap back open and a vein throbs in my forehead. Or maybe that's just the cranial trauma.

Okay, before you think badly of me, it's not just the door. Or the fact that I made a fool of myself. Or that I was running late in the first place, necessitating the fool-making. There's more at play here that you need to understand.

Reasons why I hate Leo Reyes:

1. He's tall. I don't trust tall people. Ryan is five eight in her boots, and that's pushing it. And she's my best friend. Leo is not my best friend.

2. He's a morning person. A morning person who goes for runs. *In the morning.* Worse than that, he talks about doing it like it's normal.

3. One year in middle school, his locker was directly above mine. This is unforgivable.

4. He's just . . . too much. Too pretty, too charming, too tall (did I mention that?). Too *perfect.* Teachers love him, he got elected to student council without even trying, and he's the MVP coder of the robotics team, which has awards hanging up in the school's front office. He doesn't even have to try to be the best person at this school. It's like looking at a photo that's been airbrushed to hell and back. People are meant to have flaws. When they don't, they make your animal brain go feral.

5. Once I saw him eat a banana without pulling the strings off. Like—*excuse me?*

6. New: he witnessed me run into a locked door.

So you see, nothing about this situation is ideal.

"I'm fine," I say, brushing past him and into the classroom with whatever dignity I have left. Once my back is to him, I probe my forehead gently with a wince. Oh, that's going to bruise.

Ryan is already waiting in the back, at the apex of where the desks form a U-shape. Her braids are piled up on top of her head in a thick bun, pink woven into the ends. Matching pink eye shadow pops against her dark skin, which somehow manages to work with the spider theme she has going on today. She looks more like a goth princess than someone who participates in high school student council, but after ten years of friendship and many hot glue burns, I've moved past being impressed by her outfits.

"Nice earrings," I say as I hook my foot around the chair next to her and pull it out. Eight little googly eyes stare back from the homemade spider earring dangling closest to me, their pupils wiggling slightly whenever Ryan moves her head. Ryan is an unrepentant crafter, which means her cool factor fluctuates wildly depending on whatever she's been experimenting with lately. The jury is still out on the spider earrings.

Bold words on *cool factor* from the guy who ran into the door seconds earlier, I know. Please don't remind me.

"Nice forehead," Ryan counters, either ignorant of or uninterested in my silent pleas for mercy. Typical. "Where were you?"

I forgot my backpack under my desk and had to run across campus and back again. But she doesn't need to know that. "Don't worry about it. Is Ms. Little here yet?"

"You know that makes me worry about it, right?" Ryan meets my eyes and I meet hers and she breaks, predictably, looking beseechingly up at the ceiling for some higher power to grant her the strength to endure being my best friend. It's that kind of dramatic flair that almost landed her in theater club. A fate worse than death. "I think that's her now."

Ms. Little breezes through the door, a beat-up backpack slung over one shoulder. She's young enough that it almost makes her look like a student, except for the badge on a lanyard around her neck and the existential dread in her eyes as she surveys the illustrious Rapture High student council.

Yes, someone named this town Rapture. Yes, it was the 1970s. I'll explain later.

The U-shaped desk arrangement gives her a good look at us—Ryan and me all the way in the back, me still fussing with my hair, trying to get it to obscure my forehead. Leo tilts back in his chair, one foot resting on his knee in a way that I'm sure is supposed to make him look cool, next to the twins, who are notable for hating it when you refer to them as *the twins*. As a group, I'm sure we don't look like much. I probably wouldn't want to supervise us either.

Which, yeah, how interesting is a high school student council supposed to be? But I don't think boredom is the reason Ms. Little looks distinctly unenthused to be our faculty advisor. The school year has barely started and we've already had more than one shake-up to the status quo. It probably doesn't bode well for the rest of the year, at least if you're the teacher who's supposed to be running the show.

"As you all know," Ms. Little says, facing us with all the energy of the president delivering grave news on the state of the nation, "there will be some necessary changes to the student council moving forward. For starters, I'll be your new faculty advisor." She dumps her backpack unceremoniously against the wall.

I trade a look with Ryan. Or try to. The spider wobbles at me.

"Mr. Duncan has decided to take a"—she gestures circuitously—"sabbatical."

Sabbatical is a nice word for *quit*, but I think the school is hoping he'll change his mind and come back eventually. I'm not sure if being the faculty advisor for student council is what drove him over the edge exactly, but losing two student council members within the first week of school probably didn't help. Not like they died or anything. Josh Barker moved to Arkansas because his dad's in the Air Force, and Samantha Ford got impeached for selling calculus test answer keys because *her* dad teaches the class. Maybe the idea of facing student council drama was too much for poor Mr. Duncan, but more realistically, I think he realized how sad it was that Samantha was making better money off academic dishonesty than he was off teaching. Which left Ms. Little to bravely take up the mantle of pretending to care about student council. Or at least making an attempt.

Which is fine—I have no love lost on Mr. Duncan. Mostly because he was uninteresting, but the omnipresent smell of stale cigarettes and, strangely, cheddar cheese wasn't very endearing either. More importantly, Josh and Samantha left president- and vice president–sized holes in the student council. The laws of succession mean that I was next in line for president. Which is what I wanted all along. I settled for secretary because it was better than nothing, but I guess things have a way of working themselves out. I'm sure mine isn't the first political career that started with scandal, and it certainly won't be the last.

"So." Ms. Little manages to turn the word into a sigh. She puffs out her cheeks and consults the clipboard in her hands. "Some of you will be changing positions now, to fill in our new vacancies. Seemed easiest to just move everyone up a slot, but if you'd prefer a different position . . . well, fight it out among yourselves."

"Doesn't that kind of undermine the democratic process?" Ryan says skeptically. I stomp on her foot, but I don't think she feels it under a layer of protective Doc Martens. She fiddles with the pencil behind her ear and smiles, just a little bit, just enough to let me know that she is messing with me on purpose, and she's enjoying it. I step on her boot a little harder.

This is my moment. I should have been president from the start, if student elections were won with policy instead of square chins and sparkling blue eyes. But Josh Barker's pretty-boy good looks are in Arkansas now, and it's my time to shine.

"Yes," Ms. Little says blithely. "As former secretary, Wren Martin will be our new president." I open my mouth to graciously accept. She gestures expansively . . . toward Ryan.

This happens a lot.

Ryan blinks. "I'm not Wren."

"I'm Wren," I say with a barely restrained scowl.

Ms. Little frowns. Maybe the scowl isn't as restrained as I thought. "You're Wren?" she says. "Then who's Ryan?"

"*She's* Ryan."

"I'm Leo," Leo says helpfully, "and that's Archer and Maggie." The twins wave, looking a little nonplussed. I'm not really sure how they qualified to be added to student council except by virtue of knowing Leo. I don't know how Archer even has time to be here, considering he's involved in every sport known to man. It probably should have been my job to fill the new vacancies, but I have no idea who I would have asked. So they'll have to do, I guess.

"Glad we can all get acquainted," I say quickly. "I'm Wren. I'm student council president. I accept. Thank you, thank you." Pause for applause.

Ryan does a golf clap. I shove her hands back down as I stand up.

"So, about the VP—"

"Leo Reyes," Ms. Little reads off that sheet.

I stop short with a huff. "Shouldn't I get to choose? I choose Ryan." She *did* say we could fight it out among ourselves.

"Ryan Robinson is the new secretary," Ms. Little says pointedly, raising her eyebrows when I open my mouth to argue. For someone that's *maybe* twenty-seven and chronically disinterested, she can be surprisingly intimidating when she wants to be. I guess the fighting part was an exaggeration. "Archer Min is treasurer and historian is Magnolia . . . also Min. Are you related?"

"They're twins," Leo supplies.

"They can speak for themselves," I scoff, rolling my eyes. "If they're going to be a part of student council, they should have their own opinions. Right?"

Archer and Maggie trade a look. "We're . . . twins?" Maggie says, more nonplussed than ever. "We were born at the same time. Not really an opinion. Hey, are we getting some sort of class credit for this?"

I close my eyes and exhale.

Additional reason I hate Leo Reyes:

7. He doesn't care about student council like I do. I mean, no one cares about student council like I do, but at least the others made an effort. And maybe it was because Josh was buying a passing grade in calc from Samantha, but hey, whatever works. Leo, meanwhile, has always been just *there*, sitting quietly to the side, usually typing on his laptop like whatever he's doing is more interesting than the yearly budget. Which, like, it probably *is*, but that's not why you join student council. There's a reason Leo ran for historian, and I suspect it was to put student council on his college applications without having to do all that much except type meeting notes. Which was fine before. At least he stayed out of my way.

Now he's very much in my way. Physically. The way he leans back in his chair blocks the path behind him to the front of the classroom.

"Fine," I say. "Can we get started?"

"Go wild," Ms. Little says, dropping into the swivel chair behind the teacher's desk. "Just not too wild." She looks up expectantly. "That was a joke, by the way."

Archer laughs politely.

I pull a folder out of my backpack and consider my options. The U-shape means I can either skirt awkwardly around either side to get to the front of the room, or I can sit on the desk and swing my legs around the other side of it. Considering Leo is already blocking one side—

"Don't— Okay," Ms. Little sighs as I slide over the desk and hop down on the other side. "Whatever."

I take my place at the front of the room and clear my throat. Leo is leaning back in his chair again, the wobbling irritatingly distracting. My eyes sweep the assembled council. Like I said, I care about student council. Think what you like, but it's not just because I'm a complete nerd. Or maybe it is, but Ryan wouldn't have gone along with it if I didn't have a good reason. An agenda, if you will. We had a bit of a setback when I was elected secretary, but the universe righted itself in the end. If a teenager getting suspended for selling answer keys outside the girls locker room is what it takes . . . well, what's that but divine intervention?

Or, well, close enough.

"I want to fix this school," I announce.

There's a long pause where they all stare back at me with varying shades of anticipation. A purposeful pause, for emphasis, but still, I expected a little bit of a reaction. An *About time someone did!* or a *Please, tell us more!* Instead, Ryan flashes me a little thumbs-up and Leo looks politely curious but doesn't tilt his chair forward onto four legs in awestruck wonder. So I guess that's all I'm working with right now.

Whatever. There's plenty of time to be impressed with my presidential platform. The pièce de résistance is yet to come.

"Rapture High sucks. Frankly," I say, maybe a little too frankly. I *am* the president of its student council. "Our text-books are older than we are. There are fewer teachers every year. There's the hole in the stage that that freshman fell through last year during *The Sound of Music*."

"That was so messed up," Archer murmurs, leaning over to Leo.

"And school administration *doesn't care*," I forge ahead. "They don't care about me. They don't care about you. I mean, they didn't even make us hold reelections, they just let us pick two random people to fill the vacancies." I gesture sweepingly at Maggie and Archer.

"Okay. *Random?*" Maggie scoffs.

The point, Ryan mouths, her spider earrings wiggling furiously.

Right, the point. "There are two things the administration *does* care about," I say. I hold up a finger. "They care about the robotics team." I avoid looking at Leo. Leo, the star coder of the Rapture High robotics team, who single-handedly launched robotics into relevancy here. Caring has nothing to do with the sport (science?) and everything to do with the case of shiny plaques and trophies in the front office. If Leo decided to go win a couple of badminton tour-naments tomorrow, I'm sure the principal would sell off all the little robot arms on eBay to buy the school a badminton court.

"And"—I hold up another finger—"they care about the Dance."

The. Dance. Capital-letter-D *Dance*. It has a name, but it doesn't *need* one, because it's all anyone ever talks about.

Let me explain a little bit about Rapture High School: there is absolutely nothing interesting going on here.

Okay, except for the Samantha Ford thing, but test keys are hardly the same as Harvard acceptance letters. Rapture, Florida, is a beach town, a patch of sand made viable only by tourists' propensity to visit and spend a lot of cash. There are two things available for an enterprising teenager to base their personality around: the beach and—

The Dance.

Not prom. Prom is at the end of the school year, which is the beginning of summer, which is also the beginning of tourist season. When half of the student body is pulling shifts at the Beachy Bites Ice Cream Parlor or the Holiday Inn for the season, no one really has time for it. So instead, they've collectively and culturally decided to focus their energy on a more reasonable time frame, like February, when they can all lose their absolute shit over the Valentine's Day Dance.

People start planning for the Valentine's Day Dance in *November*. Dresses, flowers, limos. They close the road outside school to non-Dance traffic just to mitigate the madness. It is, simply put, *a lot*.

And I hate it with every fiber of my being.

"I want to abolish the Valentine's Day Dance," I say with all the confidence of someone dropping an atomic bomb. "And redirect the funding into the school's infrastructure to actually improve this place for everybody who goes here after us." I manage not to drop the word *legacy*, but I want to. I want to very badly.

It doesn't quite have the impact I expected. Ms. Little laughs.

"Sorry," she says, hiding her mouth behind her hand. "I'll let you finish."

"Maybe *abolish* isn't the right word," Ryan hedges. "Maybe . . . reduce?"

"Terminate," I counter.

"Tone down."

"Obliterate."

"I have a question." Maggie raises her hand. "Before you ask us to commit social suicide . . . uh, why?"

I can see the hope leaving Ryan's eyes. I stare at Maggie, squinting incredulously. Did she not hear the first part?

"There's a *hole* in the *stage*," I say, enunciating the words like maybe she didn't understand them the first time around. "That kid broke her arm." The hole would've been cheaper to fix than the ensuing lawsuit, and *yet*.

I flip open my folder with a crisp *thwack*, my neatly stapled informational packets waiting like soldiers inside the pockets. Some people need the numbers right in front of them to understand, I get that. I've come prepared. "The money this school puts into the Dance is absolutely ridiculous." I start distributing packets like it's the first day of class. "Here you'll find the student council budget for the last five years. The Dance accounts for over fifty percent of the budget in any given year. We're blowing that on *one night*. Instead, we could be fixing the hole, or buying art supplies, or subsidizing instruments for band students who can't afford them. There's literally a thousand other things we could do with that money for the benefit of the *whole* school."

Archer shuffles his packet and clears his throat. "Well, as treasurer," he says, which I can already tell is going to get on my nerves, "I think your problem might be with the school district, dude. The student council is just here to do, like . . . fun stuff? Like dances?" He glances at Leo as if for confirmation. "I mean, it's only my first day, but that was my read on the situation."

"Fun for *who*?" I say, unable to hide the note of derision in my voice. "Gay kids? Trans kids? Poor kids? Kids who don't want to date? It's a social minefield. I mean, it's *Valentine's Day*. Somehow y'all have managed to make it worse than *prom*." I roll my eyes. "The school district won't do anything, *clearly*. So what's the point in waiting around wishing they would? We can actually do something as a student council instead of just . . . researching caterers so football players can show off to each other and get wasted in the bathrooms."

Okay, maybe a little more bitterness than I'd intended, but it's gotten the point across. Dances are only fun for *some* people, but the whole school pays for them. Not to mention everyone has to deal with the weight of the social obligation. Even *not* going is some sort of political statement at Rapture High, because it's all anyone cares about, and the administration likes it that way. The more we obsess over the Dance, the less we're thinking about our wobbly desks or how a "long-term substitute" has been teaching health class for a year and a half.

But I can change that. I mean, *we* can change that. Ryan is already on my side, of course. So that's one vote. It could be wishful thinking, but I think I see Maggie considering it too. Either that or she's still trying to figure out how to get class credit out of this.

"What if we got a sponsor?" Leo says.

Now, *that's* like a bomb going off. Maggie's head tips thoughtfully in the other direction, and even Ms. Little looks up curiously from where she's scribbling something definitely unrelated on a notepad. Leo just sits back in his chair, tapping his pen against his chin.

I freeze, my mind racing. Like I said, Leo doesn't care about student council. He mostly minds his own business, which is annoying, but I didn't expect him to pull out something even worse. A sponsor? Where did that come from? Can vice presidency really have gone to his head that quickly?

"Who is going to sponsor *the Dance*?" I scoff. "Domino's?" The Domino's that caters every event by virtue of being right next to the school, more specifically. It's to the point where I can hardly even look at pizza anymore.

It's a desperate play to derail my argument, nothing more. Typical Leo, making my life difficult just by being there. But it won't work, not this time. I have a chance, I think. I can salvage this. There's still hope.

And then he says the worst five words I've ever heard strung together in a sentence.

"What if we ask Buddy?"

2
THE APP

Last spring, Buddy took over the student population of Rapture High.

By the end of the summer, the app was national. It was all anyone could talk about. Any respite I might have gotten from being out of school was crushed by the reality of working a summer job in a tourist town, meaning I saw my classmates way too often, no matter where I went. So despite my very best efforts, I know *all* about Buddy.

Buddy is an app. It's *not* a dating app.

It swears up and down it's not a dating app, from the name to the cheerful yellow color scheme to the way the whole thing works. Buddy is a *social media* app, as it's listed in the app store, and it's supposed to be about making connections. Its whole purpose is to get past the cliques and the rumors and the societal preconceptions and connect you with people you might never speak to otherwise.

Anonymously. No pictures, no names. You answer a short survey about yourself and your interests and the app generates matches with people it thinks you might get along with. I think the name Buddy was supposed to be cutesy, but it makes me cringe any time I hear it.

It's cheesy. It's dorky. It probably would have died upon conception, except that people absolutely one hundred percent use it as a dating app.

"Why would we do that?" I ask. Well—demand. "Why would they say yes?" You don't just ask *Candy Crush* to sponsor your school dance. Do you? Maybe. I might know less about how sponsorships work than I'm going to admit right now.

Leo shrugs one shoulder, looking so nonchalant as he destroys my dreams that I want to throttle him. "We promote them, they sponsor the Dance, we can use the budget on other stuff. Everyone wins. We can make a whole thing of it," he says. "Tie it in with the Dance's theme. Like"—he gestures vaguely—"twenty-first-century masquerade."

There's a sharp intake of breath and my head whips around. I can practically see the stars in Ryan's eyes. "A masquerade . . . ," she murmurs traitorously.

No. Oh no.

"What about people who can't afford to dress up?" I say, frantically trying to rip out the plugs they're using to save this sinking ship.

"My cousin never wears her dress anymore," Ryan says, lured by the siren song of a theme and the promise of glitter.

"We could start a buy-back program for formal wear people don't want anymore. Most people only wear it a few times anyway."

"And marginalized groups?"

Maggie shrugs. "We partner with the GSA?" She says. "Buddy is technically about meeting people, not dating people, right? We could lean into the whole inclusivity, meeting-new-people thing. It would at least help."

"And—" And? And what? How do they have an answer for everything that isn't "but Wren doesn't want to"? Never mind the fact that asking a not-dating app to sponsor a high school dance is absurd. If Leo says it, somehow it makes sense. He could suggest we petition the governor for a bigger budget and everyone would nod like they were considering it.

"It's still the *Valentine's Day* Dance," I insist. "Romance is kind of implied."

"I don't know, I think Maggie has a point," Leo says. "Some people might use it like a dating app"—he sounds sheepish, as if suggesting partnering with an app for *buddies* is cool, and a *dating* app is where things start to get embarrassing—"but Buddy is supposed to be about making connections, platonic *or* romantic. I bet a lot of people don't go to the Dance because they don't have a date or don't want to ask anyone. Buddy could take the pressure off for everyone."

I—

Actually, that does make a little bit of sense. This is really getting out of hand now.

"The school gets the Dance and Wren gets his budget," Leo says again, and it sounds like a hammer hitting the last nail in my coffin. "We might even make the news."

In the span of two minutes, he's already come up with a plan better than mine, expending no effort in the process. Even when I win, he finds a way to one-up me. He's taken my platform and rearranged it in a way I can't possibly say no to without undoing everything altogether. And he's still the hero of Rapture High.

Do you understand now? Do you understand why I hate him?

"Well," Ms. Little says, "sounds good enough for me."

I have to say something. They're all looking at me expectantly, waiting for another complaint to casually solve. I should mention world hunger, just to have some good come from all this.

"*If* you can get them to agree," I say, my last weak defense. It's almost as bad as waving a white flag. "That's a pretty big *if.*"

♥

"Thanks for all your help," I deadpan, dragging my unwilling body toward the parking lot. Instead of fading, the ache in my forehead has only gotten worse, throbbing in time with my beaten and brutalized ego. I've been president of the Rapture High student council for a grand total of an hour and I've already lost control of the entire thing. *And* run into a door.

"He used the word *masquerade*, Wren," Ryan says woefully. "I can't be held responsible for what I did after that."

I grunt, unimpressed by her weakness for pizzazz and pageantry. "It doesn't matter," I say. "He'll never make it happen. That was all just a waste of time." And maybe if we *keep* wasting time on pipe dreams we'll end up with no Dance after all. Doubtful, but I have to have something to hold on to during this dark time in my life.

The afternoon is sweltering, humidity sticking to my skin like a heavy coat as we push through the double doors. Campus is nearly deserted now, except for a patch of band kids eating french fries and kicking their feet against the low wall that boxes in the quad. I recognize a few of them from class, but no one bothers to acknowledge us. The marching band is its own cult of personality, one that I would rather not mess with.

"C'mon, I'll make it up to you." Ryan puts her arm around my shoulders, pulling me in until I'm forced to walk at a sixty-degree angle. I squawk indignantly, but she only shakes me more enthusiastically. "Taco Bell. Anything you want. On the dollar menu."

"I think trying to feed someone Taco Bell is considered a criminal offense in some states, actually—"

"Wren!"

I stop, my feet planted on the concrete. Ryan keeps trying to pull me forward like she didn't hear Leo's voice, which ends with my head popping out from under her arm, pushing my hair in every direction. It's too late to smack it back into place without Leo seeing, so I settle for pretending it's not sticking up as I turn to face him. It's all about confidence. Or so I'm told.

He somehow makes even jogging seem nonchalant. He's not even breathing hard as he catches up, his hands sunk in the pockets of the hoodie he's wearing even though it's eighty-five degrees outside. "Hey," he says, stopping a respectable distance away, like I'm an alligator that might lunge. It's possible. "Can we talk?" His eyes flicker to Ryan.

Ryan is lingering, waiting to take her cue from me. She may be a craft-addicted Judas, but she's still my best friend. I nod. "I'll meet you at the car," I say. "It'll just be a minute."

"Hmm," Ryan says. "Play nice." I wince. I wish she didn't have to say everything she thought.

Leo shifts his weight, clearing his throat as we wait for Ryan to disappear around the corner. I hate that he's so tall. It's like God's personal slight against me that I have to look up when I talk to him, which might have something to do with why I avoid him.

Okay, I'm tired of waiting. I actually do want Taco Bell. "What do you—"

"I'm looking forward to working with you this year."

I blink. "What?" I say, at a loss for words. It's not something that happens a lot, but Leo Reyes doesn't look at me like this a lot, a little smile on the edge of his lips like he actually means what he said. Probably because, as mentioned, I try to avoid him.

"Student council," he says. "I'm looking forward to it. The president and vice president thing. I just wanted to . . . y'know, tell you. I think it's going to be fun."

I'm trying not to stare, but it's hard to formulate words, or even to be sure I'm hearing him correctly. He ran after me to tell me that? He thought those were words he should put together in a row and then say to me?

"The part where you single-handedly undid the core of my political platform made you think this is going to be fun?" It doesn't even come out as vehemently as I meant it to, I'm so confused. Was he not paying attention?

His eyebrows pull together, a line appearing between them. "You mean the part where I saved you from becoming the most hated person in the school and still gave you everything you wanted?" he says. He glances at the band kids as if they're going to sense my anti-Dance sentiments and descend on us.

I bristle. "I mean the part where I didn't ask for your help," I counter. What does it matter? It's not like I've ever been particularly popular, and it's my senior year anyway. What do I have to lose? "And the part where I said *Let's get rid of the Dance* and you said *What if we had a Dance so big we end up on the news?*"

He rolls his eyes, exasperated. "Why do you hate this dance so much?"

Now, that's a question I can answer. "Because it's a giant waste of money," I say, "just like your plan is a giant waste of time."

Which he *has* to know, no matter how much he's deluded the others into indulging him today. I expect him to say something defensive, or even just annoyed, either of which I would take as a minor win. Instead, he smirks. I don't even realize that he's leaned forward until he leans back again, his head tilted just enough to be condescending. The glare of the sun gives his dark hair a coppery sheen.

"You don't think I can do it," he says.

I clench my jaw. "No, Leo, I don't think you can convince a corny app to sponsor a *high school dance*." I let the words drip with as much venom as I can muster. "Don't take it personally."

Please take it personally. Please quit student council and leave me alone. Go be tall somewhere else.

"And if I do?" Leo raises his eyebrows. "You'll go along with it?"

It's a challenge. I know it's a challenge. I'm self-aware enough to know when I'm being egged on.

I'm just not smart enough not to fall for it.

"If you can get Buddy to pay for it, you can do whatever you want," I say so scathingly that it's almost lethal. Almost not a deal with the devil. Almost something that I won't regret.

Almost.

♥

My hair is still wet from the shower when I see the Twitter notification. My forehead didn't bruise, perhaps despite the two minutes I spent prodding it in the mirror. I don't really want to participate in any more social interaction for the day, online or otherwise, but curiosity gets the best of me.

I open the notification with a swipe of my thumb. On Twitter it's usually just Ryan tagging me in a cat video, or the algorithm suggesting something I don't want to see no matter how many times I try to convince it otherwise.

My heart drops. This is . . . not either of those things.

> **leo** @likethelion   1hr
> Hey @buddyappofficial any chance you'd be interested in sponsoring a high school valentine's day dance?

> **BUDDY** (: @buddyappofficial   45m
> Mind if we shoot you a DM? Our people would like to talk to your people (:

> **leo** @likethelion   40m
> Absolutely!

> **leo** @likethelion   40m
> @wrennnn Per our last conversation (:

I read the exchange three times, looking for clues in a handful of words, for some loophole that will allow me to convince myself this is definitely not happening. This is just like when social media interns for fast food companies post memes to try to win over the youths. It's just a marketing thing. It's just to look cool and relatable.

They're definitely not going to *actually* do it.

Right?

I go to Leo's profile. I follow him out of misguided social obligation, but he mostly just retweets viral videos and news articles anyway, as if he's fifty years old and not seventeen. Was he always followed by the Buddy Twitter account? Probably not. I click through to the Buddy's profile and accidentally hit the follow button in the process.

Shit. I fumble with my phone, trying to unfollow, but they follow me back almost immediately. Well, I guess it's not that hard to impress them.

My phone buzzes with an incoming text.

Ryan:
Uhhh have you been on twitter?

Me:
i saw.

Ryan:
Proper punctuation . . . oof
That bad?

Me:
you don't know the half of it.

Ryan:
Don't I?

Me:
i might have said something.
unfortunate
earlier today
i didn't think he'd actually . . . do it

Ryan:
Oh, Wrennifer

If it helps, I don't think you ever really
stood a chance

People are already starting to talk
about it on Twitter

Me:

thanks.

The little dots that indicate her typing undulate for a long moment, and I can almost hear her thinking.

Ryan:

You know Leo does KINDA have a
point
The idea is pretty ace-friendly

There it is.

What she means is *Maybe the Dance won't be so bad now*. She's trying to be helpful, or maybe just trying to assuage her guilt over going starry-eyed at the word *masquerade*, but we both know it isn't going to work. Because she knows better than anyone that I hate the Valentine's Day Dance for two reasons, and the massive drain on the budget is only one of them.

The other is that the whole school being obsessed with the Dance means that the whole school is also obsessed with dating. I mean, it's on *Valentine's Day*. What else can you expect? Deciding who to ask to the Dance is practically a blood sport, and one that's politicized to a degree only possible in a high school full of hormonal teenagers with nothing better to do.

And when you're not someone who dates, it sucks. I'm not going to pretend it doesn't, though I'm not about to tell the rest of the student council that part. I don't care if they know I'm asexual, but I don't want them to know I think about how awkward it makes the Dance this much either, because they'll only use it as an excuse not to take my points seriously. I already know that dating while asexual is harrowing, which is exactly why I don't do it. It feels like an asterisk after my name, or a warning label on the back of my head: *If you want that full Hollywood experience, look elsewhere.* So yeah, actually, it's pretty annoying that there are multiple pillars of the high school social experience that revolve around romance and, not so subtly, everything that's "supposed" to go with it. I can be annoyed about it without distracting from the fact that there's a literal hole in the auditorium stage.

So yeah, Leo does *kinda* have a point. Basing the theme on Buddy would make the romance part less mandatory and more optional, despite the whole Valentine's Day part. At least in theory. The thing is, I know it won't. Because while I may think that way, and I guess Leo thinks that way, no one else will. The Dance will be the same as it always is, with a more inclusive-sounding theme slapped on top. Pretending anything will be different just makes it more annoying. At least real dating apps are actually honest about it.

Me:

yippee

I drop my phone onto my bed and promptly face-plant next to it. It's fine. Everything is fine. There are still a thousand hurdles between Leo Reyes and total student council domination: The company's management. The school board. Ms. Little. There's still hope. I press my face more firmly into the sheets, groaning as I feel my cat curl up on the back of my head, his claws digging into my scalp.

Maybe if I'm lucky I'll suffocate before the next student council meeting.

3
THE ART OF WAR

I plant my hands on Ms. Little's desk. "You know this is ridiculous, right?"

She looks surprised to see me. Or at least, her version of surprised, which isn't much different from the bored expression she usually musters. Probably because I'm a senior and she mostly teaches freshman English.

Her students give me sideways glances as they shuffle out of the classroom, but they're all too afraid of being late to their next class to linger. That'll wear off. I'm an office TA next period, which is a school board–approved way of saying I can mostly do whatever I want.

Like corner Ms. Little before our next student council meeting.

After a night of self-pity, I've steeled myself to the fact that this isn't going to resolve itself. I need to be proactive, the way I was going to be proactive before Leo threw this very big, very annoying wrench in my plans. Yes, I told Leo I'd stay out of his way, but . . . well, that's why I'm doing this now, when he's presumably on his way to third-period chemistry on the other side of campus.

I have access to student schedules too. I use my powers only for good, never for evil.

Ms. Little looks down pointedly. "I know you're wrinkling my calendar."

I pull my hands back, squaring my shoulders. "You can't let Leo go through with this," I say. I almost say *get away with this*, like he's some sort of cartoon villain.

"I can't?" Her eyes flick back up again. "What do you want me to do? Interfere with democracy at work?"

I give her a flat look. "You teach English, not government. What do you care?"

She snorts and leans back in her chair. "You seemed to be okay with it yesterday."

I'm not sure how she interpreted *defeated, demoralized, and bitter* as *okay with it*, but I guess we all have our unique perspective. "I want what's best for the school," I hedge. "I'm just not sure that partnering with a *dating app* is . . . that." I *have* to learn how to start saying the words *dating app* in a way that doesn't make it sound like an infectious disease. I should probably stop saying them entirely, but someone ought to tell it like it is around here. "What's the PTA going to say?"

"Social media app, technically. I'm told," she says, and her tone makes it clear that she doesn't super care either way. I bite my tongue.

Okay, so we're all going to pretend it's not secretly a dating app. Fine.

"And considering half the school is talking about it," she continues, "they've probably already heard. I haven't seen any pitchforks outside yet, but there's still time."

I wince. Yeah, I'm aware. I've only been listening to people speculate about Leo's Twitter exchange all morning. Ms. Little's next class is already starting to filter in, accompanied by the dull roar of the hall chatter every time the door opens. I turn my head, trying to catch snatches of their conversations. If the rumors have filtered down to the freshmen, all hope is truly lost. This early in the year, they shouldn't be plugged in to the school rumor mill yet.

"Have you ever tried it?"

I look back. Ms. Little has her head cocked, watching me smugly. Or maybe just watching me. I've been a little on edge today. "What?"

"Have you ever tried it? The app?" She shrugs. "You're very passionate about something you've never tried."

I give her a scandalized look. "Have *you*?" I counter, feeling a bit like a fine Southern lady clutching her pearls. Since when do teachers want students to be on their phones *more*? Shouldn't they be talking about *stranger danger* and *say no to drugs* and, I don't know . . . studying?

"I have enough friends," she counter-counters.

"*Who?*" Okay, weird question. First thought is not always best thought. "That's not what I meant."

She gives me an unmoved look. "Listen, I have class in about"—she glances at the clock—"two seconds, so let me give you some advice." Ms. Little folds her hands on the desk in front of her, her fingers laced together, and looks up at me frankly. "The Dance was never going to be abolished. I know it. You know it. Maybe five, ten years from now, we as a society will have moved on from the need for high school dances. And by then you won't care, because you'll be an adult who pays taxes and has better things to worry about. But in the *meantime*"—she spreads her hands and shrugs—"there's something valuable in knowing your enemy."

"Thanks, Sun Tzu," I deadpan. So she's not going to be any help. Got it. Good to know. I turn on my heel and wade through straggling freshmen to get to the door.

I almost make it. I'm physically exiting the room when I run into Leo.

Actually, I almost clock him with the door, which is not on purpose, whatever he may think. He bends backward to avoid it, putting his hands up.

"Sorr— Oh," I say. "It's you."

His mouth quirks up on one side. "You have a problem with doors, don't you?"

Maybe I should have hit him with the door. "I have a problem with *you*," I say, stepping around him. The hall is nearly empty as the bell rings, and I'm annoyed that my carefully constructed plan to avoid him failed. "Don't you have a chemistry test today?"

Leo gives me a strange look. Ah, maybe I've said too much.

"I had to drop some papers off for Ms. Little, so Mrs. Baughman said I could arrive late. I usually finish early anyway."

"Wow. Impressive," I say dryly. Of course he can do chemistry. Perfect Leo Reyes can probably recite the periodic table backward while he juggles. *And* tweet while he does it.

"How did you know I have a chemistry test?"

"I know everything about this school," I say breezily. Okay, untrue, but at least I care enough about it to try. It's more than most people can say, including the administration. "Which is why I should have been elected student council president," I add. "And then we might not be having this conversation."

Leo laughs. "And what a shame that would be."

Is he making fun of me? I think he's making fun of me. "I'd better let you get back to important errand boy–ing," I say, hooking my hands around my backpack straps. Ms. Little can talk all she wants about knowing your enemy—no one said I have to spend time watching Leo laugh at me outside of student council too.

"Hold on," Leo says, swinging his backpack around so it hangs off his front, like he's some kind of malformed marsupial. He digs around inside it. "I was going to pass these out at the next student council meeting, but since you're here, you might want to take a look." He pulls a stapled packet of paper out of a folder.

I take it gingerly, like it might bite. "What is it?"

"It's a branding package from Buddy. Just some notes on how we would market— How are you doing that with your face?"

"It just comes naturally," I say shortly, physically unable to stop myself from looking like I'm in the act of swallowing a lemon. "How did you convince them to go along with this?" He hadn't had the decency to publicly release his negotiations on Twitter, so I can only assume he tricked them into a moment of hubris, the same way he got me. "Don't they have better things to spend their money on?"

"Well, if you read the packet . . . ," Leo says, in an imitation of me that's actually pretty good. He reaches to take it back but I snatch it away, riffling through the pages. It's longer than my AP European History study guide. "They actually just introduced a new feature that can narrow down proximity-based matches and make them school specific. They thought a sponsorship with the Dance would be a great way to promote it."

"Great," I say without enthusiasm. I've had three years to make friends with the people that go to Rapture High. I don't think an app is going to make me any more interested in the offerings. "So we're really doing this, then? Really and truly? Like, for real?"

Leo raises a finger like he's been expecting this. "You said—"

"I know what I said." I heave a sigh. I let one hand fall to my side, the packet smacking my leg with the sound of defeat. I can already see that the first page is bright yellow. Was printing these in full color really necessary?

"Wren," Leo says, rolling his eyes. "You don't *have* to do this, you know."

I perk up. "I don't?"

"You could concede the presidency to me and—"

"Not on your life," I say, gesturing with the packet. It flops in on itself. "I'm leaving. Bye."

Leo laughs softly behind me. "See you later, Wren."

♥

Let's set the scene: Me, in my bed. Dad, arguing with his tablet in the living room. Beep, sitting on a pillow next to me, his fluffy tail tickling my nose. Long-haired cats are a mistake.

It's too early to sleep, but too late to be anything but horizontal, ruining my eyes prematurely as I bathe them in harsh cellphone light. I've flipped between social media apps enough times that I'm starting to come to terms with the fact that there's nothing interesting to be found right now.

Well. I guess there's still *one* option.

I stare at the app store, the Buddy logo staring back at me like my executioner. I guess I have no one to blame but myself for finding myself here. I could have fought harder. Maybe I *should* have, but I can't ignore the fact that Leo *is* kind of right. I got my budget to improve the school. I win.

I just also lose. Story of my life.

But I'm the student council president of Rapture High, and that might not mean much outside of college applications, but it means something to me. I want to improve this school, and that means all of it. Including its beloved Valentine's Day Dance.

Even if that means going into the belly of the beast to do it. Ms. Little wasn't totally wrong, and I'm not going to let Leo run this whole show just because he knows how Buddy works and I don't.

I download the app.

The first thing it does upon opening is blind me, sending a beam of searing white light through the gloom of my bedroom and directly into my eyeballs. I search frantically for a dark mode in the settings, but if there is one, it's lost in a sea of white and yellow. Jesus. If that's the brand we're supposed to build the Dance around, we're in more trouble than I thought. It's like staring directly into the sun.

I push myself up onto my elbows, earning a disgruntled *mrpp* from Beep. There are normal log-in and registration buttons, and then, below that, a button that says [BETA] HIGH SCHOOL PROGRAM. I guess that's what Leo was talking about. I click it and reluctantly agree when it asks to access my location. A drop-down list appears, populated with the schools in the immediate area: Rapture High; St. Mark's, the private school across town; and Frank B. Bartholomew High, which is in the next town over but I guess is close enough to count. I select Rapture High and my grade and grimace when it asks me to register with my school email. I was hoping to get through this without my name attached, but I should've expected that. Anyone can *say* they attend Rapture High, especially on an app all about being anonymous. I still think the app is ridiculous, but at least it's not inherently creepy.

Finally it lets me in. Wren Martin, a bona fide Buddy user. How quickly things change.

Now for the real test. Literally. There's a survey I'm supposed to fill out about myself. It's harder than I expected.

I am

[ ] female
[X] male
[ ] nonbinary

Gender is complicated. But close enough. There's a question about pronouns below that, which is more nuanced than I expected. Still, the question after that immediately squashes any generous feelings that might have inspired.

My love language is

[ ] words of affirmation
[X] quality time
[ ] receiving gifts
[ ] acts of service
[ ] physical touch

All right, getting a little *Eat, Pray, Love* here right off the bat. I change my mind three times before moving on.

If I were a tree, I would be a(n)

[X] oak

[ ] palm
[ ] mangrove
[ ] pine

What?

I almost expect it to ask what gender I'm looking for, until I remember it's, once again, not *actually* a dating app. I'll give it some credit for not making me confront that question. I don't think the answer is *none*, so I guess the closest answer would be *all*, which sounds like a weird string of logic, but that's what I'm working with right now. I'm not even sure what I'm supposed to base my answer on, without sexual attraction to work with. Or at least that's how I assume sexual attraction works. What else would it be for?

I endure a few more questions, varying from weirdly existential to *What do you like to do in your spare time? Pick 3* before I'm prompted to put in my birthday. If this calculates matches based on star sign, I'm going to throw my phone out the window. It's not my fault I'm a Capricorn.

I hit submit, and the screen is replaced by a clock, the minute hand spinning around its face. I lean back against the headboard, my eyelids heavy. I guess if nothing else, I killed some time. Some of my valuable and finite life I'll never get back, sure, but I wasn't really going to do anything with it but scroll through TikTok anyway.

Finally the clock stops and dances cheerfully before flipping to a new screen.

It looks like any other innocuous messaging app, except for the sunshine-yellow bar across the top that says BUDDY (: big enough to be read from across the room. Beneath it are six thick bars, each a different color. No name, per Buddy's standards, but if I click on one, it takes me to the profile page. There I can see the person's age and gender, and our common interests. For instance, Green and I both thought we would be oak trees. Compelling stuff.

At the bottom of the profile I can choose to either have them removed from my suggested matches or send them a message.

I do neither of those things. I let my phone drop to my chest and slide down until I'm horizontal again, the pillow I've been leaning against flopping over onto my face. I can't say I've learned anything particularly compelling about Buddy. The only thing I've learned is that I would, if pressed, be an oak tree. Which isn't necessarily useless information, but I doubt it's going to come up any time soon. I sigh and flip the pillow off my face.

"Well, that was a waste of time," I announce into the dark. Beep purrs and smacks his tail over my nose.

4
THE MESSAGE

wake up to two message notifications from Buddy. For an instant, I think I'm having a nightmare.

The colored bars that represent my matches are right where I left them, only now two of them are darker. I open them with all the care of defusing a bomb.

Purple:
feet pics?

Green:
Hello! I hope you're having a good night. Sorry to be messaging you so late! I have insomnia due to a deviated septum, so I keep odd hours. Please don't feel pressured to reply until you're ready! Sleep is really important, as is staying hydrated! Anyway—

Oh God. What did I do that made Buddy give me these matches? I delete both of the responses. It takes five seconds for the screen to populate with two new matches. I don't even open their profiles. This was a mistake. I can barely keep up with one friend, much less make friends on demand. Though something tells me that friendship isn't what Purple and Green are looking for.

I close the app and resolve not to think about Buddy for the rest of the day, as a treat for having to see the words *feet pics?* first thing in the morning. It's a plan that lasts exactly twenty minutes, until Ryan pulls into the driveway and I get into her car.

I have a car—technically. In that it is technically a car because it has four wheels and can move under its own power most of the time. I could drive it to school, but since Ryan got her mom's hand-me-down Mazda last year and my house is on her way, I try to save my car's energy for getting me to work and back without exploding.

Last year it was great. This year Ryan's little sister is a freshman, and like many of her kind, she possesses the uncanny ability to never shut the hell up.

"She's your problem now," Ryan says when I get into the passenger seat—we established early on that riding shotgun is for best friends, not little sisters—and shoots me a bone-weary look that's a little overkill for 6:30 a.m.

Or so I think.

"Is it true?" Reed says in my ear the moment we pull out of the driveway, her face pressed against the back of my headrest.

"Actually, maybe I'll walk today—"

Ryan locks the doors.

"Is it? You have to tell me, I'm one of your constituents."

I twist in my seat to squint at her. Or try to. She's so close that I mostly get an eyeful of her nose. "Did you vote for me?"

Reed gives me an impatient look. "I'm a *freshman*," she says, enunciating the word with a regal air. "I didn't get to vote."

No, the elections were at the end of last year, when she was blessedly still in middle school. I didn't appreciate those days enough when I still had them. I press a finger to her forehead and firmly push her backward, out of my personal bubble. I can't say I've ever dreamed of having a younger sister, but Reed is kind enough to give me the experience whether I like it or not.

She drops into her seat with a huff, her seat belt snapping back into place. "But I would have," she says. "Especially if I'd known about *this*. If it's true." She pokes me in the back of the head. I try to smack her hand away, but she's too fast. "It's going to be so cool, ohmyGod. Will you please just tell me?"

"Why do you *care*?" Ryan says, finally breaking. She rests her forehead against the steering wheel as we wait at a red light. "The Dance is only for juniors and seniors!"

"Because it's cool! And you could do something about that, *by the way*, Madame Secretary." Reed kicks the back of Ryan's seat pointedly. "A big app like Buddy actually caring about Rapture High . . . *No one* cares about Rapture High. I heard it's gonna be on the news."

"*I* care about Rapture High," I say quickly. "And it's not going to be on the news. I'm not even sure it's true yet, okay?"

Buddy might be on board, but we still need permission from the principal *and* the school board before we officially have the green light. That's two additional obstacles between us and a Buddy-sponsored Dance, but considering Principal Blackburn already agreed to attend an extra student council meeting this afternoon to hear our pitch, it's not looking good for me.

No sense worrying about it right now. At 6:30 a.m., there's only one thing to do.

I lean my head back and quietly pray that Ryan crashes the car.

♥

Ryan, unfortunately, is a very good driver.

With that plan out of play, I take some old advice and try to focus on what I can change instead of what I can't. I have my budget, despite everything. I might as well use it.

So I should probably take care of that hole in the stage first, considering how big a talking point in my platform it was.

Which is how I end up in the auditorium, staring into the dusty depths of the space under the stage. Yellow caution tape crisscrosses the hole, the ends fixed with gaffer tape. Someone made an attempt, at least. It won't stop someone from falling into the hole like a cartoon character, but it's the thought that counts. Sort of.

"Do you not have any orange cones? A couple of chairs? Anything?" I say. My voice echoes back from the dark kingdom of cobwebs and folding chairs under the stage. Fortunately, the drama class is doing some sort of improv exercise in front of the stage rather than on it, chattering among themselves. I don't think this is the kind of trust fall they're supposed to be practicing.

"No one is going to do a damn thing until someone breaks another arm," Mr. Vernon says waspishly, scowling down at the hole like it's personally responsible for the poor turnout at *The Sound of Music* last year. Honestly, the element of danger might have made the show a little more engaging. "I'm only trying to expedite the process, Mr. Martin."

"So what you're saying is you want to break *more arms*?"

His mouth pinches at the corners. "If that's what it takes."

Three things to know about Mr. Vernon: he's an eighty-five-year-old in a fifty-three-year-old's body, he has an uncanny ability to stage whatever show people want to see the least at any given time, and he insists on calling everyone Mr., Ms., or, in the spirit of inclusivity, Comrade. He hands out a survey on the first day of school where you can circle your preference.

I steel myself for my first act as student council president—or at least the first one Leo Reyes isn't going to co-opt, unless he's about to swoop in here and offer to lay his overlong body across the hole.

"What if I can get you the budget to fix the hole?" I say. I can already tell from the shrewd glimmer in Mr. Vernon's eye that he intends to negotiate. This is the man who would rather half his class fall down that hole than ruin his sets with an orange cone.

"A whole new stage," he counters.

"You're pushing it."

"Mrs. Young says the dancers need an even surface."

"I'm not bartering with Mrs. Young, I'm bartering with you," I say. "*I* know the dancers have done their recitals at the community center for the past three years, and *you* know I don't have the budget to replace the entire stage."

Mr. Vernon wheezes a laugh. "What? No sponsorship from *Playbill* for the theater department?"

Oh, fantastic. Good to know the Buddy sponsorship is a joke among the faculty as well as a thorn in my side. I open my mouth to retort, but someone from his class interrupts us about a trust-fall incident. I'm left standing awkwardly over the hole while Mr. Vernon waves his arms and shouts about how the point of the trust fall is the *trust*.

I clear my throat and pull out my phone, idly swiping between apps in an attempt to look like I'm doing something important. If someone else is about to break their neck in the name of theater, I don't need to witness it.

I freeze, my thumb hovering over the screen. There's a little notification bubble over the Buddy app.

I glance upward, paranoid, but the class is too busy dodging Mr. Vernon's wild gesticulating to notice me. The last thing I want to do after Mr. Vernon's *Playbill* zinger is to entertain the whole Buddy thing again, but I hate leaving unread notifications. They haunt me like little red ghosts of messages left behind.

I jab the app with a little more force than necessary.

The bar at the top of the list is orange this time, darker than the others, to show that it has new messages.

Orange:

Hey

You are a horror

***Hottie

What? A little zip of terror goes through me before I remember there are no pictures on this app and there's no way they know anything about me—besides my star sign and my favorite fruit, I guess. Unless Buddy is some sort of Russian PSYOP who'll hack the phones of America's youth and . . . I don't know. Infiltrate our school dances, I guess.

I almost delete it out of hand, like I did the others, but something makes me pause. Why am I so afraid of this stupid app? Sure, the whole thing has been a pain in my ass, but that's Leo's fault, not Buddy's. Yeah, the idea of actually talking to real human beings on a bright-yellow app named Buddy is mortifying, but it's built around being *anonymous*. I don't *have* to actually be buddies with anyone. I click on Orange's profile and swipe down, but I don't get anything useful out of it except that he uses he/him pronouns and his love language is acts of service. Cool, I guess.

Maybe he'd be happy to know he's doing me a favor right now. I can research how the thing works and have a little fun with it at the same time. No one needs to know.

But I've got to play it cool.

. . . thanks?

Just a little crumb. We'll see what happens.

"All right," Mr. Vernon huffs, making me jump. Behind him, the class is back at trust falls, looking markedly more nervous than they did before. "What do you want, Mr. Martin? Clearly you have demands in mind."

"The student council pays to fix the hole in the stage," I say, "and we get to pick the spring musical."

He opens his mouth.

"*Not Cats*," I say quickly.

He closes his mouth and turns it into a scowl. "Is this what it's come to?" he grumbles. "Creativity and freedom stifled by the will of the student council?"

If it keeps my classmates out of furry jumpsuits, then yes. I deserve a damn medal.

"Do we have a deal, Mr. Vernon?"

♥

I finish school that day holding on to a sense of accomplishment like a lifeline. I'm doing something. I'm making a difference.

At least no one else will fall down a hole. It's better than nothing.

It's only the first month of school, which fortunately means that actual class has been syllabus-heavy and test-light, but it turns out that senior year is more than just a slew of extracurriculars and fundraisers and deadlines. Rapture High administration had the foresight to require every senior to meet with their guidance counselor twice a semester to manage those deadlines, make sure they're on track for graduation, and prepare for their bright and shining futures once they exit these hallowed halls.

Unfortunately, they also decided they didn't have the budget for guidance counselors.

So, more accurately, the seniors of Rapture High have "mentors," meaning we are assigned teachers who are forced to carve time out of their work-life balance to meet with us. I don't know if they assigned me Ms. Little since she's the student council advisor or if it's just her enduring good luck that she gets to spend more time with me.

She looks as unenthused to see me as ever when I step into her classroom, probably because she wants to get this over with and go home as badly as I do. I especially get this impression when she straightens her papers and says, "Let's get this over with so we can go home."

What can I say? I'm perceptive.

"All right, let's see. . . ." I lean against one of the student desks, my arms folded across my chest as she scans the check-in form we're supposed to fill out, scribbling notes in the different boxes. "Obviously you've been busy with student council. Very passionate about that." She raises her eyebrows at the page and underlines something. "Mr. Vernon was bragging about how you're going to have the hole fixed."

I shrug, belying the warm glow of pride in my chest. Word travels fast. "*Hero* is a big word, but . . ."

"Looks like you're taking a couple of AP classes. Your GPA is good." She puffs out her cheeks and circles something. "Have you thought about college applications yet?"

"Oh. Yeah, no." I pick invisible lint off of my sleeve with practiced nonchalance. "I'm not worried about it."

"The deadlines are usually in December," she says. "You might want to start. I don't know if you've noticed, but it's already going by fast."

"No, I mean—I'm just going to Ricky."

Rapture-Impala Community College or RICC, the school we share with the next town over, lovingly nicknamed Ricky. Affordable, close, not exactly glamorous. Everything you'd expect from a community college and a little less. The requisites for getting in are having a high school diploma and a pulse, so as long as my grades don't totally implode by graduation, I think I'm pretty safe. It's about as well-funded as Rapture High, but it's fine. Or at least good enough. It's certainly a school, I mean.

Ms. Little looks up, meeting my eyes from across her desk. "Ricky," she repeats. "You're sure?"

I scowl. "Why is that so surprising?" Plenty of people go to Ricky, or else there wouldn't be a semi-affectionate nickname for it.

"I guess you're just a little"—she gestures vaguely, swirling her hands around like she's trying to conjure the right words through dark magic—"ambitious," she settles on tactfully, and I guess I should be grateful she didn't go with *a weirdo freak* or *too high-strung to function*. "I would have thought you'd want to go to a four-year school."

"Well, you'd be wrong." I tug at my backpack straps impatiently. I knew this was going to be a waste of time, but not this bad. This could have been an email. I check the time on my phone. Ryan is waiting for me by the car.

"What do you want to study?"

"Does it matter?" I definitely sound defensive now, but it's hard to stop.

Ms. Little looks at me like I've grown a second head. "Yeah, kinda," she says with a dose of sarcasm unbecoming for her station. "That's what we're here to talk about, Wren. So talk about it."

I feel like I just swallowed a rock, and not a smooth one. I already know what she's going to say. I already know what I'm going to say. The rest of this conversation is just perfunctory. "Law."

She doesn't say *Well, that makes sense*, which is generous. Or make a joke about my career in politics, which I also appreciate. What I don't appreciate is the way she's looking at me like she's trying to read something on my face, like she can see more than I'm saying. I try to school my expression into something blank.

"So why do you want to go to Ricky?"

"What?" I expected a lecture about the amount of school needed to be a lawyer first. A reminder that this was some-thing I had to be serious about, and how community college in Rapture of all places doesn't sound very serious at all.

"Because it's affordable? Close to home? You like the mascot? Most people have a reason they want to go to the school they're applying to." She tilts her head in a half-hearted sort of shrug. "I just haven't heard you say you *want* to go to community college," she says. "You have options. There are scholarships. For something like law—"

"Listen," I cut in, and I can't help but sound annoyed. "I know everyone else is using student council to pad their college applications, but I'm not. I actually care about this stuff. I thought I got that across." By, y'know, being a high-strung weirdo freak. It's kind of my thing. "I'm going to Ricky. That's it. There's no deeper meaning. It just is what it is." I push off the desk and breeze across the room. I've already wasted enough time talking about my hopes and dreams or whatever. I've got stuff to do. I pause at the doorway and look back. "You don't need to try so hard with this mentor stuff. Really. I'm fine."

"Yeah. You seem totally fine to me," Ms. Little says blandly in that straight-faced way of hers, dropping the words at my feet and leaving me to decide what to do with them.

I turn around and leave them behind.

♥

Anyway, I promised I'd get back to the whole Rapture thing. Like I said: Rapture, Florida, is a beach town, which makes it a tourist town. I know what you've been wondering— Rapture? Was it founded by Christian evangelicals, perhaps? A doomsday cult?

Better than that: Rapture was founded by an idiot. Everyone wants their beachside Florida town to sound like an idyllic destination, but it turns out that names like Paradise and Eden were already taken or too on-the-nose, so the erstwhile founder of Rapture did what any good student on a deadline does. He cracked open a thesaurus and got to work.

Which is how you get Rapture. A feeling of intense pleasure or joy, which you'll absolutely get from visiting our beautiful beaches. Also, the end of days.

All this to say, three nights a week, I work the evening shift at the front counter of the Holiday Inn. Is it glamorous? No. Does it pay the bills? Not really, but it's easy, especially during the offseason. A Thursday night in September means I basically have the place to myself, except for the occasional late check-in or request for more towels. I don't know what the guy in 112 is doing with all those towels, nor do I want to.

Mostly I do homework on the front desk computer or dick around on my phone. So I don't really have anything better to do but notice when my phone buzzes with a Buddy notification.

Him:

Oh my God, I'm so sorry.

My friends stole my phone, I didn't even notice.

They just made this account as a joke.

Please feel free to just . . . ignore that.

I snort softly. He doesn't think I'm a horror *or* a hottie? How rude.

But it's not the response I expected, especially after *feet pics?* guy this morning. Interesting. I click his profile and scroll down, actually looking at the answers instead of just giving it the quick pass I gave it this afternoon. Nothing too exciting, really. A Scorpio (yikes), if he were a tree he would be a palm tree (still not sure what that means), and his least favorite vegetable is the cucumber (I don't remember answering that question?). And he goes to my school, apparently. I quickly mentally scroll through all the guys I'm aware of at Rapture High, but I'm not sure what having a kinship with palm trees would make someone look like. I guess the point of the app is that it's anonymous, not a guessing game.

I glance at the time. I still have an hour to kill before I can clock out, and I'll do anything to avoid being productive on company time.

Me:

its cool

mines just a joke account too

Not strictly true, but . . . close enough. And somehow less weird than the truth.

Him:

Do most people use this app as a joke?

> Me:
>
> i'd love to tell you yes, but the
> evidence tells me no
> sorry bud its just you and me out
> here trying to survive

> Him:
>
> By letting our friends make us joke
> accounts on an anonymous app?

I decide to let him assume that Ryan wrestled my phone away from me and registered my account for me. Some lies are merciful.

> Me:
>
> i said surviving, not thriving

> Him:
>
> Hahaha
>
> Well, I'll let you go
>
> Sorry for bothering you!

> Me:
>
> no worries

"Hm," I muse, closing the app again. Of course, he isn't even a real user. Won't get much useful information out of that interaction, but at least it was a halfway normal conversation. Which is kind of more than I expected from Buddy in the first place.

The desk phone rings. "Holiday Inn, front desk," I answer, for a moment forgetting to sound bored.

"About the towels . . ."

5
THE TREE

I know something is wrong the moment I step onto school grounds Friday morning. My head goes up, and I'm practically sniffing the air like a meerkat.

"Something's not right," I say ominously, one hand still on the car door like I might change my mind and get back in. Ryan kicks her door shut, signaling that I can sit wherever I want, but it's sure not going to be inside her car. Reed has already disappeared.

"Do you sense it in the Force?" Ryan asks.

I ignore the fact that she's making fun of me. My predilection for Star Wars has nothing to do with this. "Yes," I say without elaborating.

You can tell when something is going on at Rapture High—probably at any high school, or with any particularly condensed collection of human beings. It goes deeper than the rumor mill and into some sort of human instinct bordering on the psychic. Or maybe it's just the barely audible buzz of everyone talking about the same thing. Probably that. I don't really like the idea of having a psychic connection with any of these people.

There's no time to investigate further before my first-period French class, and my French isn't good enough to ask anyone what they know. But I start to have suspicions when Stephen Hannigan corners me in the hall outside second-period economics.

"What did you do?" he demands, red in the face and practically trembling with righteous fury. Or something. It's a little much for this hour of the morning, but everything about Stephen is a little much. Normally I just roll my eyes, but usually he's saying something pretentious in class, not accusing me of—

I'm not really sure what he's accusing me of, actually.

"What do *you* think I did?" I counter. Stephen's three main personality traits are the robotics team, red hair, and having a subscription to the *New Yorker*. I hate Leo because he's perfect without even trying. I hate Stephen because he tries *too hard* to be perfect.

Also, he's just . . . annoying.

"Leo quit the robotics team yesterday," Stephen says with an expression not unlike he's sucking a lemon, "and I know *you* had something to do with it."

That explains it. The cosmic ripple through the universe, the pervasive wrongness settled over the school. Like I said, the Rapture High robotics team is about the only thing the school has going for it. And if my amateur assessment is anything to go by, Leo is the only thing the team has going for *it*.

I guess if I were, say, the captain of the robotics team, I'd be worried too. Good thing that's Stephen's problem and not mine.

Yet somehow it's made *Stephen* my problem now. Do I ever get to win? "Literally how is that my fault?"

"I don't know!" Stephen hisses. "I don't know what goes on in your stupid student council meetings! But it can't be coincidence that he starts talking about this whole Buddy thing and suddenly he doesn't have time for the team anymore. So what else am I supposed to think?"

I open my mouth to say something about his lack of thinking at all, but he doesn't give me the chance to display my razor-sharp wit. He pokes me in the chest and my expression turns disgruntled. He *poked* me. Who does that?

"Fix it, Wren," he says, and the warning bell rings, reminding us that we have economics in a minute. He leaves me there with one last withering look before yanking open the classroom door.

"*Fix it, Wren*," I sneer at the door. Leave it to Leo to somehow make this my problem too.

I mean, *yes*, I'm going to talk to Leo about it. But no, not because Stephen fucking Hannigan told me to. I was going to do it anyway.

I don't get the chance to ambush him until the twenty-minute break between third and fourth periods, which is nineteen more minutes than I need to ask him if he's lost his mind.

"*Have you lost your mind?*" I hiss from the other side of a book display in the library.

Leo blinks as if he's just been visited by a vengeful ghost, a book still in his hand, midway through the process of slipping it in the drop slot. "Wren?"

"Who else would it be?" I don't mean to imply *Who else would ambush you from behind a book display*, but here we are. "I need to talk to you. Right now. Immediately."

"Behind the display?" Leo drops off his book and sidles around the edge of the display, forcing me to take a step back and arrange my expression into something appropriately scowling. The library isn't exactly the most popular place in Rapture High, and luckily it's pretty deserted even without the shadow of the display to hide behind. The rumor mill is already working overtime today. I don't need Stephen Hannigan thinking I'm his errand boy.

"Why did you quit robotics?" I demand.

Leo can't be surprised that I know—the whole school knows by now—but he looks taken aback. A peculiar expression flickers across his face. "Why do you care?" he asks, frowning. "I thought you said the school cares too much about the robotics team."

I guess I did say that a little bit. "I meant I wish it cared about other things more, not less about robotics," I hedge, walking it back like any politician would. If it weren't robotics, it would be football: At least robotics is actually relevant to education. "It's good for morale when we win something. And it's really *bad* when the star player quits for no apparent reason." Are they even called players? Teammates? Engineers? Whatever.

Leo scoffs. "I'm not the star."

I scoff back. "Stephen Hannigan seems to think you are."

Wrong move. "Did he say something to you?" Leo says sharply. He doesn't wait for an answer before sighing and running a hand through his hair. "Of course he did. This is— Never mind. I'll tell him to leave you alone."

"You don't need to do that," I say a little too quickly. The only worse thing than Stephen thinking I did what he told me to would be Stephen thinking I ran crying to Leo about it. I take a deep breath. "Just— Listen, if this is about the Buddy thing, you don't need to worry about it. I'm the student council president. I'm not going to make you do all the work just because I don't like it." And think it's stupid and a little bit degrading and overall just a huge waste of time. I can still be a professional despite all those things. I pause, waiting for him to catch my drift. "So you don't need to try to scare me into it."

Leo just stares at me for a moment, his eyebrows slowly contorting into something between confused and incredulous as the words sink in. "You think," he says slowly, "that I pretended to quit the robotics team to *threaten you*?"

Well, when you say it like that it sounds silly. "I don't know!" I huff, throwing my hands up in exasperation. "Stephen was pretty threatening this morning!" God, I need to stop mentioning Stephen Hannigan. "Maybe you thought it would make me . . . sacrifice myself for the good of the school or something."

Leo is still staring, his expression evolving along a strange path, a funny little smile twisting his mouth like he can't quite decide if he's offended or if he wants to laugh. "Wren," he says, and I can't decide which of the two emotions he settled on. "Can I tell you something?"

I blink. "I guess," I say warily.

Leo leans forward, one of his thumbs hooked around the strap of his backpack, and looks me in the eye. He has brown eyes, which I knew. I mean, it isn't a secret. I mean, they have to be some color or another. I *mean*, it's just hard not to think about when someone is forcing you to look at them. "Not everything is about you."

I can't help what my face does. I must look startled, because Leo laughs and leans back again. "I'll see you later, Wren," he says, taking a step out of the protective shadow of the book display.

I watch him go, somehow with even fewer answers than I had before. "Then why?" I call to his back, but Leo only raises his hand in a dismissive farewell as the librarian gives me an exasperated look from the front desk.

I huff. Because you know what? Whatever. I have enough problems. The Dance is my problem. Buddy is my problem. Leo Reyes and whether or not he wants to code the school's little award-winning robots is *not* my problem.

♥

We meet with Principal Blackburn in the student council classroom that afternoon. It goes more or less how I expected. Short. Brutal. Painful. I sit through it with all the grace of a deposed monarch as Leo extols the virtues of a sponsorship with Buddy and Principal Blackburn nods enthusiastically.

"Yes, absolutely. I think that's a wonderful idea. The PTA is already in agreement, but I'll discuss it with the school board on Monday," he says through his bristling mustache, still nodding. "Now, Leo, if I could talk to you for a moment—"

The meeting kind of falls apart after that, which I'm more than okay with. The thing about the Dance being in February is that we barely get a chance to breathe at the beginning of the year before we need to start planning it. We're in limbo right now, waiting for the Buddy sponsorship to be officially green-lit, but soon it'll be a flurry of caterers, decorations, and the logistics of managing a small, dancing army. If I can have one more minimally Dance-related afternoon, I'll take it.

I gladly ditch the classroom, but Ryan hangs back to talk to Maggie, so I can't exactly go very far. I lurk outside the door like a ghoul instead, fiddling pointlessly with my phone. No new messages on Buddy, from the guy the other day or otherwise. Which is for the best, though a part of me can't shake the idea I'm doing badly at this somehow. Not that I want to get a good grade in Buddy, but c'mon. Is it that I'm a Capricorn or that I'm an oak tree?

The classroom door opens and I close the app quickly, forcing it to duck back into the folder I've buried it in. I'm expecting Ryan, but it's Leo who steps out, his backpack slung over one shoulder.

He flashes me a smile that feels like he's rubbing something in. "That wasn't so bad," he says.

"Convincing Blackburn to go along with your hare-brained scheme, or listening to him beg you to come back to the robotics team?" I say dryly, our conversation in the library still at the front of my mind. I *don't* think everything is about me. I *like* it when things aren't about me. It's just that everyone else keeps dragging me into things.

If everyone did things right in the first place, I wouldn't have to be involved at all.

"Both," he says, cheerfully ignoring the bait about the robotics team. I guess he's gotten enough of that from Blackburn. He shrugs. "Mr. Blackburn gets it. He knows I've got a lot going on. With the Dance and the sponsorship and everything."

It sure didn't look like he *got it*. It looked a bit more like he was ready to get on his hands and knees and beg, but again, not my problem.

"Seems like a lot of trouble to go to over a dance," I grouse—my small, petty rebellion. The only rebellion I have left. "I hope you're happy."

"Are you?"

I look up, startled. "I— *What about me makes you think I'm happy right now?*"

He fiddles with one of his backpack straps, the end frayed like this is a common occurrence. He does that a lot, actually. I don't know when I started noticing, but now I can't stop. He's always quietly fidgeting with something—a pencil or a backpack strap or a loose thread. It makes me want to grab his hand and force it still again.

Things I hate about Leo Reyes:

1. He never stops moving. It's distracting.

"Mr. Vernon won't stop talking about how he's getting his stage fixed," Leo says. "I know that was important to you."

I hesitate. It's true. I can't say it's *not* true, especially when I'm a little pleased that Mr. Vernon is talking about it. Mr. Vernon likes to talk, so I weight the news with that in mind, but still. It's nice to be appreciated.

Am I smiling? Dammit. I force my face back into an appropriate expression.

"I figured we could forgo the vote on that," I say, brushing past the fact that maybe he's a little bit right. Maybe I'm a little bit happy. "Unless anyone really wants to see who breaks their arm this year."

The corner of his mouth twitches. "Forgo?"

I frown. "What? Is that a weird thing to say?"

Leo shrugs one shoulder. "Just very Wren Martin," he says. He doesn't specify if that means the same thing as *weird*.

Weird or not, no one can take my one victory away from me. "You might have saved the Dance," I say loftily, "but I saved this school from *Cats*."

"Not all heroes wear capes," Ryan says, pushing open the classroom door. "You know, I kind of like *Cats*."

"You like watching aviation disaster documentaries too," I say blandly, hiking up my backpack on one shoulder. *Now* we can escape. "Are we going?"

"Just one more thing," Leo says before Ryan can answer. He leans his shoulder against the wall, his arms folded across his chest. He probably thinks it makes him look cool. Or maybe he's just too tall to carry his own unreasonable height for too long unassisted. "This will take a little more planning than previous years. It's probably not feasible to meet all the time." I swear his eyes crinkle at the corners when he says *feasible*, laughing at me silently. I make sure I roll my eyes hard enough for him to notice. *Feasible* and *forgo* are not big words. "I was thinking we could probably figure out a lot of the logistics between the two of us and delegate."

I open my mouth, but Ryan is as quick as a viper, pinching me in the side before I can even think about objecting.

"Sounds great," I say, trying not to squeak.

"Sounds very presidential," Ryan agrees indulgently.

Leo's eyes flicker between the two of us, but I'm pretty sure he didn't see the pinch. Ryan is too good at bullying me to be caught that easily. "Cool," he says, flashing a smile that

I can only describe as *tentative*. It's almost disarming. "Looking forward to it."

I wait until we've rounded the corner to dig my elbow into Ryan's side. "You need shorter nails."

Ryan laughs. "You need a little sister," she says. "That was nothing."

♥

Well, that's that, then. The Dance is on. Buddy is on. And Leo and I are going to be the ones running the whole show. It's like watching the next several months of my life go down in a sunshine-yellow-and-white ball of flames.

And I'm still at school. The meeting didn't last long, but it did go long enough that Ryan's mom decided we could stick around and pick Reed up from freshman cheer practice to save her the trip. Practice that ended fifteen minutes ago. Ryan goes stomping off to get her sister's ass in gear. I, in my infinite wisdom, decide to wait rather than hike halfway across campus and back.

I choose BigTree to wait under, one of the landmarks of Rapture High. Presumably once known as the big tree. Somewhere along the way, everyone dropped the *the* and smashed the words together into a proper noun. It is, as you might assume, a very big tree.

It's also a common hang-out spot, probably the most popular besides where the smokers congregate behind the back fence, but it's deserted now. I immediately sit on one of the low-hanging branches that are usually taken, one leg curled underneath me.

I'm lucky that Ryan isn't here to look over my shoulder when a Buddy notification appears on my screen.

> Him:
>
> Hey! Sorry, me again.
>
> I wasn't entirely honest with you before.
>
> This account is a joke—I mean, it's a joke to me. But my friends were actually trying to, like, set me up with people. Because they're pushy assholes.
>
> So I guess what I'm saying is that I need a favor.

I look around a little more suspiciously than necessary, but it's just me and BigTree here. I know I should probably be stewing a little more, after having the deal more or less sealed on the Buddy sponsorship, but I can't help feeling a little self-satisfied that he messaged me again. I guess Capricorn oak trees are worth talking to after all.

> Me:
>
> set up? i thought this was for finding friends

> Him:
>
> I mean, yeah it is.
>
> I mean some people just use it differently.

They probably shouldn't, but you
know. They do.

Me:

i'm just fucking with you

i go to this school too i know how
people use it

go on

Him:

Haha, I should've known.

Can you just chat with me a bit so I
can pretend I'm actually using it?

They want me to "show my work"
haha.

It's okay if you don't want to.

Me:

aren't we chatting right now?

Him:

Yeah, but, like

You know, chatting.

Like you're supposed to do on these
apps.

I mean, you know what I mean.

I pull a face.

Me:

like sexting?

The response is immediate.

Him:

NO. God no. Not that.

Definitely not that.

Thank God. I slowly move my thumb away from the block button.

Me:

i wasn't going to

for the record

Him:

Let's just . . . move away from that

It's just, I don't know, getting to know each other

Here, I'll start

Do you have any hobbies?

Me:

i dont know, like what?

Him:

That's what you're supposed to tell me, doofus

Me:

oh well i feel real compelled to tell you my darkest secrets now

Him:

I don't think hobbies are supposed to be dark secrets

Me:

maybe if youre boring

i like to read?

Him:

Okay! We're getting somewhere.

What do you like to read?

Me:

books?

Him:

I'm starting to think you're doing this
on purpose

Me:

youre the one who asked for a
favor, you never said i had to take it
seriously

okay here, because I feel bad for you

ask it again

Him:

What kind of books do you like to
read?

Me:

Anything science fiction or fantasy! (:
Tolkien is my favorite. Kind of basic,
right? I know, but my best friend got
me into him. We watch the extended
edition LOTR movies on her birthday
every year.

How about you? What are your
favorites?

Him:

Oh.

That felt weird.

Like you were possessed by the
ghost of someone friendly and
cooperative for a second

Me:

imagine how i felt

Him:

Are you in theater?

Me:

i think this might be more creative writing

but also: god no

is that enough to appease your friends?

Him:

That should do it!

Thanks 😊

"All right, let's go." Ryan's voice makes me jump. I totter backward, slipping over the side of the branch and falling unceremoniously into the dirt, still clutching my phone to my chest. Luckily I was only three feet above the ground. The fall knocks the wind out of me instead of breaking my back like a twig.

Reed's face appears inches above mine. That girl needs to learn to respect personal space, I swear to God. "Falling is an art," she says. "That's what Coach Bailey says." She tilts her head and scrunches her nose, lowering her voice theatrically. "I don't think you've got the talent for it." She abruptly sneezes. In my face.

"Eugh!" I plant my hand on her face and push her away, groaning as my spine pops back into place. "Let's go," I wheeze, silently grateful that it's Friday.

The sooner this week ends, the better.

6
THE COLD

And then I get sick.

I wake up Saturday morning with a cough and a head so full of mucus that I can barely lift it off the pillow. I crack open one bleary eye to check the time and see a text from Ryan.

Ryan:

Hey, we're going to have to raincheck the movie. Reed woke up sick and Mom is making me stay home and wait on her

She's literally so dramatic lmaooo

Me:

reed? sick?

wow what an INTERESTING coincidence

Ryan:
Oh no . . .

Me:
Oh Yes

My head drops as I let out a muffled groan. My head is tilted awkwardly and my arm is sticking straight out, my phone still dangling over the side of the bed, but I can't summon the will to move. In a minute. Just . . . in a minute.

"Dad . . . ," I call, my voice sounding pathetically congested. "Daaaad." Beep sits at the bottom of the bed, his tail swishing as he watches me through narrowed eyes. I exhale through my mouth, my breath rattling with phlegm. "Beep, go get Dad."

Beep gets up and stretches lazily before curling up in the crook of my legs. Useless animal.

"Wren?" Dad's voice finally floats down the hall, muffled by the closed door. "You all right?"

"Don't come in," I call, which triggers a round of coughing, which makes my sinuses feel like they're about to explode. "I'm sick."

His footsteps stop abruptly.

I love my dad, but he's a germophobe. Sometimes it's less than ideal.

I clear my throat, a terrible sound not unlike rusted metal grinding against itself. "I need you to feed the chickens," I croak.

We keep chickens in the backyard. Or I do. You can see where that might not pair well with the germophobe dad.

Which he's going to have to *get over*. I can practically hear him hesitate. "Either you can feed the chickens, or I can drag my plague corpse through the whole house and do it myself," I say, summoning the last of my strength to heave a huge, crackly cough. Just to emphasize my point.

". . . I'll feed the chickens," Dad says.

I fall back asleep for a while, until I wake up hungry enough to spur me into movement. I open my bedroom door and nearly step in a bowl of cold beet soup and some kind of mineral water waiting for me there. I stare into the bowl for way too long, trying to find meaning in its murky red depths. In addition to being a germophobe and a neat freak, my dad is a health nut. Logically I know this stems from just so, so much undiagnosed anxiety. Emotionally I want a McGriddle so bad I could cry.

I Google *can cats eat beets?* real quick and then let Beep lap at the soup, taking the mineral water and retreating to the cocoon of my comforter. I don't have a TV in my room, so I settle for putting in my earbuds and looking for music that won't stab at my headache. My eyes sweep my phone's offerings dispassionately, but each app is less tolerable than the last right now. I open my email and immediately regret it when I see Leo's name staring back at me. Why is Leo *emailing* me? I don't want any email that isn't offering me something for free, or at least a coupon. Whatever, I'll deal with it later, when my brain doesn't feel like it's made of concrete. I mark it as read to clear the notification, and close the app.

What happens next is my fault for spending so much time on my phone. I should know better than to put myself in this position when I'm not in my right mind. It's the same reason you don't give a toddler a knife. It's just irresponsible.

I open the Buddy app.

Me:

why do people use this app??

i'm just trying to understand

Him:

Why are you asking me?

The guy forced on here by his friends? Am I really the expert?

Me:

idk

it was either you or the feet pics guy

Him:

Feet pics guy . . .

Me:

you see why i chose you

and you owe me a favor

tell me

Him:

What do you care?

Me:

i'm investigating

researching

i am

sick

Him:

In the head?

Me:

mind. body. spirit.

i'm going to regret this a lot when i'm
coherent again

do you like beets?

Him:

Hahaha

I'm not sure I've had beets

Do you like beets?

Me:

I hate beets

Him:

I guess people use this app to find
people who also like beets

Me:

literally???

Him:

I meant it as a metaphor, but
probably

I mean that people are able to get to
know one another without feeling so
self-conscious about what they look
like or who they know or what people
think about them

Like, you might meet someone who
also hates beets, and you never
would have known that before,
because you wouldn't have thought
to ask

It's about making connections, I
guess

Me:

and focusing on what's really
important..........vegitables

vegetables

Him:

That's exactly it

Me:

so weird

HA

i just realized it matched you with ME

Him:

You only JUST realized that?

Me:

I MEAN

the only two people who aren't here
on purpose

maybe the algorithm knew a thing or
two after all

Him:

Haha, wow, I guess so

Me:

hey, did your friends fall for it?

my acting?

Him:

What?

Oh, sort of

It's nothing against your acting.

They're just . . . stubborn

Me:

about what??

weird thing to be stubborn about

because i killed it i was convincing
as shit

Him:

I'll tell you later

Right now I think someone should
probably get some rest

Me:

haha yeah

good night

day

whatever bye

I let my phone drop onto my bed and curl sideways, my comforter pulled all the way up to block out the sun. My mind drifts aimlessly through pieces of the conversation, my eyelids heavy. I'm absolutely going to regret that later, I think again, warm with amusement at my future torment. Poor Future Wren. I'd hate to be that guy. I wonder what my friend is up to. I wonder what his name is. Maybe I should give him a nickname. I can't just call him Buddy Boy. It makes him sound like a golden retriever. Or it makes me sound eighty years old. One of the two.

Actually, I think the name Buddy is supposed to sound fun, but to me it just sounds childish. I think that's what bothers me about it, if I'm being honest with myself, which under normal circumstances I try not to be. People already think you're childish when you're asexual, or that you're not quite grown up yet, or just naive. They already don't take you seriously. It somehow makes the fact that it is pretty ace-friendly for a not-technically-dating app more annoying. I don't need a *buddy*. I don't need anyone, except for Ryan.

I definitely don't need an app to convince me that the Dance is great after all, just because it put a more chummy spin on it.

Someone should sue Buddy for being annoying. Maybe *I* should sue Buddy. That would solve a lot of problems.

Only after my fever has broken do I realize two terrible things.

1. I called him *my friend*.

And

2. he said *later*.

♥

I put a moratorium on Buddy for the rest of the weekend, and not just because I want to avoid making a fool of myself while riding a NyQuil high. The fact that I care about what this guy thinks of me at all only highlights the problem. When did I start thinking about the app as anything but a particularly inconvenient annoyance? I'm not really using it. I just have it downloaded on my phone, have an account, and talk to someone on it sometimes.

It's different.

I'm mostly recovered by the time I drop into the passenger seat of Ryan's car on Monday morning, except for a lingering ache in my head from spending the weekend with my sinuses filled with concrete. Reed, I can't help but notice, is not present.

"You could stay home, you know," Ryan says, as if sensing how wistfully I'm thinking of my bed. "Reed's going to milk this for at least another day."

"Mph," I say, my eyes closed and my head pressed back against the headrest to keep from jostling it when she takes a turn. "Student council meeting today. We're supposed to figure out how we're going to announce . . ." I lose my train of thought. "You know. The shit."

How do I know that? I don't remember. Maybe we talked about it in the meeting on Friday. Ugh, why didn't we just do it then?

Ryan snorts, and I'm not sure if she's laughing at my suffering or at the idea that we have to announce our partnership with Buddy when the whole school basically knows already. "We should just get a banner that cryptically says *the rumors are true.*"

"Probably better than whatever Leo is thinking," I mumble. My eyes snap open and I inhale sharply, suddenly filled with more life than I have been in forty-eight hours. I put my hand on her shoulder. "Ryan. Do you love me?"

She shoots me a sideways look. "Depends," she says. "Are you dying? Are you going to leave me the chickens in your will?"

I ignore her. My mind is already a mile down the road, sitting in the McDonald's drive-thru. I turn to her with stars in my eyes and hope in my heart. "Can we get a McGriddle?"

7
THE COLLISION

By the time I'm moving between fourth-period AP European history and fifth-period creative writing, I'm feeling a little more human. If I take a slug of DayQuil right before the student council meeting, I might even make it through relatively unscathed.

I should be focusing on that, particularly the unscathed part. Instead, I'm frowning at my phone as I walk down the hall, once again spending far too much time thinking about the yellow Buddy app I have hidden in a folder on my home screen.

Not that it's important that my new pen pal hasn't messaged me—I haven't messaged him either—only he said *later* and it's *later* now and I'm not sure what to do with that. I should just delete the app and move on with my life, but what if he *does* message me again? I don't want to ghost him. Maybe he just forgot. Maybe I should be grateful that he forgot. Maybe I should have stayed home today after all, because my head's clearly not in the right place.

This suspicion is confirmed when I collide with someone walking in the opposite direction.

My first thought is *Leo Reyes*, because only Leo would appear like a specter to make my day worse, but somewhere between the collision and bouncing off of a pair of pecs I realize that it can't be. Leo is built like puberty grabbed him firmly by the hair and yanked his skeleton upward, resulting in a profile that's all height and bony edges. He definitely is not the faithful follower of arm day I'm colliding with.

"Oh, sorry, man!" Archer. I should have known it would at least be someone Leo-adjacent. He manages to grab me by the shoulders before I can fall on my ass, but in the process knocks my hand with one of his overbeefed arms, sending my phone skittering down the hallway. "Oh shit! Sorry!"

I blink, dazed. I should be more concerned that Archer Min is holding me like we're on the cover of a Harlequin romance, or that my phone is now fifteen feet away on the scratched linoleum floor, but all I can do is marvel at my sudden ability to breathe through both of my nostrils again. I stare up at him in wonder. I'm not a doctor; all I know is that somehow being shaken like a rag doll has snapped something in my tortured sinuses back into place.

Archer frowns down at me. "Uhh, are you okay?"

I blink, scrambling back to my senses. Okay, Wren. It's breathing. People do it all the time. "I'm fine," I say, awkwardly disentangling myself. I take in the scope of the situation for the first time. The hall crowd is starting to thin out; the bell is probably going to ring soon. Maggie is watching me skeptically from over Archer's shoulder, probably wondering if she's going to have to save her brother from further assault and/or adoring staring. "Sorry, I wasn't paying attention. Just a little distr—"

And Leo is halfway down the hall, stooping to pick something up.

Phone.

Phone.

Phone.

One thought crystalizes in my mind, completely removed from time, and I'm as certain as I've ever been about anything: if Leo Reyes sees the Buddy app on my phone, I'm going to walk into the ocean and never come back.

I've never moved so quickly in my whole life. I launch myself across the hall, nearly taking a gaggle of freshman out with me. I practically slide to the finish line. Our fingers knock against each other as I fumble for the phone, already halfway in Leo's hand. I almost drop it three more times before I get a good grip.

Leo blinks, startled. "Oh, I was going to grab it for you—"

"Thanks," I say breathlessly, clutching my phone to my chest, hiding the screen. I spring back to my feet, my hair flopping in my eyes. "But I've got it."

He's looking at me strangely—or at least, it seems that way from what I can see of him through my bangs—which probably isn't unwarranted, considering everything about this situation. "Wren," he says, "actually, I wanted to talk—"

Right now? I can barely stay upright.

"Gottagettoclassbye!" I say, expertly dipping around him and booking it down the hallway.

♥

"You amaze me sometimes," Ryan says as she carefully cuts a picture of a dog out of an old magazine. Magazine collages again. Sometimes I suspect that Mr. Wagner doesn't actually know what *creative writing* means.

"I live to inspire," I say, dragging my glue stick mercilessly down my paper.

"What's the deal with Leo, again? I mean, I know you don't like him, but he's not going to get Buddy germs on your phone," Ryan says offhandedly. Well, I think it's offhandedly. She certainly seems to be focused on her collage, but she's crafty in more ways than one. I can't shake the feeling that this is a trap.

Either that, or the word *Buddy* makes my blood pressure spike. Obviously I left that part out of the story. I would take a bullet for Ryan Robinson, but I haven't told her about the Buddy experiment. It's all embarrassing enough as it is; I don't need her taking any lessons from Buddy Boy's nosy friends. The last thing I need is another *the Buddy idea is pretty ace-friendly!* reminder.

"We don't know that for sure," I say loftily, inelegantly dodging the real question as I cut a cat out of a Friskies ad.

I'm not sure exactly what my collage is supposed to say. So far I've just been cutting out animals and weirdly shaped lamps. I survey the classroom suspiciously and mutter, "It sure spreads like a disease." No less than three people have started eyeing us openly since Ryan said the word *Buddy*.

"Hm," she says.

"Hm," I agree. I look up to find her giving me a strange look. "What?"

Ryan shakes her head. "Nothing," she says. "I think I'm just getting a headache."

♥

It's not normal to be suspicious of a door, but when I arrive at the student council classroom that afternoon, I'm wary of it. I'm not interested in knocking with my forehead again, but this time the door definitely isn't locked. Someone's propped it open with a rubber doorstop wedged between the door and the frame rather than using it like it's meant to be used. The opening is just wide enough for voices to leak out.

I hesitate. I'm alone today—shortly after fifth period started, mine and Reed's cold abruptly caught up with Ryan and she made a hasty retreat back home. Which means I'm left to walk home today, but I don't live far from school. There are worse things. Like getting through this student council meeting on my own.

And accidentally eavesdropping on the others.

". . . it's just sad at this point," Maggie is saying. "You know what the definition of insanity is, right? Why do you keep expecting things to be different?"

I grimace. Listen, I know I don't always paint the most flattering picture of myself, but I sincerely don't want to eavesdrop on Leo and the twins. I wouldn't want anyone listening in on Ryan and me. More importantly, I need to go in there eventually, and I'm not exceptionally good at pretending everything's normal. There are many reasons I'm not in theater.

"Guys," Leo says, clearly aggrieved. Or sheepish, maybe. Exasperated? It's hard to tell without seeing his face. "It's really not that bad."

Okay, maybe I'm curious.

"It's *beyond* that bad," Archer says. "It's like watching a little puppy run into the wall. Over and over—" He cuts off with a muffled sound that I assume involves a hand planted over his face.

"I get iiit," Leo sighs. "I'm pathetic. Tell me something I don't know."

"I'll tell you that Stephen wants to kill you for quitting the robotics team," Maggie says. "If I have to hear the *we'll never make it to state now* speech from him one more time, I won't be held responsible for what I do."

"I barely had time for robotics anyway," Leo says dismissively. "Definitely not now."

"But plenty of time to run a dance."

"You know why," Archer says slyly.

"*Guys.*"

"What about that new guy?" Archer asks, switching tactics.

"It's not—there's not a new guy," Leo says, and even I can tell he's flustered. Leo, flustered? Leo, troubled with romance? Mr. Perfect himself? Oh, this is too ironic. I sidle a little closer, my back carefully to the wall. "That's just like—it's nothing. It's whatever."

"But you do like him," Maggie challenges.

"And if you like him," Archer says, "by relationship math, that means you can finally get over—"

"Fascinating stuff, right?" Ms. Little whispers.

I jump, nearly losing my phone for the second time today. I clutch it against my chest. "How long have you been there?" I hiss.

"Not as long as you," she says. She gives me a calculating look, her eyes narrowed in a way that makes me think my life might be in danger. But today she chooses mercy. She clears her throat. "Hurry up, Wren," Ms. Little calls, raising her voice as if I were halfway down the hall. "You're going to be late." She winks dispassionately and pulls open the door, disappearing inside.

I glare at the door, letting it fall closed again to preserve the act. Not that I need the help. Or that I'd really meant to eavesdrop in the first place.

Not that I care what's going on in Leo's love life either.

♥

It takes me five minutes to start wishing I'd skipped the meeting and stayed in bed today. My sinuses may have been cleared by Archer's miraculous pecs, but I'm still exhausted, and just thinking about the walk home makes me feel like I've already been hit by a truck. But here I am, putting in the effort. Leo better appreciate it.

Principal Blackburn wants to announce the Dance at a school assembly, which is horrific, but Leo promises we don't have to stand onstage, so I decide not to fight it. At least once the news is official, people might stop asking about it. Not that most people have any idea who their student council representatives are, but the ones who do are persistent. I've heard the words *Dance* and *Buddy* more in the last week than I ever would have if I'd just left well enough alone. It's true what they say about no good deed going unpunished.

We discuss a little bit about promotional stuff, but considering that's been assigned to Ryan as the certified Art Person, there's not much to actually get done today. Thank God. That McGriddle this morning really hasn't been as restorative as I thought it would be. We throw around a couple of numbers for what we can spend on decorations before Ms. Little decides to call it a day.

I shoulder my backpack sluggishly, but Leo appears in front of my desk before I can stand.

"Hey," he says shortly. Surprisingly shortly, and not just because he's over six foot. Usually Leo is . . . well, nice. Or smug, recently. Or distracted. Today he looks downright annoyed. Huh. "Did you get my email?"

I squint. We're alone, the classroom strange-looking without anyone else in it. I guess Ms. Little trusts us not to start stealing desks if left unsupervised. "I don't . . . Oh." Something sparks in the back of my mind. "The one about the meeting today?"

I vaguely remember it now, checking my email Saturday morning and deciding to deal with it later, when I felt less like death warmed over. Clearly that didn't happen.

"The one asking if you wanted to meet to discuss it before the meeting today, yeah," he says. "So you did see it." Oh, he's straight-up mad now.

I feel . . . well, I don't feel good about it. I should probably think it's funny—perfect, unflappable Leo Reyes? bothered so easily?—but I can't quite manage it. Probably because it's not just about him, it's about me, and the fact I'm student council president. I can moan and groan about the Dance all I want, but it *is* part of my job. And so far Leo has done a hell of a lot more of it than I have. I told him I would do my part and—

And, well, here I am, but just sitting through a meeting isn't exactly doing much. I'm usually not a *bare minimum* kind of person.

Leo misinterprets my silence and decides to fill it himself. "Listen, if you're not serious about this—"

"I am," I insist. "Seriously. I'm—seriously serious." And now I sound like a Dr. Seuss book. But it's true. I didn't serendipitously become student council president just to fix Mr. Vernon's stage and call it a day. There's more left to do, even if it includes the Dance.

Leo doesn't look convinced. He pins me in place with his stare, his mouth set in an unhappy line. "I have—a *lot* of other things I could be doing." He trips over the words a little. "*Robotics team* looks a lot better on college applications than *dance organizer*."

"I didn't ask you to quit the team," I say, defensive. I was told, quite explicitly, that was none of my business.

He charges ahead, like he prepared his speech ahead of time. "I'm okay with taking point on this. I get it, you're not interested in the Dance. I *get* it, you don't like me." he says. "But I'm trying to work with you here, Wren. So don't tell me you're going to do something and then change your mind."

Ah, geez. I wince. I'm not sure if it's better or worse that I didn't actually mean to be a dick this time. I could tell him that I've been sick, but somehow that feels like making an excuse, however true it might be. Dammit.

"Let's start over," I say. It's not quite an apology, but it's close. I don't like admitting when I'm wrong, especially to Leo, but I feel like I've missed a step on a staircase, throwing me all off balance. *I get it, you don't like me.* I haven't liked Leo for years, but it feels weird to hear him . . . say it. I clear my throat. "Maybe on Saturday we can get together and . . . figure stuff out." I cringe internally. I've been so disconnected from the Dance, I don't even know what needs to be figured out. "I mean it this time. One hundred percent."

Leo's expression softens. He hesitates, like he's trying to decide to believe me. That stings a bit, but I can't really blame him. "All right," he says. "Sounds good." He starts to turn away and pauses. He raises his hands sheepishly. "I didn't mean to, like, chastise you there—"

"No, like, I get it—"

"Okay, cool—"

"Cool."

We sort of nod awkwardly for a moment before he finally breaks off and heads for the door. He's got his hand on the doorknob when he stops and looks back. The other hand is threaded through his backpack strap, his thumb worrying at a ragged hole in the material. "You usually leave with Ryan, right?" he says.

"Uh," I say, my brain short-circuiting for a minute. This has been way too many things one right after another for my post-sick brain to process. "Yeah?"

"Do you need a ride?"

8
THE RIDE

Life is very strange sometimes.

That day I watched Leo Reyes heinously eat a banana with the stringy bits still on, I never would have imagined I'd one day be following him out to the student parking lot. Never would I have imagined him offering me a ride, for starters, much less me accepting it.

It's just that September in Florida is still certifiably Really Fucking Hot and I don't live *that* close to the school, at least not close enough for the walk to be in any way enjoyable. My pride is absolutely not worth sweating my ass off if there's another option. Not today.

That, and I know an olive branch when I see one. Leo's anger appears to be like a firecracker—a bit of spark, but quick to cool down. I make a note to remember that, though I'm still kind of surprised by seeing him angry at all. If I'm going to get through this year, and this dance, Leo and I are going to have to work together.

Bleh.

"This isn't the way to the student parking lot," I say as he takes us left past the art building. "Did Blackburn give you a VIP parking spot or something?"

"No, we're still headed there," Leo says, but weirdly. Subdued, almost like he's telling me a secret. I squint in his direction and realize what it is.

He's *embarrassed*.

He looks sideways and catches the look on my face. "The robotics team meets on Mondays," he says in a rush, the tips of his ears turning red. "And Tuesdays. And Fridays. I would just prefer to avoid walking past the building, if at all possible." He clears his throat. "It's not even that far out of the way."

Oh, definitely defensive. "Do you think Stephen is going to jump from the roof with a knife or something?" I ask, trying valiantly not to laugh. "Because maybe I'll walk after all."

"Oh, *funny*," Leo says, shaking his head. "He's not a *bad* guy. I mean—he's just a little too . . ."

"Annoying?"

". . . passionate," he fills in. "He cares a lot. Just sometimes too much."

He has the grace not to add *like someone else I know*, but I hear it anyway. As *if*. I'm not saying I'm normal. I'm not even saying that I'm not annoying. But I'm not *Stephen Hannigan*.

"Where's your car?" I ask, changing the subject pointedly as we round the building and finally find the student parking lot. It's still about a quarter full. In the distance, I can see the football team practicing, their jerseys the garish red-and-blue color scheme of Rapture High. And even that's not as bad as Randy the Rapture Raptor.

"Just over here," Leo says, clicking his key fob. A car beeps in response.

I turn toward the sound and nearly trip over my own feet. "*That's* your car?"

I don't know anything about cars—I don't know a 2002 Toyota Camry from a Ford Fibonacci Turbo X34-0 whatever-the-hell—but I know what expensive looks like, and Leo's car is a *beast*. I stare at the monstrous white SUV, my mouth hanging open a fraction of an inch. I'm pretty sure I'm going to have to climb into it like a tank, but I'm too dazzled to be annoyed about it. I can't see past the tinted windows, but I'd bet money the interior is leather.

Leo visibly cringes. "I got it used," he says weakly. "It's really not as expensive as it looks."

"It looks like you could invade a foreign nation in it," I say. "It looks like you *have* invaded a foreign nation and this is what you bought with all the oil money."

"I do some website coding on the side," he says awkwardly. I feel like freelance coders don't make that much, but I don't know enough about website coding to question it. "It's not a big deal."

"Better than the robotics team," I mutter.

"Oh, *haha*," he says, but he ducks his head, embarrassed again. *He's* embarrassed. Clearly he hasn't seen my car. "Get in before I change my mind."

Predictably, I have to pull myself up to slide into the black leather passenger seat. It's hot to the touch after a day spent out in the sun, but not as scalding as it should be, probably because the air-conditioning was already blowing before we got in. Of course it's got remote start and keyless entry, the whole shebang. My car barely starts when I've got the key in it.

Leo has *money*. Who knew?

I guess that's something else I should hate him for, but I don't really feel like updating the list.

I put on my seat belt and settle into the passenger seat, my backpack sitting on my lap like a shield against the awkward silence that descends as suddenly and violently as a guillotine. I didn't totally think about this part when I accepted the offer. The silence stretches like it's making itself at home between us.

I look up to find Leo staring at me. He looks a bit like a deer in headlights, his eyes a little wide and a little lost, his dark hair flopping over his forehead in what's almost a curl. "What?" I try not to sound defensive.

"Um," he says. "Where do you live?"

"Oh." Right. Yeah. Important. "Just, uh, turn right out of the parking lot and—"

At least now there's something to fill the silence, between my halting instructions and Leo persistently messing with the radio, flipping between stations trying to find one that isn't running commercials. I hear the same ad for the local used car dealership three times before I break.

"I don't not like you," I say without preamble.

Leo actually laughs, which is not what I was expecting. "Oh," he says, shooting me a sideways look, "was that not a joke?"

I scowl, which probably doesn't help my case. I've been trying to scowl less ever since he asked how I was making that face, but it's been difficult. "I dislike a lot of people, I mean," I try again. "You're not special."

"Thanks," he says dryly, but even in profile, his eyes on the road, I can see the corner of his mouth lifted in a smile. "Why? Just curious. I've always wanted to ask."

I'm not telling him about the list. I'll open the door and roll out into traffic before I tell him about the list. "Why are you being nice to me?" I counter. "If you know I don't like you."

"Because I'd like you to like me," Leo says, like he didn't even have to think about it. He clears his throat and drums his fingers against the steering wheel. "I mean—I'm not used to people not liking me." His eyes dart toward me and then away again, back toward the road.

I suppress a sigh. "Because you're perfect."

Leo nearly veers into oncoming traffic.

"Jesus!" I squawk, holding on to the door for dear life. "But you're a shitty driver! I meant people *think* you're perfect. It's annoying. That's what I don't like."

"I don't—" Leo scoffs something unintelligible. "People do *not* think I'm perfect."

"Yeah?" I counter. "Like who?"

"You."

"Doesn't count."

"Archer. Maggie," he lists. "Stephen. My brother. My mom. My—"

"Okay, okay, shut up." I flap my hands. "I'm sorry I asked."

"Me too. Kind of a depressing list."

I snort. "We're working together. And I didn't want to walk home. Liking you doesn't really need to be part of the equation. I can be a professional about it." He turns onto my street and I point out my house, trying not to think about my technically-a-car sitting in the driveway, permanently leaking oil. "Just to be clear."

He gives me another flickering sideways look, one that lingers a little longer as he pulls into the driveway. Finally he smiles, and there's a dimple in one cheek. "I can do working together," he says. "Rides might be a case-by-case basis. You can be kind of annoying sometimes."

"If Ryan can keep her immune system in check, hopefully I won't need them." I literally hop out of the car. What's the point in making a car so tall?

I shoulder my backpack and turn, one hand on the door to close it. Leo is still watching me, probably to make sure I don't twist an ankle on the way down and sue him. I hesitate. "Thanks for the ride," I say. I fidget. "So Saturday . . . ?"

"Saturday should be good," he says. His fingers drum against the steering wheel. "I'll let you know."

"Cool. Bye." I slam the door and beat a hasty retreat. I have my phone in my hand before I'm even in the house.

> Me:
>
> ryan robinson youll never believe
> what just happened

♥

I'm definitely still a little sick, because I nap for a solid two hours before I hear my dad get home. I wake up to a Buddy notification waiting for me.

> Him:
>
> So did you regret it?

> Me:
>
> which part?
>
> the feverish rambling or the asking
> your opinion on beets?

> Him:
>
> I think they kind of go hand in hand.
>
> I tried some beets yesterday.
>
> Can't say I'm a fan.

> Me:
>
> yeah they suck
>
> but to answer your question no i
> don't think so. surprisingly.
>
> i guess this anonymous thing isn't
> so bad

Him:

It would be a shame if your anti-beet
stance got out.
I'm flattered that my conversations
aren't regret-worthy.

Me:

don't be, i tell all sorts of people that

Him:

Do you?

Me:

. . . okay, not really

hey what should I call you?

Him:

Like my name?

I think that negates the purpose of an
anonymous app, doofus

Me:

no like a nickname, DOOFUS

maybe i'll just call you doofus

Him:

I don't think you will.

Me:

|:<

Him:

Why do you need to call me
anything?

Me:

idk

for the sake of clarity in my rich
internal monologue?

Him:

Is this your way of saying you want
to be friends?

Is it? I frown at my phone. It feels like letting the app win somehow. Not Leo or the Dance, strangely, which are usually the things making my life annoying, but the *app*. I don't have a lot of friends—Ryan is the only one, actually, if I'm being honest. I used to have more when I was a kid, but that was back when everything was simple, and I don't think life is going to get any simpler from here. The fact that Buddy thinks it can fix all that with a cheerful color scheme and a clever interface is just insulting.

But. Well. He's funny. A bit, I mean. And it's actually kind of nice, the being anonymous part. Rapture isn't an exceptionally big place, and except for the kids who pay to go to St. Mark's on the other side of town, we've more or less all known the same people for most of our lives. Every grade, every horrible phase better left forgotten, is stored in the social consciousness of our peers. It's hard to get to know people as the person you are now when they're just thinking about the time you got your braces caught on a chain-link fence (Ryan's story, not mine).

So maybe I like talking on the stupid app. A little bit. Sue me.

Me:

i prefer the term co-conspirator

if i'm going to be helping you satisfy your overly nosy friends

Him:

Oh, of course.

Very generous of you to offer this free service.

Me:

actually, I don't need a name, I just
need your paypal email so I can send
an invoice for services rendered

let me guess

buddyboy@gmail.com?

Him:

Buddy Boy?

Is that the name you think of me as?

Me:

NO

Him:

I don't know, I kind of like it

It's cute

😊

Me:

i'm charging you for that

9
THE ASSEMBLY

It's far too easy to talk to—okay, I'm not going to call him Buddy Boy. I won't do it.

It's far too easy to talk to *him*, my secret app-based pen pal. Secret really only because I would never, *ever* live it down if Ryan found out. Sometimes having a best friend is more risk than reward.

"You're on your phone a lot lately," Ryan observes toward the end of the week. The school assembly is slated for Friday morning, when Principal Blackburn will announce the Dance's theme, and then my first meeting with Leo is on Saturday afternoon, making for a very Dance-filled weekend. All the days in between, evidently, belong to teachers vying for their own little taste of the student council budget. Evidently Mr. Vernon's glowing review has made it around the faculty lounge. Which is great. It's what I wanted. It even makes me feel a little bit like a celebrity, warding off my eager fans as I try to get to class. But also my nerves are about ready to snap like guitar strings.

Some people (freaks) run to alleviate stress. Some do crossword puzzles or read a book or any number of semi-productive things. I, it seems, send cat videos to strangers. We all cope in different ways, I guess.

"I'm a teenager," I deadpan. "It's what we do. Haven't you seen Fox News? Something about the degradation of society."

Ryan snorts but doesn't press the issue. I think she can sense how stressed I am and doesn't want to add fuel to a fire that she'll have to put out. She's economical like that.

Friday dawns bright and early with a beam of sunlight straight to my eyeballs, cementing the certainty that today is not going to be a good day. Usually I don't mind an assembly. Except for being packed into the auditorium in unpadded seats that haven't changed in twenty years. And they're loud. And boring. And I have to see all the people I routinely try to avoid.

So assemblies are kind of hell on earth. But hey, at least I get out of class for an hour.

However, that's *normally*, and this year has been anything but normal. Listening to Principal Blackburn announce the Dance's theme will be the final nail in the coffin. Once the school hears the words from someone besides the rumor mill, there will be no taking it back. I marinate in that for a moment, letting the futility wash over me, before I force my unwilling body into motion. I'm a professional, I remind myself. A consummate professional.

Everyone already knows that the assembly will be about the Dance, confirmed by Reed chattering in my ear all the way to school, having somehow come out the other side of her cold with more vim and vigor than before. Ryan is still hanging on to her cough, but I suspect that's just so she can interrupt Reed every couple of words with a furious round of hacking. In moments like this, I remember why I love her.

The assembly for juniors and seniors is during second period, which is the one that matters for two reasons. Because I'm a senior, for starters, but also only juniors and seniors can attend the Dance anyway. Not that that stops the lower classes from buzzing about it like they're medieval peasants and the queen is coming to town.

Hidden from overzealous teachers by my classmates, I check my phone on the sly as we shuffle into the auditorium like a herd of cattle. There's a message waiting for me.

Him:
They know that everyone's on their phones during these things, right?

I startle a bit, glancing around the crowd as if I'm going to see him and flashing lights spelling out BUDDY BOY will go off. Which they don't, because he's right and half the student body has their phones out, and half of *them* are probably on Buddy too. I keep feeling like it's completely obvious what I'm doing, but I guess it's pretty anonymous after all.

Me:

they should do it movie theater style

turn off the lights so you can see

whos glowing

Him:

Please don't give them ideas

"Who are you talking to?"

I jump. Jesus, I forgot Ryan was there. She *was* fussing with her jacket, picking at one of the hand-embroidered flowers on the front. Now she's craning her neck to look over my shoulder.

"Nothing," I say, before realizing that's not even the right word to answer that question. "No one." Maybe I should lie to get her off my back, the way BB (ugh) did with his friends. Maybe I can convince her I'm catfishing someone. BB would definitely play along. He owes me one.

"You're doing it again!" Ryan says, poking my cheek.

I smack her hand away, holding my phone to my chest. "Doing what?!" I squawk, my indignity lost to the buzz of conversation that hangs over the crowd. "I'm not doing anything!"

"You keep getting all . . . smiley!" She goes for another poke but I dodge expertly out of the way, nearly running into a pole in the process. It's hard to do anything expertly when you're being swept along in a current of humanity. "It's weird."

I stick out my tongue. "Can I not *smile*?"

"Not when you've been whining about the assembly all week," she says with a flat look that tells me that she'll be just as happy as I am when the assembly is over with. Guess I didn't keep those feelings to myself as much as I thought I did. "Just curious who you're talking to. I mean, I'm right here."

Ouch. That one's . . . actually a little too true. "I text lots of people," I say loftily. "I have friends besides you, you know." Now. Technically.

"List them alphabetically," Ryan says. "And my sister doesn't count."

I snort. "Trust me, I wouldn't list your sister anyway. *Not*," I add pointedly, "that I'm listing anyone. Because it's childish. *And* you're a bully."

Ryan sighs dramatically. "Fine, keep your secrets," She waves me off in what's embarrassingly close to a meme reference. Then, after a beat. "I'll find out eventually."

"Wait, what?" She conveniently doesn't hear me as we step into the auditorium, squinting as our eyes adjust to the change in lighting. After the brightness outside the doors, the Rapture High auditorium is not unlike a cave, cool and damp and more than a little musty. A blast of air-conditioning blows in my face so hard that it actually ruffles my hair.

We're not presenting today, but being on student council means we get to (have to?) sit up front, like the second row is some sort of VIP box. Ryan and I skirt along the outside of the auditorium rather than follow the crowd down the paths that cut through the middle, siphoning them off into the different sections. Some of the teachers who have finished herding their classes are already standing along the walls.

I catch Ms. Little's eye and she raises her eyebrows. I think she's just acknowledging my existence until she gives a little jerk of her chin, summoning me over. Considering we have to walk by her to get to our seats, I don't exactly have a choice.

"Hey," she says. "I want to meet with you later."

As if I don't have enough going on right now. "About what?" I ask innocently, without slowing down.

"You know what." She raises her voice enough to be heard over the crowd as I slip away, Ryan at my back.

"What was that all about?" Ryan mutters over my shoulder.

"Probably just student council paperwork," I say, focusing a little too hard on finding our seats so she can't see the lie on my face. I know Ryan has her own opinions on my college plans, but at least she has the decency not to share them. I tell Ryan about almost everything, at least in my pre-Buddy life, but there are some things we don't talk about. Sometimes I think she's afraid to, like she knows where my bruises are but is scared to press on them too hard. But I don't know for sure. Like I said, we don't talk about it. It's better that way for the both of us.

The rest of our motley crew is already seated by the time we get to the front. Or mostly. Archer is actually standing, leaning over the back of his seat to talk to some soccer jock sitting behind him. Maggie is slouching, her jacket expertly rumpled so her phone is hidden behind the fold. Leo can't tilt the auditorium seating back, so he's settled for putting his feet up against the back of the empty seat in front of him, his freakishly long legs bent. He's also on his phone.

He looks up and drops his feet when he sees us, the rubber of his shoes slapping against the thin industrial carpeting.

"Hey," he says.

"Hey," I say.

Oh God, this is going to be weird, isn't it? It shouldn't be weird. He gave me a ride, not a kidney. What did he say exactly? That he's not used to people *not* liking him? Of course he isn't. Who wouldn't like Leo Reyes? With his white teeth and easy charm and expensive car. He's built to be liked.

Well, if he thinks it's going to be that easy, he's got another thing coming.

"*Hey*," Ryan says. She prods me in the back a little more forcefully than necessary. "Are you waiting for an engraved invitation?"

Right. I'm standing at the end of the row, holding up traffic. Which means, because I was too busy paying attention to Leo's shoes on the seat in front of him, it's too late to casually hang back so Ryan can sit next to him instead of me.

Think what you will of me, but I'm not so pathetic I would leave a buffer seat between me and Leo Reyes. Even if it means sitting close enough I can smell his laundry detergent. Which smells nice, by the way, but that doesn't mean anything. No one buys laundry detergent that doesn't smell nice. My seat squeaks as I drop into it, the hinges reminding me that they're older than I am. Maybe the auditorium needs new seats next, now that I've got the student council budget in my hands.

"Are we still good for tomorrow?" Leo says, leaning in so that our shoulders bump. I try not to jump.

"Why wouldn't we be?" I say, a little too defensively.

He shrugs one shoulder, one corner of his mouth twitching. He's laughing at me, which is annoying, but at the moment all I can think about is the mole under his left eye. When does it stop being a mole and start being a beauty mark? Not that it matters. Not that I'm thinking about it. "Because you're exceptionally good at avoiding me?"

"Worse every day," I say, and I'm not sure if I'm owning him or myself with that one. "Besides, I'm reformed. You won't be able to get rid of me now."

"Trust me, you'll live to regret that one," Ryan says, leaning over me. I try to elbow her but the hard edge of an enamel pin on her jacket protects her like a porcupine's spikes.

Principal Blackburn walks onstage, neatly avoiding the hole (I swear I hear Mr. Vernon scoff), and clears his throat loudly into the microphone three times before the noise in the auditorium starts to die down.

Principal Blackburn, simply put, looks like an old-timey sea captain. Or a U.S. president circa the early nineteenth century. A bristling gray beard dominates his face, scratching unpleasantly against the microphone with sharp bursts of static as he gets comfortable behind the podium.

"All right, everyone settle down now," he says with a heavy sigh, and another earsplitting burst of static goes a long way in shutting everyone up. "We've got a few things on the agenda to get through today. . . ."

I tune him out almost immediately, like just about everyone else in the room. Even Leo is on his phone, and he's the resident golden child. Maggie leans over to mutter something to him, but a notification distracts me before I can eavesdrop.

Him:

Have you ever noticed that
Blackburn looks

And then the notification preview cuts off. I bite the tip of my tongue. Sitting between Leo and Ryan has got me literally between a rock and a hard place. I definitely cannot be seen with Buddy open on my phone here.

I wiggle my phone, testing out angles to see if I could open it on the sly, but Ryan is already suspicious. She's watching Blackburn talk with a look in her eye that means she's actually daydreaming about something (God willing) unrelated, but I don't trust it. She may be all glitter and kitschy earrings on the outside, but she's more calculating than she looks.

There. A flicker of her eyes, checking to see what I'm doing. Dammit.

I huff and drop my phone against my middle, where at least the unread notification can't taunt me. Maybe Ryan is right, maybe I do have a problem. Or maybe I just don't want to listen to Principal Blackburn drone about school policy for fifty-five minutes. Maybe if I angle my head right, no one will be able to tell my eyes are closed. My eyelids droop. I stayed up too late last night . . . talking to BB.

Okay, yeah, I definitely have a problem.

". . . Wren Martin."

My eyes snap open again.

I raise my head slowly to find everyone looking at me—or, well, not everyone. Most people don't really know who I am, but those who do are certainly staring. Ryan is pulling a face like I've just been sentenced to death. Archer is leaning forward around Maggie so he can flash me a thumbs-up. Not very illuminating reactions. I'm forced to turn to Leo.

He looks like his eyes are about to pop out of his head. "That's not what he was supposed to say," he says. "I swear—I wrote it out for him and everything."

My heart sinks to my feet. "Leo," I say through gritted teeth. "Why is Principal Blackburn summoning me to the stage?" At least I think that's what he's doing. I'm not sure what else the awkward flapping motion he's doing at me could mean.

Leo cringes. "He . . . uh . . . wants you to tell everyone about the Dance. I can do it," Leo adds quickly, holding out his hands. He starts to get to his feet. "I'll handle it."

"No, I've got it." I wave him away and stand. The only thing worse than getting up on that stage would be watching Leo do it instead, like I'm ten years old watching my mom tell the waitress I asked for no pickles. My pride has taken so much of a beating, I'm not sure it can take much more. Besides, I took a public speaking class last semester. We mostly watched old sitcoms, but surely I absorbed something.

Still. This is going to suck.

There's an awkward pause as I shuffle past Ryan and make it up the stairs, only considering the hole in the floor for half a second. A semi-accidental trip down the stage-hole wouldn't be the worst way to get out of this. Reality is weirdly distorted on the stage, and I can't help but think that there are many, *many* reasons why I'm not a theater kid. My shoes are too loud against the scuffed wood flooring, the lights too bright in my eyes. From my new vantage point, my classmates are simultaneously small and looming, individuals lost to the mass of humanity staring at me with hundreds of blinking eyes.

Blackburn hands the podium off to me with the grace of a man handing off a bomb. The podium is a mess of papers, most of which are forms that clearly have nothing to do with the matter at hand, but I can see the press release or whatever that Leo wrote up for him half crumpled in the back. I shuffle it forward, trying to smooth out the creases with my sweaty hands.

"Uh, hello," I say, belatedly leaning closer to the mic. My voice echoes around me. God, do I really sound like that or is it just the school's cheap audio equipment? "My name is Wren. I'm the new student council president. After. Uh. You know." Why can I not talk about the change in positions without making it sound like they all died? "I'm sure you all already know why I'm up here."

Someone whoops in the back row and the auditorium ripples with excitement. Okay, they might not care about me, but they *do* care about the Dance. I take a deep breath, my confidence slightly bolstered. At least I have a captive audience.

"As you might have heard, this year the school has part-nered with the app Buddy to sponsor the Valentine's Day Dance." I nearly trip over the word *Buddy* like everyone is going to be able to tell I'm the world's biggest hypocrite, but at least I get it out without incident. This isn't so bad. This could be worse. "So this year, the theme will be Twenty-First-Century Masquerade."

The auditorium buzzes like I just kicked a nest of hornets. It's a catchy turn of phrase, I have to give Leo that. Everyone is listening now. Everyone wants to know more.

I clear my throat. "What does that mean? Well, I'll tell you." I only got a B in my public speaking class. But Mrs. Carter said what I lack in fluidity I make up for in verve. I think that's a good thing. "Every year, we spend most of our budget on putting on the Dance, but only some of us get to enjoy it. Because let's be honest, it's not a very inclusive envi-ronment. Not for queer kids, or kids who can't afford it, or even just kids who don't want to deal with the social pressure of who is going to the Dance with who." I'm editorializing a little. Focus. "The Valentine's Day Dance has always been about romance, but this year, with Buddy's help, we're going to do something a little different. Buddy is an anonymous chat app that's about making connections with people and getting to know them for who they are, not for who we *think* they are.

"By making Buddy the sponsor of this year's dance, you'll get to choose what the Dance means to you. Download the Buddy app and you'll be paired with possible matches from other juniors and seniors at Rapture High based on a short personality quiz. You can use it to look for a romantic date"—I don't add *I can't stop you*—"*or* a platonic one. Or even a group. When you arrive at the Dance, you'll be able to opt in to a feature that will reveal your true identity to your . . . buddies . . . when the clock strikes eight."

Leo *did* have a point. I'd been pretty sure he pulled the Buddy connection out of his ass when he first suggested it, but saying it out loud, I have to admit that it makes sense. Just introducing the concept changes the entire narrative of the Dance. Yeah, some people are going to ask people the traditional way and *yeah*, some people are going to use Buddy to find a date, but they don't *have* to. I guess you never really *had* to, but it felt that way. People treated it that way.

But we're trying to change things, and the most surprising part is that I think it's working. I can already see a lot of our classmates on their phones, the Buddy app on their screens like a field of little yellow daisies across the auditorium. My heart trips. It feels good to be listened to. Specifically, for something they actually like. I'm here to improve the school, not win a popularity contest, but there is something a little intoxicating about delivering news people want to hear. Is this how Leo feels all the time?

I'm afraid it goes to my head a bit.

"Because of the sponsorship, we're able to make tickets to the Dance free for all juniors and seniors." I push Leo's prepared statement aside and lean forward again, one hand bending the microphone closer. "And this year it will be held," I say, "at the Canopy."

10
THE CANOPY

A little background might be necessary.

The Canopy is actually a part of the White Sand Hotel and Resort, presumably named because *Rapture* Hotel and Resort sounds like the kind of place you go to join a doomsday cult. It's easily the fanciest hotel in Rapture, right on the water and rocking a white stone/gold accent motif that makes it look like a palace rose up out of the ocean one day. The Canopy is the hotel's restaurant and a venue for wedding receptions and business conventions, on top of being an indoor botanical garden. The entire venue is under a paneled-glass dome and filled with semitropical plants, giving it the air of a fantasy jungle with air-conditioning. It's nice. It's *really* nice.

So why *not* hold a dance there, if it's all being sponsored anyway? My eyes sweep the crowd as the auditorium bursts into applause, my mouth twisting into a grin. I understand now, in a sudden burst of clarity buoyed by the support of the crowd. Ms. Little was right; we were never going to get rid of the Dance. The school would've rioted. But this, with Buddy—it's hardly even got anything to do with Valentine's Day anymore, at least until eight o'clock hits and they find out who they've actually been talking to all along.

So if they want a Dance? I'll give them a Dance, all right. Leo may have been right about Buddy, but he's not the only one with an ace up his sleeve.

Leo is staring up at me from the crowd like he's just seen a ghost, his mouth hanging open a fraction of an inch. Not in a dazzlingly impressed kind of way. My grin falters and my eyes flicker to Ryan, who looks like she just stepped in water with socks on. Maggie? Not good. Even Archer looks a little startled.

I look up, finding Ms. Little still standing at her spot against the wall. She shakes her head slowly.

Well, *shit*.

"Keep an eye out for more information," I say quickly, a little too close to the microphone for the resulting sound to be altogether pleasant. "Thanks. Bye."

I beat a hasty retreat as Principal Blackburn comes to take over the podium. Rather than slink back down to my seat, where the rest of the student council waits, I slip behind the heavy, dusty blue curtain and disappear backstage.

I exhale shakily as Principal Blackburn mumbles the assembly to a close on the other side of the curtain. It's dark except for the emergency lights casting a thick sort of gloom over the semicircle of chairs left onstage from Mr. Vernon's last class. I shake out my hands, but there's too much adrenaline still running through my veins for them not to tremble a little bit, like I just downed a couple of shots of espresso and also ran a mile. It's fine. The lights were just bright, that's all. The crowd was happy, and that's what matters.

Right?

The door to the hallway connecting the band and choir rooms opens, and I spin on my heel. "Ryan—"

Not Ryan. Leo. It's hard to see his expression in the dark, but something about his silhouette as the door closes behind him suggests *not good.* "Wren," he says, his voice strained. *"What did you do?"*

Okay, maybe this *is* not good. Maybe this is, in fact, bad. "I thought I was helping!" I hiss back.

"This is not helping!" For a second I think he's going to grab me by the shoulders and shake me, but he settles for holding his hands up in front of him, his palms open like he's trying to manifest a solution for the new problems I just created. "How are we going to pay for the Canopy?"

I can tell from the dull roar of noise on the other side of the curtain that the assembly is letting out, but I don't have a clean getaway that doesn't involve fleeing back onto the stage. And probably falling down the hole, based on my luck so far. "Isn't that what the sponsorship is for?" Now I'm the one throwing my hands up in exasperation, though in the dark it all comes across as disjointed shadow puppets.

"That doesn't mean—"

The door to the hallway opens again and we both jump. Mr. Vernon stands silhouetted by the light from behind. He sounds annoyed as he leans in and says, "How many times do I have to tell you kids—" He stops abruptly. "Oh, Mr. Martin. Mr. Reyes."

I resist the urge to drag my hands down my face. "Mr. Vernon," I start, unsure what the next part is going to be.

"No, no," he says breezily, waving one hand. "Don't let me get in the way of young love. Can't wait for this Dance, by the way."

"*Mr. Vernon*," I sputter, and I'm grateful for the darkness hiding the flush that instantly crawls up my neck. He's already gone, comforted by the fact that if kids are making out backstage it's at least two he likes.

Not that—not that I *ever*—

"I'm going to kick more holes in that stage, I swear to *God*." I sigh, and this time I do run my hand down my face, trying to work the blood back out of it. "Anyway—where are you going?"

"We can figure it out later," Leo says quickly, already moving toward the curtain. "We're still meeting tomorrow, right?"

"Yeah, but . . ." I thought he wanted to kill me, frankly.

"I'll see you then." He disappears just as quickly as Mr. Vernon did, throwing up a hand behind him in a distracted wave.

"Okay, fine!" I call after him, annoyed. "Don't fall down the hole!" I stare at the curtain he left through, which is still swaying slightly as it settles again, like he might change his mind and reappear. He doesn't. So I just stand there in the dark like an idiot, feeling a little lost and not at all presidential.

♥

I'm not nervous to meet with Leo on Saturday, I'm just not looking forward to it. Not that I was particularly looking forward to it before, but the *Hindenburg*-level disaster that was the assembly has me a little on edge. It's enough to make me want to fake sick to get out of seeing him, but I *did* promise I would be more involved with the Dance. For better or for worse.

For worse so far, clearly.

I sigh, puffing out my cheeks and trying not to wiggle the lopsided table I've taken up residence at since the start of Ryan's shift. Starbucks seemed like a safe location when Leo and I planned the meeting—Ryan works there on the weekends, so I get a free drink as long as her manager isn't looking and I don't ask for anything too over-the-top—but now I'm regretting that there's an audience. Ryan watches me from the cash register, pursing her lips pointedly as she rings up a Frappuccino. *Where is he?*

I widen my eyes at her. *How am I supposed to know?*

The front door opens with a jingle and Leo steps in, looking like some sort of hip college freshman grabbing a coffee on his way to class, his laptop and a notebook under one arm and big noise-canceling headphones around his neck. I sit up a little straighter, the table thunking as it evens out again. I wedge my shoe against the short leg.

I watch him glance around the room before finally finding me in my corner, his hand going up in an awkward sort of wave. I start to mimic it before letting my hand flop back onto the table. Why am I waving? He already saw me.

"Hey," Leo says, a little breathless. "Sorry I'm late—what's that?" He gives the drink on the table a bemused look, like he's never been in a Starbucks before.

"It's coffee," I say. It comes out a little impatient. "It's for you." And it wasn't even free. Ryan made me pay for that one.

His eyebrows scrunch together. "There's whipped cream on it?"

"So?" That's how I like it. A chocolate Frappuccino with whipped cream and two shots of caramel. That's normal, right? "It's good. Try it." My hands twitch around my own drink, realizing I maybe should have let him order for himself. I need to stop trying to help. The attempt is only going very steeply downhill. "I'm trying to be nice, okay?"

Leo laughs and my nerves spike, threatening to make me get back into my scowling habit. I *am* trying. I'm really, *really* trying. "No, I mean—thank you. It is nice," Leo says, holding up his free hand to ward off my defensiveness. He pulls out the chair opposite me and settles down, taking a moment to unwrap his straw and sip his drink.

He's humoring me, which is annoying. But it would have also been annoying if he hadn't, so I guess that's just where we are right now.

"So—" Leo starts.

"I might have—" I say at the same time. He stops and I'm afraid that if I don't keep going I'll take the excuse to never say it, so I plow on ahead. "I might have made a mistake. With the Canopy. I should have probably . . . taken a vote . . . first."

It's not a very good apology, but it's the best one Ryan and I could agree on after we workshopped it this morning. I'm more of an *ignore my problems until they go away* kind of person, but I guess you can't do that when you're the one who made the problem in the first place. Even if you do spend seven dollars on a coffee for the person you're apologizing to.

Leo raises his eyebrows, his lips quirked in a tired smile over his drink. "You think?"

I sigh, maybe a touch more dramatically than a repentant person is supposed to. Better to just skip to the part that matters. "I'll tell everyone it was a mistake. We don't have as much funding as we thought or something. It'll be fine." I take a sip of my drink, hiding the sinking feeling that it will very much not be fine. I told the entire junior and senior classes that they were going to have the biggest dance of the year at the swankiest venue locally available. I don't care what they think of me, I think that's been well-established, but I am a little afraid they might tear me limb from limb.

Leo closes his eyes and leans on one hand, pressing his fingertips against his forehead and massaging it, looking like a sigh given human form. "I'm sorry. It's too sweet. I can't do it," he says, and for a single disorienting moment I think he means my sort-of apology. Until he pushes his drink to one side. Oh. *Well.*

Leo drops his hands in front of him, planting them on the table. "First of all, stop apologizing. It's freaking me out," he says, shaking his head. He looks up, pinning me in place with his gaze. "Tell me what you really think."

"Um." My eyes flicker to Ryan, but she seems to be caught up in a steamed milk emergency. "Well . . . I think you were right. The Buddy thing is a good idea. I think it'll work." Saying the words feels like physically pulling my own teeth, but it seems like a good place to start. "I *also* think that if we're getting money from Buddy we might as well use it on something nice. And I think that Principal Blackburn made me go up onstage with no warning, which was, like, a lot all at once. *And* I think that just because an idea isn't *your* idea doesn't mean it isn't a good one."

Okay, maybe that was a little more than he meant.

"I really was trying to help," I say stubbornly. I should at least get credit for that.

"I know," Leo says, and I blink in surprise. His mouth twists strangely, and I realize that he's trying to hide a smile. He shrugs with one shoulder. "I can tell when you're being a bitch on purpose."

Okay, this time I scowl.

Leo laughs and leans back in his chair, not back on two legs this time, but he's probably fighting the urge. "Good idea, bad idea—I don't know. But we're going to have to make it work. If we try to take it back now, they'll kill us."

"I know." I stab at my drink with my straw, breaking up the melting lumps of whipped cream. "I was thinking of myself as a martyr figure there."

"Yeah, you're not getting out of it that easily." He scoots his drink over another inch and sets his laptop on the table, cracking it open. "Archer and I will figure it out with the Buddy budget. But we have another problem."

Of course we do. I'm starting to learn that being in a governing body is just one problem after another. "What's that?"

Leo looks up from his laptop screen and says the second-most-chilling word in Rapture High's vocabulary. "Homecoming."

Okay, I actually don't care that much about homecoming. Or prom, really. Rapture High doesn't so much either, which is why the student body is significantly less annoying about it than about the Valentine's Day Dance. I think the only reason we even bother having homecoming is because of the—

The blood drains from my face. "The freshmen and the sophomores," I whisper. My back is to a wall, but I still have to resist the urge to turn around and see if Reed is lurking over my shoulder. Right now the freshmen are just excited because everyone else is, kind of like a bunch of puppies, but that's not going to last forever. Sooner or later they're going to wonder what *they're* getting. When they do, they're going to want something just as good.

Which they're not going to get, but we have to put forth some kind of effort. I don't want to face Reed if homecoming is nothing more than a gym-and-a-couple-of-bowls-of-pretzels kind of affair. Ugh.

Leo nods, looking similarly pained. "We still have to make homecoming happen. With the *normal* budget," he adds quickly, before I can get any ideas.

"So I still have to spend my budget on a dance," I say bitterly, stabbing my drink again with a little more force than necessary. "That's it? Wren still loses?"

Leo arranges his face into something that's trying to be sympathetic, but only vaguely. "Well," he says, "you did kind of do it to yourself."

I can't even scowl about that one—he's right, once again. I got myself into this mess. My pride is suffering for it, but so is the rest of the school. The hole in the stage is one thing, but Rapture High has a thousand more problems that could use that money too. I know because teachers keep finding new and creative ways to drop hints about it. Yesterday Dr. Bartlett left a note about a new projector on my AP Euro quiz.

I pause, my fingers still on my straw. I *did* get myself into this mess. But that doesn't mean I can't get myself out of it.

"Unless," I say slowly, "we can raise the money."

Leo watches me warily. Which is fair. My bright ideas don't have a very good track record so far. "Like how?"

Isn't it obvious? My mouth curls at the corners, a smile of Cheshire cat proportions sliding across my face. "A bake sale."

11
THE BAKE SALE

I love baking. It's challenging but rewarding. Precise but creative. And at the end of it you sometimes have a cake, so that already makes it better than most hobbies.

More than that, I'm *good* at it. I won second place at the community center junior baking competition in sixth grade. Which yeah, isn't exactly *MasterChef Junior*, but still, my macarons *were* perfect in every technical sense of the word. I would have gotten first place if one of the judges hadn't had a granddaughter in the competition.

So if there's one thing that can at least *help* patch this financial hole, it's a bake sale. The mighty bake sale has been the backbone of school finances since the beginning of time, and that was *without* my raspberry–white chocolate cookie bars. We've got this. *I've* got this.

And I don't really need help.

"Why does Leo have to be there?" I ask for probably the tenth time. It's mostly a rhetorical question, but I think Ryan is starting to get tired of it. I'm tired of it too, but the bake sale is tonight and I have to get my whining in while I still can. Reed has cheer practice this afternoon, which means I get the whole ride home to do it uninterrupted. "Why can't you man the club fair table with me?"

"Because my parents want to go to dinner after parent-teacher night and I like free food more than I like you," she says again, a little more impatiently than the last nine times. She gives me a sideways look as she turns right out of the student parking lot. "Stop being dramatic. It's only a couple of hours."

A couple of hours trapped behind a table in the gym next to Leo, slinging cookie bars and cupcakes and haggling with cheapskate parents. I should specify that I love the *bake* part of *bake sale*. The actual selling part is a little less exciting. But we don't have a ton of time to figure this homecoming thing out, and parent-teacher night is the best concentration of people with disposable income that we have available.

"Archer is the treasurer," I counter without conviction, sinking back into the passenger seat of her car like I might become one with the ugly upholstery. "Wouldn't it be more appropriate to have him handle money?"

"Archer has a table with the soccer team," she points out. She hesitates. "And we were in the same math class last year. I think we're better off with Leo."

I snort. "I can be bad at math too." It comes quite naturally.

"Not *this* bad."

All right, maybe she's got a point. The whole goal here is to *make* money.

My phone vibrates in the cup holder, where I stuck it when I got in the car, rattling against the hard plastic like it's announcing to the whole world that Wren Martin just got a text. I catch a glimpse of the yellow Buddy notification as I snatch it up.

"Was that me?" Ryan asks belatedly, distracted by actually watching the road.

"No, it's mine. Spam text," I say, dismissing the notification and stuffing my phone into my backpack.

I almost forget about the Buddy message entirely, the rest of the afternoon a whirlwind of flour, sugar, and preheating the oven to 350 degrees. Only after I have my cookie bars lovingly arranged in the Tupperware and ready to go do I remember I never even looked at it. I wait until we're in the car, Tupperware in my lap and Dad behind the wheel, to open it. I'm pretty confident that Dad doesn't even know what Buddy is, much less why I would be embarrassed to be on it.

Him:

So what do you think about this
Dance thing?

My heart jumps. Somehow I didn't consider that Buddy Boy and the Dance were two things that intersected. I mean,

Buddy has to do with the Dance, sure, but I guess I've been thinking of Buddy Boy as . . . different. Separate, somehow. It didn't occur to me until just this moment, my heart skittering and my palms a little sweaty, that he might want to actually meet at the Dance like everyone else. What am I supposed to say if he does?

Me:

like conceptually?

or the buddy-dance thing?

also conceptually, i guess

Him:

Considering where we're talking, I
was thinking the Buddy thing

But feel free to interpret it however
you want

And reveal myself as the number one dance-hater at Rapture High? Not likely. The whole point of this is to be anonymous. But it also means I can be a little more honest than usual.

Me:

it's kinda cool i guess

also kinda weird, but at least it takes
some of the pressure off

what do your friends think?

Him:

What do you mean?

Me:

i mean, they made you join to set you up right?

are they expecting us to meet at the dance or something?

Him:

Ohhh, that

I think they're mostly just happy to see me talking to someone on here at all, honestly. They haven't even asked about the Dance

I was kind of planning to just tell them you didn't want to do the whole reveal thing

Or maybe that your dog died and you couldn't make it or something

I frown down at my phone. Well, that's one anxiety taken care of. Still, I can't help but wonder if I should be offended. Not that I *want* to reveal my identity in the middle of the Dance, but he should want me to so I can graciously turn him down. It's an ego thing.

Me:

omg you're going to kill my DOG

i don't even have a dog and I'm offended

Him:

Desperate times call for desperate measures

You've still got time to adopt one

Me:

well now i don't think i should

since you're putting hits out on them

i guess i'll have to stick with chickens

Him:

Do you actually have chickens?

Like in your backyard?

Me:

perhaps, perhaps not

you have to be level 15 friend to find
out for sure

better start doing more quests if you
want to level up

"Wren?" Dad asks. "Where am I supposed to park?"

I pocket my phone and adjust the Tupperware of cookie bars on my lap. Time to focus. I can't think about Buddy, or Buddy Boy, or anything in between right now. Tonight, I have a bake sale to pull off.

We got here early so I could help set up the table, but the parking lot is already crawling with people here for parent-teacher night. Dad drives in fits and starts as I direct him through the ecosystem of traffic. Freshman dart like nervous deer across the road while their confused parents meander behind them, crossing diagonally so as to get in the way for as long as humanly possible. The seniors know they have college coming up, so they just walk right in front of us with little regard for where the cars are or how fast they're going.

Considering I'm about to spend the next couple of hours crammed behind a folding table with Leo, I can relate. But there are worse things I could be doing. Namely, escorting my father through the wilds of parent-teacher night.

I *told* him he didn't need to come. I almost begged him not to, because I'm almost eighteen and an honor student and have enough to deal with without him going on a parenting kick. I'm "a pleasure to have in class," I get it. I could have told him that. I did, actually.

But he's pulled into a spot at the far corner of the student parking lot, the one only the band kids usually frequent, so you can see how well that argument went.

"So where is building five?" Dad says, smoothing out the rumpled piece of paper with my schedule printed on it. I'm doing my best to herd him across campus, but my hands are full of Tupperware and he keeps stopping to consult the paper.

"I put a map at the bottom," I say, pointing with my nose. "All the buildings have big red numbers on the front. It's really pretty easy."

"Hm," he hums, unconvinced. "Can you just show me to the first classroom? Then I can figure it out."

I roll my eyes behind his back. "I told you, you didn't have to come," I say flatly.

"I wanted to come."

"I know, but . . ."

"Your mother always came to these things."

"I *know*, Dad." It comes out sharper than I really meant, but Jesus, I don't need to talk about Mom right now too. "Fine, I'll show you. Come on."

I drop him off at building five like it's the first day of kindergarten and I'm the parent, leaving him in the care of Mrs. Vogh, who teaches AP English literature. I duck out before he can think to ask me for directions to the next classroom.

I huff and finger-comb my hair into place as I trek all the way back across campus, where the club fair is being set up in the gym. The bleachers have been pushed back to make room for three long lines of folding tables, each claimed by a different sport or club and made as alluring as possible for the unspoken-for freshmen who will soon be descending on the gym. The sports teams are all stacked up right at the front, their tables draped with thick, branded tablecloths and bearing their sportsball of choice.

"Hey there!" One of the athletes springs out at me and I jump, clutching my cookie bars to my chest. "Have you considered joining— Oh, hey, Wren." Archer's salesman smile drops when he realizes it's me and I'm not about to join the soccer team, nor would he want me to. "Looking for Leo?"

"Yeah. Yes. I am," I say, trying to pretend he didn't almost give me a heart attack. I clear my throat. "I have the . . . you know." I hold up the Tupperware. My pride and joy.

Archer points. "Back corner. Good luck!"

The *back corner*? I understand the sports getting the prime real estate, but I don't like the sound of that. Something's not right here. "Thanks," I say, distracted. "And, Archer? Maybe tone down the excitement a little. They're only freshmen."

I leave him looking thoughtful with a soccer ball under one arm, the poster child for Rapture High athletics. I understand why Ryan didn't necessarily want him handling the bake sale. At least he's a hell of a soccer player.

I skirt the edge of the gym, the opposite direction from where the robotics team has a place of honor just behind the sports tables. They've pulled out all the stops, including an operating robotic arm that's currently moving wooden blocks back and forth on their table, probably trying to lure in the next young Leo from the hordes of unpolished freshmen. Somehow Stephen Hannigan's stare cuts across the gym, drilling holes in me. I twist my hand to subtly flip him off against the side of my Tupperware. I get a glimpse of his face twisting in pure offense before I turn away, hiding a smirk. His fault for staring.

It takes me longer than I expected to find our table. Archer wasn't kidding when he said the *back corner*. Our table is as far back as it can get, wedged between the wall and a table for something called the Friends Club. I squint as I get closer, and realize that what I initially took to be the world's second-saddest club is actually a club dedicated to people who enjoy watching *Friends*, the classic television sitcom, making it the number one saddest club. Someone sets out a Bluetooth speaker and starts to play the theme song, which I can only imagine will be on loop the entire night.

Fantastic. Off to a great start.

Leo is already there, fussing with the corners of our tablecloth. It's snowy white, which at least stands out among all the blue and red of the school colors, and mercifully not Buddy branded.

I don't know how he notices me over the cacophony of *I'll be there for yooooou* and chatter echoing off of the high, industrial ceiling, but he does. "Hey!" Leo says, giving the tablecloth one last tug. "All set?" He looks up and grins, his hair falling in his eyes.

I freeze.

Leo Reyes wears glasses.

Which is to say, Leo Reyes must wear contacts *usually*, because I've never seen him wear glasses before. What I mean is, I would have noticed. They're about a decade out of style, rectangular and made from dark plastic, a little too big, so they keep sliding down his nose. He pushes them back up with one knuckle.

As a look, it really should not work, outside of maybe going as a dork for Halloween. But it does.

Goddammit, it *does*.

"What?" he says.

I blink. "What?"

He frowns. "Is there something on my face?" He rubs self-consciously at his cheek.

Oh shit, I'm staring. I shouldn't be staring. That's not normal. "Should there be?" I counter defensively, which is not the correct response. I pivot, trying to make it into a joke. "Have you been sampling the product?"

And now I've made us sound like drug dealers. Flawless execution. "How did we end up all the way back here?" I try instead. Being annoyed works. That's a pretty familiar state of being. "No one is going to even notice us. Who assigned these tables?" I know no one takes the student council seriously, but you'd think we'd get at least an ounce of respect.

"I think the PTA organized the club fair," Leo says. "I mean, we got in pretty last minute. It was probably the only table left. . . ."

I narrow my eyes. "But?"

"But . . . ," he goes on reluctantly, "also Stephen's mom is the head of the PTA."

Of course. Fucking Stephen Hannigan. I roll my eyes, but there's not exactly a lot we can do about it at this point. My cookie bars will just have to speak for themselves. I set the Tupperware on the table and focus on unpacking them from their nest of wax paper. They all slid into each other, probably when Archer scared the shit out of me, so the frosting is a little wonky, but they still look delicious. That's what matters. Next to me, Leo unpacks whatever he brought to make the bake sale table look more populated. The supporting cast for my cookie bars.

Or at least, that's what I expected. I stare. "Who made those?" I say, which comes out more like a demand. I stare down at the most perfect blueberry muffins I've ever seen outside of a bakery display case. I look up sharply. "Is that a crumb topping?"

"Maggie made them," Leo says, apparently unaware of the war going on inside me. Am I jealous or impressed? Jealous that I'm impressed? My role as best baker on the student council is crumbling underneath me like a kingdom of sand.

"I didn't know she baked," I say lightly. "They look . . . amazing." I can't *lie*. Not to a muffin like that.

"Don't tell her that." Leo gives me a sideways look, his mouth tipped into a wry little smile. He shrugs. "She doesn't like you very much. It would just make her mad."

I squint at him. "Well, yeah. I picked up on that." From the way she rolls her eyes every time I make a suggestion in student council meetings and generally looks at me like I'm a bug on the sidewalk. I'm not sure *why*, actually. I mean, I've always assumed my strict anti-Dance, pro-annoyance agenda has something to do with it, but I'm starting to suspect it might go a little beyond that if Leo is mentioning it.

Which is also a little weird, now that I think about it.

"Why would you tell me that?" I say, pulling out one of the folding chairs and kicking the empty cookie bar Tupperware under the table. I take a seat. "What if it hurt my feelings?"

He gives me a sideways look. "Did it?"

"No."

"Because I knew it wouldn't." He shrugs. The school invested in rather stubby folding tables, so sitting side by side behind it, he's close enough I can feel the movement stir the air. It's too late to surreptitiously angle my seat differently. "I thought maybe we had some sort of total-honesty thing after you admitted you didn't like me in my own car."

"Huh. All right." I guess so. Why not? It's not like I care what he thinks about me. "Total honesty," I repeat, testing out the phrase. Could be fun. What is there to lose? He already knows I don't like him. I turn to him. "I was surprised to see you wearing glasses."

He looks a little startled. That's not what he expected. That, or he forgot he's wearing them. He touches the frames. "These?" Leo says. "Is it that surprising?"

"You've never worn them before." And I pay an unfortunate amount of attention to Leo Reyes. Maybe a weird amount, but it's not my fault he keeps stepping into my life, having perfect ideas and perfect hair and, for one terrible year, a locker right above mine. It's kind of hard not to notice him.

"Huh. Yeah, I mean, usually I wear contacts," he says. "I only put these on when I get home. I figured it'd be easier just to leave them on tonight."

"Well, they look . . ." *Total honesty.* " . . . nice," I finish grudgingly. I'm going to need to think more about what I'm saying if I'm going to play along. I didn't really mean to say that.

Leo smiles—not his usual smile, which is really more of a smirk, but a real one, tentative and a little surprised. "Your bar things look nice too, Wren," he says.

"Raspberry–white chocolate cookie bars," I correct him reflexively. "But, um, thank you. Let's hope everyone else agrees."

His phone rings—actually rings, which makes me jump. The only person I know who has their phone set to ring out loud is my dad.

"Oh, sorry, hold on," Leo says, getting to his feet and pushing the chair away, which makes all the cookie bars sway dangerously. There really is not enough space behind this table. Luckily for him the freshmen haven't arrived yet, so the gym is only at half of its capacity for cacophonous noise.

Like I've already established: I don't *want* to eavesdrop. I'm not willingly a person who eavesdrops. But it's a little hard not to when our table backs up to the folded bleachers, so Leo just kind of shuffles about four feet away for some illusion of privacy, his voice pitched low.

"Hey," he says. "What's up?" He pauses. "Yeah. Yeah, I can pick it up on my way home. No, it's fine." He pauses. "Emmanuel—"

I look away quickly, fussing with the arrangement of Maggie's maddeningly beautiful muffins.

Things I know about Emmanuel Reyes:

1. He's Leo's older brother.
2. He's three years older than us, so we were freshmen when Emmanuel was a senior.
3. He's probably the only person in Rapture that's more stupidly perfect than Leo. Football star, valedictorian, lead in the school play. I think he singlehandedly made high school football relevant in Rapture just by being that good at it. There's a reason that football stopped being the school's golden child when Emmanuel graduated and the robotics team took over. The Reyes brothers just have that effect.
4. He's on the phone with Leo right now.

Even as a weird little fourteen-year-old who had already chosen the guy's brother as a sworn enemy, I thought Emmanuel was cool. I still kinda do. He's like Leo if he'd never dropped that textbook on my head, cool in a peripheral kind of way instead of an annoying one.

But I definitely don't care why they're arguing on the phone. Leo's turned his back toward me, his voice lowered so I can't catch the words anymore, only the tone. Definitely arguing though. I do it enough to recognize the sound, that's for sure.

"Okay. I'll see you later. Bye." Leo turns back toward the table.

I consider making an awkward sort-of-a-joke about total honesty, but I'm not that much of an asshole. Whatever Leo and his brother were arguing about, it's certainly not my problem. I have enough problems of my own without worrying about Leo's too.

"Hey," Leo says after he's negotiated pulling out his chair again. "Total honesty?"

I give him a suspicious look. "Total honesty," I agree. *Please don't tell me about your weird argument. Please, please don't overshare with me right now.*

"I've got a bad feeling about this bake sale," he says.

I look around us, at the bleak intersection of the Friends Club and the basketball hoop. Our baked goods sit in tidy rows, waiting for whatever stragglers might wander by. My heart sinks. "Yeah," I say, "I've got that feeling too."

12
THE HAIL MARY

Fifty dollars.

An hour baking. Two and a half hours trapped in a noisy, crowded gym behind a folding table. All to make fifty dollars. And that was only because I raised the prices on my cookie bars last minute. Which, great, I'm glad a couple dozen people appreciated them, but they were the only people who even noticed our table in the first place. *Fifty dollars.* What are we supposed to buy with that? A balloon arch?

I don't want to think about it. It's too pathetic.

I try to focus on what I can control instead, in this case, convincing Ryan to go through the McDonald's drive-through on the way to school the next morning. It helps, but I'm still feeling a little hollowed out when I get called out of second period to meet with Principal Blackburn and Ms. Little in the front office and go over the final paperwork for the stage repair. That, at least, makes me feel a bit closer to alive again. *That*, at least, I've managed not to screw up. Yet.

"You're sure?" Principal Blackburn keeps asking from behind his mustache, squinting down at the numbers on the paperwork. "That's not an insignificant amount of money."

"Really sure." It'll be a *significant* amount of money when the next freshman falls through and breaks their neck, but I decide not to say that. I'm trying to be diplomatic. "That was the whole reason behind the Buddy sponsorship."

"Was it?" He scratches at his beard thoughtfully. "It might be more prudent to just make some adjustments to the theater program."

Yeah, like move the performances to the community center, just like the dance classes, and tweak the budget until eventually the theater program has been adjusted right out of the curriculum. I'm not even a theater fan and I can see the direction this is going. "Or," I say, reaching across the conference table and pushing the paperwork closer, "we could just fix the hole."

"My planning period isn't going to last forever," Ms. Little points out archly, and I don't know if she's trying to save herself from this meeting or save me from lunging across the table and signing the paperwork myself.

Principal Blackburn takes the hint. "All right, then," he says, and he signs it with a flourish. He pushes back from the table, his rolling chair squeaking. "I'll just have Kathy sign and make a copy for the student council's records." He smiles down at me in a Santa Claus kind of way. "Congratulations, Wren. Soon your hole will be all taken care of."

Well, I wish he hadn't said it like that. I force a smile as he takes the paperwork on the next leg of its journey, leaving Ms. Little and me alone in the conference room.

My instincts prickle. The front office's conference room is exactly like any other school conference room, dominated by a long table pretending to be made of real wood and surrounded by chairs with shabby off-maroon upholstery. It's not a very threatening place, except that it's always slightly too cold. But in this moment, Ms. Little sitting in the periphery of my vision, it might as well be shark-infested waters.

I see her open her mouth.

"We don't have to do the whole mentorship thing," I say, beating her to the punch. We really, really don't. "Technically we only have to meet twice a semester."

Ms. Little ignores me, probably because she knows I'm trapped here until Principal Blackburn gets back, same as she is. "I looked at your records," she says. "Your SAT scores aren't great."

What a way to open. It's a wonder she's a teacher and not in PR. I stare at the printed-on woodgrain of the table. "Oh, really? I thought they were like golf scores. The lower the better."

"I *also* know," she presses on, "that you took the test after you lost your mom."

There it is. I don't flinch, but only because I've been expecting it.

Things I don't like to talk about:

1. How my mom died
2. When my mom died
3. The fact that my mom died at all

So you can see why I haven't mentioned it before now. And why I'm really not interested in having this heart-to-heart. "Almost a year after," I correct her dismissively. Almost exactly a year. I don't even remember sitting down for the test. I should, but I don't. "I don't think the events are related."

She doesn't bother to call me a liar. "You can retake the SAT, Wren," she says instead. "If you retake it with a clearer head, get a better score—"

"Nothing changes, because community college doesn't care," I snap, finally turning to face her. She's watching me with a little frown. "So I don't know why you *do*."

The corner of her mouth twists. "Believe it or not, I didn't become a teacher for my health. Or the pay. Or because I love having parents yell at me." Well, now we're just complaining about her job. I'd rather do that, but she keeps going. "I did it because I want to help. And when I see a kid who cares so much about everything else, but not about his own future, I have to wonder why. If you really wanted to go to community college, you wouldn't talk about it like a death sentence."

"I don't—" I can feel my cheeks turning red and I can't find the right words. I grapple uselessly with them for a second. "It's not that I *don't care*."

"Then what are you afraid of?"

That, at least, I can answer. "I was afraid of losing my mom," I sneer. "And here I am."

Ms. Little doesn't flinch like I wanted her to. She doesn't drop it like I wanted her to either. "And here you are," she says. "You survived that, didn't you?"

She could have slapped me and I would have been less surprised. I stare at her, my mouth hanging open a fraction of an inch, unable to come up with a witty retort. Or a retort at all. People don't say things like that. They get uncomfortable and change the subject, or tell you that your mom is watching over you, or give you unsolicited advice so they can tell you their own sad story. They don't say *Well, you lived, didn't you?*

"You survived the worst day of your life, even when it didn't feel like you would," Ms. Little says. "And I'm willing to bet you'll survive the next one too." She leans back in her chair, one palm pressed flat against the conference table. "So what is it you're afraid of? Failing? Or succeeding?"

I force myself to come up with something to say. "Why would I be afraid of succeeding?" It's supposed to be a scoff, but it comes out too weak to even come close.

She shrugs one shoulder. "That's what you've got to figure out," she says. "I'm just here to ask the right questions."

"Well, you're good at it," I grumble, and it comes out sounding more like a compliment than I meant it to. My thumb works into a hole in the old upholstery, my fingernail digging into the seam. It's a very Leo thing to do, which should annoy me, but all I can think about is Ms. Little telling me I should download Buddy. I don't want to say she was right, but maybe she wasn't wrong. Which is to say, I can't say I regret it.

This is different though. Buddy is just a stupid app. This is—

My future, I guess. The word sits hard and cold in the pit of my stomach.

"I'll think about it," I say as the door opens and Principal Blackburn steps back into the room.

I *will* think about it. But I'm not promising anything.

♥

I should specify—I'll think about it *later*. For right now, I still have homecoming to save. Somehow.

The student council assembles in our classroom after school. For a moment we just sit there in awkward silence, staring at each other, waiting for someone else to say something. I guess that *someone else* is me. What a presidential honor.

"Well," I say, the word heavy as it flops to the ground. "The bake sale didn't exactly work."

"Yeah," Archer agrees unhelpfully. "Not really."

"It was a good idea," Ryan says, also unhelpfully. I know it was a good idea, but it still didn't *work*.

"We have to figure out something," Leo interjects, and for once I'm glad. I love wallowing and feeling bad for myself as much as the next person, but we need to move into the problem-solving phase. Again. "If we go all-out for the Dance and half-ass homecoming, it's going to look pretty bad."

"We could just raise the ticket price," Archer says.

"But the Dance is free? That would make it even worse." I sigh and rub my eyes, exhaustion making them itch. All my points about the Dance stand for homecoming too—it's still inaccessible and heteronormative and blah, blah, blah. It's hypocritical to fix one at the expense of the other. That and, yeah, the underclassmen will kill us. That's a big factor. "What if we just make it . . . not a dance?"

The words slip out of my mouth like I'm thinking out loud more than anything. My filter isn't great on a good day, but I slept like shit last night, consumed by failed bake sale ennui. Sleep-deprived, it's even worse.

Maggie sighs, resting her cheek on her fist. She gives Ms. Little an imploring look. "Do we really have to listen to the anti-dance manifesto again?"

Ms. Little waves imperiously. "Might as well."

I roll my eyes, using it as an excuse to scrape together my scattered brain cells.

"No, I mean—" I sigh again. "It just doesn't make a lot of sense for it to be a dance."

"*Why* doesn't it make sense, Wren?" Leo prompts helpfully. "Use more words."

Words and I ended our working relationship around fourth period. Now we're not even on speaking terms. "The whole thing with Buddy is making connections, right?

Romantic *or* platonic? So why are we having a whole other, entirely traditional dance? Isn't that mixing messages a little?"

Maggie doesn't look convinced. She looks done with my bullshit, actually. Or maybe just bullshit in general. "So you want to make the homecoming dance . . . not a dance," she says flatly. "How does that not make things worse? The freshmen and sophomores just don't get a dance *at all*?"

"No." I bristle. I mean, I wouldn't mind, but I lost that battle a long time ago. "They want homecoming to be special too, right? *Special* doesn't have to mean expensive, it just has to mean *different*. But we're all so hung up on the idea of a regular, traditional dance that all we can think about is limos and ice sculptures or whatever. So why not solve both problems at once? Make it less like a dance and more like . . . a party?"

"Hold on, he's kind of right though," Leo says, a thoughtful look on his face. He has his necklace around his fingers, the little gold cross pressed thoughtfully against his bottom lip. I hope he's praying and not just fidgeting, because that's probably what we need right about now.

"We could give it some sort of theme, make it more interactive. Something fun. Like . . ." He gestures vaguely.

Archer's eyes go wide and his face splits into a grin. "A rave," he says.

"Not a rave," Ms. Little butts in quickly. "Definitely not a rave."

Archer deflates a little, but where one brave man has been knocked down by a teacher invested in keeping her job, a woman rises in his place. Ryan plants her palms on her desk and actually stands, startling me.

"What if," she says, letting a pregnant pause hang in the air. It occurs to me that she's more sleep deprived than I am. Usually she saves the dramatics for me. "It was Halloween?"

"Oh no," I groan.

"Oh *yes*!" Ryan says, a mad sparkle in her eye. "Think about it—homecoming is the first week of October, and all of October is basically Halloween anyway. Everyone can wear costumes. What's more fun than that?"

I can think of a couple things, just in general, but I'm not brave enough to voice them right now. Ryan's relationship with Halloween is not to be trifled with. I know her better than I know myself, and we're about two steps away from her pulling out her sketches of whatever Halloween-themed ball gown she plans to make.

But she has a point. A Halloween theme is inherently goofy, and easy to go all-out for without actually spending that much money. All we need is that $50 from the bake sale and a trip to Party City. Round it out with the small army of inflatable yard decorations Ryan's parents have in their garage and some strategic lighting and we're basically set for A Very Spooky Homecoming.

Ms. Little pauses, one finger raised in consideration. "Halloween would be . . . okay," she says, with all the deliberation of a somewhat uncertain judge delivering a verdict. "But no sexy catgirls. Or boys. No catpeople."

The others are all nodding. "Works for me," Leo says. "Wren, was that what you had in mind?"

Not exactly, but it works, and I'm about to look a gift horse in the mouth. Besides, for all the things I'm not, I *am* a good friend. I can practically feel Ryan vibrating with excitement next to me.

So I smile sweetly and fold my hands on the desk in front of me. "It's like you read my mind."

13
THE LATE NIGHT

Him:
Are you awake?

I squint at my phone, the light searing my retinas in the dark. It's 2:30 a.m.

I have a funny relationship with sleep, and more *this sucks* funny than *haha* funny. Usually insomnia haunts me like an unimaginative ghost, rattling pots and pans and spooky chains around my head when I'm trying to get a good eight hours' sleep in. So between that and normal, choice-based bad habits, I'm used to running on pretty minimal sleep, which is why my body has adapted to make the most out of what sleep I *do* manage to get. Once I'm asleep, I'm dead to the world, like every moment spent unconscious is precious, because it kind of is.

So it's already unlikely that I'm asleep at 2:30—even more so that the Buddy notification managed to wake me up. And that's only because I set my phone on a ceramic plate, which made such a weird noise when it vibrated that it scared Beep, who dug his claws into my shoulder and bugged out of here.

Almost as good as an alarm clock.

I groan, my face halfway mashed into the pillow. I can feel sleep like a heavy blanket, just within reach. If I put the phone down now, I can still drift back. With a little luck, I might actually be well rested tomorrow, which is good, because I think I have an AP English test.

But . . .

Well. Buddy Boy never texts this late.

Me:

duh

whats up

Him:

Can't sleep

Me:

i'm familiar with the experience

any particular reason?

The typing bubble undulates for a long time. I roll over on my back and wiggle until the pillow is scrunched so I can prop my head up. Even if he doesn't say it, clearly there's something on his mind. That or he fell asleep halfway through typing it.

Not that I should care, probably—I don't even know his name. But there's no use pretending. If I didn't care, I would have flipped my phone over and gone back to sleep.

Him:
Not really

I snort. Liar. Beep jumps back onto the bed and perches on my legs, kneading them through the blanket. Evidently I'm forgiven. I hover my thumbs over the screen, trying to come up with a response that isn't *yeah fuckin' right*. No one types that long and then deletes it for no reason.

He comes up with a way to change the subject before I can.

Him:
**I guess I never told you the full story
about all this**

Me:
this?

Him:
You and me

The Buddy account thing, I mean

Me:
**i assumed your friends are just nosy
and overbearing**

**and that youre probably a
20something who can somehow
afford a 2 bedroom in manhattan
and youve got a promising career in
idk publishing but your workaholic**

lifestyle leaves no time for love
so your quirky bff has to set you
up with someone really attractive
and charming (me) but it all goes
hilariously wrong, probably because
of my personality defects (sorry)

i've seen a lot of romcoms

Him:

Wow, you got it in one

Who am I played by in the movie?

Me:

meryl streep

Him:

I was going to say Julia Roberts

Me:

they've both got the range

ok whats the real story tho

my interest is piqued

Him:

I don't know, I think I like your version
better

Just maybe not Manhattan

LA would be better

Me:

there's no accounting for taste

stop dodging the questions, meryl

Him:

It's just

No, it sounds stupid now

Me:

tell me!!!

you woke me up, you owe me

Him:

I thought you said you were already
awake?!

Oops. Beep has settled on my chest now, forcing me to
hold my phone over his body while his whiskers tickle my
nose.

Him:

Okay, fine.

So I like . . . I have a crush on this
guy. But he doesn't like me. So my
friends think I should get over it,
which is why they made me get an
account here to find someone else.

Me:

hmm

interesting

Him:

Don't say it like that

Me:

like what?!

i just said it was interesting

it actually really kind of adds to my
romcom theory, now that i think
about it

Him:

Like it's reasonable! It's weird. All of
this is weird.

Me:

HMMM

i mean

do you want to get over him?

Him:

I guess? I should, shouldn't I?

He TOLD me he doesn't like me

Me:

really?

damn

Him:

Thanks.

Me:

what else was I supposed to say!!

i just think maybe you dont want to
get over him if youre talking to me
on here and not someone like . . .

for real

The whole reason I don't date—other than the fact no one is interested and I have better things to do—is to avoid messy situations like this. Buddy Boy is charming and funny and this guy still turned him down. That doesn't leave a lot of hope for me. Life is hard enough to navigate without throwing more variables into the equation.

Me:

and you didnt really answer the
question

do you want to get over him?

Him:

I'm not sure

I'm not really sure how I'm supposed
to know

Me:

idk i guess you have to figure it out

i'm just here to ask the right
questions

Ms. Little can never know that I stole her line, or how I stare at it, squinting against the light of my phone screen in the dark. He already *knows* the answer, he just doesn't want to accept it. I can point it out to him, but I can't make him see it. He has to choose that for himself.

What is it you're afraid of? Failing? Or succeeding?

Fuck. I should have gone back to sleep.

Him:

Yeah

Maybe

I don't know

Life is hard

Me:

youre telling me

hes stupid, by the way

the guy you like

Him:

Why?

I bite my tongue again and Beep grunts unhappily, annoyed that I keep shifting underneath him. I didn't really mean to say that. Or maybe I did, but I shouldn't have. This is what I get for having conversations at 2:30 in the morning. I'm thinking too much, without enough brainpower to do it right. My hands move faster than my brain, and I have to answer for their crimes.

> Me:
> because he doesnt like you
> thats just bad taste

> Him:
> 😊

> Me:
> dont read too much into it
> i tell all my friends that

> Him:
> Don't you mean buddies? 😊

> Me:
> ok youre pushing your luck

> Him:
> Hahaha
> Okay, okay. I'll let you get some sleep, since you were nice to me

> Me:
> very magnanimous of you

I press my phone against my forehead, trying to ignore the embarrassing warmth in my cheeks, hidden in the dark. What was that all about? Since when do I say things like that? Maybe it's something to do with anonymity. Some people take the opportunity to be major assholes when there are no repercussions. I guess I'm just . . . nice.

What I don't tell him is that I think he's a little stupid too, holding out hope for someone like that. If hope is what he's really holding on to. More likely, I think everyone's a bit of an emotional masochist when it comes right down to it. Sometimes a silly little tragedy is fun, or maybe satisfying, like pressing on a bruise. Or maybe it's just distracting from something worse. I don't think his love troubles are what's keeping him up this late, but I know better than to push. Like with Leo, it's not my problem.

Maybe he's just afraid of succeeding. Of getting over his crush. Of leaving something behind.

Yeah. Maybe it's that.

I drop my phone, forgetting about Beep, who summarily decides that he's done with my bullshit. I grimace as his claws dig into my chest, his tail smacking me across the face for good measure on the way out.

Tomorrow is going to be an early morning.

14
THE HOMECOMING DANCE

I hate Halloween.

Just kidding—I love Halloween, but you were willing to believe me. Stick-in-the-mud Wren, doesn't even like Halloween. I get it. It's believable.

I love Halloween. It's fun, it's silly. There are no stakes or obligations. If I didn't hate wearing costumes, it would be the perfect holiday, and now that I'm not eight years old, I don't even have to do that anymore. Perfect. No notes. The fact that everyone has agreed to celebrate it all month long just makes it better.

But there's always a catch. It's all fun and games when you're a kid, because you're just running around soliciting candy from strangers, when every other day of the year you're expressly told *not* to do that. Then you start getting older, and the lines start blurring in weird ways. You're too old to go trick-or-treating, unless you've got a younger sibling to cart around, but you still want to do something for the holiday. And that's how the *Halloween party* is born. Two to three hours of pretending to laugh at pun-based costumes, seeing the same store-bought superhero every time you turn around, and listening to the same limited number of tangentially Halloween-related songs on loop. Truly and appropriately horrifying.

This year, homecoming is the mother of all Halloween parties.

It's also a huge hit.

I have to fight through the crowd to get anywhere, battling extraneous pieces of people's costumes the entire way. Upperclassmen usually aren't that interested in homecoming, I guess to save their energy for the Dance in a few months, but this year it feels like the whole school came out. Music shudders against the inside of my skull, reverberating off the deadly wood-floor-plus-high-ceiling combo of the gym. Sound spills out the open doors and into the night, chasing me, but at least out here there are no plastic wings poking me in the eye.

I plant my hands on the folding table set just outside the door, covered in black felt and generous amounts of fake spiderwebs. "Total honesty," I say, "if one more person asks what I'm supposed to be, I'm going to lose it. Trade with me."

Leo looks up from counting tickets behind the table. I begged for the job working the ticket table, but I was conscripted into being Ryan's personal assistant all evening instead. Friendship, sometimes, is a curse.

"Total honesty," Leo says with perfect sincerity, "you look like a feather duster. And I can't trade with you. Ryan will come looking for you anyway, and then no one will be here to watch the table."

I huff and straighten up, brushing a hand protectively down my front. I look, in simplest terms, ridiculous. But it's hard to be anything else when you're wearing a poncho made of brown feathers. "Ryan made me sew these on by hand," I say indignantly. "And everyone is basically already here. The table doesn't need to be watched."

"You tell her that," Leo counters. "I didn't know you could sew."

"I can't. But I can stab myself with a needle a lot. Which is why I deserve to sit out here on my phone for the rest of the night."

Leo laughs and leans forward, giving me a searching look. He squints. "Seriously though," he says. "Mockingjay? I'm at a loss."

I roll my eyes. "I'm a *wren*. The bird? Obviously." I told Ryan no one would get it. No one thinks that much about birds. "What are *you* supposed to be?" He's wearing all black, except for a handful of white paper starbursts pinned in apparently random places. The kind of half-assed costume you get to do when you're not friends with Ryan Robinson.

"I'm Leo," he says, gesturing to himself imperiously. "The constellation. Get it? Why are you making that face? You did the same thing with your name."

"I didn't do anything willingly," I correct him pointedly. "All of this, actually, is against my will."

"Wren!" Ryan calls, poking her head out the open door. "Come here! I need you!"

I close my eyes and shudder. "You could save me," I say, my voice heavy with the knowledge that we have two more hours before the event is over. "You know that, right? You could save me and you're choosing not to."

"I know," Leo says cheerfully, flashing his dimples. Bastard. "You'd better hurry, before she comes over here."

I heave a sigh and drag myself back to the door, where the pulse of music is like a physical thing threatening to push me back. Dante was wrong when he wrote about the circles of hell—one of them is definitely a high school dance.

Ryan is, as I predicted the moment the Halloween idea was floated, dressed to the nines. She went for some kind of spider queen this year, with a black swing dress hand-beaded with white spiderwebs that crisscross and overlap so that she looks like the dark corner of a haunted house. She's wearing a hat made to look like a spider tipped coyly to one side of her head, which should make her look like a strange take on Little Miss Muffet, but somehow she makes it work. Maybe it's a confidence thing.

She grabs me by the wrists and pulls me back into the gym. I don't resist, partly because she's still wearing her boots and I don't want to lose any toes.

"I have a surprise for you," she says gleefully.

A little too gleefully. No one ever said surprises have to be a *good* thing. "If this is about the little cannolis shaped like bones," I say warily, "I only had two."

"It's not cannoli related."

"Okay, I had five, but they're really pretty small—*mmph.*"

She grabs me by the face, her palms squishing my cheeks. I wrinkle my nose. She's been running around all night, and while I know her dress has pockets, I *also* know that she's not carrying hand sanitizer in them. I don't even want to know what gymnasium germs she's wiping on my face. "Wren," she says. "What song is this?"

I frown. "I don't—" I freeze, my head tilted. The pulse of music has faded, replaced by the dull buzz of conversation and . . . a creaking door. People on the dance floor are pausing, looking up at the speakers like there's an answer to be found there. They don't know what's about to happen yet. But I do. "Ryan. No."

She grins. "Ryan yes!"

"No!" I hiss. *"You know I love 'Monster Mash.'"*

"I do," she says, already tugging me out onto the dance floor, which is a generous term for what is really just the middle of the gym. "I do know that!"

A collective whoop goes up as the song kicks in, and my fate is sealed.

The math is simple: I don't like dances. I don't like *to* dance. I don't even like particularly loud music.

But I fucking love "Monster Mash."

Ryan drags me to the center of the dance floor, which is a war zone of glitter and flailing elbows and sharp bits of cheap plastic. I fight a smile as she pulls my arms back and forth, simulating some sort of stilted dance.

"This was unnecessary," I yell over the noise, but then the song hits the chorus, and it's all over.

"But you like it," she teases.

"But I like it," I agree with a grin, and she laughs, letting go of my wrists only to grab me by the elbows, and somehow the whole room is bouncing up and down in time with the beat. I laugh, something in my chest light and buoyant. My stupid feathered poncho reaches up and smacks me on the face with every bounce, but I hardly even notice. Ryan and I hold on to each other's arms, one of her hands committed to keeping her spider hat from flying off.

By the time the song is over I feel like I'm about to collapse, my face flushed and at least one feather stuck in my mouth, but I can't stop grinning.

"Come on," Ryan says when I make a move to leave. "One more song!"

"I need a drink!" I counter, which is true, but also if I give in now, she'll probably have me there all night. I don't know how people do this dancing thing so much. I feel like I've just done jumping jacks for three minutes and twelve seconds straight. I try not to consider that I might just not be in very good shape, due to a willful lack of exercise.

I disentangle myself from the dance floor, taking the opportunity to spit the wayward feather out of my mouth, and check my phone. I blink, surprised to find a Buddy notification. I didn't feel it vibrate.

Him:
Did you go to homecoming?

I hesitate, shaking my hair out of my eyes. Would the version of me that isn't on student council go to homecoming? Probably not, but lying seems like more trouble than it's worth. That, and I want to know why he's asking.

Me:
yeah
i'm not immune to peer pressure
why?

Him:
Just wondering
You know the art building right?

Me:
i'm familiar with it
considering i go to school here

Him:
You should check out locker A156,
toward the back. The hinge is broken
so nobody uses it.

Me:
broken lockers, my favorite. how did
you know?

Him:
There's something in it, doofus
Don't make me change my mind

My heart jumps and I stare at my phone. Does he want to—meet? Like meet-meet? Not that that's—I mean, it's *whatever*, but I don't really want to meet anyone looking like this. My cheeks are still flushed and my hair's going in just about every direction, not to mention I left half my feathers back on the dance floor. I look like a plucked chicken.

Him:
I won't be there, promise
Your secret identity is safe

Me:
your reassuring words need work
because i'm like 90% sure i'm about
to be robbed

Him:
Do you have anything worth
stealing?

Me:
i'm so not answering that

My eyes dart back to the dance floor. Ryan is still hidden somewhere among the swaying bodies. She already had her victory, so she's probably content to let me squirm away for the rest of the night, at least until it's time to clean up. I have a good window of time to slip out unnoticed.

I hesitate, torn between my curiosity and the fact that this is weird, right? It's definitely unexplored territory. What could possibly be waiting for me in a broken locker?

Whatever it is, I'm about to find out.

I sneak out the side door, through the locker rooms, to avoid getting caught by Leo on the way out. I definitely don't need to invite *that* line of questioning. Technically speaking, we're supposed to cordon off the rest of the school from wandering teenagers, but I'm a teenager with a license to wander. If I run into the custodian I can come up with some student council reason for being there.

The campus is quiet and dead compared to the dance still going in full swing behind me, the lights on the covered walkways buzzing gently. The breeze sends leaves skittering across the quad and ruffles the feathers still clinging to my poncho. It's Florida, so October isn't really *that* nice, but the cool breeze feels good after the sweaty mess of the dance floor.

I brush a mosquito off my arm and head across campus, where the art building is tucked away in one corner. It's one of the older buildings, squat and built of red brick that doesn't really go with the bland PowerPoint chic they went for with the newer buildings. I haven't had a class there since freshman year. I'm not exactly an artist.

I pull open the door and the lights flicker on with the movement. The art building isn't very big, more or less just a single hall with a classroom on either side, dented red lockers taking up the wall space between doors. I check the message again. A156 is toward the end of the hall. Also probably a really shitty locker assignment if you don't spend a lot of time taking art classes.

I can tell which locker it is without even seeing the number plaque—it hangs a little strangely, making it stand out in the line of identical doors. A broken hinge, as promised.

Me:

am I going to find drugs in here?

is this a sting?

Him:

Just open it oh my god

I smirk at my phone one last time and hook my fingers around the metal where a lock would go, then pull. The broken hinge whines sadly and the door droops, but it swings open without too much trouble.

The inside is dark and dusty, and there's definitely a cobweb somewhere in the top corner, but that's not what's important. What's important is a folded piece of lined paper. I pick it up. It was clearly torn from a spiral notebook, the handwriting neat and square.

> *A,*
>
> *Thanks for asking the right questions.*
>
> *BB*
>
> *P.S. Does this count as a quest?*

Underneath the note is a clear plastic container with a cupcake inside. A real bakery one, not from a grocery store, vanilla with white icing and mini marshmallows made to look like a little ghost. I stare down at it, the note still held between my fingertips. My heart does a funny little flip, of its own volition and without permission from me at all.

I pause and frown. I look back at the note. Heart flips again. Look away. Back at the note. *Again.*

A quest. He even remembered my stupid joke about leveling up in friendship. Every time I look down at the note, there's a full-blown butterfly garden rioting in my stomach. I hope Buddy Boy isn't secretly watching, because I actually press my hand against my chest, like I can keep my stupid heart in place. I probably look like I'm about to go into cardiac arrest.

Actually, that might be preferable to what I think might be happening. At least if my heart were the problem I could check myself into the hospital, maybe get some sense zapped back into me. But the truth is far worse than that.

I think I might have a crush.

Shit.

15
THE PROBLEM

Reasons why I cannot have a crush on Buddy Boy:

1. If anyone finds out that I've even downloaded the Buddy app I'll jump off a bridge.
2. I don't have time for this.
3. We're not *actually* using the app. I mean, technically we are, but only to fool his friends. All the talking in between is just happenstance.
4. I don't have time for this.
5. He's hung up on someone else, evidently to the degree where his friends decided that intervention was the only course of action.
   a) Someone that's not even interested . . . so not competition. Not that I'm thinking about it. Just something to consider.
6. *I don't have time for this.*

7. I don't date, so it's a moot point. A crush is an unactionable emotion in the world of Wren Martin, so there's no point in having one. It's just a waste of time that I, once again, do not have.

I scowl up at my ceiling, my hands folded over my chest so I can feel my stupid, traitorous heart beat. I feel like a microwave dinner left to thaw on the counter too long. What's left of my costume sits in the corner of my room, Beep curled up on top of it happily chewing one of the feathers. I almost didn't even have the emotional strength left to shower before collapsing onto my bed, until I remembered all the sweaty-classmate germs I probably encountered on the dance floor. I'm not a germophobe like my dad, but I do have limits, and that's one of them. Now I'm lying on my back, on top of the duvet, my hair probably drying in all sorts of interesting ways where it's smashed against my pillow.

And I can't sleep.

Addendum: I can't sleep because I can't stop thinking about that note.

Me:
A?

I don't even fully realize I've given in to the urge to text him until I'm holding my phone over my head, the screen brightness turned all the way down. Most of the homecoming cleanup we saved for tomorrow, but it's still after midnight. I'm not sure he'll even be awake. I drop my phone to my chest. Probably better if he's not.

And it buzzes with an incoming message. I whip it back up again, obliterating my corneas in the process. So much for the brightness setting.

Him:

For anonymous
Since you never gave me a name to
call you either

Me:

so instead I sound like a hacker

or a weirdo who spends too much

time on reddit

Him:

I don't have any proof that you're not
either of those things

Idiot. I smile, and immediately smack myself in the fore-head with the top of my phone. No smiling! No fond insults! Cut that shit out!

But he's waiting for me to acknowledge the rest of the note—and the cupcake, which is hidden in the back of the fridge, where my dad can't find it and question if it's gluten free. I chew on my bottom lip, squinting at the screen. I could just leave it at that, either to make him suffer or in the vain hope that I'll have some sense back in the morning. It probably didn't mean as much as I'm making it out to anyway. We had a conversation. I gave him advice, kind of.

He's just telling me he appreciated it. That's something normal people do, I'm pretty sure.

Goddammit. I start typing.

> **Me:**
> you did
>
> level up, i mean
>
> youre like level 7 now

Him:

You saw the cupcake, right?

I think it's worth at least a level 10

> **Me:**
> watch it or youll be back to level 6
>
> isn't it way past your bedtime?

Him:

Just about

Good night, A

> **Me:**
> thats not going to be a thing
>
> good night, buddy boy

♥

I do what I always do when I'm feeling lost about something.

I sit with the chickens.

Which doesn't solve any of my problems, actually, but Mom liked to say that there's something to be learned from chickens. They always look happy, that's for sure, though that could just be our flock. Four of the five are lavender

Orpingtons, which are basically fat, watermelon-loving clouds with legs. The fifth is a little copper-colored bantam that's possibly the meanest hen on earth, and responsible for a couple of scars on my forearms. But even she seems to enjoy herself when she's trying to take a chunk out of me. I like to sit with them in the afternoons and do my homework as they *buq buq buq* softly, discussing important chicken problems amongst themselves.

I spend the Sunday after homecoming with them, sitting on an overturned milk crate and tossing them corn just to watch them scratch at the dirt, their heads bobbing in a way that suggests they're not overly burdened by brains. They're good company for thinking. They don't talk back, except when they fuss at each other for stealing the best strawberry top.

But they don't have a lot of good advice, and I have too many things on my mind. The Dance. Buddy Boy. Leo. The SAT. College. My thoughts are snarled like a tangle of wires, and I can't even tell where one problem ends and the other begins. All I can think of is Ms. Little staring me down in the conference room.

What are you afraid of?

A lot of things, as it turns out. Someone needs to tell Ms. Little that asking the right questions isn't as helpful as giving someone the right answers. God.

"How has everything been?" Dad asks later when I'm standing at the fridge, trying to decide between oat milk and almond milk before moving on to which specific brand. Dad likes to have options when it comes to his nondairy dairy products. "Have you been . . . good?"

I blink, the synapses in my brain connecting after a long pause. I didn't exactly get a lot of sleep last night. It's a good question. The right question, Ms. Little might say obnoxiously.

Have I been good?

I have a crush on a guy who has a crush (unrequited) on someone else, and also I have no idea who he really is. It's almost Shakespearean.

Except that I kind of *do* know who he is, and that's the problem. I mean, I don't know his name or how tall he is or his eye color, but I know he usually doesn't stay up late but he does when something's on his mind, and he says *doofus* like he's ninety years old, and sometimes I say things just to set him up for jokes I know are coming. I know the person without all the baggage of reality, him distilled into thoughts and words and choices.

But he doesn't know me. I mean, he knows my weird Star Wars opinions and my feelings on beets, but he doesn't know the reason I *can't* have a crush on him. I'm okay with being asexual—I've really never seen anyone and thought *Wow, I really wish I experienced sexual attraction*—but it would be naive to pretend it doesn't complicate things. Society has made it *abundantly* clear how important sex is to just about everyone else, and . . .

What am I afraid of? The question nags at me again. I'm afraid of getting rejected. Easy. And pretty reasonable, I think. I don't want someone to look at me and tell me my sexuality is a deal breaker. I don't want to be pressured or to be a disappointment. I want to be Wren and I want that to be enough, and that's not going to happen. Not for Buddy Boy or for college or for anything. I couldn't even become student council president except on a technicality.

And so far I've been doing perfectly fine ignoring all that. Now I'm sitting with chickens and having crushes on strangers and, at this moment specifically, staring off into space while holding a carton of oat milk in one hand, and my dad is still watching me expectantly.

"Wren?" Dad prompts, his eyebrows pulling together. Evidently staring blankly at oat milk isn't his definition of *good*. Hypocrite. He's the one who loves the stuff.

"Fine," I say belatedly, putting the oat milk back after all. "Why wouldn't I be fine?"

Because I'm spending time with the chickens, but he won't say that. Dad doesn't do confrontation of any kind. He approaches any risky topic sideways, like he's trying to pounce on it, but he's like a tiger on the tundra, and all the flashy warnings make it extremely easy to get around. Sometimes I feel bad for exploiting his inability to communicate, but—like father, like son—I also don't particularly want to have this conversation. Unlike him, I don't feel the need to try to have it anyway.

He thinks it's about something worse, of course. Which is unfortunate, but not enough for me to assure him that no, Dad, I'm just mourning the fact that I have a crush. Like normal, well-adjusted kids do. Don't worry about it.

"No reason," he says quickly. He hesitates, and I dawdle at the fridge like I'm still considering my options. Waiting him out is also a valid strategic move. "Your teacher told me you were thinking about sticking around after graduation."

"Who?" I demand. Pointlessly—it was Ms. Little, obviously. I should tell him she's *a* teacher, not *my* teacher, but I switch tactics instead. "When?"

"At parent-teacher night." Dad gives me an owlish look. Of course. I've been so caught up with the bake sale and homecoming and *crushes* that I forgot Dad went to parent-teacher night, much less that teachers actually talked to him. "I was just surprised. I thought you couldn't wait to get out of Rapture."

I bite the tip of my tongue to stop myself from snapping. The year after my mom died I would have given my right arm to get out of Rapture and be anywhere besides a town built of memories. If I had been a senior then, I probably would have applied to the University of Alaska just to get out.

But now—I don't know. Things change. Maybe I'm used to the memories now. Maybe I don't want to let them go.

Why does everyone think it's their business?

"I'm full of surprises," I say, shutting down the topic like flipping a switch. For all his faults, Dad can take a hint.

"I guess so." He flashes me an uncertain smile, and I can't help the spike of resentment. It's not fair. He's trying, in his own way. But Mom wouldn't have let me get away with that bullshit answer. He lingers for a moment longer. "If you weren't fine, you know you could tell me, right?"

"Right," I say. "But I am fine."

"Right."

"Cool." I close the fridge and pretend to check the time. "I'd better get to work. See ya, Dad."

16
THE INVITATION

The weird thing about having a Halloween homecoming at the beginning of the month is that when it's over, we still have an entire month of Halloween left. I mean, October.

And I've got enough to keep my mind occupied, even without counting Buddy Boy and any inconvenient feelings. We might have pulled off homecoming, but that just means the Dance is looming on the horizon. Four months in the future for everyone else means *right now* for those of us planning it, and if I have to comb any more sites for decorations in the exact shade of Buddy yellow, I'm going to start pulling my hair out.

So the last thing I have time to worry about is Ms. Little. Our mentorship check-in isn't until the end of November, but I decide to cut her off at the pass. If only to keep her from talking to my dad again.

"Here," I say, dropping a five-pound book onto her desk. Ambushing her between classes probably doesn't count as a meeting, technically speaking, but I want to get this over with as quickly as possible. "Happy?"

Ms. Little looks down at the book. "'*SAT Test Prep Study Guide*,'" she reads without inflection. She tilts her head. "From 2012?" There's definitely an inflection on that part.

"It's the only copy the library had." Which says more about the state of the Rapture High library than about me. "It's math. I don't think that much has changed."

"Hm," she says succinctly.

"That's it? 'Hm'?" A little more enthusiasm would've been nice. "Isn't this what you wanted?"

She shrugs. "Anyone can check out a book. And it has to be what *you* want, Wren. I'm just here to—"

"Ask the right questions," I say impatiently. "Yeah, yeah. You can stop saying that."

She gives me a strange look. "I've said it *once*."

Right. I'm the one who keeps saying it. Well, whose fault is that? I plant my hand on top of the book. "There's one catch," I say heavily. "I'll read it, but you keep this between us. No more talking to my dad about my life choices. Deal?"

One corner of her mouth twists reluctantly. "He seemed surprised you wanted to stick around Rapture," she says, which is distinctly *not* an agreement. "It might help to talk to him about it. Get his opinion."

I hesitate. "It's what he would do. It's what he *did*," I say brusquely, recovering.

"Nothing wrong with that." Ms. Little shrugs with one shoulder. "You don't seem to take after him though."

I love my dad. Really, I do. But yeah, the resemblance is not striking. He'd be happy if you put him in a hamster wheel for the rest of his days, so long as it was well sanitized and had a steady supply of granola. I . . . well, I don't know. It's complicated. I heft the book up off her desk, cradling it in my arms like a particularly dense baby. "Do we have a deal or not?"

"Fine, fine. Deal," she says, rolling her eyes. "Now get to class, would you?"

I think I believe her. Enough to cross one thing off the to-do list, at least. I step back into the hall, wondering when exactly I'm going to have time to uphold my end of the bargain. Why are these books so *thick*?

I barely have time to flip the book around and hide the cover against my chest when I spot Maggie down the hall. Not that I'm embarrassed, exactly. I just don't want anyone to know I bombed the SAT in the first place, even less the reason *why*, and I'll die quietly if they find out. But I'm not *embarrassed*.

I sidestep so I can dodge her, but Maggie only maneuvers around a clump of sophomores to meet me there. She shoves a black-and-orange invitation into my hands.

"What's this?" I say, staring down at it like it might bite. Considering what Leo said about Maggie, it's possible. I'm supposed to be on my way to AP European history, but I'm having trouble being concerned. Dr. Bartlett is so old, apathetic, or both that a wild elephant could walk into class five minutes late and he wouldn't even look up.

"It's an invitation," Maggie says with the barest shred of patience, somehow managing to look down her nose at me despite being shorter. "Archer and I are throwing a Halloween party. Seniors only." She flicks back her hair and looks askance down the hall, as if daring a bold junior to question the decision.

"Okay." I just stand there, holding the invitation by my fingertips while cartoon bats grin at me from the front of it. "Am I supposed to give it to someone?"

Maggie scowls. "It's for you, idiot." She snatches the invitation back, folds it in half, and tucks it between the pages of my book. My heart jumps, afraid she'll question what it is, but she doesn't even blink. "Don't read too much into it. I know Ryan would just pick you as her plus-one anyway. I'm just getting ahead of the game."

"Thanks," I say blandly, pulling the invitation out again. "But no thanks." I hand it back.

Or try to. Maggie just stares me down until I awkwardly let my hand drop again, still holding the folded invitation.

"I don't like Halloween parties," I say awkwardly, like I need an excuse to not want to spend several hours at the Min house, following Ryan like a shadow. I was able to survive homecoming because I had work to do, and even then it was a close thing.

"Then don't come." Maggie shrugs. "But tell Leo that I tried to be nice."

"Leo asked you to be nice to me?" I say incredulously, but Maggie is already gone, lost in the rapidly thinning crowd as time runs out before the next period starts. I frown after her, the invitation still hanging limply in my hand. Leo pretty matter-of-factly dropped the *Maggie doesn't like you* thing. I didn't care, and I was kind of under the impression he didn't either. Unless he's trying to promote some unity among student council, but I think that's Ms. Little's job. And she's got enough on her plate just harassing me.

"Huh," I say as the bell rings.

♥

And that's that on the subject of Halloween parties.

Until it's not.

I'm sitting with the chickens again, the SAT book open on a milk crate next to me, when I feel my phone vibrate. I try not to look at my phone when I'm hanging out with them—I feel like chicken-based wisdom is by nature anti-technology—but one of the lavender Orpingtons has been sitting in my lap for the better part of a half hour, and it's starting to become a hostage situation.

She clucks unhappily as I shift my weight to wiggle my phone out of my pocket. She eyeballs me critically but doesn't give up her spot.

Him:

Did you hear about the seniors-only
Halloween party?

Me:

yeah

why?

Him:

Just was surprised you didn't have
an opinion on it

Given (a) Halloween (b) party and (c)
Halloween party

Me:

omg I don't hate halloween

why does everyone think that

Him:

I kind of got the feeling you don't like
most holidays

Me:

an unfair assessment

i mean don't get me wrong some are
more pointless than others

but I only hate-hate the fourth of july

Him:

Why the 4th of July??

Me:

i don't like the fourth of july. its loud,
and hot, and irritating, and american
imperialism gets everywhere

Him:

Is that a Star Wars reference?

Me:

you weren't supposed to notice that

Him:

Nerd

A lot of things go into a bad decision. It's a domino effect of fate. One that, even in retrospect, I'm powerless to avoid. It's impossible to tell what domino tips me over the edge. Maybe it's because I'm sitting with the chickens, which always puts me in a good mood. Maybe I'm quietly pleased he got my stupid *Attack of the Clones* reference. Maybe I just have an idiot crush and I'm out of my mind.

Me:

are you going to the party?

since you love halloween so much

Him:

Yeah, probably

Are you?

Me:

probably not

unless you want to

unless you want to go together i mean

I stare at my phone like it might bite me, my eyes wide, but it's too late to take it back. I really just did that. The SAT book was one thing, but this is—there are victims to this sort of thing. Me, mainly. Because I'm pretty sure I'm going to have a heart attack no matter which way he answers.

Him:

Oh

I mean

Sorry, I don't want this to be

awkward. It's just that like

This is going to sound so fake but
like, my life isn't really great right
now? It's just . . . complicated

And it's like here I can be someone
else, without a complicated life, and
I'm afraid if I mix them together it'll
take the good things here and it'll all
just kind of be . . . bad soup. Does
that make sense?

Okay, it definitely doesn't

I guess I just like me being me and
you being you on this stupid app
without having to be a real person too

Is that selfish?

My heart is sitting in my throat, my mouth dry, and oh my God, he just keeps typing. Why does he keep typing? Why have I yet to sink into the earth's cold embrace, where I belong? I guess I should be glad that his reason is a *him* problem and not a *me* problem, but I'm too busy trying to smother my fight-or-flight instinct to think about gratitude.

I'm not proud of this: I panic.

Me:

oh yeah of course

i thought your friends might ask
about it, i mean

Him:

Oh! Haha, I misunderstood
I thought you were asking if I actually
wanted to go together
Wow that's embarrassing

oh haha yeah sorry i didn't explain
that right

I slither sideways, all the will to live leaving my body, sending the chicken on my lap clucking furiously into the air. Dad finds me lying on the ground, staring pensively at a blade of grass. At least three chickens are perched on my legs. I'm considering changing my name and leaving the country. I don't know what Ms. Little is talking about—I have lots of ideas about my future.

I shift my head to stare at Dad's feet as he comes to stand over me.

"You all right?" he asks, looking down. Probably having a crisis about his son lying in the dirt, much less covered in chickens. I don't know how to tell him that sometimes bacteria can be cathartic.

"Doing great, Dad," I say. I spit out a blade of grass trying to journey into my mouth.

"Okay," he says doubtfully. He starts to turn away but pauses. "Hey, Wren?"

"Yeah, Dad?"

"Do me a favor and put those clothes in the wash when you come in."

That's actually not too bad. Maybe he's starting to get over the germophobe thing. Yeah, right. And maybe my life isn't a complete disaster. Hope springs eternal. "Will do."

♥

And that's that on the subject of Halloween parties.

Until it's not.

I pick up an extra shift at work on Halloween, because why not. The problem with cheap teenage labor is that they tend to all call out at the same opportune times—in this case, Halloween and the day after—so it's pretty easy to be the hero Holiday Inn needs.

It's also the first day of a cold snap, which is its own kind of novelty. You never really know what to expect from October in Florida. The weather ranges from "ugh, still pretty warm" to "oh, this is kind of nice, actually." *Cold* is rare, at least our idea of it, and probably a sign of climate change, but that doesn't stop me from enjoying it. It'll only last for a couple of days before it's hot and sweaty again, so I might as well.

I inhale deeply as I step outside at the end of my shift, leaving behind the Holiday Inn lobby smells and embracing the cold night air. There won't be many sexy cat girls/boys/ people running around tonight, that's for sure. Not that there's much overlap in the demographics of sexy cat costumes and trick-or-treaters. I hope.

I'm wondering if I've hidden my stash of nonvegan, very GMO, terrible-bad candy well enough that Dad won't throw it out, when I notice Ryan's Mazda sitting in the parking lot. I stop in my tracks. I'm pretty sure that's Ryan's Mazda, at least. That dent on the back door looks extremely familiar.

But Ryan wouldn't be here, at my place of business, because Ryan is supposed to be at the Mins' Halloween party. That I am definitely not supposed to be at. So therefore, this cannot be Ryan's Mazda.

The window starts to roll down.

"Oh Jesus," I mutter. I see her spider hat before I see anything else. This will not be good.

"Wren!"

I jog across the parking lot, digging in my backpack for my keys. Of course they've fallen straight to the bottom. If I can just make a quick getaway now, I can pretend I didn't see—

"Wren! Stop running!" Ryan manages to back out of the parking spot and pull up behind me in the time it takes me to wrestle my car keys from the bottom of my bag. She leans out the driver's-side window like she's catcalling me, her spider hat threatening to fall off. She's wearing the same costume she did for homecoming, except she's wearing a jacket over the spiderweb dress. "Get in the car!"

"I told you, I'm not going to the party!" I say, exasperated. We've only had this conversation about ten times. Ryan might not know specifically *why* I'm not going, but there are plenty of other, non-crush-related reasons that should satisfy her. Like the fact that I just got off work and I'm wearing a Holiday Inn–branded hoodie instead of a costume. Or that I notably and famously hate Halloween parties. Both very good reasons.

But neither so good as the fact that Buddy Boy is going to be there.

Which is fine. I mean, we go to the same school. We probably pass each other in the hallway every day. There's no reason a party would be any different. Especially not a party I kinda sorta asked him to and got kinda sorta rejected.

Especially especially because I won't be there.

"Wrennn." Ryan is practically falling out the window now. The car creeps steadily forward, following me down the aisle, toward the desolate corner where the staff parks. "I told my mom you were coming."

"I didn't consent to being part of your web of lies."

"She wouldn't let me go alone!"

"Bring your sister."

"It's seniors only."

"That's really sad for you."

"Wren." I realize she's stopped the car, waiting several feet behind me. Something in her voice makes the hair on the back of my neck prickle. It's not a full moon, but I can't shake the sudden feeling I'm in danger. Maybe it's the way she's looking at me, one eyebrow raised, her mouth set in steely determination. "I didn't want to have to do this to you."

I narrow my eyes, trying not to let my trepidation show. "Do your worst."

Very slowly—very deliberately—Ryan holds up a bag of Reese's Peanut Butter Cup pumpkins. Family size.

"Maybe this will change your mind," she says with all the sly confidence of a poker player displaying a winning hand.

17
THE PARTY

I go to the party.

I was always going to go to the party—I can't say no to Ryan. She knows that. I know that. Just like I know that if I'm going to accept the inevitable, I might as well get something out of it. Holding out until the last moment means:

a) She can't make me wear a costume. I go along with these things because Ryan's parents seem to think she's a ticking time bomb of teenage bad decisions. That's not even a little bit true, and if it were, I'd hardly be able to stop her, but I guess they're firm believers in the power of the buddy system. But that love and sacrifice only go so far. I'm not wearing a costume twice in one year.

b) I get to ride shotgun with a bag of my favorite candy sitting on my lap like a baby, or a puppy, or something equally precious. If you lived with my father, you'd understand. This level of sugar is considered contraband in the Martin household.

A net win if you run the numbers, I think, but it sure doesn't feel like it when we pull up to the party. Or rather, park down the street half a block away from the party and trudge up to the address listed on the invitation.

"There's no way they actually live here," I say, squinting up at the town house and double-checking that the number is right. I knew as soon as we turned in to it that this couldn't be their neighborhood, the streets filled with perfect white townhomes like rows of teeth. Between the strict uniformity and the relative proximity to the beach, it's the sort of place you live when you're a thirtysomething lawyer or a lifestyle blogger. Not where you let your teenage kids throw a party.

"Sounds like a good mystery to explore inside. C'mon, my legs are freezing," Ryan says, shooing me up the stairs. A paper sign covered in grinning bats is taped to the front door, welcoming us. I take a deep breath, enjoying one last lungful of the cold night air.

And then I'm knee-deep in party. The interior of the town house is just as nice as the carefully manicured garden outside it, all monochrome and modern art. A waist-high ceramic statue of some sort of twisting fetus shape stands sentry by the front door, cementing my theory that the twins don't actually live here. Archer Min could never look at something so fragile on a daily basis and not accidentally knock it over with a soccer ball.

"Hey, Wren!" Archer appears in front of me as if summoned, and I step back, almost taking the fetus sculpture out myself. According to the invitation, the party is "costumes optional," but Archer clearly thought to set an example. Which is to say that he's dressed as Rocky from *The Rocky Horror Picture Show*, which is to also say that he's wearing gold booty shorts and not much else.

"Aren't you cold?" I squeak, searching for something normal to say and coming up with that instead. I look around desperately, but Ryan has abandoned me. I can only generously assume she was blinded by the shine of the lights off Archer's metallic ass.

"You made it!" Archer says, completely ignoring the question. Or maybe he just didn't hear it. Music is pulsing from somewhere else in the house, but Archer is also holding a plastic cup that's tipping just enough to give me the feeling he's already refilled it a couple of times tonight. So it's that kind of party. If Ryan's parents were here, there would be heart attacks all around. "Have you seen Leo?"

I pause my search for exit routes to give him a strange look. "Why would I have seen Leo?" I say. "I just got here. I've barely seen you." On second thought, I've actually seen far, far too much of him. I look up at the ceiling to avoid making eye contact with his pecs. Why do you need that much upper-body strength to play soccer?

"Oh. Yeah, that makes sense." Archer sounds confused. "He just seemed kinda bummed, so I thought he might have run into you."

"What?" I break my staring contest with the ceiling fan, disgruntled. "So when he's in a bad mood it's my fault?"

Archer pulls a face. "Never mind!" he says a little too loudly. "Hey, did you get a drink yet?" Without much choice, I stiffly let Archer steer me deeper into the town house.

Okay, the party isn't *that* bad. I mean, it's loud and crowded and I see most of these people all day every day at school, so I don't really need to see them outside of it, playing beer pong on a kitchen table and shedding the more fragile parts of their costumes. But I have my Reese's pumpkins tucked securely in the pocket of my hoodie like a lumpy chocolate kangaroo joey, and a cup of something red that Archer foisted on me. I also get to make pointed eye contact with Maggie from across the stylishly open-concept living room, and she looks mildly disappointed that I showed up. So there's that.

Yeah, not really worth it, but I have to take whatever silver lining I can get. There's not even a dog.

I make it about fifteen minutes before my phone buzzes.

Him:

I'm starting to see why you're anti–
Halloween party

My nerves jump. *Shit.* I've been so caught up in hating parties, I forgot why I specifically hate this party. Is Buddy

Boy here? Now? Texting me? I shoot a surreptitious glance around the room, but a teenager on their phone isn't really the damning piece of evidence I want it to be. Even someone on their phone with Buddy pulled up doesn't mean a damn thing, because of Leo and all his bright ideas. All I know is that I desperately hope he's not the guy dressed as a hot dog, with his mustard starting to fall off.

I do another quick scan of the room. Buddy may be a common sight among the Rapture High senior population, but *I* can't be caught on it. Sometimes being me is exhausting.

Me:

not shaping up to be all you hoped
and dreamed for?

Him:

Honestly, mostly I've been going out
and buying ice

Me:

ice? its freezing out

make them go chip it off the ground

Him:

Hahaha

It's not THAT cold

Me:

maybe not physically

but emotionally

Him:

You might have a point

So what did you end up doing
tonight?

I freeze, guiltily clutching my phone in the middle of the party I said I definitely wasn't going to. What am I supposed to say *now*?

For a terrible, vindictive instant, I think about telling the truth.

And immediately think better of it. And then what? I spend the rest of the party walking on eggshells, waiting to be picked out of the crowd somehow? Then again, he specifically *didn't* want to know who I am, so maybe he wouldn't look at all. And then I'm just the asshole who couldn't respect his boundaries.

So I guess I'm a liar instead.

> Me:
>
> decided to pick up an extra shift at work
>
> exciting right

> Him:
>
> Riveting

> Me:
>
> hey, you know what i tell myself?
>
> at least i'm not out buying ice

> Him:
>
> You know what, I think you win this one

I smile half-heartedly, but I can't quite muster the will to do our usual back-and-forth. Why do I feel so guilty? I'm lying to spare *his* feelings. That's got to be worth something when they weigh my sins or whatever.

Well, one more lie won't hurt.

Me:

speaking of, I think they want me to
"work"

Him:

Ew

Me:

right

enjoy your ice party

Him:

I'll try my best

I sigh and pocket my phone, turning back to the sliding glass door. The music is too loud now, the town house too small. Sometimes—and this is very gross and sentimental and I'm begging you not to hold it against me—when Buddy Boy and I are texting, it's like the rest of the world drops away, or at least gets a little quieter. Closing the app and putting away my phone feels like stepping from the shade back out into sunlight.

Bleh, I'm getting poetic. That's never a good sign. I look over my shoulder to make sure Ryan isn't watching and slip out the door into the night air.

The backyard is narrow and long and dominated by a similarly shaped pool, lit purple by shimmering underwater lights. I send a quiet prayer of thanks to whoever might be listening that it's evidently not heated, or else the party would have spilled out here by now. Instead, the patio is deserted. A temperature below seventy degrees for the first time in eight months is enough to keep everyone inside.

"Nice costume."

"Jesus!" I jump. Okay, *almost* everyone. I didn't notice Leo sitting at the edge of the patio, half hidden in shadow, like some kind of supervillain. Though now that I'm actually looking, the light from the pool is reflected back at him, the ripple of the water shimmering against his skin. Okay, maybe I wasn't paying enough attention. That one's on me.

Leo grins at my reaction, but his heart doesn't quite seem to be in it. I hesitate, considering whether I should go back inside—and do what? Pretend I got lost looking for the bathroom?—or just roll with it. Normally I would do the classic *fake a text and turn around* maneuver, but remembering Archer's comment makes me look a little closer. Leo *does* look a little bummed. And is sitting on the patio in the cold wearing jeans and a T-shirt with a logo for a band I don't recognize. Not even a costume, unless he's going as some obscure-band groupie.

Ah, fuck it. I cross the patio and take a seat next to him, where there's a step down into the pool area. I stuff my hand into my hoodie pocket and it comes out with two Reese's pumpkins.

"Here," I say, handing him one.

Leo stares at it like he's never seen one before. "What's that for?"

"It's Halloween. Usually people give out candy on Halloween," I say. "Don't tell anyone, but I've got a bunch of them." I rustle my hoodie pocket.

He gives me a puzzled little smile, but he takes it, setting down his phone to fiddle with the wrapper but not quite opening it. "Thanks?" he says, still sounding not quite certain. "Maggie didn't think you were going to come."

Maggie and Leo talk about ol' Wren a lot, don't they? Or maybe they don't; maybe she just mentioned it when she told Leo that she'd dutifully invited me like she was supposed to (which I still haven't all the way figured out why). Still. Weird. "I'm susceptible to bribes." I shrug one shoulder and gesture with my cup. "Plus I've got whatever this is."

Leo gives it a sideways look. "Careful. Archer makes it pretty strong."

"There's alcohol in this?"

He looks alarmed for a split second and I laugh, nearly spilling my drink.

"I'm messing with you," I say, holding the cup up to my lips. "This stuff tastes like lighter fluid. Don't worry, Ryan is driving." Ryan's not a drinker. Sophomore year, she had a shot of whiskey from her grandparents' liquor cabinet and immediately snorted it out her nose. Like I said, her parents really don't have anything to worry about from her. Her sister is a different story.

Leo huffs a soft laugh. "That's good," he says. "Last time I drove you home, you told me all about how you hate me."

"Revisionist history. You *asked*." I think. Maybe. It was a while ago. "And I think you called me annoying."

"You have to admit," Leo says, "you're not *not* annoying."

"I'll drink to that." I take a sip of my drink, which tastes like a red Jolly Rancher dissolved in paint thinner. But it's getting better. Kind of like a Stockholm syndrome situation. "So what's your problem?"

Leo pauses. He's unwrapped his Reese's pumpkin and broken it in half (new reason to hate Leo Reyes—who eats candy like that?) and is considering the pieces. Or he was. Now he's considering me. "Who says I have a problem?"

I make a show of looking around the empty backyard. "I guess you must just like the company out here," I say. "And aren't you cold?" Florida cold is not the same cold most everyone else experiences, but I still can't believe he's wearing short sleeves. I've seen him in hoodies when it's eighty-five degrees out.

"You're here too," he points out, ignoring my climate-based question.

"Yeah, well, we've already established that I have problems."

That startles a laugh out of him. He looks away quickly, taking a contemplative bite of his Reese's. I squint. Who thinks this much about candy? I'm torn between wanting to take it back and wanting to give him another one, to see if he does it every time.

"I guess I have problems too," he says grudgingly, looking out at the pool.

That I find hard to believe. Leo Reyes? Problems? Isn't he too tall and perfect for those? "Like?"

I don't know why I said that. Archer's drink must be stronger than I thought.

Leo gives me a sideways look, hesitation plain on his face. He opens his mouth, then seems to reconsider whatever he was about to say. "I don't . . . I don't know. I guess that's the problem. I don't know what I want. Or what I'm supposed to do. Or anything." He says it like a confession, but I can't shake the certainty that this isn't the only thing on his mind. I guess he can have more than one problem. I certainly do.

I huff softly into the lip of my cup. "Yeah, tell me about it," I grumble.

His look turns incredulous. "You?" he says. "You know exactly what you want."

"I mean, I know what I want from *high school*," I say, gesturing circuitously with my cup. Do I really come across that confident? I always thought it was more like melodramatic. "But in case you haven't noticed, high school is almost over. None of this actually matters. I mean—it matters, but it doesn't *matter* matter. You know?" This drink is pretty strong, actually.

There's a smile in his voice. "Well, now I'm not sure."

"I mean . . ." I mean that high school ends, and life after goes on and on until you die. I mean that the last time something ended, it was the life I had as someone with a mom. I still don't know who I'm supposed to be after that, almost two years later. Because I can't be the same. Sometimes things happen and you can never be the same—you don't get the choice.

But I don't know how to be anyone else either.

"I don't know what I mean," I say instead of all that. I'm thinking about his phone call with his brother again. Fighting with your sibling is a normal thing, at least as far as my experience with the Robinson sisters goes, but it's weird to think about people as perfect as Leo and Emmanuel Reyes fighting. Then again, maybe that's what this is about. Maybe it's hard, being only the second-most perfect. Maybe Leo doesn't know who he is either. "How are we supposed to figure it out? How old are you, anyway—seventeen? Eighteen? We should have at least until we're, like, thirty."

"Almost eighteen. My birthday is in two weeks," he says.

"A Scorpio? My condolences."

Now he laughs. "Shut up," he says with a grin, and it's like he's actually present for the first time all night. Like he was in black-and-white before, despite the purple glow of the pool lights, and for a minute he's now in color. I look away quickly, hiding behind another sip of my drink. "I thought you were supposed to be helping with my problems?"

"I think I was actually just pointing them out."

"Yeah, well," he says. "I'm glad it's not just me."

"Nah. You're not that special."

Leo shakes his head with a smile and starts on the second half of his Reese's, and I take the opportunity to watch him out of the corner of my eye. He looks tired. Not sleepy tired, which my drink is starting to make me, but a tired I'm a little more acquainted with. The worn-down kind of tired, when you're like a pencil-top eraser that's gotten so flat the metal is starting to scratch the paper. The lights from the pool dance across his face, purpling the bags under his eyes. Huh. Maybe he can't sleep either.

He glances up and catches me looking. Shit. It's too late to turn away now. We sit there, trapped in an iron-clad moment of staring and staring back that seems to go on for an eternity. I'm not sure what it means or what to do or why my heart is beating so fast, so I open my mouth—

And say the first thing that comes to mind.

"Archer and Maggie don't really live here, do they?" I blurt out.

And like that, whatever weird magnetic moment just happened lies dead on the ground. Leo blinks. "It's their aunt's place," he says, looking a little dazed. Or bewildered. Probably from my radical subject change. God, I want to stick my head in the pool and not come up for air. "She spends half the year in Beijing for work, so she lets them use it."

As if on cue, there's a muted crash from inside the house, followed by the sound of breaking glass. I wince, imagining the fetus sculpture in pieces across the foyer.

"*Archer!*" Maggie's voice cuts through the ensuing guilty silence.

"Yeah," I say. "That's what I thought."

♥

Ryan drops me off at home with the promise she'll drive me to work tomorrow so I can retrieve my car. It's late by the time I crawl into bed, exhausted and confused and still a little tipsy. It's not fair that Leo's problems only made me think of my own after I've tried so hard for so long to ignore them.

I know it makes me sound like a coward. I know problems don't go away just because you refuse to look at them, but it's the difference between protecting a bruise and hitting it with a hammer. It's easier to pretend nothing has changed than to acknowledge the ways things have already changed. The ways they're still changing.

I turn the light on and sit up, then pull the SAT prep book off my bedside table and hold it in my lap. The glossy cover is creased at the corners, battered from over a decade of use. It's as thick as a brick, but the gray pages are thin and soft at the edges as I flip them against the pad of my thumb. The math is simple: If I don't take the SAT, I don't have to worry about getting into a college that *isn't* community college. I'll stay in Rapture. I'll keep doing what I've been doing, just at a slightly different location. It's as easy as that, a non-action. All I have to do is put the book away and I'll never have to decide if I should stay or I should go. A lot of people do it. There's nothing wrong with it.

But it doesn't feel *right* either.

I take my phone in my hand and flip it over twice before I open the Buddy app. I don't want anyone to know about this—not Ryan, not my dad, and I wish Ms. Little didn't know—but I don't think I can do it on my own either. I think about Leo, caught in his own snare of indecision. It's hard to know what direction to go in without someone to tell you which way is up.

And to Buddy Boy, all I am is Anonymous.

Me:

what do you think about regret?

For a moment I'm afraid he might be asleep and I'll have to have this conversation in the morning, when I'll be all the way sober and much less contemplative. But he hasn't been sleeping well lately either.

Him:

That's a big question for 12:30 a.m.

What do you mean, exactly?

Me:

i'm not really sure

i'm just thinking like

do you ever have a decision to make

and you know what the right choice is

but that choice is the scary one?

so you don't want to make it?

Him:

Yeah, I do

Me:

i guess i'm just wondering if i'll regret
not making the choice

and if thats scarier

Him:

I guess you don't know until you're
there

But it kind of sounds to me like
you've already made the decision

Me:

yeah

maybe i have

18
THE QUESTION

Like Archer Min and an expensive piece of modern art, October crashes into November.

And shit gets *real*.

November first, it's like the entirety of Rapture High goes on Valentine's Day Dance lockdown. Meaning, this year, they go on Buddy lockdown. You can't walk six feet on campus without seeing the app on someone's phone.

Ugh.

"Have you tried it yet?" Reed asks in the car one morning, her chin resting on the back of my seat. "Mom said I'm not allowed, but she doesn't know I changed the email on my Apple account—*don't* tell her." She shoots a suspicious look at Ryan, who rolls her eyes.

"You're a freshman," I say in lieu of answering. "You can't even go to the Dance. Why bother?"

"Because it's fun!" Reed flicks my ear and I swat at her. "Maybe I'll fall in *love*."

"I doubt it," I say, trying not to shift uncomfortably in my seat. I fuss with the zipper on my backpack. "It's not meant for falling in *love*."

"Okay, but, like," she says flatly, "for real."

"Okay, for real," I say, twisting around to look at her, "you won't because you're annoying and— *Ow!*"

"Will you two stop fighting?" Ryan complains from the driver's seat. "I feel like a single mother of two right now."

I huff and face forward again, rubbing my shoulder where Reed pinched it. "It's an algorithm anyway, not a magic wand. It probably just matches people at random."

I'm probably right, but what I don't like is that it *worked*. I know it's a coincidence that I got matched with Buddy Boy, who by some terrible turn of events turned out to be funny and sweet and annoyingly charming, but that's not going to save my skin if anyone on student council finds out about him. I realize belatedly how stupid I was to ask him to go to the party with me. Did I really think it would be as easy talking to him in person as it is over text? And how did I intend to explain why I was meeting some random guy there anyway? Ryan would have sniffed out my bullshit in an instant.

Which might still be a threat. I sneak a look in her direction, but she's not as suspicious as I feared. She's mostly watching the road, which is a good thing.

But like a Greek tragedy, my hubris gets the best of me.

"Have you?" I ask.

It takes Ryan a moment to realize that I'm talking to her. She blinks and glances sideways. "What? Me?" she says. "Have I what?"

"Tried the app." I'm not going to say the name out loud if I don't have to. Someday I'll sue the developers for emotional damages.

Listen, I know I'm tempting fate. I know I physically cannot shut up about how embarrassing it would be if someone found out that I, Wren Stick-in-the-Mud Martin, used and enjoyed the Buddy app. But.

But Ryan is my best friend, and the sheer depth of my embarrassment is at war with my need to tell her everything, and has been since I realized that this crush is here to stay. It feels like way too much has happened in too short a period of time, and I don't know what to do with any of it. Sort of, kind of asking Buddy Boy out and getting shot down, lying about going to the party and then feeling bad about it, the way Leo and I locked eyes by the pool . . .

It's all a little confusing. And none of it is covered in my SAT prep book.

But me being me, I can't just *tell* her all that. So I try to go at it sideways instead. I've learned a few things from my dad's nonconfrontational style of parenting.

"I mean, I guess one of us should be familiar with the app, if we're going to be taking their money," I say lightly, trying to make the question less weird.

"Oh, uh. No, I haven't tried it," Ryan says, fiddling with her fuzzy pom-pom earrings as she pulls up to a stoplight. "Mom doesn't want us to, so. Y'know."

A little alarm rings in the back of my head. Yeah, I can believe Ryan is subjected to the same dating rules as her fourteen-year-old sister, but I *can't* believe she would actually listen. Ryan isn't exactly a rebel, but she's well versed in circumnavigating the rules. The Halloween Bribery Incident was not the first of its kind.

"Right," I say, trying to hide my curiosity. I'm not going to ask with Reed in the car, I'm not an animal, but I keep rolling that thought around in the back of my head. Ryan was only ever anti-Dance on my behalf, and we all saw how quickly that went out the window once Leo pulled out the word *masquerade*. I know Ryan Robinson better than probably anyone, but I don't know what she would have against Buddy. If she hasn't downloaded the app, it's because she really doesn't want to, not even out of passing curiosity or research for the Dance. Huh.

Ryan is keeping secrets and Leo is having problems and Maggie is being nice to me, apparently as a favor to Leo for some reason. At least Archer, I'm pretty sure, is only thinking about soccer at any given time. I should thank him for that. I should have appreciated his simplicity sooner.

Reed disappears the moment Ryan pulls into a parking spot, before the car even completely stops moving. I don't know if I had that much energy as a freshman, but I doubt it. Definitely not before seven a.m.

But I'm grateful if it means I can actually ask Ryan about Buddy without her little sister around. I do still want to tell her, as painlessly as possible, about the Buddy Boy thing, but for the moment, that problem has taken a back seat to the fact that Ryan is lying. And Ryan and I don't lie to each other.

This is the part where I point out she's never *asked* me if I signed up for Buddy out of spite and ended up accidentally crushing on some random guy. If she did, I would be honest. Obviously.

She just hasn't asked that very specific question yet.

"Hey," I say as casually and off-the-cuff as possible, "so about—"

"I've actually got to run by the library before class," Ryan says breezily.

"But—"

"Melissa wants me to drop off some photography club forms."

"Who's Melissa?"

"I'll catch you later."

And then she's gone, leaving a Ryan-shaped puff of dust in her wake. My teeth click together as I close my mouth, and I turn it into a frown.

Weird. *Definitely* weird.

I heave a dramatic sigh that she's not around to appreciate and head to my first-period class.

♥

Ryan isn't the only person on my mind.

Actually, there are a lot of people on my mind. It's November now, which means Thanksgiving, which means it's basically Christmas. Which means Dad is even twitchier than normal, through the terrible combination of the holidays and flu season.

But the real problem is Leo.

Why is it always Leo?

I shouldn't be thinking about our conversation by the pool this much. If you take it out and look at it (which I have), there were barely enough words exchanged for it to legally be considered a conversation. But lo and behold, I find my mind circling back around again and again, like a canoe with one paddle.

Because the problem is that it wasn't *just* Halloween. Halloween was merely the catalyst. Now it's *all the time*. I always thought Leo Reyes was annoyingly perfect, and he still kind of is, but now that I've seen the cracks, I can't stop. I notice the way his eyes wander out the window during student council meetings and the way he's fidgeting with his cross necklace more, making it jingle against itself like a bell on a cat's collar. He's even stopped mentioning the Dance outside of meetings, as if the bake sale–homecoming double-header sucked up all the energy he had for tormenting me. That, or something else is on his mind.

Yeah, I feel bad for him. So what? I have a heart, you know. And it's made of gold.

So I follow him into the bathroom.

Which isn't ideal, obviously, but he's harder to track down than a guy that tall should be, especially since he's been missing days of school lately. Not that big a deal for anyone else, but weird for a guy who got the perfect attendance award every year of middle school. Also annoying for anyone trying to find an opportunity to corner him. So when I catch a glimpse of him stepping into the bathroom between classes, I follow him. I open my mouth—

To find the bathroom empty.

I close my mouth again, frowning at the empty room. One of the stalls is closed, but I don't see any feet under it or hear any bathroom sounds that I'd rather not think about.

"Leo?" I say tentatively.

"Oh, it's you." The stall door opens and I jump, my heart about catapulting from my chest. Leo steps out, peeking around the stall door. "Hey."

I stare at him, squinting incredulously. "Were you . . . hiding?" And not from me? Should I be insulted?

Leo looks embarrassed, dropping his hands from the stall door as if he can pretend he wasn't just clutching it like a stage curtain. "Yes. No. I mean, a bit." He scratches the back of his head sheepishly. "I thought you were Stephen."

"You were hiding from *Stephen Hannigan*." I pause. "Wow, that is embarrassing."

"Stop." He rolls his eyes, exasperated. "You only hate him because you're the same person."

Okay, *now* I'm insulted.

"We lost the regional qualifier yesterday," Leo says. "The robotics team. So I'm just . . . avoiding him for a little while."

"In the bathroom."

"In the bathroom," he repeats. Not for the first time this week, he looks exhausted. "I didn't say I was proud of it."

"I guess I've done worse." Probably. I can't think of anything right now, but I don't want to rule it out. "Anyway, I need to talk to you. About the Canopy."

I can see the gears in his brain realigning. "Okay," he says warily. "What about it?"

I take a deep breath.

"Ryan's cousin had her wedding at the Canopy last year, and I guess when you're considering booking the place, they have, like, a tasting menu," I say, trying not to spit it all out in a rush. Casual. I can be casual. "So you can try the appetizers and stuff. Totally free, so long as you end up using their catering. And since we've already booked them . . ." I gesture vaguely, hoping he'll fill in the blank.

Leo's eyebrows pull together. "We've already booked them . . . so we don't have to try the catering?"

"No, I—" I barely resist the urge to drag a hand down my face. This is the guy all the teachers fawn over? The genius who cost Stephen his big robotics win? "I mean we should take *advantage* of that and get *free food.*" Do I have to spell it out? Put together a PowerPoint presentation? My cheeks are uncomfortably warm. I really didn't think this conversation would take so long or go so awkwardly. Or be held in the middle of a bathroom. I'm going to be late for my appointment to dig my own grave and bury myself in it.

Leo blinks owlishly. "You and me?" he says, actually pointing to his own chest.

"We're the president and vice president," I say stiffly. "It only makes sense."

"Oh," he says. "Yeah. Of course."

"'Of course' as in you're interested?" I press. I need to end this conversation. I need, need, need to end this conversation.

"Yes." He clears his throat. "Yeah. Sounds fun."

"Cool."

"Cool."

Okay, Wren, exit stage left. "I'll text you the details," I say as breezily as I can, stepping backward so I can push the door open with my elbow. "Don't take it personally, by the way," I add, before I can stop myself. Even my rash moments of benevolence only go so far. "I just really like free food."

"Right," Leo says, and I swear I see the ghost of a smile cross his face, reminding me why I subjected myself to all this in the first place. Well, I think with a spark of satisfaction. Mission accomplished. At least my death by awkward wasn't in vain. "Who doesn't?"

19
THE GRIFT

We go out to dinner on Friday night.

Which feels *weird* to say, because it's factually true, but not like *that*. Leo Reyes and I go to a tasting menu appointment at the Canopy at four thirty on a Friday afternoon because it's free and I'm tired of looking at his sad eyes, and free food is one universal thing that makes people happy.

There. That's more accurate.

The White Sand Hotel and Resort sits right on the beach like a sand castle, the sunlight gleaming off its windowpanes like they're made of gold instead of glass. There are a half-dozen resorts along the beach, but White Sand is Rapture's crown jewel, and far and away the most extravagant. It's the sort of place where even breathing feels expensive. They would never hire me, despite my extensive hotel reception-ist experience. Though that might be more because I'm seventeen and complain about tourists like it's part of my job description.

Maybe that's why I'm so defensive when I feel Leo staring at me. "What?" I demand.

He shakes his head. "I just can't believe you're wearing that."

Oh my God, he's still on that. I let him drive, under the guise of not wanting to find parking for two cars. His white SUV fits in a lot better with the parking lot crowd than my barely-a-car would, not to mention my air-conditioning is on the fritz (again) just in time for the typical up-and-down autumn temperature to go back up again. The downsides are:

1. There's no easy escape if this goes badly, and
2. Leo can't shut up about my outfit.

"Most people dress up to come here," he says.

"How am I not dressed up?" I smooth the front of my shirt. "It's a button-down, isn't it?"

"It's *yellow plaid*," he says, looking me up and down again, like he can't comprehend something as visually offensive as yellow plaid. Personally, I don't get the problem. It even has long sleeves, though I might have ruined the effect a little by rolling them up to my elbows. But it's, like, eighty degrees out, so that's not exactly my fault.

Leo, of course, looks like he's here for a business-casual meeting, which I was not expecting. He was wearing a plain T-shirt and a hooded jacket at school, so I wasn't really prepared for the dark jeans/black blazer/red Converse combination that makes him look like he's got this at four thirty and a mixer for Silicon Valley young professionals at five o'clock.

I should have known he'd find a way to be Leo perfect for something that was my idea in the first place. He was a little slow on the uptake this time, but he always gets there eventually.

"What?" Leo says. Oh great, now I'm the one staring.

"*I just can't believe you're wearing that*," I mimic, and he rolls his eyes.

Luckily the hospitality employee, a twentysomething named Marie with a blond bob and a bright smile, appears at that opportune moment to whisk us away on a journey through all the Canopy restaurant has to offer our event. To her credit, her smile doesn't waver as she takes us in, despite being clearly uncertain. I like to believe our age is what trips her up, not the yellow plaid.

She consults her clipboard. "Wren and Leo M—"

"That's us," I say, flashing a blinding smile of my own. She actually squints a little. "Ready to go."

We have to go through the entire sales pitch before they'll let us get to the good part. We tour the Canopy's ballroom and get handed different pamphlets every time we pass through a door, nodding as Marie details how life-changing their venue is. It really is beautiful. The ballroom is made to look like a Venetian garden, with artfully rough-hewn flagstones on the floor and wooden arches overhead, so choked with climbing ivy and wisteria that you almost can't see the glass ceiling. I'm not really sure how we're supposed to get it to go with the tacky friendship-app theme, but that sounds like a Leo problem. I just collect pamphlets and smile.

Finally Marie seats us at a table in the actual restaurant, which is dead at this time of day except for a couple of clusters of early-bird specials. She sticks us at a table near the kitchen, but in a place like the Canopy, even that is impressive. The late-afternoon sun simmers through the glass-domed ceiling, making the air seem to sparkle as golden light dapples the plant life that gives the place its name.

"Do you think people would like the duck crostini appetizer?" I muse, consulting the tasting menu that Marie left for us to consider. "I want to try it."

It takes me a minute, engrossed in the menu, to realize Leo hasn't responded.

I look up to find him frowning at the stack of pamphlets we've collected, scrutinizing the top one like it's a calculus exam. My nerves prickle, a silent warning crawling up my neck.

Okay. This might not be good.

"Wren," he says slowly, making my name into something closer to an accusation.

Definitely not good.

Finally Leo looks up, his face a fascinating combination of incredulity and confusion. He holds up one of the pamphlets, a classy white-and-gold number with overwrought looping script. "Why does this say"—he turns it around to read it—"Mr. and Mr. Wren and Leo Martin?"

Ah, shit.

"Okay," I say, holding the menu up like a shield. "I can explain."

"You knew about this?" Leo hisses, all cautious confusion going completely out the window. He leans across the table like someone's going to overhear us. I don't know how to tell him that anyone out to dinner at four thirty is not going to have ears good enough to hear us from across the restaurant. "Wren, *why do they think we're getting married*?"

I want to press my forehead against the elegant white tablecloth. They personalized the *brochure*? This is what happens when people have more money than sense. Disaster. "In my defense, you weren't supposed to find out about that part."

"*Wren.*"

"They only do the tasting menu for weddings!" I say, dropping the menu and throwing my hands up in exasperation. Okay, too much gesticulation. Need to scale that back before someone *does* notice and wonders if the wedding is about to be called off. I lean across the table and lower my voice. "And I was going to do it with Ryan, but you've looked like such a kicked puppy lately, I thought it might cheer you up."

"I—I'm not—" He seems to give up on denying his kicked-puppery. He huffs instead. "So this is *my* fault?"

I roll my eyes as emphatically as possible. "It's your *fault* that you're being *weird* about it."

"What about this isn't weird?"

"It didn't have to be."

"Wren." Leo folds his hands on the table in front of him like he's delivering an unfortunate diagnosis. "How exactly were we supposed to get away with this when we're not, in fact, booking catering for a wedding?"

Well . . .

Well. It's too late now.

I spot Marie making her way back to our table, clutching another handful of pamphlets. Shit. "Do you want your free duck crostini or not?" I hiss. I lean back in my chair and pick up the menu again, clearing my throat. I steal a look at Leo. "Just be cool."

He gives me a withering look that luckily Marie misses, Leo's back being to her, and I decide that this is the last time I go out of my way to be nice. If I hadn't given in to a moment of compassion, Mr. and Mrs. Wren and Ryan Robinson would be enjoying a delightful round of duck crostini and having a good laugh right about now and definitely not worrying about how we were going to convince the Canopy that a high school dance is actually a wedding.

"How are we doing?" Marie asks, arriving at our table with all the presence of a sunlamp. I have to admit, I admire her endurance. My face would hurt from all the smiling by now. "Any questions about the menu, or are we ready to get started?"

Better take control of the situation again. If we get kicked out before the dessert round, I'll never forgive him. "I—"

"Ready to go," Leo says, and my eyes dart sideways, startled. It's like flipping a switch—*What the hell is going on?* Leo has been traded in for the smooth, easy-confidence Leo who fits the blazer look. Foolishly, I'm struck by a moment of satisfaction. Well, at least he's getting on board. We can save the *You were right* and *Thanks for the great idea* for later.

I should have known better. If there's one thing I've learned, it's that Leo Reyes doesn't let anything go unanswered.

"Marie," he says, and he has a way of being so casually charming that it's infuriating. With anyone else, they'd be trying too hard. Leo makes it look incidental. "Have we told you how we met yet?"

I freeze.

Marie looks a little surprised, probably because I've so far spent the entire experience carefully redirecting any reference to our upcoming "wedding." But like any good salesperson, she loves a good opening. "You *haven't*," she says indulgently, when she's supposed to be telling us all about the chicken, fish, and vegetarian options. "Let me guess—there's a story?"

"Not a very exciting one," I say hurriedly, smashing my heel into Leo's toes under the table. "Hardly worth mentioning."

His eyelid twitches, but his smile doesn't waver. "Oh, it's so funny though," he says. "We actually met on Buddy. Would you believe? Have you heard of it?"

My heart skips a beat. My foot slips off his shoe, hitting the ground with a thump that's just a little too loud, but still enough to jump-start my heart. Jesus, I thought—No, Leo absolutely does not know about my Buddy misadventures. He's just making fun of how much I hate it. He's trying to annoy me, not scare the crap out of me. Ironically, I'm so relieved that he doesn't even succeed.

"Really?" Marie leans in with wide eyes. Okay, she's definitely playing it up. People meeting on an app isn't that surprising. She laughs. "Oh, I've heard all about it. I've never met someone who met their partner there. But clearly it worked!"

"Clearly," I say dryly.

"Clearly," Leo repeats. "What can we say? High school sweethearts." And he reaches out and puts his hand over mine. I drop the menu again.

Okay. Well. He didn't— That level of acting isn't quite necessary.

His eyes meet mine, and there's a smirk toying at the corner of his mouth. Oh, I think. He's not trying to annoy me—or, well, he *is* annoying me, but there's more to it than that. He's issuing a challenge and waiting to see if I take the bait.

I bite the tip of my tongue. Well, we're already *here*. And I'm not a coward.

I flip over Leo's hand and hold it sweetly, squeezing his fingers a little too tight. I ramp up the wattage on my smile. "If you think that's funny," I say, "just wait until you hear about our color scheme."

♥

By the time we've gotten through tasting three courses and dessert, Leo and I have constructed a complex fictional life including a wedding color scheme (yellow and white, the Buddy colors), two cats (Harry and Houdini), and the name of our future child (Birdie). I'm actually impressed we manage to keep it all straight, at least enough that Marie doesn't seem to suspect it's all bullshit (though I suspect she doesn't get paid enough to care).

Leo, to his credit, waits until the car doors are firmly shut to say anything.

Well. *Say* is an overstatement: he leans forward to rest his forehead on the steering wheel and laughs so hard that I think he's going to cry.

It takes him a solid minute to come up for air, red in the face and wheezing. "Mr. and Mr. Wren and Leo Martin," he says between gasps.

"We are never speaking of this again," I say, gesturing expansively with my sheaf of pamphlets to hide the fact that I'm struggling not to laugh. "Ever. Never ever. No one needs to know."

"Well, I'm definitely not going to tell anyone I let you give me your last name," Leo says with a grin, starting the car. Every so often his shoulders tremble with delayed hiccups of laughter. "Leo Martin? *Really?*"

"What's wrong with my name?"

He raises his eyebrows and gives me a sideways look. "*Wren Martin.* Your name is just two different animals."

"I—" I never thought of it like that. Oh God. It feels worse to point out that technically the animal is spelled *marten.* "Shut up," I huff, and he grins wider.

It's just getting dark by the time Leo pulls up to my house, and I'm surprised how disappointed I am that the evening is ending. I'm pretty sure that once I step out of the car, my brain will convince itself that this was all an extensive fever dream, in order to protect my sanity.

"I have to admit, Wren," Leo says, "you sure know how to throw a curveball."

Oh, now I'm *embarrassed*? At least we're not in the middle of the restaurant. I pay an inordinate amount of attention to unbuckling my seat belt. "Well," I say with a tenuous amount of grace. "You know me. Wild card."

Leo laughs softly and I stuff the pamphlets under my arm, already considering how to shove them to the bottom of the trash so Dad doesn't notice. Not that my dad typically digs through the trash like a rat man, but better safe than sorry.

I have my hand on the door when Leo speaks again.

"Thanks," he says, and there's a weight to his voice that makes me look back. He's staring at the steering wheel, his thumbnail worrying at the space where two pieces meet. "For trying to cheer me up. It was…" He tilts his head and scrunches his nose, considering. "… nice, I think. Minus the lying."

"You're welcome. Minus the lying," I concede. I climb out of his giant SUV.

I barely make it to the driveway before I hear the window rolling down. I brace myself. The energy in the car was getting dangerously close to a heart-to-heart, and I don't have any of Archer's horrible punch to help me through it now.

"By the way," Leo says, leaning out the window. "Don't worry about our friend Marie calling you for a follow-up. I just paid for the tasting."

The righteous indignation must show on my face, because he laughs. "It was supposed to be free!" I argue, brandishing the pamphlets. *"That was the grift!"* That's half the fun! What's the point in a grift if you just pay for it!"

"Wren," he says, somehow managing to be absolutely sincere while still clearly laughing at my outrage, "if I have to pay eighty dollars to not explain to Ms. Little why the Dance is being booked under a fake wedding, it'll be worth every penny."

All right, maybe I didn't think that part all the way through. But the point stands.

"You've got a lot to learn." I shake my head, turning back toward the house to hide the smile inching across my face. Dammit. It's not funny that he ruined my grift. It's definitely not funny that Leo and I just pretended to be engaged for an afternoon.

"Yeah," Leo says. "I guess so."

Except it is. Just a little bit. I had fun being fake engaged to Leo for a couple of hours. Don't think I'm happy about it.

♥

It all feels like a weird dream when I wake up the next morning, but most things feel that way when it's seven a.m. on a Saturday. I skip Starbucks and roll my car through the McDonald's drive-through for a cup of black coffee, with one sugar to make it palatable. Sometimes you need a cold, hard dose of reality.

This is one of those days.

The SAT is being held in one of the first-floor math classrooms. I get there too early, before the doors are even opened, though I can see the shadows of proctors lurking inside. I'm still not sure about this, but once I registered, I couldn't back out without losing my fifty bucks. I guess it's a good enough reason to be standing here, clutching my coffee like a lifeline, trying to pretend I'm not nervous.

I have no reason to be nervous. I get good grades. I take AP classes. I even studied the prep book, though maybe not as much as I should have. I should be fine. Or at least decent.

But all I can think about is the last time I was here, staring down at my paper booklet, the proctor's voice droning in my ear. I remember all the details now. My pencil, the weight of it in my hand, the texture of the paper. The way when I wrote my name the *M* came out crooked. I remember thinking that my mom was dead and I was just sitting there, taking a test like it was something that mattered. It was real—the pencil, the paper, the crooked stroke of my name— and my mom just . . . wasn't. She just wasn't. Not anymore.

"What are you doing here?"

I blink, snapped back into the present. Stephen Hannigan stares back at me, looking entirely too cosmopolitan for the setting. Who wears a white button-down to the SAT? Between the gray cardigan and the fancy thermos, he looks like he got lost on his way to a librarian convention.

I stare at him for a beat too long, my mouth hanging open a fraction of an inch. I can't think about last year, or the year before that. Just this brief slip has thrown me entirely off my game. Maybe that's why I'm a little too honest. "I'm here to take the SAT," I say.

Which, like, obviously. But it feels weird to say it out loud. I didn't even tell Ryan I signed up to take it again. Or Ms. Little, but only because I didn't want her to be smug about it. Stephen is the last person I want to know that I bombed the test so badly I need to retake it just to get a reasonable score. Part of the problem with doing well in school is that people expect you to *always* do well in school. It makes it worse when you don't.

There's a beat of sickly silence, and then Stephen takes a sip of his coffee. "Yeah, me too," he says, and for a moment I'm surprised, before he keeps going. "I think I can scrape up at least an extra hundred this time, but we'll see. I'd like at least a fourteen hundred, since I'm clearly not going to have Robotics World Champion to put on my application." It comes out more bitter than my coffee.

What am I supposed to say to that? Since when do Stephen and I shoot the shit about college applications like we're friends? I was under the impression that we're acquaintances bordering on enemies. "Oh. Yeah," I say awkwardly, for lack of anything better. I fiddle restlessly with the plastic lid to my coffee cup. His reusable thermos is making me feel guilty about the future landfill in my hand. "Sorry about the regionals thing," I offer. "I think Leo feels bad."

Stephen's eyes narrow slightly at Leo's name, and I immediately regret saying it. "Did he tell you that?" he demands.

"He implied it." By hiding in the bathroom. I decide not to mention that part.

Stephen's still giving me a suspicious look, his mouth pinched at the corners like his coffee is too bitter. "Yeah, well," he says, taking out his phone in a clear indication of *I'm done talking now.* "He should."

Maybe some people have more important things going on than padding your college application, I want to sneer, before I abruptly rein myself back in. Why am I defending Leo? I don't care what Stephen Hannigan thinks about me, much less what he thinks about other people. I took Leo out once to get the sad look off his face, and he managed to throw a wrench into that plan. That doesn't mean I have to go around defending his honor.

Still, I can't help but give Stephen a little sideways glare—until I catch a familiar flash of yellow on his phone screen.

"You're on Buddy?" I demand.

He looks up from his phone, startled. He curls the screen away from me to hide the messages, but I've been spending too much time staring at that interface not to recognize it. "Yeah. So what?" Stephen says, looking at me like I might make a grab for his phone. "It's for *your* Dance."

First of all, it's not *my* Dance. If anything, it's Leo's Dance. But I'm not thinking about that. I'm thinking about the sickly realization that Buddy Boy, *my* Buddy Boy, is someone I go to school with.

Which I knew, obviously—that's the whole point of this special school feature—but somehow it never quite clicked until I found myself staring down the realization that Buddy Boy could very well be Stephen Hannigan.

No. No, absolutely not. I'm not thinking about that, because I have a test to take, and if I have to confront the possibility that there's any universe, any situation, any possibility where I might have a crush on Stephen fucking Hannigan, I'll delete the app and let Buddy Boy think I was lost at sea.

"Nothing," I say a little too quickly. "Just taking a survey. For student council."

"Right." Stephen gives me a strange look, as if he weren't the one who started this conversation in the first place.

I'm saved, ironically, by the SAT. One of the proctors opens the door, finally letting us inside. Somehow the classroom, just as small and beige as it was the day before, is more intimidating now.

"Well," Stephen says, locking his phone, already in hand for when we'll have to leave them with the proctor. "Good luck, I guess."

"Yeah," I say faintly. "You too."

20
THE INVESTIGATION

And so we come to Thanksgiving.

Almost. For me, Thanksgiving comes in two parts. One is the normal day-of Thanksgiving, where we drive to my grandmother's house in Tallahassee. There I participate in such riveting holiday events as:

1. Watching my uncle yell at football
2. Pretending to be interested in my older cousin's multilevel marketing scheme
3. Fielding awkward questions from my younger cousin
4. Trying to enjoy at least slightly dry turkey while knowing that my dad is silently tabulating how many juice cleanses he'll need to recover from this one
5. Bonus, this year: waiting, excruciatingly, for my SAT scores to come in

It's different, without my mom. Kinda like sitting next to an empty chair, waiting for someone to come sit down, but they never do. You don't mention it—what's there to say about an empty chair?—but you don't put the chair away either. You just sit with it. I guess a lot about losing someone is just sitting with it. There's not much else you can do.

A lot of holidays hit like that now. That's why I like the fake ones more. Like, for instance, Robinsonsgiving.

Some backstory: For the week of Thanksgiving, Ryan's family takes advantage of our time off from school and drives up to Atlanta, where they spend the holiday with Ryan's aunt. All very wholesome and fun, except that Aunt Stephanie is a vegan. Which is fine. For her. Ryan's dad has different opinions on the subject.

So every year on the Saturday before Thanksgiving, the Robinson family has their own pre-Thanksgiving to get it out of their systems before their weeklong vegan getaway. Turkey and gravy, sweet potato casserole with marshmallows on top, stuffing with bacon bits. The whole shebang. And I, being a charming and lovable fixture in Ryan's life, am always invited.

Normally this means a day of cooking and eating and puzzles, the most baffling of the Robinson family traditions, but this year, it also presents a unique opportunity: I'm going to find out Ryan's beef with Buddy, and why she's hiding it from me (Buddy's number one enemy, supposedly), or die trying.

Even if that means doing a thousand-piece puzzle of the Death Star with Reed while Ryan and her parents work in the kitchen. I've been banned from the kitchen since the (accidental!) Great Microwave Fire, and I think Reed was banned at birth just as a precaution.

"I can't believe I let you pick the puzzle," Reed says for the sixtieth or seventieth time, her cheek propped on one fist while she listlessly sorts through puzzle pieces. There are two piles: a small one of black pieces and a mound of varying shades of gray. "The Murder Ball is stupid anyway."

"It's the *Death Star*," I correct her. "And of course it's stupid. But it's a stupid *cultural icon*. And the puzzle thing is *your* tradition. I just bring what I'm told."

"It's *Mom's* tradition," she says haughtily. "I'm as much a prisoner here as you are. Now get back to work on finding the edge pieces. We're on a deadline."

Yeah, we *are* on a deadline. Or I am, at least. I glance behind me, where Ryan and her dad are peering into the open oven like they're going to find divine prophecy written in the turkey grease. The ranking of those who know Ryan Robinson best goes like this:

1. Me, her best friend, light of her life
2. Her little sister, annoying but tenacious

This, of course, makes Reed and me natural enemies, even besides her habits of kicking the back of my seat at seven in the morning and giving me colds. It's the only way to maintain balance in the universe. If we were to team up and combine our knowledge . . .

Well. The effects would be devastating.

Which is why I need to grill her before Ryan looks up from the mashed potatoes long enough to realize what I'm doing.

I lean across the table, pretending to inspect the corner we've managed to put together. Reed looks up at me with narrowed eyes.

"You'd better be focusing on those edges."

"You know she was lying, right?" I say quickly, my voice hushed.

Reed is obnoxious and loud and overall an annoying little human being—but she's smart. She catches on quick. I see confusion flip to understanding as her eyes dart toward the kitchen. "About what?" she asks, her voice just as low.

"About Buddy," I say.

She squints at me. I swear, this girl has the memory of a gnat.

"In the car," I say impatiently. "The other day? She said she never downloaded it?"

"Oh. Ohhhhh," Reed says, and I mash together two puzzle pieces so it looks like we just made a discovery. "So you think she actually *did* download it?"

"Maybe." I move the pieces around in a way that looks purposeful, but really I need the excuse to look away. Okay, so maybe I feel a *little* guilty about looping Reed in on this, but desperate times call for desperate measures. It'll be fine. Like I said, memory of a gnat. "But I need your help finding out."

"Oh?" She cocks her head, one eyebrow arching dangerously. "What's in it for me?"

I bite the tip of my tongue. I prepared for this, but that doesn't mean I like it. "Twenty dollars."

The eyebrow comes down into a scowl. "Try again."

Worth a shot. "Fine," I say through gritted teeth. "I'll get you into the Dance."

Her scowl blooms into a shit-eating grin. "And get me a date with a hot senior boy," she says loftily.

"I think that might be illegal."

"Hot junior boy."

"What makes you think I know any hot boys?" I ask, exasperated. I'm not exactly an expert on hot, but I suspect Reed and I have different standards.

"You know Leo," she says loftily.

I narrow my eyes. "That's my offer. Take it or leave it."

"Fine, keep them all for yourself." She sighs and brushes her hair over her shoulder imperiously. "I'll do it."

"I'll get you into the Dance *if you succeed*," I add quickly. "If she catches you, all bets are off and I pretend we've never met."

"Wren." She gives me a look of pure contempt. "I'm her sister. I could steal her phone in my sleep."

♥

Dinner lasts ten years. I can hardly focus on my turkey, probably because Reed keeps shooting me significant looks, which Ryan definitely notices but won't say anything about in front of their parents. So *she* just shoots me weird looks too, until the three of us are just making bug eyes at each other across the table. It doesn't go unnoticed.

Mrs. Robinson sighs. "I love you all dearly," she says, "but you kids are *strange*."

That's probably why we get out of finishing the puzzle, which is usually a capital crime in the Robinson household, but it doesn't get us out of doing the dishes. I'm still loading the dishwasher when Reed sidles up to me.

"You remember our deal?" she says out of the side of her mouth, and it takes everything I have not to roll my eyes.

"Yes," I say. "I remember. It was an hour ago." I don't know why she thinks I'm about to double-cross her at any moment. Getting her into the Dance is actually the least annoying thing she could ask for, except for maybe the twenty dollars. If I'm really lucky, she might shut up about it in the car now that she's gotten what she wanted.

"Good." Her eyes dart around the room, even though we're alone in the kitchen. "You have five minutes. Dad always makes Ryan set up the karaoke machine because he can't figure it out." She hands off Ryan's phone like we're international spies.

I must be a little caught up in the atmosphere too, because I nod stiffly and slip it into my back pocket. "Finish this for me," I say, handing her a dirty plate. I dart away before she can protest.

I nearly collide with Mrs. Robinson on the way out of the kitchen, executing what's almost a pirouette in order to slide sideways through the door.

"Someone's in a hurry," she remarks, clearly still confused from dinner. I feel bad for her sometimes. It can't be easy having both Ryan and Reed Robinson under one roof. And then they go and invite me in. On purpose.

"Just got to go grab something!" I say in a rush, disappearing down the hallway. I hesitate there, peeking around the corner to make sure no one is coming after me.

Safe. I duck out of sight, my back pressed against the wall. I could hide in the bathroom, but I don't really want to offend the Robinsons' cooking by spending too much time in their bathroom right after dinner. It should only take a second anyway. I'll do it here, where I can hear anyone coming.

I hesitate, Ryan's phone in one hand. Okay, now that I'm here, I'm starting to feel bad. *Really* bad. Which is a problem, because I've already done half the crime. But it's not like you can be only halfway guilty, right? I'm not really a math guy, but I think at a certain point it's more economical to just go through with it.

I unlock her phone, because of course I know her passcode. If it helps, she knows mine too. That's what happens when you've been best friends this long. Her background is a picture of Beep, since she can't have a cat due to her dad's being allergic. Beep's slitted eyes regard me with withering judgment.

I flip through her phone so fast I nearly cut my thumb on a chip in her screen protector, looking for that damning yellow-and-white app. I check her folders too, since I keep mine buried in one between the Starbucks and Dunkin' apps. And I find . . .

Nothing.

I frown down at her phone, feeling strangely disappointed. So Ryan isn't secretly harboring a crush on an anonymous classmate through a gimmicky not-dating app. I guess that's just . . . me.

Hm.

I sigh and darken the screen again. I guess I'll unpack that emotion later. In the meantime, I need to establish some plausible deniability before Ryan realizes her phone is missing. I cross the hall and open the door to her bedroom.

Only to find Ryan already standing there, staring intently down at a cellphone.

My first thought is: *Ha! I knew it!*

My second thought is: *Wait. I'm holding Ryan's phone.*

"Is that my phone?" I accuse, jabbing a finger in her direction.

"Is that *my* phone?" Ryan counters, pointing back.

We stand there for a moment, staring at each other like two deer in headlights and/or two gunslingers in the Wild West. I'm so caught up in the shock of us catching each other red-handed that I can barely process the fact that my phone has a hell of a lot more damning evidence on it than hers does.

Ryan just looks baffled. "How did you—" She closes her eyes. "Reed."

"That *rat*." Oh, I'm going to *kill* her. I knew she was chaotic, but I didn't expect her to be savvy enough to play us both at the same time. "What did you promise her?"

Ryan's lips thin, and her eyes dart guiltily around the room. "That I'd get her into the Dance." Finally she meets my eyes. "You too?"

"Me too," I agree. "I guess she figured she'd cover all her bases."

We drop our accusatory fingers simultaneously, settling into an awkward silence. I can practically see the same gears turning in her mind that are turning in mine. I *could* be mad, but so could she, and considering we committed the exact same crime, I guess we just . . . cancel each other out.

But also, *she's* the one who actually found something. I can see it on her face. She found the Buddy app, but she doesn't want to say it, not unless I say it first. I try to remember the last conversation Buddy Boy and I had, but it doesn't matter. Ryan knows me, and she knows that conversation thread is about the same thing as looking at my squishy, bleeding heart. If I decide to trade phones and never discuss it again, I think she'll follow my lead. *If.*

Well. This is what I wanted, isn't it? The truth?

I toss her phone on the bed. It bounces once and I flop down next to it, pressing my face into the purple duvet before I roll onto my back. After a moment, the bed creaks as she follows suit. I turn my head, and the queen-sized bed is big enough that we're face-to-face, our legs dangling off opposite sides.

"So," I say.

"So," she agrees.

A thousand things I could say, but I take the easiest route first. Typical. "You really didn't download the app?" I say, squinting.

She meets me with an incredulous look. "Why say it like that? You're the one who thinks it's stupid."

"Because it is," I say without missing a beat. "But . . . I don't know. I thought you'd be into that."

"Stupid stuff?" Ryan says blandly.

I elbow her shoulder and she laughs, pushing my arm away.

"I did download it for, like, a week," she says, without the air of confession that I would have said it with. "I thought the idea was really cool, and you were being so dramatic about it, I thought maybe I could show you it wasn't so bad. But it felt like everyone I talked to was trying to find a date, and I decided I just . . . wasn't interested."

"In Buddy?"

"In dating."

"Oh." I fold my hands over my chest and look up, tracing the popcorn ceiling with my eyes. "Like, ever? Like in an aromantic way?" I used to wonder if I was aromantic too, if it went hand in hand with asexuality like some sort of two-for-one-special. For some people it might. I was never really sure, but these feelings toward Buddy Boy are the final nail in that coffin. I'm almost tempted to think that it would be easier if I were, but I cringe internally at the thought. I know better than that. The world already acts like you're broken for not experiencing sexual attraction, and it's practically *designed* around the idea of the romantic relationship. No, I don't think that's very easy at all.

"Maybe." She shrugs again and the bed shakes a little. "I guess. I never needed a word for it, really."

I frown at the ceiling, rubbing the material of my shirt between my thumb and forefinger. I've always liked having the word *asexual*. I like how it makes me feel like I belong somewhere even when the rest of the world thinks I'm not quite right. But I guess for some people it's more comfortable opting out of having a box entirely. "I didn't know that," I say awkwardly. Awkward because what I really sound like is *Why didn't you tell me?*, even if I don't mean to. I know how it is. Sometimes things don't feel worth saying, or else are too hard to say, or too awkward. Even before your best friend starts going through your phone.

"It's not a *disease*, you clown," Ryan says, but she's grinning. She pushes my shoulder. "You don't have to be all somber about it."

"I'm *not*," I say, pushing her back, but relief unspools quietly in my chest. I *think* she kind of just came out to me, and I don't want to mess that up. But I guess coming out doesn't always have to be dramatic. Sometimes it just is what it is. Still, I glance at her shyly. "But, like, if you *do* want to talk about it—you know I get it, right?" I fidget with the hem of my shirt again. "The being something by not being something?" At least, that's how I've always thought about it. It feels weird, defining yourself by the absence of something. Sometimes I wonder if I would have ever realized my asexuality needed a label if the world didn't keep telling me it did.

"I know," Ryan says, her smile quirking one corner of her mouth. "I know I can talk to you about anything, Wren." She pauses, and her expression turns sly. "Even if you are a hopeless little romantic."

My head whips sideways so fast my bangs fall across my eyes. I push them back with a huff. "I am *not*," I protest.

"You are *so*," she says, giving me a look like I've lost my mind. "You write novel-length fan fiction about Star Wars characters."

"I—" I sputter. "That's different."

"I read it, Wren," she says flatly. "It's not different." She reaches out and pokes me between the eyes. "But that's not what you want to talk about."

I purse my lips. Speaking of things that are hard to say out loud. "You saw the conversation?"

"Yeah," she says, a little sheepish. "I mean, I had a feeling, but I kept waiting for you to say something and you just *wouldn't*."

I wrinkle my nose. "I was kind of waiting to find out you were hilariously in the exact same situation so we could laugh about it and I could not be embarrassed by making a fool of myself," I say in one breath.

She smiles wryly. "Sorry to let you down on that one, pal." Ryan grunts and pulls herself up, sitting cross-legged on the bed. She tugs on my shirt until I reluctantly do the same. I'm not sure what the science of it is, but I'm pretty sure heart-to-hearts are easier to have horizontally. "So?" she says, leaning forward, her elbows on her knees. "How do you feel about it?"

"About what?"

"Having a big squishy crush."

"Don't say that *word*," I groan, looking beseechingly up at the ceiling. "Terrible," I say after a moment's deliberation. Her eyebrows come back down, her forehead furrowing in the middle. She doesn't believe me. Okay, I don't believe me either. "Good," I amend. "Good in a terrible way. Does that make sense?"

"You never make sense," she says, but she's smiling. She scrunches her nose, clearly on the edge of a decision. "Can I tell you something you're not gonna like?"

Well, when you put it that way. "I guess," I say warily.

"It's been . . . nice," Ryan says, "seeing you happy."

She's right, I don't like it. I don't like the idea that anyone, even (especially?) someone I love as much as Ryan, could tell I *wasn't* happy. Guilt cuts me like a knife to the chest. Does she think she wasn't enough? That I needed someone else? "I wasn't—"

She's already waving me off. "No, I mean—" She pinches her lips together, trying to find the right words. "It's been nice seeing you excited about something. Something that *doesn't* have to do with student council."

Have I been that bad? I open my mouth to ask, but I already know she's right. She's just saying the same things Ms. Little did, in a different order. What have I *really* looked forward to, before it was waiting for a message from Buddy Boy? When my mom got sick, the future became something inevitable. And when she died, the future just . . . ended, I guess. Everything got stuck in place, and I got used to it. My crush on Buddy Boy, the SAT, college—they're all the same. They're all something that could make my life different. Make *me* different.

And that scares the hell out of me.

"So," Ryan says gently. Probably because I've been staring at her as I do mental handsprings through an emotional revelation. "Are you going to spill your guts about this guy or what?"

"*Well*," I say, my hands on my knees. I take a deep breath. There's a lot, actually, that I should catch her up on. "Let's get one thing straight: none of this was supposed to happen."

21
THE ANNIVERSARY

Ryan:

I didnt realize how bad this had gotten

How extreme

It's like I'm losing my best friend . . .

Sometimes I can still hear his voice . . .

Me:

oh my god i was IN THE BATHROOM

you are so annoying i should never have told you anything

Ryan:

Sure, I definitely believe you

I definitely believe you weren't on Buddy

Absolutely convinced

Me:

go enjoy aunt stephanie's tofurky and
let me have some peace

Ryan:

Okay, rude

Tell him I said hi 😊

Me:

thanks i will absolutely not do that

Yeah, she caught me. Obviously. Give me a break.
I switch back to Buddy.

Him:

I can't believe you're anti dog

Me:

im not ANTI dog im just not PRO dog

you'd reconsider too if you had my
cousins chihuahua panting in your
face

stinky

Him:

So you're a cat person then?

Me:

cat person first

then chicken person

then . . . idk. im leaving my options
open

Him:

So you DO have chickens?

Me:

i didn't say that

but i will say chickens are the
superior animals

are they stinky? yes. do they live
outside? also yes. eggs? a bonus.

its the perfect arrangement

Him:
It's just not the same.

Icee shoves his nose in my face for the fifth time in an hour, his bug eyes glistening wetly. I'm not exactly sure why my cousin named her dog *Icee*, but I can only assume it has something to do with his uncontrollable shivering. Seems a little cruel to me, but no one's asking.

No one at real Thanksgiving is asking me anything, luckily—anymore. Thanksgiving turkey has faded into post-turkey football, and I've managed to survive mostly unscathed. Dad somehow got himself roped into pretending to care about the game, but I'm not enough of a hero to fall on that sword with him. Instead, I've managed to seclude myself in my grandma's spare bedroom, glued to my phone and more than happily playing the typical teenager. Damn kids.

Considering Buddy Boy has been replying almost immediately, I get the feeling we're on the same wavelength.

Which is probably why I decide to push my luck. That, and spilling all my secrets to Ryan has got me thinking. She's right: talking to him *does* make me happy. And maybe I'm a little afraid of that—or a lot afraid of that, depending on the day—but maybe I shouldn't let that stop me either.

Maybe.

Me:

i forgot to tell you i fucked up and my
best friend noticed the buddy app on
my phone

Him:

Really?!

Did they say anything about it?

Me:

omg obviously

which i guess is my fault for making a
big deal about NOT downloading it

and also your fault for not letting me
delete it

Him:

Wow, the sacrifices you've made just
to talk to me

Heroic

Me:

i know

Him:

So what did you say?

I bite the tip of my tongue and sink deeper into the pullout couch. Obviously I brought this up on purpose. Obviously my big horrible crush is pathetic. Obviously I should tell him something close to the truth, which is that I downloaded Buddy to see what the big deal was and accidentally found the one normal person on the whole app, and we've had a big laugh about it.

Obviously I do not do that.

Me:

idk i panicked

she assumed it was for the dance

thing and i just kind of let her

Him:

I guess that was a pretty reasonable
assumption

God, sometimes I want to strangle him. I settle for shaking my phone instead, pretending it's his anonymous little neck. I'm *trying*, but he won't pick up what I'm putting down. *How* am I not being obvious enough? Oh no . . . someone thought we were planning to go to the Dance together. . . . Haha, how awkward. . . . Jesus Christ, if I was in a nineties teen sitcom I'd be twirling my hair and chewing bubble gum. How many more injustices do I have to submit to before he realizes what I'm almost-not-really saying? Or before I give up and move on with my life?

I rest my phone against my forehead and sigh. Yeah. Good question.

Me:

yeah, so thanks for that

shes a bit of a romantic, unfortunately

shes basically got the wedding
planned

She's going to kill me if she ever sees this, is what she is.

Him:

Oh, good to know. I'll have to start
suit shopping

What are our colors?

Me:

yellow and white obviously

Him:

Obviously

Me:

maybe we can get a buddy
sponsorship

be on a commercial or something

And then he goes quiet for one minute. Two minutes. Five.
I resist the urge to smack my phone against my forehead until
I either come to my senses or sustain enough brain damage
that I can't remember making a fool of myself. What's with me
and marriage lately? First Leo at the Canopy and now this.

It takes him thirty-seven minutes to message me back.

Him:

Sorry! Had to help with the dishes

And then he changes the subject.
My life is a joke.

♥

I get my SAT results on November 30.

I did pretty well. Well enough, I guess. I think about
Stephen sniffing about wanting to add another hundred to

his score, but I'm just glad mine has four digits. I stare at the paper with the breakdown of my score for a long time. I should be happy. Or proud. Or something. Instead, I mostly feel nauseous.

I thought the test was going to be the hard part, but I also thought the test didn't really matter. I took it to prove to Ms. Little I wasn't afraid, and that should have been it. I don't *have* to do anything with the score. I certainly don't have to use it to apply to college.

It's November 30. The deadline for applications for the fall semester at Florida State is December 1.

Which is also the day my mom died.

Listen, I'm not exactly religious or spiritual or anything, really. I don't believe in signs or greater meanings. December 1st is just a day. One day out of three hundred and sixty-five, burned into my mind like the world's shittiest holiday that only me and a handful of other people know about.

But it's impossible not to think about her, and me, and what I'm doing here. Because I know what I'm doing. I'm waiting. I'm waiting for my life to go back to what it was, waiting for my mom to come back, waiting to start my life again. Those things aren't going to happen. I graduate from high school, I go to community college, and—what? I live in my same room, I go to my night shift at the Holiday Inn, I go to class. That's it, I guess. Nothing changes, but nothing stays the same either. I already know what I should do. What I want to do, past all the grief and the fear like an old, familiar bruise. No one has to ask the right question.

I submit the application. I don't have to decide right now—maybe I won't even get in—but at least I won't regret that I didn't give myself the option.

I think Mom would want me to do that much.

I message Buddy Boy, late enough that it's obviously an insomnia night for both of us. He's one of the things on my mind, but he doesn't know that, and I don't want him to think I'm ignoring him tomorrow.

Me:

hey if i'm quiet tomorrow dont take it personally

its kind of A Day

Him:

An important day?

Or a bad one?

Me:

both i guess?

not a good one

Him:

Okay

Take care of yourself

Me:

i'll try my best.

I can't think of a joke.

I turn my phone off before I go to bed and sleep in late. When I do get up, I drag my blanket behind me like a cape out to the living room, where my dad is already sitting on the couch. He's got a Starbucks cup on the coffee table, something with a lot of whipped cream and caramel drizzle—that's how you know it's December 1st. It's the kind of day where—well, you take care of yourself. Or at least he takes care of me.

I think it helps him to take care of someone, and it helps me to be taken care of. I don't think we let each other do that enough.

I crawl onto the couch next to him and press my face against his shoulder. Dad picks up the remote.

"Original trilogy or prequels first?"

"Original," I say. "I'm a purist."

I hear him smile. "I know."

♥

December 2, I get a message that leads me back to the broken locker at the back of the art building. I go during my TA period, so there's no one around.

There's another cupcake inside, with a note taped to its clear plastic container. This cupcake is vanilla with white icing and little orange and red leaves piped around the edge. Delicate black icing declares *It's Fall, Y'all!* in the center. I flip open a torn piece of notebook paper.

> *It's important to take care of yourself*
> *But sometimes you need a little help (:*
>
> —*BB*

22
THE GARAGE

"We can work on it in my garage," Leo suggests. "My dad has power tools."

Ms. Little frowns. "I don't know if I can officially sign off on that."

Archer perks up. "I know how to use a saw!"

"I definitely can't sign off on *that*."

"It's made of cardboard," Ryan says, leaning over my desk. "What are we sawing?"

"I'm not sure," I say, "but I can't wait to find out."

That's Monday's student council meeting. Weirdly, it's not about the Dance.

Weirdly because with the Dance in two and a half months, there are still a thousand things for us to do. We're planning a whole bundle of initiatives—my word choice, it sounds cool—to tie into the Buddy sponsorship and make the Dance more accessible. The formal wear drive is the big one, and the one that requires the most lead time, but for some incomprehensible reason we have to put important things like that on hold for a minute to focus on . . .

. . . the Rapture High Winter Village.

Every year, for reasons unknowable, Rapture High purchases a fleet of cardboard houses and gives one to every student organization and team to decorate. The houses are then assembled on the football field as the Winter Village. People donate five dollars to stroll through the village, eat small candy canes, and buy overpriced hot chocolate from the band kids. The houses are only about five feet tall, so the whole thing ends up looking like a town built for somewhat-shorter-than-average people. The houses are also wildly inconsistent. Some people barely paint theirs, while last year the robotics team had a solar-powered windmill covered in lights attached to theirs. I wonder whose idea that was.

That's how we all end up at Leo's place the following Saturday morning, wearing our best painting clothes and carrying an air of grim determination. There's an official vote at the end of the Winter Village for the best house and an unofficial vote for the worst. Not that there's a prize, but the worst ones end up in TikTok compilations, so we're trying to avoid that, if at all possible.

Ryan whistles as she parks next to the mailbox. "Nice car," she says, eyeing Leo's oversized white SUV in that car-person kind of way. Unfortunately, Ryan's dad is into Formula 1 racing, and she's never recovered from a childhood of car stuff.

I gesture dismissively before she can start talking about engines or whatever. "Don't mention it. He gets all embarrassed."

"How do you know?"

Hm. I've said too much. I climb out of the car before I can reveal any more unexpected Leo trivia, like absolutely anything that happened the afternoon we went to the Canopy.

Having seen Leo's giant car, I expected the Reyes household to be similarly over-the-top, more in line with the condo from the Halloween party than with my house. But it's . . . normal. It's a humble three-bedroom suburban house, not that different from mine, white with turquoise trim and a big metal gecko next to the front door, giving it a very Florida vibe. But in a cute way, not a Florida-Man-headline kind of way.

Leo has rolled up the garage door and already assembled the cardboard house on a tarp inside. I squint at the garage as Ryan and I walk up the driveway. Of course Leo is someone with a clean garage. I've never trusted people with clean garages. If you don't know what I'm talking about, it's probably because you have a clean garage.

Maggie and Archer are already there. They stand to one side with Leo, considering their blank slate with varying degrees of intensity.

"We need a theme," Maggie says without preamble. She turns to me. "What's our theme?"

"Uh." I'm not used to Maggie talking to me willingly, much less offering me decisions to make. "Why do I have to choose?"

"You're the president."

"So I'm only the president when you don't want to make a decision?"

"Yeah, basically."

"Okay, okay," Leo says, interrupting us before the situation can devolve any further. "I think we can all agree that the theme can't be Christmas."

We all murmur in agreement. Yeah, of course, obviously. While the Winter Village strives to be as inclusive and secular as possible, at least half the houses end up with a phoned-in Santa theme. Though admittedly everyone kind of expects the nativity scene from Bible club.

"Hanukkah?" Archer suggests.

"Are any of us Jewish?" Ryan says skeptically, and we all murmur again.

A sampling of our finer ideas:

1. ~~Winter~~ We live in Florida. Next.
2. ~~Solstice~~ No one can decide what that would look like.
3. ~~Grinchmas~~ That's just Christmas but the Grinch is there.
4. ~~Bigfoot~~ What?
5. ~~Krampus~~ Better than Bigfoot, but again—*what?* Also, still Christmas themed.

We don't really decide on a theme so much as have only one left.

"This is weird," Maggie says for the third time.

"It's *ironic*," says Archer, my unexpected sidekick. He gestures broadly with a paintbrush, almost taking his sister out with a swatch of yellow paint.

"I just feel like *capitalism* still counts as being Christmas related," Leo says skeptically, scratching his head at the mock-up Ryan put together. "I mean, at least kinda."

"Do you have any *better* ideas?" I say dryly. An Amazon/late-stage-capitalism theme is a *bit* on the nose, I'll admit, but I don't have any better ideas, and this is the closest we've come to a consensus. In retrospect, we should have settled on a theme at the meeting on Monday, but hindsight is twenty-twenty. "Ms. Little is going to love it. Trust me."

"Yeah, because she's weird," Maggie says.

"I still like Krampus," Ryan throws out there, and there's enough anti-Krampus agreement that at least we're all on the same page again.

Ryan takes over after that, regardless of the lack of Krampus. As is always my role in these kinds of events, I follow in her wake and paint our cardboard house as assigned. Luckily she knows I don't have an artistic bone in my body, so she assigns Maggie to the trickier parts. It's nice, falling into familiar roles after the weirdness surrounding Robinsonsgiving and the mutual phone thievery. As unnecessarily convoluted as that whole situation was in all ways, I'm glad I told Ryan about Buddy Boy and the SAT and all the complicated emotions threatening to clog my arteries. It's like a weight has been lifted off my chest.

Except now I can't even check the time on my phone without earning a significant look. Because she knows I'm checking for Buddy messages, even when I'm *not* (I am), I'm *focusing* (I'm not) on this very important project that I care *deeply* about (I don't). Eventually I just pocket my phone and accept that I'm going to be painting a gray wall for half the morning. BB hasn't even messaged me back, so I *guess* it doesn't matter.

Unfortunately, this means I have too much time to pay attention to Leo.

It's not that I'm nosy. I'm just curious. It's my fatal flaw, or at least one of many. He's wearing his glasses again, which is distracting in a way I can't quite put my finger on, except for how annoying it is that he makes the look work even though it went out of style years ago. He paints with laser focus, a smudge of gray paint on one cheek and the tip of his tongue sticking out between his teeth as he paints inside the pencil lines Ryan drew for us.

It feels weirdly personal, being at his house. It was personal being in his car too, but in a more awkward way, and that was before I noticed something was up with him. I thought I'd concluded that Leo's problems were his own, but I guess I threw that decision out the window when I started inviting him to fake weddings to get him to stop looking so sad. He looks less sad now, but I think he's just gotten better at hiding it. I'm not sure. I can't decide if I want to look closer or look away.

"What?"

I startle, nearly dropping my paintbrush. "What?" I counter.

Leo gives me a sideways look. "You're staring at me."

"Because you've got paint on your face," I scoff, savagely dabbing at a patchy spot in front of me. Why is this cheapo paint so thin? God. "Are you painting with your eyes closed?"

He gives me a baffled little smile, but mercifully the door into his house opens before he can think of a response. We all freeze like meerkats, as if we've been caught doing lines of cocaine off the washing machine instead of painting a cardboard box. All of us except Leo, who springs to his feet so fast that he drops his paintbrush. It hits the ground and a splatter of gray paint completes an improbable arc that flies up and splatters across my cheek. I let out an undignified squeak. I don't know how he did that on purpose, but I'm pretty sure he did.

I turn to glare after him but stop short. He's standing at the door, one foot on the concrete step that leads into the house, one hand on the doorframe. A woman leans out of the house, her hand on the inside. They're obviously related—they have the same tan skin and Roman nose—but she's not his mom, who I've seen on the periphery of every school play and fundraiser for just about my whole life. His aunt, maybe, or an older cousin.

Whatever complicated feelings I have toward eavesdropping don't matter, because they're speaking in Spanish. I knew I shouldn't take French. Not that I understand much French either.

I'm staring again. I tear my eyes away, only to find Maggie glaring at me from the other side of the cardboard house. There are little windows cut into each side of it, giving her a clear view through the center so she can shoot daggers directly into my heart.

I give her a look back. *What?*

She narrows her eyes.

I shake my head and roll my eyes.

Maggie stands abruptly, so that I can only see her waist through the windows. Her grubby painting shirt is still stylishly tucked into her sweatpants, which feels like a level of fashion unfit for the occasion.

"Let's get pizza for lunch," she all but announces. Leo looks back, his aunt (cousin?) disappearing into the house as the conversation ends. "Wren and I will go."

"We will?" I say.

"You will?" Leo says, looking vaguely alarmed.

I stand up, leaving my brush on the tarp. My knees complain as if I'm eighty years old. "Why me?" I complain just as loud. "Why not your brother?"

"Why not you?" She challenges me with her eyes, like she's the alpha dog at the junkyard and I'm a puppy that's wandered in off the street. I meet her stare for about half a second before backing down. Pizza isn't worth my life.

"Why not me?" I agree.

♥

Maggie and Archer share a dark red Toyota Corolla that I think is a hand-me-down from their older sister. It drives pretty well, except for the screeching sound every time Maggie takes a corner like it's the Daytona 500 and she's gonna lose it all if she doesn't win One Last Race.

It's cool out today, enough that the chill hasn't burned off even though it's well into the afternoon. It makes working in the garage nice, but the car has been baking in the sun. I'm itching to turn on the air-conditioning, just a little bit, but I'm convinced that Maggie will smack my hand away if I try. She doesn't even turn on the radio, so we're just sitting in awkward silence, listening to the sound of the engine.

"Can I just—" I reach for the radio.

"What are you doing?" Maggie says abruptly, which is the verbal equivalent of slapping my hand away. I let it drop.

"Uh," I say, wondering how long we'll have to be gone before Ryan reports my kidnapping to the police, "I wanted to put on some music?"

She gives me an exasperated look with enough force to melt flesh from bone. "Not the *radio*," she says. "With Leo."

Haha, what?

"Okay," I say warily. "Now I'm confused."

There is no *with Leo*. There is no *with Leo* anything. What would I do *with Leo*? Besides the Canopy, but there's no way he told her about that. I think. I was embarrassed by the whole thing and it was *my* idea. I'm pretty sure we're both taking that one to our graves.

Not that it was, like, a thing, but I could see how it might be misinterpreted as one. Especially if your name is Maggie Min and you hate my guts for some/many reasons.

"Are you into him?" Maggie says bluntly. She pairs it with a sharp right-hand turn, altogether making me feel like I've been forcibly ejected from the car.

"Into *Leo*?" I wheeze, and I actually put my hand to my chest, which is something I've got to stop doing. "What are you talking about?"

Into Leo? I'm not into *anyone*—okay, maybe I'm "into" Buddy Boy, I guess, but that's embarrassing and unlikely in a completely different way. It also doesn't feel entirely . . . real. At least not in a scary way, or a way that's *actually* going to lead to anything, which goes a long way toward explaining how I got into that mess in the first place. As much as I keep dropping hints, I don't think I would ever be so bold if I expected it to go anywhere. It's just for fun, like playing at something I'll never have in real life. I might as well enjoy it while I can.

But that has *nothing* to do with *Leo*.

It's impressive how Maggie manages to give me a significant look and drive at the same time, not that traffic is particularly challenging on a Saturday afternoon. She steers with one hand and holds up the other, ticking off points with her fingers as she goes. "Let's see. There's the extra student council meetings, just the two of you—"

"His idea."

"The bake sale—"

"For the greater good."

"You were alone together at the Halloween party—"

Okay, my idea. "That was a fluke."

"The weird honesty thing—"

"What does that have to do with anything?" If my cheeks are a little warm, it's because the car is stuffy. But also I didn't realize anyone had noticed us doing that.

She gives me a flat look, her expression merciless. "It's flirting."

"It's not flirting." Is it? No. It's not. I think I would know if it was flirting. Right?

Maggie ignores me. She gestures flippantly with one hand. "Especially since you keep staring at him like you've never seen him before."

He had paint on his face. I almost say it, but I close my mouth at the last moment, so abruptly that my teeth click together in a way that has nothing to do with Maggie's reckless turns. I *have* been paying a little too much attention. I could find ten different ways to justify it, but Maggie's not going to listen to any of them, so there's not really a point. As wrong as she may be, when she puts it like that, the evidence does sound pretty damning.

Is *that* why she doesn't like me?

"Are *you* into Leo?" I ask, sounding incredulous and, weirdly, a little offended.

"*Me?*" Now she sounds offended. "Ew, he's like my brother. Another one."

"Then why are you so mad at me?" I'm legitimately confused now. Not that I think I'm some universally likable person like Leo wants to be, but clearly the reason for Maggie's dislike is Leo-centric. Which makes sense, I guess, thinking back to all the times he ran interference between us, but it's still not something I was expecting. If she's going to hate me, it might as well be for something I did. I can give her options.

"Because—" Maggie cuts herself off, pursing her lips like Ryan's mom does when she really wants to swear but is too much of a responsible adult to do it in front of us. Maggie looks like she wants to say something too, but I don't think she's holding back a swear word. She drums her fingers against the steering wheel. "Like I said. Leo is like a brother to me. I'm just trying to watch out for him." She side-eyes me. "Don't hurt him. Or I'll hurt you."

I squirm uncomfortably in my seat. "Well, don't worry," I say, with a confidence that sounds fake even to me. "The last thing I'm gonna do is hurt Leo Reyes."

23
THE SOB STORY

Needless to say, lunch is pretty fucking awkward. Maggie ignores me as soon as we get out of the car, me balancing a stack of Little Caesars pizzas while she carries a single two-liter of Coke. Ryan is too absorbed in her work to notice my desperate glances, but Leo has plenty of glances of his own. His eyes keep ping-ponging between Maggie and me. Not that I notice. Because I'm decidedly not looking at him.

Oh God, what *does* he think? Does he know why Maggie cornered me? Is that why he's so nervous? Or maybe he's just wondering why she wanted to spend time with me, which is reasonable. I need to lie down and not move for several hours.

Maybe I should just ask him. Total honesty, right?

No. No, definitely not that.

We still have to finish this stupid cardboard house, so after we eat, we wipe the pizza grease off our hands and get back to work. I'm actually doing pretty good at pretending Leo and Maggie don't exist, when I have to go and ruin it.

"Um," I say awkwardly. "Bathroom?" I do a little finger-guns thing. I don't know why, but it's too late to take it back. I wish I could.

"Oh," Leo says. "Yeah, let me show you." We shuffle awkwardly until Leo finds a way to step around both me and the paint without knocking anything over and incurring Ryan's wrath.

Leo's house smells like lemon floor polish. Normally I distrust people whose houses are too clean (like their garages), but Leo's manages to look comfortable. Lived-in. I can hear the TV on in the living room and see a flicker of movement as Leo leads me down a narrow hall, the walls covered in framed photographs. I catch glimpses of Leo from various stages of life, equally represented with his brother, Emmanuel, who seems to live in a football jersey. I want to stop and look, but after my conversation/reading of the riot act with Maggie, that doesn't seem like a good decision.

"First door on the left," Leo says, and once again we engage in an awkward shuffle as I scurry past him.

I, as you might imagine, go to the bathroom, which isn't something that needs to be gone into in detail about. It should have been a wholly unremarkable experience. It is, until I wash my hands and then lean forward against the sink to peer into the mirror, inspecting a pimple that's been threatening to form, when something catches my eye. In the mirror I can see a little trash can tucked into the corner behind me, the kind we can't have at home because Beep likes to knock them over. And in it is an empty orange pill bottle. Only half of the label is visible, but it's enough to make me stop. I shouldn't look. It's definitely unethical to look. But just half a name is recognizable enough to make my stomach drop to my feet.

Of course I look.

♥

"I'm not feeling very well," I say, even though the cardboard house is half finished and my gray wall is still patchy under one and half coats of paint. "I'm going to have my dad come pick me up."

"I—" Leo starts.

"I'll take you home," Ryan says, reading my mood like a barometer. A *Ryan Robinson in her crafting zone* trance is not to be broken lightly, but she's still my best friend. She knows what's up.

Ryan's car is sun-warmed and a little musty, but I like it better than the crisp air outside. I like the familiar beige plastic siding on the passenger-side door and all the little stains on the upholstery that are probably my fault but I don't remember making.

"Did Maggie say something?" Ryan asks when we're down the street and I'm curled up in my seat, one knee up so that my chin can rest on it.

"No." I roll my eyes. "I mean, yes. But it doesn't matter."

"Is everything okay?" She sounds hesitant now, like she's stepping out onto a frozen-over pond and she doesn't want to see it crack. I don't like it, but it's not her fault, it's mine. Maybe I am as fragile as she's afraid I am.

"Fine," I say, and it might be a lie. I'm not sure yet. "Just . . . you know. One of those days."

Ryan knows me. She knows when something's not right, and she usually can tell why. This isn't new Buddy bullshit. This, unfortunately, is something very familiar between the two of us. We don't talk about it. We never talk about it. Sometimes I wish we would, but it's not that easy. If I want to talk about my mom, I'm going to have to be the one to bring it up.

And I'm not very good at that.

"Yeah" is all she says. "I know."

♥

Leo notices me avoiding him.

He'd have to be an idiot not to, and he might be a lot of things, but he's not that. It's probably pretty obvious when I stay home on Monday to avoid the student council meeting. It's definitely obvious every day after that. We only have one class together, which should make it easy, but it turns out that I see Leo a *lot* on any given day. In the hall. In the quad. In the library, the cafeteria, the front office. Rapture High isn't an overly large school, but, like, dear God. More than once I nearly sprain an ankle ducking away to avoid him at the end of the hall.

I know it can't last. We've still got a Dance to put together, and there's too much work to be done to avoid him forever. But that doesn't stop me from trying.

It's Saturday, and I'm cleaning the chicken coop. It's my firm belief that everyone should do at least two things, for the sake of being well-rounded, and those are (1) work customer service and (2) clean a chicken coop. There's just something humbling about scraping up a tremendous amount of chicken crap while the offenders stare at you with intense interest, hoping you're hiding strawberry tops some-where in your back pocket.

It's not the state I want to be receiving any guests in. I'm not really expecting to, until there's a voice behind me.

"Hey."

I jump, which makes the chickens briefly burst into the air, clucking furiously and ruffling their feathers. I spin around, almost putting my hand to my chest before I remember that I've been mucking around in chicken crap for the better part of an hour. I feel like a walking biohazard.

Meanwhile, Leo looks completely normal, except that he's standing in my backyard. I just blink at him, my sense of reality desperately trying to regain equilibrium.

"How did you get here?" I ask, more baffled than accusatory. It sounds like I think he teleported.

He shifts his weight awkwardly. "Your dad let me in."

"I mean—how do you know where I live?"

He frowns. "I've dropped you off here, like, twice."

Oh. Right. I shake my head, flipping my hair out of my eyes, and wipe my hands on my pants. They're already going straight in the wash when I'm done; there's no reason a little more salmonella would hurt. The fact that I'm wearing my coop-cleaning outfit, which consists of yellow sweatpants and a purple T-shirt from a school fundraiser three years ago, is a little more mortifying.

"So. Uh." I start to lean against the coop and then think better of it, in an aborted motion that ends up being more awkward than if I'd just followed through. I squint in the sunlight. "What's up?"

"Well," Leo says, "I was wondering why you're avoiding me like the plague." I open my mouth, but he holds up a hand to stop me, and somehow it actually works. "I thought about asking you, but that didn't seem like it would go anywhere, considering . . . you." Okay, well, yeah. But that doesn't mean he has to say it. "So I started thinking about when it started. When we were painting the Winter Village house, right? I thought maybe it was something Maggie said . . ." I wonder if he can see the terror in my eyes. God, what did Maggie say to him? ". . . And then I found this." He pulls something out of his pocket.

My heart twists. He holds up an empty orange pill bottle. I open my mouth again.

And I sigh.

All right, I guess we're doing this.

I leave the chickens to scratch in the dirt and cross the yard. Our backyard is mostly empty, except for the tall oak in the corner and the chicken coop. There's a sliding glass door that leads into the house, and a square of mottled concrete that plays host to a small collection of failing patio furniture. I ignore the sun-bleached Adirondack chairs and sit on the edge of the concrete, my legs stretched out in the patchy grass. Leo hesitates, but eventually he settles down next to me, his arms folded across his knees, pill bottle still held loosely in one hand. We sit in silence for a minute, watching the chickens go about their little chicken lives.

"I'm not sick," Leo says finally, throwing it out there like a bone. "For the record."

I roll my eyes, but I don't look at him. "I know it's not yours. Your name isn't on it," I say. I didn't want to look at the name at all, but it was kind of unavoidable, and that's what I get for being nosy. I've been trying not to think about it, the way I try not to think about a lot of things that really matter, but especially the bad ones. Still, it keeps flashing through my mind, unwanted, black text on a white label. I try to push the memory away again, but Leo is still sitting next to me. Waiting. "And you look too good. I mean healthy. I mean—" I press my lips together and exhale through my nose, trying to put together my disordered thoughts. "I mean, I'd know if it was yours. That's the stuff they give you when other stuff stops working. Trust me. I know."

That's what they do with cancer. We should know a better way by now, but I guess we don't. You throw progressively worse things at the worst thing of them all and you hope that it works, or at least works for a little while. And it does, sometimes, until it doesn't. Or it does, sometimes, until it hurts more than it helps.

"My mom," I say, my voice stilted. "Two years ago now."

It's like prying the words out from behind my teeth. Like I said, Ryan and I don't talk about it. But that's because Ryan has only ever lost her golden retriever, and while Puppuccino was a great dog, it's hardly the same. She can't talk about stuff like this. She can only listen.

It's different when someone actually gets it. *My mom.* I hardly even say the words anymore, afraid that people might ask questions, but even more afraid of talking about her in the past tense. It's its own kind of grief, cutting her out of my life because it hurts too much not to. I get the feeling I don't have to explain that to Leo.

I think he needs me to talk about it. I think I need me to talk about it too.

Leo is quiet for a long moment, twisting the pill bottle around in his hands, his thumbs pressed against the plastic. "My brother," he says. He presses his thumbs against the bottle a little harder. "Emmanuel. It's—" He clears his throat. "It's, you know. It's not good."

It's the bags under his eyes and the way he's started getting distracted by nothing, his easy charm cracked like it's been left out in the sun too long. It's that he'll miss school sometimes, never for more than a day or so, but I didn't really suspect why until I saw that bottle. Or maybe I did, maybe I saw something I recognized there, but I didn't want to think about what it really meant. I feel stupid now, thinking about how much I wrote it off as his perfect life and his perfect brother and that maybe Leo just wasn't perfect enough and that was the problem. I should have known better. Cancer doesn't care who you are or how young you are or that you were the best football player Rapture High ever saw. It certainly doesn't care how many people love you.

"That fucking sucks," I say.

Leo laughs, and then laughs again, like he surprised himself the first time. "Most people don't say that."

I huff a laugh. "Am I wrong?"

"No. You're right. It really fucking sucks." He shakes his head. "Thank you. For not saying you're sorry. That's what everyone says."

It is what everyone says, and I never know what to say back. *It's okay*—no, it's not okay. *Thanks*—for what? It's not fair that they get a script and I don't.

"Usually it's a character flaw of mine."

"Yeah, usually it's really fucking annoying," he says, but his lips twitch in a smile.

"I am sorry that I avoided you," I say, resisting the urge to twitch. I pull at a hole in the knee of my pants, fraying the edge a little worse. "I just got a little freaked out." It's scary, seeing a piece of yourself reflected back in another person like that. Especially the worst part of your life. Especially when that other person is Leo Reyes, who's supposed to be perfect and infuriating and too tall.

Well, at least he's still too tall.

"I know," he says, more gently than he usually does when he's acting like he knows all about me. "I almost didn't come." His eyes are fixed somewhere on the dirt between two chickens, his thumbnail digging into the ridges of the pill bottle cap. "I probably shouldn't have ambushed you."

I shrug a little. "Sometimes I need a little push," I admit. Like to take the SAT. To apply to college. Even to download Buddy, though I still can't believe how spectacularly that plan went awry. I couldn't have guessed the app would work as intended.

He's quiet for a moment. "I didn't know you had chickens." He says it like he's extending an olive branch. Or at least trying to move past this *admitting our faults* thing.

I shrug. "A lot of people have chickens." I could leave it at that. I almost want to, but I've already decided to be honest. "They were my mom's. She loved birds. She even named her birds after birds." I point to where a cluster of them are looking at something in the dirt. Probably a bug. "That big one is Grand Admiral Thrush. The one next to her is Lieutenant Emu."

"They have ranks?"

"Well, it's called a pecking order for a reason."

"Of course," Leo says. He laughs softly to himself, barely more than a puff of breath. "Is that why you're named Wren?"

"It could have been worse." I wrinkle my nose. "She liked Robin better, but my dad said no."

Leo laughs. "He didn't want you to be Batman's sidekick?"

"Leotards and capes would not have been a good look for me," I say dryly, and it's like the tension that's been living in my chest all week is finally loosening by degrees. The air is a little easier to breathe now. Even if it smells like chicken shit. "Hey," I say, bumping his knee with mine. "Total honesty?"

He eyes me uncertainly. "Total honesty," he agrees after a beat.

"I know I can be a dick," I say, and it's a testament to the strange, reserved energy in the air that I don't get a smart-ass remark about that. "But I get it. I get this. I wish I'd had someone to talk about it with, who knew what it was like to go through it all." Or maybe I don't. Maybe I would have been afraid, looking at someone who had already gone through what I could scarcely imagine. But Leo is at least going to have the option. I can do that much, even if it feels like picking off a scab too early. The wound is still raw underneath.

I swallow the lump in my throat. "You know I'm here if you need me, right?"

Leo meets my eyes, and it's like that moment by the pool again: we're locked into the space of seconds like they're an eternity. I almost want to look away, but more than that, I want him to know that I'm being sincere. I wish I knew what he's thinking.

"I know," he says at last, his voice a little hoarse. "I know."

24
THE (SWEATER) PARTY

Well, that fucking happened, didn't it?

Buddy Boy doesn't text me later that night, but I keep myself up late just fine on my own. I lie in bed and stare at the ceiling, the lights off but my phone upside down on my chest, the screen a little halo of light in the darkness. I keep picking it up, swiping listlessly, and putting it down again, uncertain what I'm even trying to do. Not sleep, certainly. I have realistic expectations about that.

It feels weird that Leo knows now—about my mom. About me, really. There are a lot of reasons I avoid telling people. It's too personal in a way that can't be avoided, like cracking open my chest to show off the wound where my heart should be. And then they know, and I know that they know, and I know they're looking at me and feeling bad for me and watching, waiting for me to break, hoping they don't step on my toes. It . . . well, it fucking sucks.

But I guess Leo is different. I guess Leo has his own problems to think about.

I pick up my phone again.

Me:
i think maybe you were right

Him:
Who is this?

Me:
???

Him:
The Anonymous I know would never admit someone else was right

Me:
omg shut up

and stop calling me that, the fbi are going to think I'm a superhacker or whatever

Him:
Haha

Okay, I'm done

Now what was I right about?

Me:
nvm you lost the right to know

Him:
That's okay, at least I know I was right about something

Me:
you are so annoying i swear

its like

can i tell you something personal?

Him:

Only if you want to

Me:

so i have this thing where like

i'm asexual

you know what that means right

Him:

Yeah

I'm pretty plugged into the LGBT
community, as a card-carrying
member

It's a little shock of relief that I wasn't expecting, both saying it out loud (well, you get the idea) and him accepting it. Some people don't think asexual or aromantic people count as queer, or just not queer *enough* without another letter tacked on, and—well, it's a shitty feeling, being told that you don't belong by people who are supposed to know what it's like to be treated like there's something wrong with you. I guess the fact that I'm clearly crushing on a guy counts for something, but if people like that are going to treat being queer like a club, I don't want to get in on a technicality. You shouldn't have to experience attraction to get through the door. It's way more complicated than that.

I didn't think BB would be like that, but I'm really glad to know he's not.

Me:

so its like

i don't really let myself think about
relationships because

idk it just sucks that i know there are
people who arent going to be ok with
that

and its not like i can even be mad
about it

like everyone is going to want
different things and theyre allowed to

Him:

I guess I can't say you're wrong

But I think just as many people
would be okay with it

Me:

i guess

but it still feels like something i have
to ASK and its humiliating

like i'm a house with a bad roof and
i have to disclose it before anyone
signs any paperwork

Him:

Well, I don't know what I was right
about

But I definitely don't think you're a
house with a bad roof

Me:

idk i'm not making any sense

i guess i just feel safe here and i
appreciate that

and i was just thinking that maybe
you were right

about keeping this and real life
separate

it's kind of nice i guess

not having to be a real person all the
time

He's quiet for a long time, and I stare at my phone in the dark. I don't know what I'm doing. Maybe I just had to say it, in a way I haven't said it to anyone, even Ryan. Maybe what I'm saying is it's hard being seen. It's really, really hard. I think about Leo seeing me and me seeing Leo and what I'm supposed to do with that, and I think that Buddy Boy was right about wanting to keep things anonymous between us.

It's worth it, having someplace where I can be someone other than Wren Martin, even just a little bit. Even if it means Buddy Boy will always be Buddy Boy, which is the worst name imaginable, and never quite real life. It's safer that way. For the both of us.

Him:

It'd be nice if being a real person was easier

But I'm glad we can not be real people together

I sigh so loud that Beep does one of his signature beeps and stalks to the end of the bed. I ignore him. *It's worth it*, I remind myself. It's not just easier this way, it's better. For the both of us. I should feel relieved, but all I taste is disappointment, heavy and bitter and entirely of my own making.

It *is* better this way. I guess I was just hoping he would disagree.

♥

Winter break arrives quickly and mercifully. I still have nightmares where I'm trapped in the Rapture High Winter Village during the zombie apocalypse, but at least when I wake up from them, I don't have to get myself ready and go to school. At this point, I'll take what I can get.

The last week before break was a whirlwind of prep for the Dance, and pre-Dance events, and the Winter Village on top of all that. Which meant I spent a lot of time around Leo but also I didn't. As in we were in the same room at some point almost every day, but also the rest of student council was there, and *also* also we were all so wrapped up in event logistics that I didn't really have time to feel awkward about it. Figuring out how to work this new element of Leo into my day-to-day worldview, I decide, can wait until January.

First there's Christmas Eve.

What do I accomplish in the time between break starting and Christmas Eve? Nothing. We all know I do nothing. I lie on my back like a sad turtle and play video games while covered in cat hair and crumbs from the illegal gluten-full cookies I don't tell my dad about. I'm not proud of it, but also I deserve it. Let me have this.

Anyway. Christmas Eve.

Navigating the holidays and grief combined is what can only be described as a minefield. Nothing is the same as it was, and the things that *are* the same are hard to look at. A part of you wants to pretend that the holiday doesn't exist—that all the holiday Starbucks cups and corny music is some mass delusion—but as much as your therapist might say you don't *have* to do anything, reality is a bit more complicated than that. So you do . . . something. You get it over with and punch your holiday ticket to satisfy whatever societal demons you've got on your back.

For us, that means the Robinson Family Ugly Sweater Party.

My family has never been particularly religious, aside from some token attempts at vague Christianity during my childhood whenever my grandmother was in town. When I was little, I would leave out cookies and milk for Santa and we would watch *Home Alone*, because it was, and remains, my favorite Christmas movie. My parents would let me open one gift and it was always socks, but with a fun pattern on them, just so I could complain about getting socks for Christmas. The last pair I got had chickens on them. I wore them a lot for a while, in the beginning, but now I save them for Christmas.

We don't do that anymore. My dad and I didn't talk about it, didn't make any sort of official decision. We just don't. I'm not sure we could if we tried.

Instead, we spend Christmas Eve at the Robinsons' house. The Robinsons *are* religious, and it is a *thing* for them, to the point where they go to midnight service. Rather than getting a nap in before that, like normal people, every year they hold an ugly sweater party to kill time before they go to welcome Baby Jesus into the world.

Normally I'm all about Robinson family events, because I love the Robinson family, minus Reed sometimes. *Normally!* But this year isn't normal, because this year, Aunt Stephanie is coming down from Atlanta, and bringing the Cousins with her.

Ryan's cousins are fine. I mean, Ryan thinks Nicolette walks on water just because she's a couple years older and goes to a women's college in Massachusetts, and Caleb is thirteen and in the middle of an intense anime phase. But it's fine. Really.

"You're being dramatic," Ryan says.

"I said it's fine," I say, fiddling with my phone even though Buddy Boy isn't texting me back. Probably because he's busy. Probably because it's Christmas Eve. That makes sense, but it doesn't change the fact that I need him to save me from the party I'm about to be dragged into.

"That's what you say when it's not fine." I'm lying on my back on her bed, so I can't see the look on her face, but I can hear the pointed stare.

"Sometimes it's like we're married," I say, and this time I can hear the eye roll. I drop my phone on the bed and prop myself up on my elbows. "Fine, but the first time I hear you tell Nicolette that something is *sooo coooool* I'm gonna barf—*mmph!*"

She hits me directly in the face with my ugly sweater of choice, and I flop back dramatically, like it was a bullet. "Wren, shut up and put on the Sonic sweater."

♥

My ugly sweater of choice features Sonic the Hedgehog. I'm not sure if the funny part is supposed to be the fact that I've never partaken in the Sonic franchise, or just the fact that it's an eye-searing shade of blue, but it's what Ryan had decided on by the time we were leaving Target. *I* wanted the one with a shaggy llama on the front with a pocket meant to hold a drink or assorted peppermints, but that only got me an impassioned rant about the "fake" ugly sweater industry, so Sonic it is.

I slouch through the party, trying not to look like a gaudy wall decoration. It's brisk outside, but not nearly cold enough for twenty people to be wearing sweaters inside, so they've got the air-conditioning running to preserve the illusion. At least there's no snow machine this year. I pick at the buffet table like a vulture on a corpse, eyeing the shrimp platter with undue consideration so I can pretend that I don't notice Ryan's cousin Caleb hovering at my elbow. I don't know why he thinks I'm cool when no one else in the world does. I'm not sure how to make him stop either.

"Do you watch anime?" Caleb asks, his hovering intensifying.

"No," I lie.

Ryan sits next to Nicolette at the dinner table, laughing at something I didn't catch. Nicolette is wearing a cream-colored turtleneck, because people who go to women's colleges in Massachusetts are too cool for ugly sweaters, I guess. Or maybe that's just what constitutes as ugly in New England. It makes her look like the personification of the *Dead Poets Society*.

"Have you seen *Fullmetal Alchemist*?" Caleb is inches away now. He's also thirteen and as tall as I am.

Ryan laughs again and leans her elbow on the table, doing everything but twirling braids around her finger. "That's sooo cool. . . ."

Okay, time for some fresh air.

"Can you hold this?" I say, foisting my plate of half-eaten crackers into Caleb's hands. I flee the scene before he can object.

I use my superior knowledge of the Robinson house to slip away, ducking through the kitchen and circling back through the living room, where I get lost in the pack of dads. I don't know if there's a Big Game for Christmas, but somehow they all end up congregating and talking about sports anyway. Dad always ends up caught in their field of gravity, tempted by masculine camaraderie even though he doesn't know anything about football. Or maybe he does now. Eventually he's got to just start learning by osmosis.

I escape out the side door, into the cool embrace of the night air. I take a deep breath—and cough. It smells like garbage can and cigarette smoke.

Ryan's Aunt Stephanie looks back at me owlishly from where she's leaning against the house, smoking a cigarette. I stare back.

"Do not tell my sister about this," she says quickly.

"Okay," I squeak, and I beat a hasty retreat toward the front of the house. I don't know if it makes sense to be both militantly vegan and also a smoker, but I'm not about to stick around and mull it over with her.

The driveway is filled with cars, which provide a nice cover for me if anyone comes looking—specifically Caleb. I doubt Ryan will pull herself out of Nicolette Fan Club mode any time soon. My dad's old black SUV sits at the end of the driveway, so I lean against the bumper, my legs stretched out in front of me. Even with the AC on, the house was stuffy. Outside, it's pitch black even though it's only six thirty, and I'm actually a little glad to have the sweater on, even if the sleeves are still pushed up to my elbows. I take out my phone and flip it restlessly in my hand. Still no messages from Buddy Boy. I suppose he's "making holiday memories" with his "beloved family."

Bastard.

Movement catches my eye and I look up. There's a figure running down the street, not on the sidewalk but in the gutter. Or jogging, actually. Running would imply they're being chased, but even from a distance, this seems to be more of a physical fitness sort of situation, which is just as bad. I squint. The Robinsons' street is pretty well lit, between the streetlamps and the Christmas lights, but from this distance, all I can really tell is that the jogger is human.

Probably. I guess I shouldn't rule out Christmas demon just yet.

I squint a little harder. There's actually something a little familiar about that Christmas demon.

My sneaking suspicion has evolved into full-on conspiracy theorizing by the time I can see that it is in fact Leo Reyes jogging down Ryan's street. Jogging right toward me, though I don't think he's noticed me yet.

I consider slinking away, but there's the risk he would notice me, and I'm still feeling just guilty enough about avoiding him before that it keeps me in place, waiting for him to pass by. His face is flushed and his hair flopping in every direction, except where it's slicked back with sweat. It should make him look like a mess, but instead it gives him this annoying hypercompetent vibe that I assume is something you learn when you start jogging. I certainly wouldn't know.

I see the moment he notices me, because he actually does a double take. I expect him to take AirPods out of his ears or something, but he's not wearing any. He's jogging *without* music. Dear God.

He's wearing basketball shorts and a faded T-shirt from some long-forgotten Fun Run. He pulls up the hem to wipe the sweat off his face, which is disgusting. I look away politely and scratch the back of my neck.

"Hey," he says, out of breath, and when I look back again he's fully clothed. He seems surprised to see me loitering outside a random house.

"Hey," I say, like this isn't weird. I dig the heel of my shoe into a seam in the concrete.

Leo looks up at the house behind me. "Your vacation home?" he asks, also pretending this isn't weird, a wry twist to his lips even though he's still breathing hard and sweating everywhere.

"Yeah, but I let Ryan and her family live here."

"Very magnanimous of you."

"I know." I side-eye him, finally rounding the corner on how weird it is that he's standing here and coming to see the fuller picture. No one jogs on Christmas Eve because they're feeling good and emotionally stable. Or I'm sure some people do (as much as anyone who jogs can be called stable), but not Leo. "I'd invite you in, but it's an ugly sweater party." I pluck at my Sonic sweater. "They're really serious about the dress code."

Leo laughs. "Damn. I'd invite you to jog, but I don't think you're the type."

"Absolutely not," I say, but I slide off the bumper, hitting the ground with a little hop. I glance back at the house to make sure no one's come looking for me. Which they haven't. I consider shooting Ryan a preemptive text but decide against it. I've got my phone. If they wonder where I've gone, they can find me.

I'm not really sure where I'm going anyway.

I set off down the road, walking in the gutter, my hands in pockets. I actually hear Leo pause behind me before he makes some kind of decision. His stupidly long legs make it easy for him to catch up.

"You're ruining my rhythm," Leo says blandly, falling into step next to me.

"No one said you had to hang back with me," I counter, and I smother a triumphant smile when he huffs softly but doesn't make any move to speed up. We walk in silence for a moment, except for the steady crunch of our shoes against the asphalt. I wonder if he's cold in his T-shirt, now that he's slowed down, but he doesn't seem to notice the chill. Figures. "So what's the deal?" I say at last.

I can feel him look at me sideways, from the corner of his eye. "Who says there's a deal?"

I gesture flippantly. "It's Christmas Eve, and you wear a cross," I say, gesturing to my chest where a necklace would lie, if I were a necklace kind of guy. "There's a deal."

"Crucifix, technically." He reaches up to touch the *crucifix* he wears on a gold chain around his neck. Not that I noticed he wears it, but . . . well, obviously I did. He's practically been chewing on it the last couple of months. "My family always goes to Mass on Christmas Eve," he says. "It just felt like . . . a lot. So I pretended to be sick."

"And went jogging?" I shoot him an incredulous look. "I'm not sure which sin is worse, that or the lying."

He rolls his eyes. "So what's *your* deal?"

Fair is fair. I shrug. "Don't really like parties," I say. "Don't really like Christmas—don't start."

He frowns. "Start what?"

Oh fuck, Buddy Boy is the one who makes fun of me for not liking holidays, not Leo. "Nothing," I say quickly. "That and Ryan's thirteen-year-old cousin thinks I'm cool."

Leo laughs—the kind where he throws his head back a little bit, like it surprised him. "I don't know where he got that idea," he says with a sly grin. "You must be pretty desperate, if you'd rather spend Christmas Eve with me."

It's certainly not an image I would ever have predicted, Leo and I walking side by side on the street, lit up in Technicolor by Christmas lights in the dark. A part of me doesn't quite believe it now, but there's something comfortable in the space between us. Understanding, I guess. Maybe neither of us ever thought this is where we'd end up, but we both have places we'd rather not be. I guess that's a good enough reason to be right where we are.

"It could always be worse," I say. "I could be jogging."

25
THE PARK

We go to Atlantis.

It's actually called Webber Park. When Ryan and I hit middle school, it was the first place our moms let us go alone. It's in the middle of Ryan's neighborhood, so it really wasn't that wild a privilege, but it felt like one at the time. The park used to be known for its aging plastic playground and the ditch neighborhood kids liked to roll down, but a couple of years ago they filled in the ditch and replaced the playground. Now it's aggressively under-the-sea themed and Ryan and I are too old to go to the park and think of it as freedom. So we call it Atlantis and only come back to eat ice cream on the swings sometimes.

It looks like a ghost town, lit up by a couple of anemic streetlamps and completely deserted, considering it's Christmas Eve and most people have better things to do. I make a beeline for the climbing dome, my footsteps crunching in the mulch. It's the only piece of equipment left from before the renovation, a big dome made of rubber-covered steel triangles I guess held up better than the plastic slides. In accordance with the theme, they slapped a big plastic octopus on top, its legs bent to make little buckets you can sit in at the top of the dome. The effect is rather thronelike.

Leo lingers on the edge, where wooden beams separate the mulch from the grass, looking like a vampire waiting to be invited in. A slightly perplexed vampire. Or maybe charmed. Probably charmed.

"The sweater really completes the look," he says wryly.

"Of what? A king?" I spread my hands and gesture to my playground kingdom. The octopus-throne is only just big enough for me to fit without concern of getting stuck there. Or at least without an *abundance* of concern. I wiggle, trying to get comfortable. "An octopus king?"

"Or a twelve-year-old," Leo offers.

I roll my eyes. "You have the rest of your miserable life to jog. Get on the playground."

He rolls his eyes right back, exaggerating it to make sure I see, but he actually listens. He walks over to the cluster of slides and climbing ropes made to look like a sunken pirate ship, appraising it like it might reach out and bite him. He looks up at the monkey bars.

"Hey," he says, throwing a look over his shoulder. "Watch this." He reaches up and wraps his hands around the bars, his feet still planted firmly on the ground.

Oh, that bastard.

"Wow, your ability to grow over six feet is sooo impressive," I say. "I can't believe I taught you to find your inner child again and this is how you repay me."

Leo laughs and pulls himself up, somehow folding his body so that he's able to climb on top of the monkey bars, his legs dangling down in the gap. Okay, that part was a *little* impressive. I guess.

"Why don't you play a sport?" I ask. "I mean, if you love exercise or whatever. Get a scholarship like all those sportspeople do." I tip my head back, studying him, imperious. "Too skinny for football. Do you have to be a meathead for soccer, or is that just Archer?" I pause. "I say *meathead* with all the love in the world." Considering he's the only twin that likes me, I should probably be a little nicer.

Leo laughs and leans back, lying across the monkey bars, his arms folded behind his head. There's no way it's comfortable, but he doesn't seem to mind. "I used to run cross-country," he says, "but I hurt my knee at the end of sophomore year, and after my brother got sick, I didn't really have time." He shrugs, and I hear the strange hesitance in mentioning his brother, like talking about it out loud only speaks the sickness into existence. "I still like to jog, though. It's kind of one of those things that's more enjoyable when you don't have to do it."

I remember the knee brace, vaguely. It must have been right before summer break, and if my time math is correct, it was the summer after my mom died, so I wasn't paying that much attention to anyone or anything. I wrinkle my nose, going for levity. "Can't relate."

Leo is quiet for a long moment, idly kicking his legs over open air. His head is tilted back like he's looking up at the stars, even though from where he's lying, he's probably getting an eyeful of light bulb from the streetlamps. "What are you doing after graduation?" he asks.

My heart skips a beat. Has Ms. Little been talking to him too? No—most seniors talk about graduation. "I applied for FSU," I say, trying to make the words sound casual. Florida State is the closest state school to Rapture—half our class applied—but it's the first time I've actually said the words. I won't find out if I got in until February, but I still check my application every few days, to be sure I actually submitted it and it wasn't just a weird dream. "But I might just go to Ricky instead," I hedge, losing my nerve. Rapture-Impala Community College will always be there for me. The problem is that's starting to sound more like a threat than a promise. It's already occurred to me that if I don't get accepted to FSU I've done all this emotional turmoil bullshit for nothing.

I look over to find that Leo has turned his head toward me, his eyes narrowed thoughtfully. "You're really good at not answering the question," he says conversationally.

"I did answer the question!" Listen, I'll own it when I'm being annoying, but this time I was actually cooperating. He doesn't even know how much he should appreciate the mental gymnastics it took to get the words out. "If you didn't get the right answer, then ask what you really want to know."

Leo pushes himself up again, so that he's leaning back on his arms, braced against one of the bars. "What do you want to do?" he asks. "Like, *really* do."

"Like, my hopes and dreams?" I deadpan.

"Like, your hopes and dreams," he confirms.

I hesitate, chewing on my bottom lip. "I want to be a lawyer," I say grudgingly. "I want to work in DC and be a civil rights lawyer."

The corner of Leo's mouth quirks upward. "Will we have a President Martin someday?"

I scoff. "I'm hoping to die without ordering any drone strikes on foreign nations, so that's a no from me. Student council president will have to do."

Leo laughs and looks up at the sky again, his shoulders bunched and his head tilted back, somehow both tense and at ease at the same time. He's quiet for so long I think he's going to make me ask. Finally he says to the sky, "I got into UCLA. Computer programming. Full-ride scholarship and everything."

"Oh." I can see the map of the country in my head, Rapture a little dot on the Florida panhandle. Los Angeles seems awfully far away. On scholarship too. Robotics team must've made for a helluva résumé. "Congrats." I pause. "You didn't answer the question though." He said he got a scholarship, not what he's actually going to *do*.

He rolls his head to give me a Look and I raise my eyebrows in response. "Annoying, isn't it?" I say, wrinkling my nose.

"Very." He pauses again, but this time he's looking at me, and the moment drags enough that I have to bite down on the urge to twitch. I don't think he's even looking at me so much as he's lost in his own thoughts, but it doesn't make his gaze any less heavy. "I thought I knew what I wanted," he confesses. "I thought I wanted to get away and be somewhere else. Someone else. Away from all the bad memories and the hard things and from just feeling so pointless and helpless. But . . ." He gestures half-heartedly, letting the unfinished thought drift out into the night. His eyes focus again, and he's definitely looking at me now, a crease appearing between his eyebrows. "Do you think that's running away?"

This is not the night I was expecting when Ryan stuffed a violently blue sweater over my head. I dig my thumbnail into a seam in the molded plastic, and I think about Buddy Boy, weirdly. About what he said, I mean. About wanting to be someone else, without all the complications of real life we don't get to choose. I was only fifteen when my life took a nosedive; I didn't really have the option to run away. But Leo does.

I wiggle out of my seat and climb off the dome. This doesn't seem like the kind of conversation to have while sitting on an octopus. Leo looks down from his vantage point on top of the monkey bars, and for a split second it looks like he's afraid to come down—not like he's going to twist his ankle and ruin his nonexistent cross-country career all over again, but like he's safe up there. Safe from a conversation that *he* started, I might add.

But I get it. Sometimes you have to say things you don't want to. You can finally push the words out, but that doesn't mean you don't desperately want to pull them back in.

He swings his legs one last time and then hops down through the gap between bars, the mulch crunching under his feet. It looks like the chill is finally starting to get to him, though not as much as it should. He rubs his arm.

"It feels like I'm trapped, sometimes," he says in a low voice. He stops rubbing his arm, but he hangs on to his elbow, one arm crossed protectively over his middle, making him seem smaller. "Or . . . I don't know. It's weird, isn't it? Knowing that something bad is going to happen in—what? Six months? A year? The doctors don't *quite* say it, but . . ."

"But you know," I fill in.

"But you know," he agrees, every word heavy. "And I'm afraid of it."

The silence settles between us. I fold my arms over my chest, pulling my sleeves over my hands and tucking my cold fingers against my rib cage. It's strange, hearing him talk about the things I went through two years ago now. It's hard to even remember that time in my life sometimes, like watching myself through textured glass. I can see the shapes of my old self, but not the details. Some memories hurt too much to look at head-on.

"I'm afraid . . . ," Leo starts, before looking away. He starts to laugh, then seems to remember there's nothing to laugh at. "I'm afraid of having regrets, I guess."

Regret. Just the word is like a poke in the eye. I've been thinking about regret a lot lately. We're standing under the monkey bars now, just loitering there, like the world's strangest business meeting. The chill is starting to seep into my skin, but going back to the party feels absurd now. I want to tell him I'm afraid too. Of staying, of leaving. Of never figuring out which is the right thing to do. But I don't think that'll help. I think about Ms. Little, and about Buddy Boy too. I don't think Leo is waiting to be told what to do. He already knows.

I think he's waiting for someone to ask the right question.

"Do you *want* to go?" I ask. "Or do you just want to leave?"

They're not the same question. It's different from what Ms. Little asked me, but the idea is the same. I didn't wantto hear it then—I'm not sure I want to hear it now—but she was right. I didn't *want* to go to community college. I was just too afraid to leave.

I'm still afraid, but I'm starting to think that the feeling doesn't go away. The brave part is doing the hard thing anyway.

"Maybe ten years from now you'll regret whatever you chose. Maybe not. People make mistakes—you can't be perfect all the time." I was hoping that would make him smile, but it doesn't. He just watches me, looking like he's holding his own heart in his hands and doesn't know what to do with it. "You'll always have regrets. I think it's human nature or something. But you're doing your best. We're all doing our best. I guess it's . . ." I shrug, losing steam. "I guess it's all we can do."

I look up and meet his eyes. The streetlamps cast strange shadows, one eye gold where it catches the light and the other dark. He opens his mouth, closes it, and opens it again. I dig my knuckles into my ribs.

"*Wren!*"

"Oh, Jesus," I huff. The tension is broken by Ryan, her sweater sparkling like a beacon down the street. I have my location shared with Ryan, because of course I do, but I was hoping she'd be too proud to chase me down in front of too-cool Nicolette. But Nicolette is with her . . . and Caleb.

I turn to Leo. "Do you watch anime?" I ask grimly.

"Um." Leo's eyes flutter. "I've seen *Fullmetal Alchemist*?"

"That's what I was afraid you'd say." I turn to face my fate. "You'd better get jogging. Trust me."

♥

While Ryan is in church, waiting for Baby Jesus to be born, I'm in bed, staring at my phone. I didn't want to tell Leo that it's his fault I'm not getting any sleep tonight, but it kind of is.

You'll always have regrets.

I'm such a dipshit. Why didn't I say *You'll always make the right decision and it'll be great*? That's much more comforting advice, specifically to me, staring at my phone like the apps are going to rearrange themselves and tell me what to do. I've already decided that Buddy Boy is better off staying in the app, at a safe distance. That I wouldn't know what to do with anything more than that, except mess it up. It's the good choice, maybe. It's the easy choice, definitely.

But what do I *want*?

I hit the Buddy app with my thumb. The time reads 12:03 a.m. Somewhere across town, Ryan is watching a couple of costumed ten-year-olds cradle a plastic baby.

Me:

merry christmas buddy boy

I assumed he must be asleep, but three undulating dots appear at the bottom of the screen almost immediately.

Him:

Merry Christmas <3

I stare at the little heart until my screen goes dark, assuming I've fallen asleep and forgotten about it. I let my phone tip forward and thump on my chest, my hands resting uselessly on top of it.

Bah humbug.

26
THE NEW YEAR

New Year's Eve. The final hurdle in the holiday triathlon. Normally, once I've managed this, I'm in the clear—I can relax without having to worry about smiling through holidays I haven't really been interested in since my mom died. This year I've got the Dance looming on the horizon, but I'm trying to take my challenges one at a time.

I pick up the evening shift for NYE, since, much like Halloween, no one wants it. No one wants the midnight shift either, but I'm not that magnanimous, and they won't let me work that late until I'm eighteen anyway. I'm loitering outside the front entrance with Jerry, my favorite maintenance guy. He's not supposed to smoke where hotel guests can see him, but he does anyway, leaning against a giant decorative planter so the palm fronds sort of almost obscure him from the doors. They don't stop the entrance from smelling like an ashtray though.

Being work friends is more like being co-hostages, but Jerry always rigs the vending machine to give me free Cokes, so he's pretty all right.

"Big plans tonight?" Jerry asks in his pack-a-day rasp.

"A party," I say with a shrug. "Just waiting on my ride."

He takes a drag and squints at the parking lot. "The one that's been driving in circles?"

"That's the one." I sip my Coke. "She'll figure it out soon."

It takes Ryan another two spins around the parking lot before she pulls up in front of the entrance. She rolls down the passenger window and leans out to frown at me.

"You got off work five minutes ago," she says. "Why aren't you walking to your car?"

I take a long drink. "Because I knew you were going to be here." I was counting on it, actually. She's not the only one with schemes.

"Why would I be here?" Ryan says, affronted, even though she is, in fact, here.

"Because the twins are having a New Year's Eve party," I say blithely, opening the passenger door. I set my backpack on the floor, bracketed between my legs. I always bring a backpack to work, but tonight the cargo is a little more delicate than usual.

"How did you know the twins were having a New Year's Eve party?"

"Leo told me."

"Leo told you?" Now she's given up on disgruntled and is just surprised.

Shit. Ryan might know about Buddy Boy, but she doesn't know about this weird new . . . understanding? friendship, dare I say it? between Leo and me. It's hard to tell the story without revealing more about Leo than I comfortably can, not to mention the tremendous amounts of crow I'd have to eat about hanging out with Leo Reyes, student council vice president and perpetual thorn in my side. So yeah, I haven't mentioned it. I'm trying to keep fewer secrets from my best friend, but I'm still a work in progress.

I pretend I didn't hear her. Instead, I throw a wave over my shoulder. "See ya, Jerry."

He raises a hand in return and goes back to his cigarette, shaking his head.

Ryan gives me a flat stare as I shut the door behind me and buckle in. "You could have told me you wanted to go to the party," she says.

"*Want* is a strong word."

"You could have told me you were *willing* to go to the party."

"I could have," I say. "But then you wouldn't have bribed me. Oh." I pull a Starbucks latte out of the cup holder. Whipped cream, chocolate drizzle, sprinkles. The works. Impressive. She probably got it for free from work, but I can still appreciate the effort. She must really want to go to this party. I feign surprise. "For me?"

Ryan heaves a sigh and puts the car in drive.

♥

The twins' New Year's Eve party is at their aunt's town house again. There's a new statue by the door to replace the one Archer broke at the last party, this one mercifully less fetus-like. Either their aunt appreciated the replacement or she never noticed the difference. I get the feeling she's not that invested in the decor if she keeps letting Archer and Maggie throw parties here.

Only about half our senior class is here, which is better than the Halloween party, but the music is just as loud. This time I'm smart enough to decline when Archer offers me something mysterious in a red cup—I've been speaking a little too freely around Leo as it is, and that's when I've been sober. No need to find out what drunk Wren has to say. He's an idiot.

"Hey," Ryan says in my ear, leaning on my shoulder. She's not drinking either, she just likes these sorts of events in a way I physically can't. High on life or whatever. It takes everything I have to love her despite it. "Do you think he's here?"

"Who?" I say, turning my head only to get a mouthful of her braids.

"Your friend," she says, pulling back enough that I can stare at her blankly. She raises her eyebrows. "The guy. Your guy. You know." She leans in again. "The Buddy guy?"

"Don't say that so loud!" I hiss, immediately scanning the room. As if anyone could hear over the thumping bass of the music, but I don't *know* that no one here can read lips. Now is not the time to find out.

Ryan rolls her eyes exaggeratedly, just to make sure I get the picture. "Then keep up! *Do* you think he's here?" she presses. Literally. It is way too warm and there are way too many bodies in this place for her to be draping herself over my shoulders. "He goes to our school, right?"

"Yes—I mean, he does go to our school—I don't know if— Why does it matter?" I huff, planting my hand on her cheek and pushing her away. I adjust my backpack strap self-consciously with my other hand. She's more like her sister than she thinks. No concept of personal space.

She's undaunted. "I just think it's interesting," she says, the words distorted by her smooshed cheek. "That you're here. And he's here. Very interesting." She waggles her eyebrows.

I drop my hand, dodging out of the way before she can lean back into me.

"Nothing about anything is *interesting*. I don't even know if he's here," I say with a scowl. "You're enjoying this way too much."

"Of course I am." Ryan grins. "This is like a soap opera."

"I regret telling you anything about my life, ever."

"You love me," she says, resting her head on my shoulder again, only to pick it up and frown. "Why didn't you leave your backpack in the car?"

"Never know when you might need it," I say, and promptly shove my Starbucks bribe into her hands. "Hold this. I have to go to the bathroom."

The good thing about the bathroom excuse is that usually people believe you. Bad thing is that if you spend too long in there, their minds start going to undesirable places, but I'm hoping Ryan is distracted by the party, even if it means probably losing my drink.

Listen: sometimes I make bad decisions. I know this may surprise you. Usually I try to run them by Ryan first, so at least if they're bona fide bad decisions I can pin the blame on her for not stopping me.

But the problem is I'm not sure if this is a bad decision yet. I'm still in the process of figuring that out. And right now the process involves sitting on the cold tile in the town house's austere guest bathroom, my backpack on my lap and my phone in my hands. There's a reason I was so cooperative this time, though Ryan doesn't need to know that—I still want my bribe. But there's a grander plan in motion here.

Me:
new years plans?

It takes him a minute to respond.

Him:
Graduate, grow a year older, maybe
do some traveling
You know, the usual

Me:
you know the pedantic thing is only
cute when i do it right

Him:

I thought I'd try it on for size

Is NYE an acceptable holiday?

Me:

i'm not sure it completely counts as
a holiday

Him:

Which is what makes it acceptable?

Me:

youre catching on

Him:

That must be why you have time to
talk to me

Me:

dont take it personally

i'm pretending i'm not at a party

There's a flicker of moving dots—he's typing. And then he's not. I bite the tip of my tongue. I probably should have just asked if he was at the party, like a normal person, but that didn't quite work out the last time I tried. That, and I don't want to push, especially after I dramatically told him we were better off staying anonymous. I may not be here to see him, and maybe I still mean it, about staying anonymous, but my whole plan hinges on him being here, so I can't really avoid asking.

The point is, it's up to him whether he wants me to know if he's here or not. *If* he's actually here. His choice, for better or for worse.

But I don't want to have any regrets.

I'm weighing the bad versus good decision all over again when my phone vibrates.

Him:
What party?

I sit up a little straighter, the tile floor digging into my tailbone. Play it cool. Casual. Like I'm not hiding in the bathroom at said party, hunched over my phone like a gargoyle.

Me:
the min twins

jesus i never said the two words together before. rhyme not intended and not my fault

Him:
Oh really?

That's funny, so am I

I knew it. I shake my phone in savage victory, nearly sending it flying across the bathroom. I bite the tip of my tongue. Play it cool, play it cool, play it cool.

Me:
wow its almost like we go to the same high school

are you the guy wearing basketball shorts and tube socks?

be honest

Him:
Wouldn't you like to know 😊

Oh my God.

I stand up, almost dumping my backpack in the process. Okay, that was—that was definitely flirting. Or something. You don't just *platonically* winky-face. Right?

Well, Ryan and I do all the time, actually, but that's different. This is—well, I don't know what this is exactly. But it's making my palms sweaty.

No time to think about that now. It's time for phase two.

I unzip my backpack and double-check its cargo before I hook it over my shoulder and reenter the party, which is even louder after the shelter of the bathroom. I blink rapidly as my eyes adjust to the dim lighting that someone decided was atmospheric, my gaze sweeping the crowd. Where *is* Archer? Usually he just kind of appears in front of me, typically when I'm least expecting him. I can't pull off phase two without him.

I'm craning my neck, one hand hooked around my backpack strap, when I bump into someone from behind.

"Oh," Leo says, turning around. "Hey, Wren. You made it."

"Hm? Oh, yeah. Hey," I say, momentarily distracted. "Sorry, wasn't paying attention—are you going somewhere?" We're standing in the foyer. It seemed like a good starting point for my sweep—Archer could be anywhere, so I have to do this strategically. I didn't expect to find Leo here.

"Oh, just to get more ice," he says, holding up his car keys. He hesitates. "Do you want to come with?"

Never in a thousand years would I have expected Leo Reyes to invite me to go on an ice run with him, and never in a million would I have thought I'd actually kind of regret saying no. I guess New Year's Eve really is a night for miracles. Too bad I don't have time for them. I'm in the middle of something, and I'm on a time crunch.

"I'm actually looking for Archer," I say. "Have you seen him?"

I can see the question plain on his face: Wren? Looking for *Archer*? You're probably wondering the same thing. Hold tight. All will be revealed soon.

Well, not to Leo, but luckily he doesn't hold that against me. He nods toward the back sliding glass door. "I saw him out by the pool a minute ago."

"Awesome. Thanks." I clap him on the shoulder like I'm his football coach, but I disappear before I can waste time being mortified. The sliding glass door is open, letting the somewhat cooler air outside equalize the collected body heat inside. The backyard is significantly more populated than it was during the Halloween party. We're hours away from January, but we're still in Florida, and the brief chill we enjoyed around Christmas has faded away into weather that's mostly just been damp.

"Archer. Hey," I say, snapping to catch his attention. He's in the middle of some story that involves big animated gestures. "C'mere."

Archer Min, being a darling boy that I don't appreciate enough, drops everything to stroll on over.

"Wren! I didn't know you were coming," he says with a grin, clapping me on the shoulder hard enough that I stumble a bit. Maybe he's where I picked up the shoulder-clapping. "What's up?"

I draw him off to the side, away from a cluster of people trying to play beer pong on a patio table. "I need your help," I say. "I need you to be a distraction. Get everyone out of the house for a minute."

"Cool, sounds fun," Archer says, already nodding. "But, uh, why?"

I swing my backpack around and unzip the top. "Don't worry about why," I say, even as I reach my hand inside. I pull out a long box, just enough that the corner pokes out between the zipper teeth, so he can see they're fireworks. Variety pack. His eyes light up like it's Christmas all over again. I smirk. "Just worry about these."

Archer grins. "I'm your man."

27
THE FIREWORKS

The plan is simple. Buddy Boy's love language is clearly cake-based. Twice now he's given me a fancy cupcake via dead drop. It's probably about time I return the favor.

Unfortunately, the venue tonight is a little trickier than a broken high school locker, so I have to get a bit more creative. Archer is providing the distraction, which will buy me time to plant it without anyone noticing me. The only question that remains is *where*. It needs to be accessible enough that I (and Buddy Boy, for that matter) can get to it, but not so accessible that someone random scores a free cupcake. I don't need the stoners sniffing it out.

My first thought is the kitchen, but I axe that plan immediately. It's too open concept, with a breakfast bar that offers a view of the living room. Great from a real estate perspective, not so much from a secret agent one. And I don't have a ton of time. I realize a little too late I should have given Archer the fireworks *after* I picked a location.

That part is working, at least. After Archer loudly announced his intention to set off fireworks in the street, most of the party followed him out there, either to watch him blow off a couple of fingers or to blow off a couple of their own. The stragglers are pretty easy to navigate around. Most of them are clustered out back or in the living room, playing Mario Kart.

As I'm scouting the kitchen, a door catches my eye, and it's like a light bulb appears over my head. The kitchen is out, but there's still the next best thing: the pantry.

Now, my pantry consists of a closet next to the kitchen, but I don't own a town house or spend most of my time doing business in Beijing, so the Mins' aunt is working with something a little fancier. Her pantry is more like a *walk-in* closet. Perfect.

Throwing one last look over my shoulder, I open the door and slip in. I have to slap the wall a little to find the light switch, which is what sheds some light on my next mistake.

She doesn't have any food.

Which makes sense, I guess, considering she both (a) is out of town most of the year and (b) lets her niece and nephew have the run of the place, so obviously she doesn't use a lot of forethought. So there goes my idea of hiding the cupcake behind some rice and beans. I glare at the empty shelves . . . and then tilt my head upward.

Well. The highest shelf might work.

I carefully pull the cupcake out of my backpack. I made it myself, which is unbearably embarrassing, but I swear it's more arrogance than romance. My cookie bars didn't get much of a chance to shine at the bake sale, so it's time for a redemption arc: lemon-lavender cupcake with cream cheese frosting, but I like to call it *perfection*. The fact that I had to put it in an old plastic Chinese takeout container is a little less elegant.

I set it on the highest shelf I can reach, then put my foot on the lowest, testing its strength. Luckily for me, the shelves are made of wood, which means they're fairly solid. It only groans a little when I test my weight on it.

I need five seconds to boost myself up and slide the cupcake onto the highest shelf, where it'll be hidden from direct line of sight. Five seconds. Easy.

I've just started to push myself up when the door opens.

"Oh my God," Ryan says. "What are you doing?!"

I drop back down hurriedly. Too hurriedly. My ankle rolls and sends me toppling backward, arms pinwheeling cartoonishly. Ryan only barely manages to catch me under the arms, like this is the world's worst trust fall. I hold the cupcake straight up in the air, miraculously unharmed.

I flap my elbows furiously, disentangling myself. "Shut the door!" I hiss. So much for stealth. "What are you doing here?"

Even with two people in it, the pantry feels palatial. We could probably ballroom dance. Instead, I have to face the incredulous look Ryan is serving me. "I heard noises. I thought they might have rats in here."

"And you were going to do what? Fight them off?"

Ryan rolls her eyes. "Will you just tell me why we're in the pantry, already?"

I straighten my back and tilt my head imperiously. "I'm flirting," I say with as much grace as I can muster. "I think. Now, will you be my spotter?"

"You're—" Ryan closes her eyes and exhales through her nose. "You know what? Never mind. It's probably better not to ask."

"That's the spirit." I clap her on the shoulder, which is apparently something I do now. "Don't let me fall."

♥

And then all there is to do is trigger stage two, and wait.

Archer finishes with the fireworks sooner than I expected, but I'm done by the time people start to filter back inside, thankfully with all their body parts. I'm not sure if Archer still has his eyebrows, but I didn't hear any sirens, so nothing could have gone too wrong.

I'm ready to go ahead with phase three, which is to tell Buddy Boy about the planted surprise, but Ryan refuses to be shaken off that easily. She follows me into the backyard, so close that she steps on the back of my shoes.

"So he *is* here," she says smugly, leaning closer every time I move to take out my phone. She straightens up abruptly, her eyebrows furrowing. "Is that why you were so willing to go to the party?"

"You were going to make me go anyway," I said defensively, holding my phone up to my chest. ". . . But the possibility that he would be here had something to do with it."

"You *rat*." She ruffles my hair and I squawk, ducking out from under her hand. I pat my hair back down again and she smirks. "What? Afraid he might see you? *Is* he going to see you?"

"No! I mean—probably, but he's not going to know it's me." My cheeks are getting warm now, but that could just be the fire pit. Probably just the fire pit. "That's why I hid the cupcake. So we can stay anonymous."

"Oh," Ryan says, understanding dawning on her face. A little too *much* understanding. The concept really wasn't that difficult. "Until the Dance."

I blink rapidly. "What?"

"So you can stay anonymous until the Dance," Ryan says. "You know, like the whole point of the Buddy tie-in? Is that not what you were going for?"

"Uh." Not exactly. Probably. I guess. Somehow Buddy Boy's *separate from real life* manifesto feels like a lot to explain right now. Honestly, I'm not sure what I *am* going for, even though I just went for it. A lot depends on what happens next. "It's complicated."

Luckily Maggie catches Ryan's attention and pulls her away from bullying me, which is the first and likely the only time Maggie has ever done me a favor. I stake out a patio chair around the firepit and plant one foot on the cushion, casually hiding my phone.

Me:
hey you should check out the pantry
when you get the chance

that makes it sound like a trap. its not
a trap.

Him:
You know that makes it sound even
more like a trap, right?

Me:
are you gonna go or not?

i'm not spying, promise

Him:
Did you get something for me?

Me:
only one way to find out

Him:
I was kidding! You didn't have to get
anything for me

Me:
i guess it you dont want it i can give
it to one of my many other buddy
acquaintances

Him:
I didn't say THAT

That was a joke, right?

Me:
omg just go look idiot

I tilt my head back and look up at the sky. A few stars manage to peek through the light pollution, and in the distance someone is setting off fireworks, even though we still have twenty minutes to go. People are starting to wander outside for midnight, the Times Square ball drop playing on a TV on the patio. I try to ignore them—it doesn't seem fair to try to guess at Buddy Boy's identity through the process of elimination. It also sounds like a one-way ticket to losing my mind.

Ryan had a point, which is something I try not to say too often. *The Dance.* It's so obvious. I should ask Buddy Boy to the Dance. The thought is so unlike me that it makes me want to dunk my head in the pool, but the solution is too clear to deny. I could just use Buddy like a normal person and ask him to the Dance, where we reveal our identities under the gaudy Buddy-sponsored lights of the Canopy and live happily ever after. Or at least figure out what's going on between the two of us. I've already had my awkward coming-out talk with him, so that's out of the way. Ryan will make fun of me for the rest of my life and Leo will want to strangle me after my entire anti-Buddy campaign, but I can live with that. Probably. Maybe Buddy Boy hasn't changed his mind about wanting to keep things simple, but maybe he has. I won't know until I ask. Blah blah, no regrets, whatever.

But that's something to worry about next year. Haha.

My phone buzzes and my heart jumps in response.

Him:

How the hell did you reach up there?

Me:

i'm really tall

Him:

Really?

Me:

in someone's immortal words:

wouldn't you like to know (;

Him:

Haha

Thank you, really. That was really
sweet

Me:

yeah well

i owed you a couple

Him:

Holy shit this is really good

Me:

don't act so surprised!

"You look happy," Ryan says over my shoulder. I don't give her the satisfaction of jumping out of my skin, but it's a close call.

"The mission was a success," I say, tilting my head to look up at her. "*And* he complimented my baking."

"A direct path to Wren Martin's heart." She hands me a plastic champagne flute. "It's almost countdown time."

"My favorite part. It means we get to go home soon," I say, but through a self-satisfied smile. There's a warmth in my chest that doesn't have anything to do with the merrily crackling fire pit. I take a sip of my drink and frown. "Sparkling grape juice? You could have gotten me the real champagne."

Ryan flicks my ear. "You're supposed to wait until it's midnight, numbskull."

Just about everyone is clustered on the back patio as the ball begins to drop, Times Square in miniature. I don't join the countdown, because I'm tragically too cool to participate in group activities, but I nod in sync as a handful of over-eager fireworks pop off above us, spraying the night with burning green and gold embers. On the TV, the giant glittering ball sinks in slow motion.

And like that, the year is over. Ryan grabs me around the shoulders and plants a kiss on my cheek and I laugh, trying not to spill my drink. I've never really gotten why the New Year's kiss is a thing, but the people around us take to the tradition like you assume a group of hormonally charged teenagers can. Some with a little too much gusto.

I turn my head to make a joke about it to Ryan when something catches my eye. Some*one*. Which they shouldn't have. Among a crowd of at least thirty people pressed together around the pool, there's no reason I should spot Leo Reyes, clear on the opposite side of the patio. There's no reason I should notice him, no reason I should care. There's especially no reason I should care that he's in the middle of locking lips with Stephen Hannigan.

Absolutely no reason at all.

"Oh my God, Wren," Ryan says, yanking my glass upright again. "You're getting grape juice, like, everywhere."

28
THE DECISION

Reasons why I hate Stephen Hannigan:

1. He thinks he's the smartest person in the room. Always.
2. Leo once said we have the same personality, which is *not* true.
3. He thinks robotics team is more important than anything else.
4. And he's the captain of the robotics team, so he's probably spent a lot of time with Leo. Like, a significant amount. They probably know each other really well, even if Leo has spent most of the school year avoiding the quitting-robotics fallout. Which he wouldn't have done if he didn't care what Stephen thinks.

And, as of the new year:

5.   He kissed Leo Reyes.

Which I shouldn't care about. Leo can do whatever he wants. Who he does or does not kiss is so not my business, or my problem, or anything to do with me. But if I did care, I'd think that he could at least pick someone . . . better.

Stephen Hannigan? Come on.

. . . Okay. Did you believe that? I would believe that. Or at least I might if I didn't have the singular misfortune of living in my own head. And from this vantage point, I know there's a pretty good reason why I can't stop thinking about it.

I'm absurdly, ridiculously, intensely *jealous*.

Yeah. I'm going to need some help to figure this one out.

♥

New Year's Day was on a Friday this year, so we're back at school on Monday. It's the last day of calm before the storm—we get one day to adjust to the new semester and then we have to hit the ground running to finish up the Dance prep, not to mention the actual event itself. I'm already exhausted just thinking about it.

The first day back, everyone is still trying to remember their routines, including the teachers, but I'm more distracted than usual as I wait for the bell to ring at the end of second period.

I'm up and out of my seat before it even stops ringing, bullying my way through the hall with my backpack thumping against my rib cage. Third period is still my TA period in the front office, where I'm so beloved and supervision is so laissez-faire I don't even bother to check in before I head to the library. I'll sign in later and fudge the times. For now, I have an investigation to mount.

You would think Ryan would be the person I'd go to in these troubling situations, and usually you'd be right, but I'm afraid she just doesn't have the qualifications for this one. Or maybe she's *over*qualified. I don't need someone who knows Wren Martin, I need someone who can be objective and honest and all those qualities I try to avoid, because they suck. I need someone who doesn't even like me.

The Rapture High library is a squat gray building that sits in the middle of campus like a box someone set down and forgot about for roughly thirty years. The carpet is thin, the air is musty, and the lights have dead flies caught in them. It's great.

And conveniently, Maggie is the library TA during third period. I don't like to throw around the word *fate* often, but sometimes it all just falls into place.

I find her shelving books in the nonfiction section, between *technology* and *ghosts*.

"Can I talk to you?" I ask, planting one hand on the shelf and the other on my hip. Shit. Started off too strong there. I drop my hand from the shelf. "I mean—hey. How are you? Can we talk?"

Maggie looks up from the book she's shelving, her expression so devastatingly unimpressed that my pride almost has me turning around and walking away. But I need to at least *try*, even if she decides not to humor me.

"Talk?" She squints as if she's never heard of the concept before. "Me? With you? About how you gave my brother fireworks?"

Archer, you *snitch*. Okay, fine. So I'm going to have to cut to the heart of the matter, then. "About Leo."

Now she's listening.

Actually, now she's glaring, eyeing me warily, like a predator unsure if I'm a harmless snack or poisonous. "What *about* Leo?"

I take a deep breath, steeling myself. "Last month, in the car," I say, "were you . . . giving me the shovel talk? About Leo?"

It sounds ridiculous, even as I say it. I've made it very clear how I felt about Leo. At least before things got complicated, but that's a very recent development. There's no way anyone would think—

"Yeah," Maggie says. She sets the book down and turns to face me. "Wait, did you *just* get that? Just now?"

"I don't know! I thought . . ." Actually, I don't know what I thought. In retrospect it's pretty obvious, right down to and most importantly *Are you into him?*, but at the time the idea was so wildly outside of my reality I didn't even consider it. "Am I into Leo?"

I can hardly even believe I'm saying the words. *Leo.* Perfect Leo Reyes, who I've hated ever since he accidentally (allegedly) dropped a textbook on my head in seventh grade, when I had the misfortune of having a bottom locker. The darling of every class he's ever been in, lauded hero of the robotics team and some kind of coding prodigy, who manages to get straight As and do student council on the side *and* help his sick brother. Who pushes back when I try to get my way and is funnier than I expected. Tall, handsome, just plain *nice* Leo Reyes. Who I think about, it turns out, quite a lot.

In retrospect, I guess I should have seen this coming.

"Oh my God." Maggie heaves the deepest sigh I've heard in my life and drags a hand down her face. "Why are we having this conversation?"

I look sideways at the entrance to the library, like Leo himself is going to come strolling through any moment, even though I know for a fact he should be in chemistry right now. It occurs to me that it might mean something that I know his class schedule. "Have I *always* been into Leo?" I say, increasingly distressed, asking myself as much as her. "I need someone who will be honest with me. Who isn't afraid of hurting my feelings." I run a hand through my hair, pushing it back from my forehead. "I—I mean, we've been spending more time together, but it's just student council stuff." Except it isn't. Even heart-to-hearts aside, I'm not sure the fake engagement dinner strictly counts as a club activity. "But then I saw him with Stephen Hannigan and—"

"Don't even get me started on the Stephen thing," Maggie says shortly, holding up a hand to stop me. She glances toward the front circulation desk, where the librarian is wrestling with a broken laptop. "All right," she says grudgingly, steering her cart away. "C'mon."

Maggie leads me into the bowels of the library, which isn't very far, but it serves its purpose. The nonfiction stacks are tall and dense, like a forest that hasn't seen any visitors in a while. Considering the globe decorating the end of the stack still features the USSR, I don't have to wonder why this section doesn't see much use.

"All right," Maggie says again, parking the book cart between us and leaning forward to rest her elbows on the handle. "You have ten minutes. What do you want to know?"

I wet my lips with the tip of my tongue. My plans didn't really stretch this far. There wasn't really a scenario where she actually listened. "Is Leo into *me*?"

"Violation of bro code," Maggie says immediately, gesturing dismissively. "Next question."

Shit. Fair though.

"How did you know I was into Leo?" How did she know before *I* did? Even saying the words now feels weird, but I can hardly deny it at this point.

"This conversation is physically nauseating me, I want you to know," she says flatly. She flips her hair over her shoulder, surveying the dusty titles boxing us in. "I mean, I already told you in the car, but it's your time." She shrugs. "The way you guys keep ending up alone together. And the honesty thing. And the way you keep staring at him. The fact that you noticed the Stephen thing *at all*."

"Okay, yeah, I got that one, thanks." I huff and fold my arms over my chest. Fine. So it was obvious. I'm just stupid. What else is new! I still have time left before Maggie kicks me out. "What's with the Stephen thing?"

I never thought I'd find someone Maggie hates more than me, or something we have in common besides student council. Judging by the look on her face, Stephen Hannigan manages to fulfill both. "It's annoying, is what it is," she says, which doesn't really explain anything at all. She looks around surreptitiously, even though we're penned in on either side by books, and few people are in the library during class. She chews on her bottom lip, clearly deliberating. Finally she leans in conspiratorially. Instinctively I lean in too.

"Stephen has had a crush on Leo since freshman year. But here's the thing," Maggie says, her voice hushed, "and if you say any of this to him, I'll pull your eyeballs out through your nose."

Evocative. "Understood."

"Leo has this guy he's been talking to on Buddy," she says. "All anonymous, you know the schtick. They're basically dating, but they can't say who they are until the Dance, obviously. Stephen's the one who made a move on *him*, so now Leo thinks it was, like, some sort of *hint* that Stephen was this anonymous guy all along, and it's, like, whatever." Maggie rolls her eyes.

My stomach drops.

Leo has a Buddy account. Of course he does. I mean, it would be weird if he didn't. He probably had to, as part of the sponsorship agreement. That would make sense. I think.

I can't be jealous this time. Or at least, I think I can't. I mean, I have a Buddy account too, though that's a secret that will remain between Ryan, Buddy Boy, and me until my deathbed. I mean, I was flirting via cupcake when I realized I liked Leo at all. So I definitely can't be jealous. That wouldn't be fair.

I want to tear my hair out for other, unrelated reasons. Definitely.

"Wait, do you not think it's Stephen?" I say, backtracking through my furious snarl of complicated emotions to actually listen to how she worded it. I *know* Stephen has a Buddy account, I saw it myself. I'm struggling to talk myself into believing it could be anyone *but* Stephen.

"I *hope* it's not Stephen," Maggie says. "Or Leo has worse taste than I thought." For some reason she gives me a pointed look up and down. What's *that* supposed to mean?

That Leo *is* into me?

"Anyway, time's up. This conversation never happened." She takes hold of her book cart and pushes it forward, forcing me to flatten myself against the stacks to keep from getting my toes run over. She stops at the end of the aisle and looks back over her shoulder. "And, Wren? My point from the car stands. If you hurt him I'll—"

"Rip my eyeballs out through my nostrils," I finish blandly. "Got it."

Her mouth quirks upward in a smirk. "You're smarter than you look." She shrugs and turns back. "And you're not Stephen Hannigan. I'll give you that much."

I think that's as close to a compliment as I'm ever going to get from her.

♥

I don't know what to do.

I don't know what to do, and I'm rapidly running out of time to figure it out. The Dance is like a ticking time bomb on the horizon, but even that's a false deadline. The Dance is when this whole Buddy thing finally comes to an end and everyone's matches reveal themselves, but I have to make a decision *before* that. Most people don't wait until the day of to ask someone to the Dance. Not to mention the logistics involved, like if Buddy Boy even intends to let Buddy reveal his identity at all. I guess I won't know until I ask, which is the whole problem. I still don't even *want* to go to the Dance, but I have to in any scenario, so no use dwelling on that.

So do I ask Buddy Boy?

Or do I ask Leo?

Or do I go back to my simple, easy plan of spending the rest of my life with Ryan and a few chickens? I was okay with that before. I'm definitely starting to see the appeal again.

I literally never thought I would be in this position. This position being:

1. Going to the Dance.
2. Wanting to ask someone else to go to the Dance with me
3. Wanting to ask *two* people to the Dance, resulting in some horrible love triangle. Love quadrangle, if you count Stephen Hannigan, which I don't.

Life is truly a nightmare.

I sigh and crawl out of bed, where I've been languishing for the better part of an hour now. It's dark, but it's not too late. I throw on my jacket and a pair of flip-flops, which is a horrible outfit but also a very Floridian one. Not my best look, but I've done worse.

"I'm going for a walk," I say, dodging Beep as he slinks between my legs, pretending he hasn't been fed.

Dad looks up from where he's squinting at the TV, somehow looking even more baffled than he was at *90 Day Fiancé*. For someone so health conscious, he sure consumes a lot of garbage TV. "You're going for a walk?" he repeats.

"Yeah," I say. "I do that sometimes."

"Do you?"

No, but I need to clear my head, and maybe Leo had the right idea. Because evidently I can't go two minutes without thinking about Leo. God, it's like I have a disease.

"I do now," I say defensively.

"Okay," Dad says, still sounding skeptical. "Well . . . have fun."

It's brisk outside, the air just cold enough to feel good when I breathe in deep. It's dark, but streetlamps flood the road with artificial light, and half the houses still have Christmas lights up. My flip-flops smack rhythmically against the pavement, a slumped-over snowman inflatable watching me sadly as I walk past. I'm not sure when the clarity and peace of mind are supposed to kick in, but I haven't even made it to the end of the block, so maybe I'm expecting too much.

My feet take me to the edge of my neighborhood, where the land dips down to a small pond. It's a retention pond, to collect excess rainwater, and there are definitely alligators in there, but in the moonlight it almost looks like a peaceful nature preserve. Or at least, close enough. My mom used to take me here when I was little, to feed white bread to the ducks. I don't think that's very good for the ducks, but it's too late to apologize to them now.

I sit down on the little bridge that spans a narrow part of the pond, my legs dangling over the edge, my toes pointed up to keep my flip-flops from flip-flopping off into the water. I lean over the metal railing, tucking the steel bar under my armpits, and take out my phone.

Buddy Boy has been talking about what movie he should watch, but I think he can tell my heart's not totally in it, especially after I failed to rise to the Star Wars bait. I should try harder, but I can't help but feel guilty, like I should make a decision before I talk to either of them. Like I'm on the fucking *Bachelor* and I only have one rose or something. I don't know, I've never seen *The Bachelor*.

My phone buzzes with a new message.

Him:
Are you okay?

Shit, he noticed.

Me:
fine

just contemplative

Him:
Sounds terrible

Me:
you have no idea

Him:
Do you mind if I contemplate too?

Me:
contemplate away

Him:
It's about you, fair warning

Me:
me??

My heart jumps into my throat. What does *that* mean?

Him:
Still want to hear it?

Me:
no i want to live in agonizing
ignorance forever
tell me, doofus

Him:

Doofus? You stole that one from me

Me:

maybe so

Him:

I was just thinking about . . .

I'm sorry about how weird I've been

About keeping you up late and
making you talk to me and everything

Even though I'm just some stranger

Me:

omg you didnt make me do anything

idiot

if i didn't want to talk to you don't
you think i would've deleted the app

Him:

I know, I know

I wish we could have met under
normal circumstances I guess

I stare down at my phone, the night wind cold on the back of my neck. What if we hadn't met on Buddy? What if I knew his face or his name or anything besides the text on the screen? What if we didn't go to the same high school, what if I went away to college and we met in English 101, or studied at the same coffee shop? What then? I might not have even looked twice, and if I did, I probably would have been too afraid to do anything about it.

But I didn't. We didn't. I met him on Buddy, where I don't even know his name.

Him:

Then again, I guess maybe we
already have

Weird to think about, right?

Passing each other in the hall and
not even knowing it

I like Buddy Boy, I like him a lot, but I don't *know* him. Not the ugly parts, the hard parts, the parts no one wants to look at. We're careful to keep that true. It's like he said—on Buddy, he doesn't have to be a real person, and he's right. I saw the appeal of that too. I still do. I thought I could live in a bubble, where nothing ever changed. I thought I'd be safe that way. But that would mean nothing ever got better either.

And you can't hide from reality forever.

I close the app and open my contacts.

"Are you dying?" Ryan demands, picking up on the second ring.

I hold the phone away from my ear. Jesus, she's loud. "No?"

"Oh." There's a rustle from her end of the line. "Then why are you calling me? You never call me."

"I . . ." My mouth goes dry, and the wind ruffles my hair. The air is cold, but there's a spark, buried deep in my chest, that's warm. I laugh at the absurdity of it all, and something ripples distantly on the pond. "I think I'm going to ask Leo to the Dance."

29
THE PRACTICE RUN

But before we can tackle the Dance, there's still the lead-up to the Dance.

Thank God. I need the time to process, much less actually do something about the earth-shattering decision I've just made. Unfortunately, all the hubub also means there's literally nowhere I can look without being reminded of Buddy, the Dance, or, most frequently, both. It also means that I'm spending every afternoon after school either working at work for (a little) money, or working at school for no money at all.

The upside is there's enough to be done that we've had to employ a divide-and-conquer method. Naturally, I'm paired with Ryan, which (don't tell her this) I actually find myself a *little* disappointed about. Don't get me wrong—I would physically implode if I had to spend an extended amount of time around Leo right now, especially alone, but . . . that doesn't mean I don't *want* to.

What can I say? Feelings are confusing.

Our major project is the formal wear drive. Ryan proposed it as a buy-back program, but Ms. Little axed that on account of it sounding like we're dealing with firearms, and I voted against using any of our budget to pay for clothes, sponsorship money or not. So it's more of a donation thing instead, with the bonus of getting a coupon for a free pizza at the local Domino's. I honestly didn't really expect it to work.

More fool me, because evidently the good people of Rapture have:

1. A lot of formal wear lying around
2. A leftover sense of school spirit and charity
3. A deep, abiding love for Domino's pizza

People have been donating all through last semester, which leaves Ryan's garage looking like a thrift store the day after prom, and us the poor, wayward souls tasked with sorting through it.

"So walk me through it again," Ryan says as she wrestles with a hanger caught in a particularly strappy dress. "Why are you asking Leo to the Dance?"

I sigh and sit on a cardboard box, cushioned by a nest of slightly dusty suit coats. "Because I have horrible, squishy feelings for him. How many times are you going to make me say that?"

"And you just now realized that?" Ryan presses. "All of a sudden?"

I open my mouth and then stop. "Why did you say it like that? *Just now?*" Her eyes dart away, and she's suddenly deeply invested in the dress's tangled straps. "When did *you* realize it?"

"Well . . . you know . . ." She purses her lips thoughtfully, her eyes on the ceiling. "Right about . . ."

"Ryan Robinson."

"Junior year," she says, with the air of having a tooth extracted. She gestures vaguely. "Last winter, roundabouts."

"Last— *Why didn't you say anything?*" I squawk, with an expansive gesture that knocks a dress off its hanger. I bat it away, tangled in layers of pink chiffon. When I emerge again Ryan is watching me with a look of exaggerated patience.

"Oh yeah—'Hey, Wren, have you ever considered there might be a *reason* you're obsessed with Leo Reyes? One that *doesn't* have to do with the textbook he accidentally dropped on your head five years ago?'" she says. "What would you have said about that back in September?"

Now it's my turn to purse my lips, feeling like I just sucked on a lemon. I hate when she's right. "No comment."

"Exactly."

I roll my eyes. "Okay, well. I got there eventually. So why are you so surprised?"

"I'm not *surprised*," she says, finally wrestling the dress into shape. "Actually, I'm a little surprised you're planning on doing something about it." She hangs it on the *maybe* bar. Or at least, I think it's the maybes. She's set up a complex sliding scale of usability to rank the donations that I don't totally understand. "But whatever happened to the Buddy guy you were all wild about?"

I chew on my bottom lip and take great pains to put the fallen dress back on the hanger. Two can play at the *working to avoid eye contact* game. "Nothing happened to him," I say cagily. "I just . . . made a decision, I guess." I decide to leave out the moonlight on the retention pond, the wind in my hair, etc. I don't need to set the whole scene. "I thought that being anonymous meant I could be myself on Buddy, but it really means being who I *wish* I was. The Wren without any problems, who can pretend to be normal. Around Leo I'm just . . . me. For better or worse." Usually worse. I exhale softly. "And he still keeps hanging around, so that's got to be worth something."

When I look up, she's smiling. "What?" I say defensively.

"Nothing," Ryan says, hanging up another dress. A *definitely maybe* this time. "You're just so cute."

I scowl theatrically. "I am not cute." I kick her ankle as she walks past.

She retaliates by reaching out to tweak my chin. "*So cute.*" She makes a kissy face and ducks away, laughing, when I move to flick her nose. "And the ace stuff?"

My heart sinks just a bit. Yeah, that problem is still there, that anxiety chewing on my heart from the inside. "I don't know," I confess. "I guess I'll just have to—"

"Trust that if he really likes the real you, it means accepting every part of you?"

"—die."

"Or that." Ryan rolls her eyes, far too secure that she's right to argue with me. "So do you think he'll say yes?"

Well, that's where things get interesting. Because it's not just about *my* decision here, despite all the blood, sweat, and tears that went into arriving at this conclusion. It takes two to tango, and this *is* a dance. My heart rate picks up speed a little, but not in an uncomfortable way. In an . . . exciting way, I guess. Ryan was right, back at Robinsonsgiving. It has been a long time since I've really been excited about something. It's been a long time since I've let myself have something to be excited *about*. The fact that it could all implode is more than a little terrifying.

"I mean . . . I think so?" I grimace. "Maybe? I never thought about it before, *obviously*, but he *did* ask Maggie to be nice to me. And at the time I was, like, wow, that's weird, but what if it's because he likes me? And he keeps hanging out with me, which was annoying at first, but— Oh my God, *stop*. I'm being serious!"

Ryan is full-on grinning now. "I didn't say anything," she says innocently, practically wearing a halo. Yeah, right. She doesn't have to say anything. I've known Ryan Robinson long enough to read her aura alone. "I think . . . you have . . ." She pauses cryptically, squinting. "A good chance. But you didn't hear that from me."

My heart jumps. Stupid thing. "Did he say something to you?" I demand.

"No one says anything to me," she says blithely. "I just have a working set of eyes."

"Oh yeah? And how can you tell?" I say flatly. "Did you take a class?" And can I take it too?

"Not quite," she says, gesturing with a hanger. "I'm just the world's leading expert on Wren Martin."

She's right about that. It's what makes her dangerous. "It might not matter anyway," I say, for some reason now playing devil's advocate against myself. I've been doing that, waffling like I can maybe still talk myself out of it. Maybe I can go live in the woods and eat opossums. Or become a monk. I have *options*. "Maggie said he's been talking to some guy on Buddy." Better not mention Stephen, I decide. And not because the thought of him and Leo kissing on New Year's Eve makes me want to break the plastic hanger in my hands in half. Which isn't a good sign toward the monk career path.

"I mean, so are you," she points out. "That doesn't mean anything."

"Yeah, I guess." I don't want to let it show and encourage her too much, but hearing her say that is more of a relief than I expected. The idea of Leo turning me down for someone he's never met—or, God forbid, Stephen Hannigan—is soul crushing. I probably *would* go become an opossum-eating monk. I take a deep breath and slide off the box, hopping to my feet. "All right, Professor," I say. "Help me figure out how I'm going to do this."

She blinks. "Do what?"

"How am I going to ask Leo to the Dance?" Because it's not going to be easy. Because nothing in my life is *easy*, specifically not things that involve both dances and Leo Reyes. "Help me practice. You be me."

"Okay, *this* I'm not qualified for," she says, but she grabs one of the suit jackets anyway and shrugs it on. It fits as awkwardly as possible, too short in the arms and too wide in the shoulders. "*You* be you. I'll be Leo. And . . . *action*." She claps in my face like a clapboard.

"I— What are you doing with your face?" She's leaning against one of the clothes racks, angling her face upward and pouting toward the corner of the garage. "You look like you're waiting to get cataract surgery."

"I'm being tall and handsome," she counters out of the corner of her mouth. "Now ask me out. I won't wait around forever, you know."

I'm definitely the stupid one for thinking this was a good idea, but that's hardly new. I should be used to the feeling by now. Might as well roll with it in the safety of a dress-laden garage, where no one else can witness this.

I clear my throat and walk up to her as casually as I can, except I can't remember where I usually put my hands, so I end up hooking my thumbs in the front pockets of my jeans like the world's most awkward cowboy. I try to imagine Leo squinting at Ryan's garage instead.

I clear my throat again. I sound like I have a hairball. "Hey." My voice comes out too high.

Ryan-Leo turns toward me, her lips still pushed out in a ridiculous pout. "Hey," she says, her voice pitched deeper than any normal human speaks. "What's up, Wren?"

"Oh . . . just thinking about the Dance. . . ." I gesture vaguely and end up looking like a flight attendant.

"About how much you hate it." She nods.

I scowl. "No."

"About how much you hate me?"

This is so stupid. "No!"

"Oh? You don't hate me?" Ryan's eyes sparkle mischievously. "Then what is it, Wren Martin? Have you . . . written me a *Pride and Prejudice*–worthy declaration of love, perhaps?" She tosses her braids over her shoulder dramatically. "Like in your favorite movie, starring Kiera Knightley?"

"Not my *favorite*." But top ten. Maybe top five. I snort, unable to help the grin tugging at the corners of my mouth. I clench my fist dramatically. "Leo Reyes, you have bewitched me body and soul—"

"Dance with me, Wren!" Ryan throws her arms around my shoulders and I laugh, stumbling. "Let us dance the night away!" She's starting to break character, giggling so hard we both shake. We waltz clumsily through the half-curated racks of clothes. Or try to waltz. I think it's closer to joint-flailing than dancing. I spin on my toe and she dips me so deep that my hair brushes the concrete floor.

"Just so you know," I say, trusting her not to let me fall and crack my head open, "you were of no help whatsoever."

Ryan laughs. "But you love me anyway."

"But I love you anyway," I agree.

30
THE TWIST

Then, naturally, everything goes wrong.

"Serious question," I say, my hands planted on the desk. "Why are you trying to ruin my life?"

Ms. Little looks up at me with a blandly patient expression I'm pretty sure she exaggerates just to mess with me. She scribbles out a sentence on the paper she's grading without even looking at it. "I don't think college is going to ruin your life," she says. "Which I politely haven't mentioned, by the way."

"That's not—" I sputter, my cheeks going pink. She has gotten off my back about the college thing, but I suspect its only because she knows I took the SAT. I haven't told her I put in my application for FSU, and I don't really intend to. Maybe she was right, but I don't want her to know that. More than that, I don't want to have to tell her if I don't get in. "I'm talking about the event schedule."

"Oh. Well. I know you're a conscientious objector," she says, "but if you didn't want to work on the Valentine's Day Dance, you really should have stepped down from student council president in, like, October."

"I've been working on Dance stuff!" I object. I flap my hands, which probably looks more like I'm fighting off bees than clearing the air. "It's not about the Dance—I mean, it is—it's just that . . ." I falter, looking for a good excuse. "I've been working with Archer for the Love Locks."

We *all* had to come up with an idea for events, both to drum up hype and to uphold our end of the bargain with the sponsorship. Including me. So Ryan is doing the formal wear drive. Archer is personally dressing up as a bumblebee and delivering candygrams to different classrooms. And I'm doing Love Locks.

What are Love Locks? Right now, mostly a pain in my ass.

"And now Archer is busy. So you're working with Leo," she says. "What's the big deal?"

I may have a newfound openness in talking about my love life, or having a love life at all, but only out of necessity. Ms. Little and I are not about to have that conversation. More than likely, it would result in a race to see who could throw themselves out the window first. Or worse, she might have more advice.

Yes, I secretly wished I was working with Leo on the formal wear drive instead of Ryan. *Yes*, I'll combust if I have to work with him now. Like I said, feelings are confusing.

"We could be killed in a devastating accident and leave the student council without leadership," I say, with an entirely straight face. "There should always be a designated survivor."

Ms. Little stares at me incredulously. Did I expect that to work? No. But I didn't expect anything else I might say to work either, so it might as well be something she wasn't expecting.

"Right," Ms. Little says, circling an 81% at the top of the paper and then moving on to the next in the pile. "I think that's just a risk we'll have to take. Archer is busy. You've got Leo."

Dread sinks into my bones and threatens to drag me through the crust of the Earth. I think the Love Locks are a good idea. Cheesy, yeah, but I think we boarded the cheesy train a long time ago. I stole the idea from an article on *BuzzFeed* I saw about the Pont des Arts, a bridge in Paris where couples used to fasten a padlock to symbolize their enduring love or whatever. It was actually super dangerous for the structural integrity of the bridge, but luckily we can't really get a bridge into the gym anyway, so we settled for a length of chain-link fence.

It's simple: Someone buys a numbered combination lock and any one of our preapproved treats—chocolates, lollipops, or these cheap little stuffed bears with wonky eyes. They write whatever they want on the card, put it all in a mesh bag, and then lock the whole thing somewhere on the fence. Then they give their Buddy buddy the number on the lock and the combination to open it, so they can then anonymously enjoy their treat.

Did I also steal the idea from Buddy Boy's cupcake thing? A little. Would I have liked to come up with a more neutral name than Love Locks? Yes, but that's what the real thing is called, so we're pushing the "all different kinds of love" angle instead to fit the Buddy theme better. You can love your friends too, after all. That's why I'm buying Ryan a lock with the weirdest-looking stuffed bear I can find attached to it.

It's pretty easy as far as school events go, except for one thing: given the nature of the event, students have an entire week to buy locks and retrieve them, which means our little booth needs to be staffed every day, before and after school, both to sell locks and, about 40 percent of the time, to explain how to open them. *Which means . . .*

A lot of Wren and Leo time. Once, not that long ago, that would have been a bad thing. Now it's a bad thing, but for radically different reasons, namely that every time I think about my resolve to ask him to the Dance, it triggers my fight-or-flight response. I need to just get through this week. One week, and then I ask Leo to the Dance on Friday, when the Love Locks event wraps up. That way, whatever the answer, I don't have to sit next to him for a whole week and pretend everything is normal.

It's going to be a long week.

DAY ONE

Monday, day one, we get there early to make sure everything we set up Friday is still in place. The fence looks like a makeshift tennis net in the middle of the gym, held in place by concrete feet the custodians made for it. It's easy to avoid eye contact with Leo, mostly because I'm literally half asleep. I miscount change three times before he takes over the money-handling part, and I'm relegated to crabbily explaining how to operate a combination lock. Most people haven't used one since middle school, sure, but unfortunately, I left my abundance of patience and understanding back at home.

DAY TWO

I get to the booth—a card table with a yellow vinyl tablecloth thrown over it, let's call it what it is—to find a twenty-four-ounce cup of coffee waiting there, steaming gently. I stare at it.

"What's that?" I ask, pointing at it like it's radioactive.

Leo looks up from where he's counting the till—a metal lockbox Ms. Little dug out of some closet. "It's coffee," he says, and his smile quirks. "Thought you might need it."

My heart quirks in response. I don't even know what that means, but it does it.

By the afternoon shift, word has started getting out about Love Locks, so we're slammed way past the time we're supposed to close up for the day. By the time the gym clears out and we're able to put away the lockbox, the school is a ghost town as Leo and I drag ourselves to the parking lot.

"Is that your car?" Leo asks.

It says a lot that I'm too exhausted to even realize he's stopped to witness me unlocking my car, which is an elaborate process that involves jiggling the handle, kicking the bottom of the door, and forcibly inserting the key before the door can pop out of place again. "Uh," I say, "in the technical sense of the word." I shrug, embarrassment starting to catch up with me. I desperately need a new one, but I can't seem to justify spending the money when all I do is drive to work and back. Usually. "Ryan said she doesn't love me enough to give me a ride to school an hour early."

Not that I want to listen to Reed chatter at that hour of the morning anyway. There's not enough coffee in the world.

"Oh." Leo fiddles with the strap of his backpack, his monstrous SUV in the background. "I can give you a ride tomorrow, if you want."

"Oh," I say. And then, before I can think better of it: "Yeah, sure. Thanks."

Leo offers me a tentative smile. "We're going to the same place anyway." He waves and finally turns toward his car.

My car door pops open and smacks me in the leg, punishing me for my infidelity.

DAY THREE

Leo shows up in my driveway with another giant coffee waiting in the cup holder.

"Sorry, it's just black," he asks. "I couldn't remember what that sugary thing you like is. Is that okay?"

It's horrible, but I'll drink anything caffeinated when the sun hasn't even risen yet. Also, considering he's giving me rides and providing me with the caffeination, not really a good time to complain.

"Perfect," I say. "Helps me stay mean."

Leo laughs.

I'm doing homework during my TA period when Ryan texts me. She has ceramics third period, and Ms. Bogowski is legendary and beloved for not caring if you have your phone out during class.

Ryan:

Why did Leo ask me what your coffee order is?

DAY FOUR

Thursday morning, Leo brings a Starbucks Frappuccino with whipped cream and caramel drizzle. I die quietly in the passenger seat.

The back half of the week means that most people have already bought their Love Locks, to pretty decent financial success on our part, and now the objects of their affection are coming to collect. Unfortunately, the students of Rapture High School still fail to understand the mysterious workings of the combination lock.

I also get a message.

Him:

Question

Scale 1 to 10 how uncool is the love
locks thing?

I glance sideways at Leo, but he's on his phone too,
equally checked out. We get to close up shop soon, and most
people have filtered out of the gym for the afternoon, except
for a couple of frustrated students still struggling with spinning their lock faces just right. I decide not to help them
until they ask for it.

Me:

10

Him:

10 meaning very cool and fun?

Me:

Omg you didn't get me one, did you?

That's so sweet! (: <3 <3 <3

is that what you expected me to say

Him:

It's scary when you do that

Like you're being possessed

Me:

they call me the ghost of valentine's
day past

Him:

But if I DID get you one

Hypothetically

The combination would be 13-45-20,
lock 78

My heart jumps, entirely of its own accord. Buddy Boy was *here*. Buddy Boy probably bought a lock from me and I probably glared at him because it was probably 6:30 a.m. and I'm definitely thinking about this way too much. But, like, holy shit.

The guilt hits me a moment later, a one-two punch. I still haven't quite figured out the ethics of having a crush on Leo and Buddy Boy at the same time. I mean, it's allowed, I guess, no one can stop me, but I can't shake the feeling I'm leading Buddy Boy on somehow. Even if he's the one who has consistently maintained his distance, that seems to be changing. Especially now that he's gotten me a *love lock*.

I'm still thinking about it when Leo and I close up the booth for the day. That's the other problem: How the hell am I supposed to check the fence for lock 78 without Leo noticing?

In the end, it doesn't take that much creative thinking, actually.

"Shit," I say when we're halfway to the parking lot. I pat my pockets. "I forgot my phone."

Leo turns back. "Oh, I—"

"You go start the car," I say quickly. "I've just got to run and grab it."

Luckily the gym stays unlocked since the custodians have to come through, so I'm able to sneak back in without any actual sneaking involved. The trick will be moving quickly, before Leo starts to wonder where the hell my phone could be that it's taking me so long to retrieve it.

I scan the fence, searching the locks for a 78 written in silver Sharpie on the face. The length of fence we got a hold of is only about twelve feet long and half picked-over by this late in the week. Locks sit in patchy clusters along the chain link, holding pink mesh bags with their goodies inside. Everyone had better come for the rest of them by this time tomorrow, or Leo and I are going to be spending a lot of time combing through the combination master list to pop the things off. I'm pretty sure the maintenance department wants the fence back.

There. Number 78. I jump forward, my hands shaking with a spike of adrenaline as I spin the lock's face. I have to put in the combination twice before I get it right, yanking the lock open so that it drops its little bag. I shove the lock and the bag in my hoodie pocket without looking and jog all the way back to Leo's car.

I take the bag out of my pocket at the first available opportunity, standing on my front porch after Leo's driven away. It's light and thin—not one of the ugly stuffed bears, thank God. I glance over my shoulder like a fugitive and pull the drawstring open, shaking the contents into my palm.

Oh. It's a key chain with a plastic cupcake on the end. It's sparkling and pink, clearly meant for seven-year-old girls. It even smells like vanilla.

There's a little note taped to the key ring.

> *Guess I've kind of locked myself into this brand, huh?*
>
> —*BB*

I laugh softly, twirling the key chain around my finger so that the little cupcake bounces across my knuckles. I look behind me, as if Leo might have reappeared in my driveway, but he hasn't. That doesn't stop him from sitting in the back of my mind though. I've already made my decision, but stuff like this sure as hell doesn't help. I toy with the key chain while I'm doing my homework that night, bouncing it against the back of my hand until I finally break and pick up my phone, opening the Buddy app.

Me:
there are worse brands to have

Him:
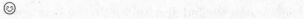

31
THE DAWN OF THE
FINAL DAY

Friday arrives like a punch to the gut—suddenly, and in a way that leaves my stomach aching. I consider bailing on booth duty altogether, but implying that I spent the morning puking probably isn't the best way to soften Leo up to go to the Dance with me.

I'm not sure when exactly I'm supposed to spring the question. I spent the night before toying with the cupcake key chain, rethinking and deciding and rethinking again. A three-dollar key chain doesn't change any of the reasons I chose to ask Leo instead of Buddy Boy, but it sure as hell doesn't make me feel any better about it. I consider not going to the Dance at all, but I'm the student council president, and the only thing worse than attending the Dance would be letting them run it without me.

Reasons why Wren Martin can't sleep:

1. What if Leo says no?
2. What if Leo says *yes*?
3. What the hell is Buddy Boy planning? His words say no, but his actions say yes, and I have no idea if he plans to reveal his identity on the day of the Dance. And I sure as hell don't know how to ask.
4. Stephen Hannigan exists and goes to our school.
5. The Valentine's Day Dance is, obviously, February 14.
6. FSU acceptance decisions come out on February 15.

It's a lot. Like, *a lot* a lot. I need coffee, and not just because I got up an hour earlier.

I can cross two things off the list, at least: I'm going to ask Leo. I'm going to ask him *today*.

Just . . . at the end of the day.

When we close up the Love Locks booth there are still about twenty locks attached to the fence, so we haul out the three-ring binder that serves as the master list, where I carefully recorded the number of each lock and its combination, specifically for contingencies such as this. Ms. Little forbade using bolt cutters to get the job done.

It's actually kind of soothing, especially on my rattled nerves. Leo reads off combinations and I turn the locks, drop the lock into a cardboard box, and split the spurned treats between us. I have an ugly bear poking out of the pocket of each side of my hoodie, and I've eaten about half a pound of chocolate hearts already, when Leo speaks up.

"Kind of sad," he says, looking up at the locks we have left from where he's sitting on a plastic chair with the binder open in his lap. "That no one cared enough to come get them, I mean."

I scoff. "We sold this stuff for like, five dollars," I say, glancing down. Yes, I have to stand on a stool to get the locks at the top. No, I don't want to talk about it. "It's not an engagement ring."

"Yeah, I guess," Leo says, standing. He tugs thoughtfully on one of the locks still on the fence, the master list tucked under one arm. "It just sucks that some people are going to be left wondering and not even know who stood them up. I didn't think about that happening."

I never would have noticed this side of Leo before we started working together—the thoughtful one stuck in his own head, who pulls on locks like one of the pink mesh bags might hold solutions to his problems. Who feels bad about the idea of people getting stood up, just because of his sponsorship scheme. I'm staring again—I'm aware of it now, at least—but he hasn't noticed yet. He's fiddling with the lock face, turning it so that it clicks, without any real attempt to unlock it. Normally I'd be annoyed, since we still have ten locks to pull off, but right now I can't think about anything but my heart in my throat.

Finally he feels the weight of my stare and looks over, and there's really nothing dramatic to say about the lights of the gym on his hair or the fact that I'm standing on a stupid footstool, but my mouth is suddenly very dry. So I open my mouth and finally just spit it out.

"Do you want to go to the Dance with me?"

Time stops.

And then Leo blinks. "What?"

I clear my throat. "Do you want to go to the Dance with me?" I pass it off as causal, or at least try to. Like I haven't been thinking about this with varying degrees of torment since New Year's Eve. Like it's, y'know, no big deal, whatever. "I mean, if you want." Obviously if he wants. I already said that. Idiot.

"I . . ." Leo's mouth hangs open for a moment, like he had the right words but lost them. I kind of wish they'd stayed lost, because the next words out of his mouth are: "I . . . can't."

"You . . . can't?" I repeat, too confused to stop myself. Not *don't want to.* Not *won't.*

Can't?

"Um." My brain fizzles, struggling to regain cognitive function. "Okay." I step off the footstool and gesture vaguely with what ends up looking like finger guns. I trip a little over the stool as I try to step around it. Cool. Great. My life is going perfectly. Every fear and anxiety about rejection is coming home to roost. Good to see them again. "Worth a try! Anyway, I'm just gonna—go check on—something else. Somewhere else. Don't worry about it."

"Wren, wait—" Leo grimaces, reaching out as if he would stop me if he were a little closer. For a moment I'm afraid that if I keep going he's going to chase me down, like he's running through the airport and I'm about to go start a new life in New York City. But if this is a Lifetime romantic comedy, it needs some fucking work. "I should— I owe you an explanation."

"You really don't."

"Wren."

"I'd rather you didn't."

"I founded Buddy."

"Wait, *what?*" I turn to him, incredulous, the mortification of being rejected briefly and momentarily forgotten in how completely surreal the moment is. "You *what?*"

Leo fidgets with the binder, looking uncomfortable under the bright gym lights. "I founded Buddy. Coded it, mostly, I mean. I ended up selling it to this tech company wanting to break into social media but—it's mine. A bit. I'm still on the board." He's starting to lose steam, his voice getting weak. "I own a percentage and . . . stuff."

"Sorry, I—" I step away from the footstool, before I trip over it and we end up having to have this conversation in the hospital. "You— Why are you telling me this?" As much as there is to process about this information, why is it suddenly so important to tell me *right now*?

He looks helpless, his eyes so wide and liquid that *I* actually feel bad. "Because I came up with Buddy . . . because of you."

I open my mouth.

"I mean, there were *other* reasons," he says in a rush, borderline babbling. "Obviously I've been coding for the robotics team, but I got really, really into it when I hurt my knee. It was kind of more of an experiment. I didn't expect anything to come of it. But I figured it was a good thing—I could help with my brother's medical bills, and the car is nice, though I guess it is a little big, and—"

"Okay. Hold on. Slow down." I hold up a hand. "Rewind to the part about any of that having to do with *me*."

He stares at me for a good ten seconds, his mouth open a fraction of an inch. The silence seems to stretch on forever before he closes his mouth again, biting his bottom lip. "Because you hated me," he says awkwardly, his shoulders moving in some sort of shrug. "Nothing I did seemed to make you *not* hate me, and all I could think was that we're all so stuck on our first impressions, we don't let ourselves get to know people as they are now. So I came up with Buddy. Because I . . . wanted that."

Another pause. "Because . . . I've kind of been in love with you," he says, grimacing, "for a while."

Okay, no, that's—that doesn't sound right. I blink, the gears in my brain grinding against one another as it calibrates to this new information. "I— Since *when*?"

He looks at the ceiling, is mentally tabulating how long he's been afflicted. "Since I had the locker over yours in seventh grade."

"I— *You dropped a book on my head.*"

Leo rolls his eyes. "Don't be so dramatic," he says, somewhere between a laugh and a sigh. "It wasn't a textbook, it was my planner. It was made of paper."

I roll my eyes right back. The moment is so absurd I want to laugh, but the sound gets stuck in my throat. "Yeah, *I'm* being the dramatic one." I feel like he's hit me over the head with a textbook all over again, for real this time. Like a chemistry textbook. Or world history. The pieces of what he's saying are slowly starting to connect, and I'm not sure where that leaves me. Us. Either/or. "Wait, so—if you created Buddy, that means you spent your *own money*"—he opens his mouth to argue—"the *company's* money to *torment me* all year with this *stupid Dance* . . . because you're in love with me?" I squint.

Leo throws his hands in the air in exasperation. Or he tries to—the three-ring binder he's holding makes it a bit difficult. I still get the idea. "I wasn't *tormenting* you. I *thought* I was giving you what you wanted. You got your budget and everyone else got the Dance. And I kinda thought you were coming around to it."

I fidget with one of the bears in my hoodie pocket. I wish I hadn't stuck them there now. "Yeah," I say reluctantly. "Maybe I was." I'm still not a fan of the whole concept of the Valentine's Day Dance and its popularity and every string attached, but some things have been fun. I guess. "I guess that brings me to question two," I say, gesturing impatiently. "Because you're in love with me . . . you can't go to the Dance with me?"

Okay, clearly I have bigger things to be concerned about than who Leo goes to the Dance with, but I'm not really sure what to do at this point. The only way out of this conversation is to bring it full circle.

"Because I want to say yes," Leo says, and my heart jumps, but he's got that helpless expression on his face again. "Because you're funny and—well, I don't know about cool."

"Now you're just kicking me when I'm down," I say.

He cracks a smile, like I hoped he would. "See? You just say things that no one else would, like it's nothing, and I love that, but . . ." He sighs and scratches at his forehead, using the excuse to duck his head. "But I've been thinking a lot, a *lot*, about what I want and what I need, and . . ." He looks up with a rueful little smile. ". . . and when I look at the numbers, Wren, I can't be sure that you wouldn't hurt me. And I don't know how much hurt I can afford right now."

My heart sinks, and it's not so much shock as it is understanding. Because he's right. Because I've hated him, or at least I thought I did, for the last five years. Because I've been rude and dismissive and openly combative. Because I haven't given him a reason to believe otherwise. Here I thought I could swoop in, five years late to my own feelings, and get everything I wanted. But I guess he's tired of waiting.

It's not his fault, how much it stings. He doesn't know how many times I've imagined this conversation in different ways with different people, half of them imaginary and most of them a lot less kind about it. It's actually a little funny, in a cruel irony kind of way. It's not because I'm asexual—this time it's the rest of me that's the problem.

Maybe I'll laugh about it later.

"I'm sorry," he says softly.

I shake my head. "Thanks," I say, trying to ignore the way my heart seems to weigh a thousand pounds, threatening to drag me to the floor. "Really. You didn't have to tell me all that."

He opens his mouth to say something.

"But I'm glad you did," I interrupt. "I think I, y'know, probably needed to hear it. Builds character. Or whatever." I muster a half-hearted smile. I clear my throat and jerk my thumb toward the door. "I, uh, actually told Ryan to wait around in case this went badly, so I'm just gonna go . . . find her before she leaves."

"Okay," Leo says. He looks absolutely miserable, which should make me feel better, but it makes me feel worse. Somehow *him* rejecting *me* is still my fault. It should annoy me, but I'm starting to think it's less a symptom of perfect Leo Reyes and more the fallout of imperfect Wren Martin. "I'll finish up here."

I grab my backpack from where it's slouched against the folded tables and hesitate. "See you later, Leo," I say over my shoulder, not quite looking back.

A beat. "See you later, Wren."

32
THE VALENTINE'S DAY DANCE

All that time spent agonizing over my feelings, over who to pick. All that soul-searching about right questions and allowing myself to say the answers I really mean, even if the answer is the hard one. All that, blown up in my face, and I have no one to blame but myself for lighting the fuse.

And I feel . . . okay.

Like really, legitimately *okay*. I poke and prod at the feeling, trying to get it to change into a more recognizable shape. I feel . . . disappointed, yeah. Embarrassed. Regretful. But those things are all on the surface, and underneath them, it's like a knot of tension that's been living in my chest has loosened. It's still there and still just as heavy, but it's not holding itself as tight as it was before. I plucked up the courage to ask Leo to the Dance, and he turned me down in a way I couldn't have even imagined. At the beginning of the school year, I would been three steps away from changing my name and leaving the country. Or walking into the Gulf of Mexico and letting the crabs carry me away.

But all that happened, and the world hasn't ended.

Not like after my mom died. I hated it then, the way the sun still rose and birds still sang and people still talked about the latest season of whatever was on HBO as if nothing had changed. Everything seems inconsequential after something like that, yet I'd been ten times more afraid of it, like once you're hurt that badly once, you realize you can get hurt again, and more pain is the very last thing you can stand. So you try to protect yourself.

But I took the SAT. I applied for college. I asked Leo Reyes to the Dance.

And I survived every one of them.

It's weird. It's *really* weird. I kind of feel like I deserve a medal, or at least a good grade in life-altering revelations, but no one's giving them out. So I guess I'll have to settle for the dubious reward of having grown as a person, whether I wanted to or not.

But that doesn't mean I'm having *fun*.

The good news is that we purposely scheduled Love Locks for the last week of January, as a big almost-Dance-time event. The bad news is that I still have *two* terrible weeks to pretend Leo and I didn't have the most awkward conversation known to man.

I succeed. Mostly. It helps that I'm a consummate professional (yeah, right) and also there's still a metric ton of stuff to nail down before the Dance. So I throw myself into it with reckless abandon, wielding my clipboard like a weapon against slackers and catering professionals who can't get back to you in a reasonable time frame. It's fine.

Except I can't even look at the word *Buddy*, much less all the tastefully branded (as tasteful as anything sunshine-yellow can be) tablecloths, without feeling vaguely nauseous. Because while I had my big emotional journey about getting turned down, I still have to reckon with everything *else* Leo said. Like the fact I've been so horrible to him he went and created a whole app about it. A whole app he convinced to sponsor the Dance all to help *me*.

It's nice. *Too* nice. It should be on the list of things I hate him for, but instead it just makes me feel like human garbage every time I see the little yellow icon smiling back at me.

And I *still* have to do the Dance.

"I don't want to go."

"You have to go."

"But I don't want to."

"Wren."

I mash my face into the comforter of Ryan's bed, like I can sink into and disappear into another, bed-themed world. Unfortunately Ryan is prepared for this. She grabs me by the ankles and pulls back, so I slide off the end like a dead eel, taking the comforter with me. It flops on top of me.

Ryan pulls the comforter off like a magician revealing a bedraggled pigeon. I squint in the light.

"Put that back," I complain. "I'm going to take a nap."

"What you're going to do is get up and come help make this dance happen," Ryan says, sounding remarkably like her mother. "Because you know why?"

I sigh dejectedly. *"Why?"*

"Because (a), everyone is going to think you're a petty bitch if you don't."

"I *am* a petty bitch."

"Because (b), *Leo* is going to think you're still moping about him."

"I *am* moping."

"And because (c), if you *don't*"—Ryan leans in close, her voice dropping to a menacing level—"I'll tell my parents that *you* offered to drive Reed to the Dance."

I narrow my eyes. "You wouldn't." The Dance doesn't start for another five hours, but the music in Reed's room is already shaking the walls as she gets dressed, her ill-gotten ticket in hand. She already tried to get us to let three of her freshman friends go with her, but we haggled it down to a plus-one.

Ryan's eyebrow twitches upward. "Wouldn't I?"

♥

Rapture High's Valentine's Day Dance arrives like a hurricane—after much anticipation and with devastating effects to the entire city. Normally it takes place in the gym, resulting in the road outside the school being shut down and a rented trolley shuttling people from a nearby field-turned-parking-lot to avoid any vehicular manslaughter on the big day.

This isn't a normal year, thanks in part to my bright idea. The White Sand Hotel and Resort, the proud owner of the Canopy, is no stranger to events. But I don't think they're quite ready for this.

It's chaos—but controlled chaos, thanks to my clipboard and many unsightly personality traits geared toward managerial potential. February is hardly peak tourist season, so we're mostly dealing with the locals, who all remember their own Dance fondly, though maybe less fondly as a massive shoal of high school students descends upon them. The hotel insisted on valet parking only, which means we had to pay through the nose to cover the cost for everyone, or else make my *the Dance should be accessible for everyone* stance a lie. Luckily my Love Locks event made a pretty good profit, because I'm sure as hell not using any more Buddy money.

Leo money. Ugh. Not going to think about that right now.

Best to think about anything *but* Leo, which is easier said than done when the whole event is Buddy themed. Decked out in yellow and white and black, the place looks like a beehive exploded. Ryan keeps insisting that the black accents are elegant, but I don't quite see it.

I duck to the side, away from where well-dressed teenagers are being funneled from the valet circle into the Canopy's ballroom. Patterned lights sit nestled between elegant potted ferns, pointed at the wall for a dramatic effect that makes it feel like walking through a neon fever dream. I tuck myself next to one, my phone held in one hand.

The Buddy app open, of course, like everyone else in the place, even though it's too early. We sent out an email with the exact instructions, but Maggie had big sandwich boards printed and placed outside the doors to be safe. The Buddy devs (Leo) coded a Rapture High exclusive option users could opt into. The user enters their name and picture, then chooses the conversation partner (or partners, if they cast the net wide) they want to meet up with. At eight o'clock, when the dance is in full swing, the app will reveal the identity of each user's personal mysterious stranger.

Lips will lock, hearts will be broken, feet will dance all night. It'll be an evening for the history books.

And Buddy Boy still hasn't said a damn thing.

Bet you're wondering what happened with him. Well, the good news is that I'm not so completely faithless I went running to him the moment Leo stopped being an option. The points about Buddy Boy that stood before still stand now, and I'm too busy licking my wounds to consider another stab at romance. Clearly I've got enough about myself I need to figure out before I drag anyone else into my life.

Besides, I already asked Buddy Boy to drop his anonymity once before, and he didn't want to. Which is fine, like I said, but the weird thing is that he hasn't said *anything* about the reveal at the Dance, not even to specify that he'd rather not participate. I've mentioned it a couple of times in passing— it's kind of impossible not to, considering how it has engulfed life as we know it for at least a week leading up to the actual dance—but so far Buddy Boy has acted like it's got nothing to do with us. Which maybe it doesn't, but it's still confusing to wrestle with.

I sigh, staring down at my phone. Not even a single message today. I'm really not sure how to take that.

"Hey, slacker."

I jump, nearly knocking over the potted fern. Maggie is standing in front of me, hand on her hip, looking impatient. Or looking like Maggie, really. She always looks kind of impatient.

She also looks good tonight, which I'm loath to admit. She's wearing a suit that looks more appropriate for accepting an Oscar than attending a high school dance, but she pulls it off, so there's not much else I can say about that. The rose-gold sequined blouse she's wearing under it glitters every time she moves. It matches the half-mask that sits on her nose, doing absolutely nothing to obscure her identity. I don't super get the point, but I've always thought the idea of a masquerade doesn't make a ton of sense.

"Are you going to get changed or what?" she says.

We came in T-shirts and jeans for the set-up, but except for the fashionably late kids, the Dance has basically started. Except— "I did change," I say, affronted. "What's wrong with this?"

Maggie frowns. "It's *yellow plaid*."

No, I didn't wear the same outfit from my fake dinner date with Leo on purpose. That would be petty and weird. The truth is that (a) it's legitimately the nicest shirt I own, and (b) I'm stupid. I didn't even realize the correlation until I was already changed.

"And a bow tie," I say defensively, pointing at my neck. The red bow tie goes with the red stripes in the plaid, and I won't hear otherwise.

"Right," she says, looking me up and down again for good measure. "Well, get inside. We've got work to do."

"I know, I know." I pocket my phone, trying not to be disappointed that there's still no notification bubble over the Buddy app. Maybe Buddy Boy hasn't said anything *because* he's afraid I'll want to talk about the Dance. I suppress a sigh. I'm never talking to boys ever again. Or girls, except Ryan. Or anyone else. If I get lonely, I'll get a dog, like a sensible person.

"Hey, Maggie," I say, looking up. She looks over her shoulder, clearly ready to be back in the ballroom, but I don't really want to yell this over the music in there. "Sorry I was such a dick to Leo. And about the Dance."

Maggie gives me a measured look, her face unreadable. "Yeah, he told me what happened."

I cringe. Of course he did. "Cool," I say. "Well, I'm sorry. I know that's why you don't like me, so . . . just thought I'd say it."

"Did you tell him?"

I blink. "Tell him what?"

She looks at me like I'm stupid. "Did you tell Leo that you're sorry?"

"I . . ." I scroll back through the memory of That Conversation. Did I? I've certainly thought a lot about what he said since then, but at the time I was mostly trying to escape. "I . . . guess not?"

Maggie rolls her eyes. "Give it a try, idiot," she says. "After you make sure the drinks table isn't absolute chaos." She hesitates, raising one finger like she's just remembered something. "For the record, I think you're right about the Dance."

I blink. "Excuse me?

She shrugs. "I think you're right," she repeats. "It's a waste of money. You don't even want to know how much I paid for this suit."

"I—so—" God, I wish people would stop telling me stuff. I was not meant to process this many thoughts at once. "So you were pro-Dance all year solely to spite me," I say, "because I was rude to Leo, who I didn't even know was in love with me?"

"Hm. I guess when you put it like that . . . ," Maggie muses. "Yeah, more or less." She turns on her heel and disappears back into the ballroom.

I catch a glimpse of my reflection in one of the mirrored bronze panels that artistically line the wall. "My life is a joke," I tell the warped Wren staring back at me. He doesn't look very sympathetic.

33
THE BEACH

I haven't changed my mind: the Valentine's Day Dance and the overblown, love-drunk, drama-riddled obsession that consumes Rapture High is pointless at best, actively a waste of resources at worst. The fact that this year it succeeded in a way no one thought was possible and got its claws in me only makes it that much worse.

But maybe I'm just a little proud of how it came out.

The Canopy's ballroom is beautiful in its own right, but tonight it's draped with yellow and white lights intertwined with climbing vines. Great swaths of ivory fabric cross the ceiling, the lights dappling them like psychedelic starlight. Glass double doors bracket the room, the pair on the far end leading out to the Canopy's famous glass-domed garden. Staff in white vests linger unobtrusively among the plants, making sure no one stomps all over the flower beds. The unsung heroes of the night. I hope they know I appreciate them; the security deposit was almost as bad as the cost for the venue.

Not thinking about the money, I remind myself firmly. Not thinking about Leo.

The Dance itself is plenty distracting. Music shudders through the speakers, making it too loud to even think. Teachers and parent volunteers mingle along the perimeter, only the most daring of them venturing close enough to the center to break up dancing that's getting a little too R-rated. My rounds take me past where Ms. Little lurks in one corner.

"I did it, you know," I say, leaning in so she can hear me over the music. "Applied."

"Good," she says, which isn't exactly an overwhelming response, but I can see one corner of her mouth twisting with a barely suppressed smile. "Are you going to go?"

"I don't know if I'm accepted yet."

"Not what I asked."

I roll my eyes. Clearly she chooses her questions deliberately. And has more faith in how I look on paper than I do. Being able to put *student council president* sure didn't hurt my chances, though. "Yeah," I say, looking away, out over the dance floor. "I think I will."

Which means leaving my dad and Beep and Rapture, the last place where I knew my mom and where she knew me. Ryan too, if she ends up getting into Georgia Tech like she wants. It scares me, knowing that my life will change like that but not knowing what shape it'll be in.

Still, I'm excited to find out.

"Good," Ms. Little says, and she smiles for real this time, even if it comes across like she didn't mean to. She nods. "If it's what you want."

Yeah, I think it is.

I leave her there to supervise from the sidelines and dive back into the chaos. All things considered, it's going pretty well. No one's broken an ankle wearing high heels or thrown up in a potted plant. Though the night is still young, and Ryan's already walked in on a group of girls sneaking sips from a flask in the bathroom. I'll take the win while I still can.

There's only one thing that's bothering me.

I catch Archer by the elbow. "Have you seen Leo?" I yell over the music. Archer is wearing a suit almost identical to his sister's, except his bow tie is sequined instead of his shirt. I wasn't sure how useful he was going to be when the rubber hit the road, but it turns out his athlete's stamina and near-endless supply of enthusiasm make him perfect for running an event. I don't think I've seen him stand still for the last four hours.

"No," Archer yells back. "Have you seen him?"

Okay, maybe not perfect. "Why would I ask you if I had?"

He shrugs. "Maybe you were taking a survey?"

"Never mind," I say, releasing him. He takes off like a shot again, to manage a minor crisis that seems to be unfolding at the drinks table. I should probably follow him, but I'm too busy scanning the crowd.

It's easy to miss someone in the mass of formal wear, masquerade masks, and questionable dance moves, the lighting low and the music distracting, but as student council members trying to keep this function functioning, we all move in similar orbits. Shouldn't I have run into Leo by now? It's been at least an hour since I saw him last, and that was when people were still arriving. It's not like there isn't enough to do. So where the hell is he?

"Hey." Ryan appears next to me. Her outfit tonight has nothing on her spider dress from homecoming, but the abundance of bumblebees tries its best to make up for the lack of spiders. I see why she insisted on the black accents now. Her '50s-style skirt wrinkles against me as she leans in. "Have you seen Leo?"

At least I'm not the only one wondering. Maggie is behind Ryan, pensively looking out at the dance floor, so it seems safe to say that she doesn't know either. "No," I say. "Food poisoning?" I offer.

"Ew."

"Yeah, forget I said it." My phone buzzes in my pocket. I pull it out. "Hold on, that might be him."

And I freeze.

There's a Buddy notification waiting for me, the little yellow-and-white icon somehow startling even in the middle of an aggressively Buddy-themed room. It actually makes it feel even more portentous, especially as the deadline on the Buddy identity reveal crawls closer. Butterflies twist themselves into knots in my stomach. I almost don't even want to open it, but I swipe the message with my thumb.

Him:

Hey, so I'm just going to write this all out and send it before I lose my nerve.

I know that neither of us really meant to end up on Buddy. I was going to delete it, because it was embarrassing, and I didn't want to bother you anymore. But I liked talking to you. A lot. It was so easy, when everything else felt hard. It was like I could be a different person here, where things were easy and uncomplicated. So I was afraid. I was afraid of how much I liked you, and I was afraid to show you the real me. Maybe you wouldn't like me when it wasn't just a silly game. Or maybe once you were a part of my real life, that would go wrong too.

But I'm tired of running away from the things I'm afraid of. I don't think you can live that way.

Or at least, I don't want to.

If you want to meet, I'm on the beach outside the hotel. Sorry that's like, super dramatic. It's just a little crowded in there. If you don't, that's fine too.

Either way, thank you for being my
friend.

Okay, sorry, that was sappy.
Anyway, if the answer is no, just say
something about Star Wars and we'll
forget it ever happened.

"Shit," I say eloquently.

"What is it? Leo?" Ryan says, leaning in to look at my
phone, but I pocket it again.

"Everything's fine," I say before her mind can leap to the
worst possible conclusion. "I've just got to go do something."

Right now. My feet are confused, unsure why we're not
already moving, already there on the beach. There are too
many thoughts racing through my head, so my mind settles
for going completely blank instead.

I make a move to leave, but Maggie steps in front of me.
She holds out her suit jacket. "Here," she says. "If you're
going to do something dramatic and romantic, you might as
well look like you tried even a little bit."

I stop short, staring. "Why are you . . ." Someone once
told me not to look a gift horse in the mouth. I'm assuming
the same goes for formal wear. "How do you know it'll fit?"

Not for the first time that night, her eyes look me up and
down condescendingly. "Wren," she says flatly. "Trust me.
I know."

I bite back a scowl. No time to get fussy about short
jokes now. "Thanks," I say, taking it from her. "Now I really
gotta go."

♥

The White Sand Hotel and Resort sits right on the water, where it offers beach access in addition to its multiple swimming pools. The Canopy has a balcony that looks out over the sand, with a narrow staircase that leads down to the beach. The water is beautiful tonight, inky black except for the silver crests of the lazy tide reflecting the moonlight.

It's also *cold*, because it's *February* and the weather decided to remember that today. I'm grateful for Maggie's jacket for more than one reason.

I take the stairs two at a time, threatening to trip and break my neck on the way down. When I finally get to the beach, I stagger like I'm the one who's been hitting the flask in the bathroom. I don't know if you've ever tried it, but dress shoes aren't really made with beaches in mind. I get fed up and take them off, the sand is soft and cold beneath my feet.

There's one plus to the evening being wholly unsuitable for the beach: it's practically deserted. There are a few clusters of people along the coastline, a couple of them probably drifted out from the Dance, but only one of the figures is alone. He sits in the sand, facing the water, his elbows resting on his knees.

I slow down as I get closer, just a little bit out of breath. Finally, I stop. I don't make a pretty picture, my hair tossed by the cold wind and my shoes hanging from one hand, wearing a jacket that doesn't *quite* fit, thank you very much. I check my bow tie with one hand. At least that's still straight.

I clear my throat. "Hey."

There's a moment, suspended in time, my heart in my throat, when nothing happens. It's too late to change my mind, but it almost feels like I still could. I could step out of the scene, go back to the Dance, and leave this whole weird situation behind me. It would probably be easier. Because a lot of things are starting to come together in the back of my mind, realizations falling into place one after another like dominoes. Because I recognize the slope of those shoulders, and the figure's overlong legs. Because a lot of things are suddenly starting to make sense.

I don't think I want to be anywhere else but right here.

Leo looks back.

He jumps to his feet, kicking up sand. He looks good, because of course he looks good. Leo Reyes could come out of surgery looking good, though I'm starting to realize I might be biased. He's wearing a dark blue suit over a white collared shirt, which should be a boring look but comes across as timeless instead. Even covered in sand.

Even if he's looking at me like *that*.

"Wren, not right now," Leo says, his voice terse. His eyes flicker behind me back toward the hotel, his expression cagey, bordering on annoyed. "Can it wait? I'm—I'm in the middle of something."

"Um." I'm not sure what to say. "Not really."

He stares at me for a second, his expression frozen, before he shakes his head. "Well, it's going to have to. Go back to the Dance. I'll find you guys later."

"Leo, I—"

"*Seriously*, Wren," he snaps. I don't think I've ever heard Leo *snap* before. At least not like this, his voice raw and impatient. "I can't deal with you right now." He stoops to pick up his own shoes, similarly defeated by the sand, and starts to march down the beach.

God. It's like I've swallowed my own tongue. Say something. *Say something!*

"Leo!" I call after him.

He doesn't listen. Of course he doesn't.

"Goddammit," I mutter, and I pull out my phone.

Me:

please come back

Leo stops.

He turns slowly, the wind ruffling his hair, phone still in one hand, so that the glow of the screen casts weird shadows where the moonlight doesn't touch. It's hard to see his expression, but I think he's confused. I do the only thing I can think of: I wave.

I drop my hand belatedly. Okay, that was stupid.

It works. Leo walks back slowly, shoes still dangling from two fingers. That means I get to watch in real time as his expression morphs from confused to baffled to incredulous, which all sound similar but manage to be extremely distinct from where I'm standing.

"You don't have a Buddy account," he says when he's close enough. "I would know if you had a Buddy account."

"Did you check?" Is that something he can do?

"That would be a violation of the privacy policy," Leo says faintly. "But—" He lets it drop abruptly. Obviously I have a Buddy account. Quite obviously.

We stare at each other for a long moment. It's quiet except for the whisper of the waves and my own thundering heart. I try to come up with the right thing to say, but the words keep slipping through my fingers. Bastards.

"When did you figure out it was me?" Leo says at last.

"Um. I started suspecting about ten minutes ago," I say. "When I knew for sure? About two."

Leo laughs, but I don't think he actually finds it very funny. He drops his shoes in the sand and runs a hand through his hair, turning away. "This is . . ." He trips over the words. "Not what I expected."

I wince when he's not looking. Yeah, I guess it's not.

"Well," he says, laughing again. This time I can tell that it's nervous. "I feel stupid, I guess. I should—I'll just—"

"Leo, wait." I drop my shoes as well, taking a step forward so that he has no choice but to look at me instead of where he's been looking, down at the sand. I take a deep breath. "I'm sorry."

He blinks. "You're what?"

"I'm sorry for how I treated you," I say, swallowing the lump in my throat. "I'm sorry for how I acted. I was jealous. You're tall and athletic and friendly, and everyone seems to love you, so it was like—like I thought I should hate you, to restore some stupid cosmic balance to the universe. I was an idiot. And I guess I just got used to it." My shoulders slump, like the words are something physical that's finally left my body. "I shouldn't have done it and I'm sorry."

His eyes are liquid in the half-light, his mouth hanging open a fraction of an inch. "Wren, I . . ."

"I realized that you're not perfect. I mean, you're still tall, but"—Jesus, I'm really babbling now—"but you get anxious and annoyed and you have problems, real problems. But you still manage to be kind and caring and funny, and I guess I'm still jealous, but I don't hate you for it anymore. I . . ." I clear my throat, my face warm. "I wish I could be more like that."

Leo's mouth is closed, his lips twisted in something of a rueful smile. "You forgot the part where I lied about being an app developer to fund a high school dance so the boy I liked wouldn't commit social suicide," he points out. "Not exactly a positive trait."

"Oh, well, brag about it." I roll my eyes, a smile tugging stubbornly on the corner of my mouth. "I don't know if I'll ever be that good."

Leo laughs for real this time, and the sound is warmer than the glow of the hotel lights looking over the beach.

"I'm so stupid," he says, shaking his head, but he's smiling, just a little bit. "I really thought Anonymous was the way to get over you."

"Well, you were right after all," I say. "About being able to get to know someone for real, without everything else getting in the way." I pause. "But you were still only my second choice," I continue with a shrug. "You were going strong for a while there, but this guy named Leo really came out of nowhere to take the lead."

He grins, suddenly bashful but valiantly pretending not to be. "Yeah, well," he says, "for a while there I actually thought you were—"

"I know who you thought I was," I interrupt, "and I'm going to forgive you for it."

Leo laughs. "Sorry."

This time, the silence is warm despite the cut of the wind. It's comfortable, nestled between what was and what still might be. I almost don't want it to end. I don't want to figure out what happens after this, who we are to each other and maybe even to ourselves. I just want to be here.

Leo nods at the hotel. "Do you want to go back to the Dance?" he says, a tentative offer there. Him and me at the Dance. Buddy Boy and Anonymous. Or maybe just Leo and Wren.

"God no," I say, and I pick up my shoes again. I set off down the beach at a leisurely pace, the sand cold between my toes and the wind at my back.

There's a beat of hesitation; then I hear Leo behind me, jogging to catch up. He falls into step next to me. Comfortable, but close enough that I can feel the warmth of his arm next to mine.

I give him a sideways look. "That was so *Pride and Prejudice*," I say.

Leo rewards me with a grin. "Not Padme and Anakin?" he says, raising his eyebrows, and it's strange, having a Buddy

Boy conversation with Leo, here out loud with our real voices, but I think it might be something I could get used to. I think he might feel the same. I guess there's time to figure it out.

I snort. "What? No. Han and Leia, maybe."

"Only if I get to be Han."

"You *get* to be Leia," I say, waving emphatically. Leo catches my hand, and I try not to let the surprise show on my face when he doesn't let go of it. He lets our hands drop to hang between us, and my cheeks definitely go warm when he laces our fingers together. Oh! Okay. I guess I could get used to that. I try to pretend I'm not blushing like a fine Victorian lady showing her ankle for the first time, but judging from his sly smile, I don't think it works. I poke him in the side with my elbow. "You're the smart one, I'm the cool one. That's always how this has worked."

"I'm not sure about *that.* . . ."

34
THE END

The end.

Just kidding, I'm not that much of an asshole. I know you want a little more than that.

Like every year, the Dance ends, and *poof!* It's entirely over. Almost like it never even happened, except for the posters that need to be taken down and the pictures on social media. It's one of the reasons I've always hated it. All that money and time and trouble, and that's *it*?

I guess this year is a little different.

"Do you want to go to prom?" Leo asks, and laughs before the words are even all the way out of his mouth, probably at the disgusted look I throw him. I'm starting to think he says ridiculous things just to get me to pull faces at him.

"That's a trick question," I say. "We *have* to go to prom. The thing won't organize itself."

But that's not for a couple more months.

In the meantime, my power as student council president reigns supreme. The auditorium stage will be fixed for the spring musical—*Les Misérables*, not *Cats*—with enough money left over to replace most of the stage lights that burned out last year. What I'll do next is kept in check only by Ms. Little and the will of the student council, but considering Ryan is my best friend and I'm dating the vice president, I'm feeling pretty good about getting the majority vote.

Yeah, I'm dating the vice president. There's probably something unethical about that, but that's politics, baby!

Unfortunately the vice president always likes to get to student council meetings early, like some kind of dweeb, which means we're stuck waiting for the rest of the council members, not to mention Ms. Little, to show up. But there are worse ways to kill time.

Today, for instance, I've made a lounge chair from my limited resources: reclining in the teacher's swivel chair, my feet up on Leo's lap.

"I think I've decided what to do about college," Leo says, changing the subject. He's pretending to do something on his phone, but I've started to pick up on when he's faking it. I have a little more practice reading Leo's moods than I realized.

"Oh yeah?" I say casually. Leo doesn't talk about his brother a lot, and I don't push him to—all of this is a little too new, and the subject a little too painful. We are getting pretty good at talking around it, though.

"Yeah," he says. "I think I'm going to postpone my enrollment at UCLA for a year. Stick around for a bit. Help out at home."

"That sounds like a good idea," I say, which I would have said either way. It's his decision, though I can't help remembering what Buddy Boy said about not running away from the things that scare him anymore. I know he's afraid for his brother, and afraid for himself, and I know the way the ground beneath your feet is never quite as stable as it was once you realize how unpredictable life is.

Sometimes you need to wait. Sometimes you can't anymore. I found out the day after the Dance that I got into Florida State on a partial scholarship. So I guess that's where I'll be in the fall, for better or for worse. For the better, I hope.

But there's still a little while before I need to worry about that.

"What are you going to do?" I needle him, poking his stomach with my shoe. "Take a gap year? Grow your hair out long? Get really into the smell of patchouli?"

Leo laughs and unties my shoe, which feels like a punishment unbefitting the crime. It's still kind of surreal, equating Leo and Buddy Boy. Sometimes Leo will reference a conversation I had with Buddy Boy, or I'll get a text and expect to see a Buddy notification. I pretend I deleted the Buddy app from my phone, but really I just hid it in a different folder, an archive of a very strange time. Sometimes I like to scroll back through the messages, retroactively picking up on little

Leo things. Sometimes the similarities are embarrassingly obvious. Whatever, it worked out in the end. Sue me.

The weird part is how long I spent agonizing over the choice between Leo and Buddy Boy, Buddy Boy and Leo. I thought I chose Leo because he was more real, more honest, more complicated, the same way Leo chose Anonymous because he was something different and uncertain after too many years of quietly pining after, well, *me*. I'm still not sure what it means that all four of us turned out to be the same two people, but I think it's something kind of messy. Something about how people can be more than one thing, and sometimes choices aren't that easy to define. I think I kind of like it.

I like *this*. Leo has talked a bit about when he realized he was gay, how it felt to be different in the shadow of his seemingly perfect football-star brother. How you can accept a part of yourself and still struggle with the feeling that it means you're not enough somehow. How the right people will like you not despite it, but because of it. He's good at that—managing to say the things I need to hear but still don't quite like to talk about.

"I'm keeping my options open," Leo says with a grin, pulling me back into reality. He goes for my other shoe as I half-heartedly try to kick his hand away. "But those are some great ideas."

I momentarily forget that my chair has wheels and I laugh as it unexpectedly slips sideways, nearly dumping me out of it. I grab the desk for stability. "What if I told you I was allergic to patchouli?"

"I don't think you can be allergic to patchouli," he says, finally catching my shoelace enough to untie it. Bastard. "But I'd say that's very tragic to hear."

I pull my feet away and plant them on the ground, steadying the wobbling office chair. I'll need to give it up soon. We've only got a couple of minutes before our entourage shows up.

But that's enough time for one more thing. I lean forward. "Hey," I say. "Come closer."

Leo gives me a sideways look, clearly fearing retaliation. "Why?" he says warily.

"I have a secret to tell you. C'mere."

He looks around the empty classroom. "Why do you have to whisper?

"Because it's a secret, doofus."

He grins, because I picked up *doofus* from him and he won't let me forget it. He leans forward, humoring me. "Okay, what—"

I close the distance and kiss him, my hand on his cheek so I can feel it get warm. Leo likes to say things so I can pretend to be annoyed. I like to embarrass him, and it turns out that Leo Reyes is very embarrassed by PDA.

Reasons why I like Leo Reyes:

1.   He's easy to embarrass. Before, I would have thought someone like Leo would have nothing to be embarrassed about, but I didn't know the leverage I had over him

2. He likes Star Wars. Not the prequels, which is a pretty basic take if you ask me, but I'm trying not to hold it against him.

3. He's tall. I know that was a bad thing before, but it's a good thing now. Shut up.

4. He laughs a lot, even at the dumb shit I say. Ryan says what that's done to my ego is irreparable.

5. He likes me, all of me, for some reason.

6. He doesn't mention that time he saw me run into a locked door, but I think he probably forgot about it. He makes fun of me for plenty of other things, but I'm usually asking for it.

7. He doesn't notice when the classroom door opens.

"Oh my God," Maggie says. "Can we *not*?"

I laugh as Leo ducks his head, blushing furiously. "You knew that was going to happen," he hisses.

"Am I psychic now?" I say, ignoring the fact that my cheeks are a little warm too. But it was worth it.

"Wait, did I miss something?" Archer says, poking his head through the door. It's been three weeks since the Dance, but he still hasn't quite caught on to the Wren/Leo thing.

"Don't worry about it," Ryan says, patting his shoulder like she's a long-suffering veteran of the war of my romantic pursuits. "Ignorance is bliss."

"Dramatic," I accuse.

"Shrimp," she counters blithely.

"Rude—"

"All right, all right," Ms. Little says, sweeping into the room with her usual deathly lack of enthusiasm. "Save the teenager theatrics for later, I didn't buy a ticket. Let's get this meeting over with." She pauses at the front of the classroom. "And get out of my chair."

ACKNOWLEDGMENTS

Just the fact I get to write these a second time is amazing, and I'll never stop being grateful for everyone who was a part of this journey from messy Google Doc to real, actual book.

A huge thanks to my agent, Cate Hart, for being Wren's first champion. My editor, Ashley Hearn, and editorial assistant, Zoie Konneker, for helping me bring out the heart of Wren that I didn't know was there yet. Illustrator Cherriielle and designer Lily Steele for the beautiful cover. Michelle and Terry, and the entire marketing team at Peachtree, as well as publicists Sara DiSalvo and Bree Martinez for helping throw Wren out into the world.

As always, I couldn't have done anything without my family. My mom, who was *my* first champion, and my brother, who probably inspired a bit of Wren's chaos, now that I'm thinking about it. My dad, my nana and papa, and my entire family, who have always been there for me. Augie and Dino for being my editing meltdown sounding boards, but also all my other friends and their unique brands of chaos: Susannah, Lena, Charlie, Tiff, Annamarie, Soraya, Mel, Roxy, and Wendy.

And I guess a thank you to Wren too—I wrote this book in 2020, which tells you only a fraction of what was going on in my life at that point, and he's been with me every step of the way since then. I'm not saying he *didn't* occasionally make me want to pull my hair out, but we went through a lot together, and I'm so grateful to get to share him.

ABOUT THE AUTHOR

AMANDA DEWITT is an author and librarian, ensuring that she spends as much time around books as possible. She also enjoys *Star Wars*, Dungeons & Dragons-ing, and even more writing—just not whatever it is she really should be writing. She graduated from the University of South Florida with a master's in library and information science. She lives in Clearwater, Florida, with her dogs, cats, and assortment of chickens.

amandadewitt.com

Find Amanda on Instagram @am.dewitt
or Twitter @AmandaMDeWitt.